Lily In The Valley

In the valley of heartbreak, love still blooms.

The Double Back Diaries
Book 2

Alexandrea LeChelle

Contents

Content Warning

This story touches on grief, parental loss, family conflict, and the ache of heartbreak. While it is ultimately about love, healing, and the courage to begin again, there may be moments that feel heavy. Please honor your own peace. Pause, breathe, or step away when you need to. Your well-being matters more than finishing these pages. This story isn't going anywhere. When you're ready, I hope it reminds you that even through heartbreak, light and love remain within reach.

Dedication

To everyone who has ever rebuilt themselves after heartbreak, this story is proof you can bloom again. For the valleys we must walk through, and the light we discover waiting on the other side, may these pages remind you that even in your lowest seasons, the roots of who you are run deep, and love has a way of finding you still. There is beauty ahead, there is healing within, and there is always another sunrise waiting to carry you home.

Prologue

Summer 2002 - New Orleans, LA

"Come on here, Khalil," Ms. Sonya called from the back of her flower shop. She was busy working on a peace lily arrangement for an upcoming funeral. Ms. Sonya was tall, towering over me like the Power Rangers I watched on Saturday mornings, minus the ninja moves. Her voice meant business with a hint of sweetness laced around it, like cough syrup with a pinch of sugar added to help the bite. She turned from the arrangement, going to the register where my father and I waited.

"Ms. Sonya, thank you for watching my son," my father said, pulling out his wallet and thumbing through a few bills. "If it wasn't for you, I wouldn't be able to work these extra hours at the plant."

"Kevin, go ahead and put that money up. I love watching Khalil." Ms. Sonya turned to me, rubbing a hand through my head of thick curls. "It's like having my grandbaby around."

"Thank you again. Khalil, go back there and make yourself useful. I'm sure it's something Ms. Sonya need sweeping."

"Yessir," I said, grabbing my backpack filled with my snacks and Hot Wheels and heading to the back workroom. Each time I came back here, my eyes widened with wonder. Weathered wooden shelves lined the back wall with pots and vases, all different shapes and sizes took residence.

My nose tickled, trying to take in the scent of every flower she had stocked. The air was a sweet mix of roses, lilies, and something spicy I couldn't put my finger on. Before I knew it, a fit of sneezes blew from my nose. Walking over to the desk in the corner of the room, I grabbed a tissue and blew my nose. I could hear a faint discussion between my father and Ms. Sonya.

"You heard anything from Toya yet? It's a shame what that girl did, leaving y'all like that," Ms. Sonya snuffed.

"No. You know all her people long gone." My father let out a deep sigh. "It's been four years, Ms. Sonya. I don't think she coming back. It's my fault. She told me this wasn't the life she wanted. Settling down and raising a family. But I pressed her anyway."

"Naw. It take two people to make a baby. If that's not what she wanted, she had options. Besides, you and I both know what the real problem is. Until that monkey get off her back, ain't nothing we can do."

"You right. Let me get going. My sister will pick him up when she get off her shift at Charity Hospital."

I tuned out their goodbyes, going back to settle myself in the chair by the desk. The only thing I knew about my mother was that we shared the same face, same eyes, same hair. I only knew that from the one picture of us my father kept hidden in his nightstand. She looked so sad, like she'd gotten the wrong presents for Christmas. I didn't even know kids were supposed to have mothers until I realized my best friend, Xavier, always had his mom around.

I took the Hubig pie out of my backpack, peeling the wrapper back and savoring the sweetness of the fried hand pie. The squeaky door opened, Ms. Sonya's big and bright smile lit up the room just like the sunlight dancing on the stained-glass vases. She got back to work on the arrangement, moving slowly, as if not to wake someone sleeping. I watched her pick up a big, shiny leaf, tucking it gently into a wicker pot with a white flower that stood tall and proud. I liked that flower. It looked like it was reaching up to catch the light streaming through the side windows.

"Ms. Sonya, how come people always give those flowers to people when somebody die?" I asked, placing my half-eaten pie on the desk.

"Well, you see, peace lilies symbolize peace, hope, and rebirth. The death of a person can be a hard thing to go through, even harder for the ones they leave behind." Ms. Sonya kept adding little white flowers around the big one, and some green stuff that looked fuzzy. It made me sad, but I didn't know why. "I think they show that even in the darkest of times, you can still have a little bit of beauty around. As long as you take care of them, love on them, they'll last a lifetime."

"Do all flowers mean something?" I asked, walking over to meet Ms. Sonya at her worktable. I took in the ribbon the color of moonlight that she wrapped around the basket. She scribbled a message on a small card, then tucked it between the white petals.

"Yeah," she responded, stepping back to look at her work. "I can show you some in the shop and tell you what they represent."

"Sure." I stayed out of the way while Ms. Sonya cleaned up her station. The more I stared at the arrangement, the more it made me want to hug my mom. It was pretty and sad all at the same time. I wondered what it would feel like to be in her embrace. Would her skin be soft and smooth like the petals? Or cushiony like the moss pieces covering the dirt? Maybe she had claws on her fingers, like my Aunt Brenda, that would scratch my sides like the wicker of the basket.

When I looked up at Ms. Sonya, she gave me a small smile, her eyes kind but a little shiny, like they had water in them. "Come on, get your pie, and let's take a walk through the store."

We moved from the back workroom to the front of the shop; Ms. Sonya hoofing, me following behind like a shadow.

"Let's start with these," she said, grabbing a few pink and

white flowers with never-ending petals. "Camellias are all about admiration and perfection. You give someone one of these, you telling them you think they perfect just the way they are."

Gently, I touched one of the soft petals. Maybe my mama left because she felt like she couldn't be the perfect mother for me. I wondered if she knew I'd accept her any way she was, even with the monkey on her back.

Next, Ms. Sonya grabbed a big, bright sunflower from another bucket. "Now, sunflowers are special. They twist and turn to make sure they facing whichever way the sun goes. Like the people here in New Orleans. We could be dealing with the worst of hurricanes, but we still gon' laissez les bon temps rouler."

"So, if you give somebody sunflowers, it mean y'all about to have a good time?"

She chuckled. "Maybe. They also mean you're loyal to that person. You adore them."

"Oh, like a best friend?" I shook my head. "Ms. Sonya, I ain't giving Zay no flowers. That's lame."

"Boy, you crazy." She laughed, walking us over to a table filled with roses in different shades of bright colors. "You know what these are?"

"Yeah, roses. My teacher got some for Valentine's Day last year. What they mean?" I asked, leaning on the table, noticing the sharp thorns on the stem.

"Roses tell their own story. I know you know red ones mean love. But yellow," she started pulling a yellow stem from the center. "These mean friendship and joy."

I stared at the flowers, taking in their scent. "So, I could give these to a girl, and be like I gave you these 'cause you my friend?"

Ms. Sonya raised her eyebrow, looking at me suspiciously. "Khalil, you got some girl you sniffing around?"

"No, ma'am. Not right now. I'm just taking notes for later." I laughed off.

"Umm huh." She smirked. We walked past a low shelf filled with shrubs with some tiny flower buds that looked like weeds.

"What are those?"

"Those are sweet olive shrubs. Tough little things. They can take any kind of beating and still bloom. Just like us. No matter the hurricane or floods, we always come back, stronger and prettier."

"What's your favorite flower, Ms. Sonya?"

"I love me some lilies. Which one you like?"

I thought back over all the meanings she'd told me. The roses and sunflowers were cool. So were the sweet olive bushes. They didn't do anything for me. I thought about the lily arrangement she was working on early, and how she said they stood for purity and restored souls. It was what I hoped my mama found after she left.

"I think I like lilies, too."

Ms. Sonya walked over to a bucket closest to the register and picked a bold pink flower with white edges and dark spots. "Here. You can have this one. Now, go get your backpack. I got some food at the house you can have for dinner. Your auntie said she'd be a little late picking you up."

"Ms. Sonya, what kind of monkey my mama got on her back?" I asked, breaking into the silence of the kitchen, save for the small TV on the kitchen counter. I pushed around the food on my plate, a healthy heaping of greens and neckbones over rice. "It's not a gorilla I hope. Them things big as hell. That might break her back, huh?"

"Boy, watch your mouth. I know your daddy taught you better than that," she scolded, swatting the side of my head. "And no. It's not a gorilla, but it's just as heavy."

"So like an orangutan?"

Ms. Sonya let out a laugh from deep in her belly. "Yeah, like an orangutan, I guess." She stopped eating and stared at me, a thought going back and forth between her eyes. "You been thinking about your mama, Khalil?"

"Yeah, a little bit. I don't know much about her. My daddy don't talk about her either." I picked some meat from the neckbones, letting the savory flavor linger on my tongue as I chewed.

"Stop eating with your fingers." Ms. Sonya passed me a napkin. "And listen to this. Sometimes, people go through things, and it's nothing we can do about it but let them go through it. We can want to save somebody from hurting, but if they ain't ready to be saved, that's just got to be it. You hear me?"

I shook my head. "Do you think she'll ever come back?"

"I don't know and–" Screeching tires and the front door opening startled the both of us. Ms. Sonya rose from the table, grabbing a nearby knife. I followed close behind, sticking close to the walls.

Ms. Sonya's daughter, Charisse, walked into the house, holding the hand of her daughter, Kelly. She looked sad and a bit confused, like how I felt whenever I thought about where my mama was.

Ms. Sonya didn't look happy, which was rare. She normally had a smile as warm as a summer night in New Orleans.

"Girl, what the hell you doing here? And, why you slamming doors like you ain't got a lick of sense?"

"Mama, not now. I'm not in the mood." Charisse huffed through the house, dropping off the duffel on her shoulders by the stairs.

"You got some damn nerve, walking in here like you pay the damn bills. And why you got this girl on the road, late as it is?"

"Mama, I can't take it. I am done dealing with his big-headed ass."

"Y'all go watch TV in the kitchen. Kelly girl, I'm gonna come make you a plate in a second. Fix you some Kool-Aid."

The two of us walked back to the kitchen, Kelly looking at the floor the entire way. She stayed quiet as she poured herself a glass of the sweet red drink, then walked over to sit next to me at the kitchen table. Silently, we watched the reruns of *The Jamie Foxx Show*.

"You alright?" I asked, finishing my plate of food.

"Yeah," she replied. Her voice was soft, but firm. It reminded me of when you had to say thank you when someone gave you a birthday card with no money in it. Back in the front room, we could hear Kelly's mother and grandmother going at it. They were talking loudly, but I could tell they were trying not to. It was something about Kelly's dad and her mother needing a break from his big-headed ass.

"You sure you okay?" I asked, turning the volume down on the TV. "And don't lie."

Kelly sighed. "It's my mom and dad," she murmured, her voice barely above a whisper. "They're always arguing. I hate it."

I frowned, hating anything that made the girl before me sad. I thought for a moment, then reached into my backpack hanging on the back of my chair. I pulled out a bag of Hot Cheetos. "Want to know something about these chips?" I asked, hoping to distract her.

She looked at me, her eyes lighting up for the first time since she walked in the door. "What's that?"

"They're magic," I said, nodding as seriously as I could. "When you eat them, they make you feel better. Don't believe me, try it for yourself." I opened the bag, holding it out to her with a hopeful smile.

The giggles that left her mouth made my heart feel funny, like when I eat all my Halloween candy and need to get the zoomies out. She took a chip and popped it into her mouth, her eyes closing at the spicy taste.

"You feel it working?" I asked eagerly.

"I think so." She laughed again, music to my ears. "I think I need to get some more to be sure."

I placed the bag on the table, and we each took turns grabbing chip after chip. We continued watching the show, munching away as Jamie Foxx's antics washed over us. After a few more laughs, I felt brave enough to scoot my chair closer to Kelly. I grabbed the lily Ms. Sonya had given me back at the flower shop.

"Here," I said, offering Kelly the flower. "For extra magic."

She took the lily, her smile genuine this time. "Thank you, Khalil. For this and the chips. It made me smile."

I beamed, proud of myself for cheering her up. "Anytime I can I will, Lily-girl." Kelly gave me a double take then shook her head, letting the accidental nickname I let slip roll off her shoulders.

We turned our attention back to the show, except this time we were sitting a little closer, our shoulders brushing each other each time we laughed. The kitchen was filled with a quiet comfort of a shared friendship. I looked over at Kelly, her snaggle-toothed smile now reaching her eyes. Secretly, I hoped that maybe, just maybe, I could always be the one to make her smile, no matter how big the arguments at her home might be.

Part One

"*The First Time Ever I Saw Your Face*"

Roberta Flack

Chapter 1

Kelly

You learn a lot about people when they were vulnerable–hooked up to IVs, tucked into hospital beds, trying not to let fear show on their little faces. You learned a lot about yourself, too. Like how, despite everything I thought I wanted when I was younger, whether it was cheer captain, top of my class, or a whole wall of trophies, I didn't really feel like I was doing anything important until I made this tiny six-year-old with a custom Bratz bonnet laugh in the middle of her chemo treatment.

"I'm serious, Lavender," I said, perched on the edge of her bed, pulling a silly face. "If you want your stuffed unicorn to qualify for a medical license, she will have to pass the board exam."

Lavender giggled, her little hand clutching her IV pole like it was a favorite doll. "She already knows everything! She watches Grey's Anatomy with my mom."

I gasped. "Well, that explains it. She's obviously overqualified." It was the smallest exchange, but in this job the small ones mattered most.

"Dr. Reid!" one of the nurses called from the nurses' station, lifting a clipboard in my direction. I smiled and gave Lavender's hand a gentle squeeze before I stood.

"I'll come back and check on Unicorn's progress after lunch, okay?"

"Okay!" she chirped. "Tell her she better not fail," she added with a fierce look.

"Message received."

Back at the nurses' station, I signed off on a few patient charts, waved at Dr. Benavidez, and ignored the way one of the new residents did a double-take as I walked by. I didn't mean to walk like I owned the hospital. But when you're confident, you didn't exactly shrink yourself for the comfort of others.

Besides, the white coat just hit differently when you earned it.

"Kelly, you staying late for the grand rounds?" one of my co-residents, Janelle, asked as she flipped through a chart beside me.

"I was thinking about it, but I promised my mom I'd stop by her place."

She arched an eyebrow. "Everything okay?"

I shrugged quickly, eyes flicking down to the clipboard in my hands. "Same mess, different day. My parents have been doing this petty push-and-pull thing for as long as I can remember. I'm trying not to get roped in."

Janelle winced. "Oof. Been there. I can't stand when grown folks act like kids."

"Exactly. I'm twenty-eight. I shouldn't still be dodging their guilt trips like dodgeballs in middle school."

We exchanged a knowing look before parting ways. I headed to the locker room, stripped off my scrubs, and changed into a fitted black tank top and baggy jeans that hugged the round curve of my ass just so. The outfit said, "I'm off the clock but still the best-dressed person in the room."

On my way out, I checked my phone and saw I had a text from my dad.

DADDY-O

Heard you're going to your mom's. Again.
When are you gonna spend some time with
your old man?

I rolled my eyes. I'm sure the "again" was meant to be drawn out like I was some disloyal teenager sneaking out to crash at a boyfriend's house. I debated calling him back but decided against it.

If he was truly hurt, he knew where to find me.

MY MOM LIVED in a Mediterranean-style townhouse in the Houston Heights area. It was beautiful with its exposed wooden beams, stone arches, and cream exterior. It was a far cry from the brick mini-mansion my parents shared before their latest split. Her bachelorette pad had a kind of modern aesthetic that influencers would sell a kidney for. It was a little much for someone who claimed to hate "all that modern mess," but Charisse Reid was nothing if not a contradiction.

As I pulled up, I spotted my dad's car in the driveway.

Of course.

I parked anyway. I wasn't about to play hide-and-seek over grown folks' drama.

When I got on the porch, the door opened before I could even knock. My dad stepped out, dressed in one of his too-expensive polos and cologne that hit my nose before he even said a word.

"Hey, baby girl."

"Hey, Daddy," I said, giving him a quick kiss on the cheek. He lingered, eyes scanning me like he was trying to read between the lines of my outfit.

"You look tired. Been working too hard again?"

"Residency is supposed to be hard," I said lightly. "I'm fine."

He nodded, but his eyes drifted to the front door. "I just think it's funny–"

Lord.

"–how you always find time to come see your mama, but I haven't seen you in weeks."

"It hasn't been weeks," I groaned. "I just saw you at Nessa and Zay's engagement party."

"It's been eleven days since that," he corrected like he'd been counting. "And before that, it was weeks."

I sighed, shifting my weight. "Daddy, I'm not picking sides."

"You don't have to say it, Kelly. Actions speak louder than words."

I hated when he did this. Turned every visit into a referendum. Like loving one parent meant betraying the other.

"Look, I'm here now, okay? I'll call you later this week. Maybe we can grab lunch."

His expression softened a little, but the weight in his eyes didn't lift. "Alright. Just...don't forget who taught you everything you know."

I blinked. "Really?"

"I'm just saying." He opened his car door, shook his head like I'd already failed some unspoken test, and drove off.

I stood on the porch for a second, trying not to feel guilty, and then I went inside.

My mom was in the kitchen with a glass of wine and a silk head wrap that matched her lipstick. She looked up as I walked in, flashing a smile that didn't quite reach her eyes.

"Did your father say something slick on the way out?"

"When does he not?" I tossed my bag on the stool and went straight to the fridge. "He gave me the usual guilt trip. Said I've been favoring you."

She snorted. "Because you come here and I feed you? That man still thinks the world revolves around him."

I popped open a sparkling water and leaned against the

counter. "Y'all need to just divorce already. Aren't you tired of this back-and-forth bullshit?"

"Kelly Reid, watch that damn mouth of yours. You may be taller than me, but I'll drag you down to my level before washing your mouth out with soap myself. I'm not one of your little friends."

"Weren't we throwing back mimosas just last weekend," I questioned, shrugging my shoulders.

"Watch it." Her mouth tightened, giving me the look. You know the one. Eyes tight, mouth pursed. The one Black mothers gave right before they popped you with a slipper. "It's not that simple, Lily girl."

"It is. File the papers, celebrate your freedom, and then let me show what it means to be outside. We can take a girls' trip."

She laughed, but it was laced with something tired. "I don't know if my idea of fun still looks like yours."

"You don't have to match me shot for shot, Mama. Just come have fun. You've earned it."

She studied me for a long second. "Why are you so pressed about me getting a divorce?"

"I'm pressed about you being happy. And I'm tired of being the emotional referee between you and Daddy."

That made her quiet. She ran a hand along my jawline, her palm cradling my face for a second. She took a sip of wine, eyes settling on some far-off place in her head.

"I'll think about it," she said finally.

I nodded, even though I knew what she meant.

You didn't rush a woman like Charisse Reid. You just planted the seed and hoped it grew.

Chapter 2

Kelly

I STAYED AT MY MOM'S LONG ENOUGH TO EAT TWO servings of her shrimp and grits, refill her wine, and threaten to hide her phone if she answered another call from my father. The usual. By the time I got home, the sky had deepened into a soft violet-blue hue that always made me feel a little nostalgic. Like I was supposed to be sitting on my grandma's porch in cutoff shorts, eating a red cold cup, and talking trash with her and her friends, mastering my spades game. Instead, I was in my house, pulling off my earrings and mentally switching gears from "daughter suck in the middle" back to "future pediatric oncologist baddie with goals."

I dropped onto my couch; my laptop balanced on my thigh and my phone in one hand. The group FaceTime rang before I could even text them to say I was home.

The screen split into four familiar faces: Nyah, with her over-sized bonnet, wine glass, and bowl of popcorn, was waiting for the drama to unfold; Lynn, already halfway through a glass of wine, had the ring light on like she was about to film a YouTube tutorial; and Vanessa, all fresh-faced, with her baby hair slicked and that mysterious smile she got when she was up to something.

"Hey y'all," I cheered, comforted by their voices.

"I haven't heard from y'all all day! I was about to send out a search party!" Vanessa pouted from the chaos of her cluttered studio.

Nyah's laughter rang out from her chic, minimalist kitchen. "As if you'd ever leave your sanctuary, Nessa. How were your rounds today, Kelly?"

"Yes, spill the tea, including whatever happened with that sexy Dr. Blackwood," Lynn chimed in from amidst a backdrop of law books, her braids swinging slightly.

I chuckled, the warmth of my friends washing over me. "You know, just the usual chaos. But, hey, nothing a little wine can't fix, right?" I held up my glass, filled with sparkling rosé, prompting virtual clinks against the camera from my friends.

Our conversation flowed effortlessly, shifting from recaps of the engagement party to Nyah's current grievances with her husband. I laughed more deeply than I had in weeks, letting my usually guarded demeanor melt away under the safety of our sisterhood.

"So, Kelly, you're finally ready to admit you're in a relationship," Nessa teased. "Or are you still claiming 'busy saving lives' as an excuse?"

I rolled my eyes playfully, smirking. "I don't know why y'all think I'm in a relationship. I'm in a faithful marriage with my job, and let me tell you. It's the most demanding spouse ever."

"Well, at least that spouse is dependable. Can't say the same for some of the real ones out here," Nyah complained.

"Then leave, Nyah," I suggested, waiting for whatever excuse my friend would give this time around.

"It's not that bad," she voiced, looking off into the distance. "Y'all know how I get when I'm PMS-ing."

"Ugh, tell me about it. I had to sit through three meetings today with the worst cramps," Lynn whined. "Nessa, I know you made a pan of brownies. I'm coming over tomorrow to indulge and watch black rom-coms."

"I, uh, forgot to make them." Vanessa walked away from the phone. I was puzzled. How could she forget about the brownies? The THC-infused goodies were a staple to our sisterhood ever since our cycles synced after college. "We should make something else. And I found these mocktail recipes that taste almost like the real thing on social media."

I bet this bitch is pregnant.

"What gives, Nessa? You're being weird." Lynn asked, peering over her large frames. "Why would I drink a fake drink when I could have the real thing?"

Vanessa smiled even wider, biting her bottom lip like she was trying to keep it in. "Okay, okay – I wanted to tell y'all in person, but I couldn't wait anymore."

She held up a roll of black-and-white images with small white text that said, *"Baby Morris."*

My jaw dropped.

"I know that's not what I think it is!" I shrieked, immediately sitting up straighter.

"Bitch!" Lynn screamed. "You're pregnant?"

Vanessa nodded, grinning so big she could barely contain her excitement. "Nine weeks today. We heard the heartbeat this morning." All to be heard was the spinning of my ceiling fan and a kid's show echoing in the distance from somewhere deep inside Nyah's house.

"Nessa," Nyah gasped. "Girl, spill it. I need the details."

"Wait–" I counted back ten weeks, mentally replaying every event, every get-together, every drink that touched Vanessa's lips during that time. "How the hell are you ten weeks? You were just drinking at your engagement party."

"And your gallery opening," Lynn added.

"I pretended to drink. Zay finished it for me." Vanessa laughed, tears in her eyes. "I told Zay we'd wait until I was out of the first semester, y'all are my sisters, so y'all don't count."

"Aww, Nessa," Lynn cooed, ever the softie of our group. "I'm so happy for you. You and Zay."

Nyah nodded. "Another baby," she squealed. "TJ's getting so big, I can't wait to have another one around to cuddle."

I smiled, too, fighting to make it reach my eyes. If there was anything I hated about myself, it was that even in happy times, there was a piece of me that stood off to the side, arms crossed, like it deserved to sit out of the fun. Of course, I was thrilled for my sister, but something tugged at me. I shook off the feeling, leaning closer to the screen, letting my friend's excitement wash over me.

"And before y'all start fighting over who's the godmother, just know that's my baby," I said, sipping my wine. "Nessa, you're going to be an amazing mother," I added, with more warmth in my voice than the alcohol hitting my chest.

"I hope so," she said, looking down at her still-flat stomach. "Honestly, I just hope I don't fuck them up. It didn't feel real all these weeks. But hearing the 'whoosh, whoosh, whoosh' sealed it for me. Last year was so tough. I felt like I was crying every other–"

"That's because you were crying every other day," Lynn said, cutting her off.

"Anyways." Vanessa rolled her eyes and continued. "But this year...It feels like everything is lining up for me."

There it was again–an annoying buzzing in my soul, a gnat flying around, evading my attempts to squash it. Everyone else's puzzle pieces were snapping into place while mine were jumbled in the box.

But at least I had a box with all the right pieces, while others were left to scrounge the deepest, darkest basement, looking for a piece of the cover to determine how it should fit. I have things going for me. I was damn good at what I did, respected, the one younger residents came to for advice. But for the past year, I felt I was on autopilot, all the years of living up to the expectations of being me – being the best, hardworking, smiling on cue even though I was crumbling inside. It was as if my limbic system had decided to go on vacation even though the rest of my brain denied its PTO request.

"Speaking of life changes," Nyah said. "Kelly, have you heard back about your fellowship match?"

"Nope," I said, shaking my head. "They announced results will be emailed next week."

"Girl, you know you got it. Look at her," Lynn said, pointing to her screen. "She's not even stressed about it."

"That part," Vanessa added.

I smiled with my heart this time. "Thanks, y'all. I'm just ready to know. I've worked my whole life for this moment. I just need the universe to take me a little further."

"It will, Kelly," Lynn said. "The universe always shows up for bad bitches."

We stayed on the phone a little while longer until I grew tired of my friends' thinly veiled attempts to get answers to what was going on between Khalil and me. Nothing was going on. Well, nothing that needed to be shared with anyone that wasn't Khalil or me. After I said goodnight, I sat in my thoughts, staring at the black screen of my laptop. I tapped the keyboard, the screen lighting in the dim light of my living room. My rank order list confirmation stared back at me—each hospital chiseled in stone, waiting to decide my destiny. I'd spent countless hours deciding the order after several interviews nationwide, much to my father's chagrin.

I'd chosen Boston Children's Hospital, Johns Hopkins Children's Center, Texas Children's Hospital, Lucile Packard Children's Hospital, and Seattle Children's Hospital. In a little over a week, I'd have my answer. I should have closed my laptop and gone to bed. Instead, I searched my computer files and opened the document that included my personal statement. I reread the first line, each word a building block to my own personal scripture: *My goal is not just to treat illness but to preserve hope, especially in children, where a little joy goes a long way.*

Ugh, these words, my voice. Honest, but a little too preachy, a little too polished. Would the selection committee read it and see what work I put into living these words daily? Would they see the woman who stayed late, reading bedtime stories to her patients? Would they see the woman who brought stickers and silly socks during each round? The one who didn't flinch when parents broke down in her arms after hearing there was nothing we could do to save their precious baby. Or would they see another high-achiever ticking off boxes, ready to add another title to their name?

I closed the laptop and threw myself back on the couch, Disney princess-style, arm draped over my forehead. My phone buzzed.

Khalil.

I smiled before I picked up. I'd been trying for years to fight this feeling, but something about seeing his name made my breath hitch each time. Not because I had feelings for him–though he was always fine, even more so with age, and had a voice that curled around your spine, spellbinding drawl that made you think you were in a dream–but because he *saw* me. Not Kelly Reid. Not the valedictorian. Not the fun one. Not the doctor. *Lily-girl.*

I swiped to answer his FaceTime. "What you want, Big Head?"

"Shit, at least you know." He laughed into the phone. There was a long pause, long enough to feel intimate. "You good?"

I hesitated, then said, "I'm tired."

"Long shift?" he asked. "Them ankle-biters finally getting to you?"

"Haha. More like long life." I sighed. "I went to my mama's for dinner. My dad was walking out as I pulled up. Gave me the usual guilt trip."

"Man, I know that's your dad, but he's a clown. All he been doing the past few months is making you and your mama feel bad for his sorry ass." Khalil sucked his teeth.

"Exactly. I'm just...over it. And did you know Nessa's pregnant?"

"No shit?"

"You didn't know?" I asked, pouring myself another glass of wine. "Well, I'm sure Zay will tell you now. They were trying to wait until she's out of the first trimester." I paused, letting the fermented grapes marinate my tongue. "She's so happy. Like *really* happy."

He was quiet, letting my comments linger in the air. "That hit you a little different, huh?"

I nodded before realizing he couldn't see me since I'd placed my phone on the cushion next to me. "Yeah. I don't understand it. It's not envy. There's no fiber in my body calling out for a baby...I know things are working out in my favor, but I don't get excited about them anymore. Like really excited. Like the joy oozing from Nessa's pores when she told us about the baby. Or how Lynn talks our ears off when she finalizes a contract or meets a new guy."

"It's because you don't let yourself get excited, Lily-girl. I know you. You move and move, never allowing yourself time to think about what you've accomplished."

"You think you know me so well." I smirked, fiddling with the frayed edges of the throw blanket draped across the edge of my lap.

He laughed, a deep-hearted chuckle that stirred something deep within me. He paused a moment, as if reflecting, before speaking again. "I do know you. You're the most capable woman I know, Kelly. When you walk in a room, people can't help but stare and fall in line with the energy you bring. You set the tone."

I swallowed. "How do you always know what to say?"

"Because I know you. Even if you trying to dip out on me and move halfway across the country." He laughed again, this time with less enthusiasm. "What am I going to do without my big dog around?" he laughed, trying to play off whatever feelings he was having. I looked at Khalil through my phone screen, his smile wavering just a touch, even though all thirty-two of his pearly whites were on display.

"I don't know," I said, rolling my eyes. One minute Khalil could be so sincere, almost heartbreakingly sweet. The next, he was full of jokes and silly little games that kept you at arm's length. "Find someone else to force your horrible movie choices on."

"Shut the hell up. Everybody and they mama know *Leprechaun in the Hood* is a classic."

"*The Wood* is a classic. *Training Day* is a classic. Hell, *Tales From the Hood* is a classic," I replied, standing and grabbing my phone and wine glass in the process. "Nobody's checking for an evil leprechaun harassing people because they stole his gold."

"That's what they asses get. They shouldn't have stolen his shit."

I deadpanned at Khalil through my phone. It was then I noticed the snug black t-shirt he wore with his gold Cuban link chains. "Where are you going this time of night?"

"You already know. Me and one of my frats about to link up for a bit." He cheesed into the camera.

"Hmph. Have fun I guess." I poured myself more wine before heading back over to my sofa.

"What, you gon' miss me?" He sat his phone down and peered into my soul it felt. "Say the word, I'm all yours." The way he bit his lip was distracting, the subtle glint of gold from the grills on his lower teeth catching my eyes.

"Khalil, you flatter yourself too much." I took a swig of my wine; my mouth having gone dry. "Let me not keep you from dogging out the women of Houston. I'll talk to you later."

Khalil let out two barks before picking his phone off the counter. "You know me, Lily-girl. That's the only way I know how to be. Especially since you ain't trying to put me on a leash."

I nearly choked at his last comments. "Bye, Khalil," I said, ending the call, staring at the ceiling, my phone pressed to my chest like it could hold his voice a little longer. I didn't know what fresh set of drama tomorrow would bring, didn't know if my top match would be the one, didn't know why Nessa's news triggered a sadness in me, or why Khalil going out festered like a wound on my pinky toe. I grabbed my cell phone, typing out a quick message to Lynn.

ME

Come pick me up. We're going out tonight.

LYNNIE-MAE

I know you're up to something, but I'm down.
Be there in an hour.

Chapter 3

Khalil

As I stepped into the dimly lit lounge, the DJ had the floor jumping with his set consisting of Boosie, Future, and Sauce Walka. The bass pulsed like a second heartbeat under my skin, mixing with the low buzz of laughter and conversation. It didn't matter that it was a Thursday night. The spot was alive with energy. Cologne, perfume, and weed hung in the air like the quiet suspension of tension before a storm.

Maverick Washington waved from a booth near the back, his white teeth and dark skin gleaming under the violet-blue LED lights. I weaved through the crowd, dapped up a few familiar faces, and slid into the booth beside him.

"Man, what up, Mav?" I clapped him on the back, our fraternity handshake flowing out of us like second nature.

"Shit, finally catching a break from traveling." He laughed, signaling the waitress with a nod. "That jet lag life ain't cute no more. Got me thinking about settling down somewhere."

We ordered drinks and fell into easy conversation. I updated him on EcoVision, the community centers Zay and I were renovating with Nessa's parents' foundation. Mav told me about his latest tech projects, his move from Silicon Valley back to Texas, and how Houston was starting to feel like home. I fully understood what he meant. Something about how the city made you slow down but speed up. It had me considering putting down some roots myself. I had my career; all I was missing were the flowers to bring some life to the foundation I'd created.

As Mav spoke, my eyes drifted toward the bar where a woman caught my attention. She was about 5'6", cocoa-butter skin, weave flowing down her back in soft waves. Her dress clung to her like a second skin. Although I preferred women with a little more height, a little more presence, there was something about the way she smiled at the bartender that made me stand up.

"I see you, bruh." Mav chuckled. "Send me a signal if you dipping out early."

I made my way to the bar, casually leaning in until she turned to notice me.

"What's your name?" I asked, eyes steady, voice smooth.

She turned, smiling like she'd already decided I was hers. "Tasha. What's yours?"

"Is that your real name, or one of the fake ones y'all females give out to avoid stalkers?"

She laughed playfully. "Depends on what you plan on doing with it."

We slid into conversation, her responses quick, almost rehearsed. She was all hands and flirty laughs, leaning in close to emphasize I had all her attention, begging to ensure she had all of mine. I kept it light, tossing her a few half-smiles and letting my gaze drift when she was lost in her own storytelling. My phone buzzed with a text from Kelly.

LILY-GIRL

What poor unfortunate soul have you trapped so far?

ME

Chill out Lily-girl. Go to sleep.

"Who's texting you?" Tasha asked, her tone clipped but bright, a sharp thorn kissed with sugar.

"Just a friend checking in."

She smiled, too wide, too bright. "Tell your friend you're in good hands."

I chuckled, pocketing my phone. "Is that right?"

Tasha ran a manicured hand down my arm, but I barely registered it. Kelly's name still lit up my mind. My phone buzzed again in my pocket. I tapped my thumb on the edge of the bar as Tasha continued talking. About what, I couldn't tell you. While she droned on, I slid my phone out of my pocket.

LILY-GIRL

I guess that's a yes. I hope she's cuter than the last girl.

ME

It could be you, but you playing around.

Seriously, get some rest. You been working your ass off.

LILY-GIRL

You can be halfway decent sometimes. Almost makes me think you could be my man.

The last text caught me off guard. Froze me right there at the bar. I bit my lip, struggling to keep the grin threatening to consume my face at bay. Turning toward Tasha, I nodded at whatever she was saying, not entirely hearing her. She was still running off at the mouth when another woman approached her her sister, slightly shorter, same cocoa-butter skin, only her face had a little more edge to it.

"Tasha! I broke my damn heel. Damn these cheap-ass shoes." She looked me over, smirking at her sister. "Who is this?"

"I'm-" I started to answer before Tasha cut me off.

"This is Khalil," she said, resting her hand on my chest. "He's been keeping me company while I waited for you."

"Nice to meet you, Khalil. I'm Courtney."

I nodded. "Y'all wanna join me and my homeboy? He's over in that booth."

Courtney's eyes widened. "Is that Maverick Washington?"

"Yeah, we went to high school together."

"You know Maverick Washington?" Courtney was stunned as she continued looking over at our booth.

Even I was shocked that she knew my friend. While he'd played in the NFL for a few years, he'd always kept a low profile. Lived under the radar, clocked into practice and games until he'd made enough to start his own tech firm, then retired. I'd consulted him several times when Zay and I were starting our company, used him to make connections and get investors.

"Who's Maverick Washington?" Tasha asked, leaning into my side.

"Girl, I swear. You wouldn't know a diamond from a moissanite," her sister replied.

The sisters followed me. At the booth, football took center stage, and while Courtney dazzled Maverick with her knowledge of his stats, Tasha focused her energy on me.

I kept my responses brief, distracted by the itch crawling up my spine. Then, I smelled it.

Citrus, warm skin, and trouble.

Her voice floated above me like silk and smoke. "Look who we have here."

My muscle tightened, and I knew without turning who it was.

Lily-girl.

I turned slowly, and there she stood, statuesque, stealing the air in the room with her presence. Her legs, thick and toned from the delicate heels gracing her feet, went on for days. Her body was wrapped in a sheer printed dress that stopped just beneath the curve of her ass, one so soft and round yet defied gravity. The nude bodysuit underneath lifted her breasts just right, the apex staring me right in the face. I looked away to meet Kelly's gaze. Her eyes crackled like a blazing fire, daring me to react.

I didn't blink.

"What's happening," I said, letting my gaze stay locked with hers. "What y'all doing here?"

She was radiant, confident, her usual sly smirk playing on her soft, glossed lips. Lynn stood beside her, grinning like she already knew the chaos brewing. She sipped the drink in her hand, biting the black straw as she looked between Kelly and me.

"Khalil, stop being rude and introduce your friends," Kelly said sweetly, using the charming mask she'd perfected over her lifetime. Only now, in this moment, her tone was challenge wrapped in cotton candy.

I hesitated, my brain stalling.

She arched a brow, smile still in place, already clocking my fumble. "You know what, excuse him. I'm Kelly, and this is Lynn." She leaned over me, extending her hand to the women between Maverick and me. Her essence stole the little bit of resolve I had left, rendering me speechless.

"Courtney," the football sister piped up. "And this is my sister, Tasha?"

"Courtney and Tasha. How cute. Is Tasha short for something?"

The women engaged in their own conversation. Maverick raised an eyebrow at me, silently mouthing, *You good?*

I nodded, but barely.

As Kelly and Lynn sat at the table, Kelly took a seat opposite me, crossing her legs with deliberate ease. Tasha reached for my arm again, but I shifted just enough for her to miss without bringing attention to the movement.

Why?

I was single. Yeah, Kelly and I had an understanding. Part of that understanding was that neither of us belonged to each other.

And still, sitting here with Tasha trying to stake her claim, Kelly looking smug, catching everything. You'd think I was a child being caught red-handed. As if the teacher invited my mother to observe me in class, waiting for me to continue being the class clown. I shook my head, ridding myself of the unnecessary guilt clawing away inside of my chest.

I looked around the table, settling on the beauty before me. I couldn't take my eyes off Kelly. The way she laughed with Lynn, Tasha, and Courtney. The way she embraced both women, genuinely interested in having a good time with them. The way she ignored me on purpose, I was sure. The curve of her neck when she tossed her hair over her shoulder.

She was magnetic.

She knew it.

I knew it.

An hour passed like minutes with her in my space. Eventually, she and Lynn left our booth, taking to the dancefloor with Tasha and Courtney. She danced with strangers, hips swaying, ass bouncing, her eyes catching mine across the floor. Every look she threw me was gasoline on fire.

"So that's Dr. Kelly Reid?" Maverick mused beside me. "I see why you ain't been able to lock that one down."

I smacked my lips, taking a sip of the fresh glass of whiskey. "The fuck is that supposed to mean?"

"This little back and forth thing," Maverick started. "I see why Zay says he stays out of it."

"We don't have a back and forth thing. What's understood doesn't need to be explained."

He chuckled, choking on his drink. "Okay. When she end up with somebody who done playing games, don't say I didn't warn you."

"Like I told Zay a few months back, I'm done playing games. I'm waiting for her now."

"Nah. If you see something you want, you better get it before it's gone."

I looked back at the dancefloor, my eyes finding the tall beauty among the crowd. When Kelly walked toward the restroom, I followed.

The hallway was narrow, dimly lit. She turned the corner and paused, sensing me behind her.

"Khalil." Her voice was velvety smooth and held a tinge of warning.

"Why you keep playing with me like I won't remind you what the deal is," I said, stepping into her space.

"Remind me of what?" She tilted her chin, giving me a full view of her delicate features. Almond-shaped brown eyes ablaze with mischief, framed with thick lashes fanning her cheekbones. Her button nose was punctuated with full, soft lips. Skin as smooth as petals. But her mouth, sharp as thorns.

My hands found her waist, pulled her flush against me. "That I'm the man that had you screaming my name two months ago. Still ain't got my card back."

Her breath caught, but she didn't move away. Her eyes narrowed, dropping to my lips then back to my eyes. I felt the subtle rise and fall of her chest, her breasts pressed against me, begging for my attention.

Instead, she whispered into my ear, "You think one good night makes you unforgettable."

"Nah. You and I both know it hasn't been just one night," I murmured, brushing my lips over her cheek. "Besides, every night you're the one that's unforgettable. Been hooked since the first taste."

Her hand splayed over my chest, her fingers curling into the black fabric. Her mouth moved to mine, hovering like a honeybee. I licked my lips, thirsty for a taste. We stayed like that, charged and teetering while the music continued in the main part of the lounge.

Then she slipped from my embrace.

"Don't follow me unless you ready to back it up," she tossed over her shoulder, slinking away into the crowd.

She didn't have to say it twice.

I laughed, looking to the floor. Running a hand over my jaw, I walked back to the booth I shared with Maverick. Tasha and Courtney had made their way back as well. Courtney was still going on about Maverick's previous career, curious about life in the limelight.

"Khalil, I thought you'd left," Tasha said, breaking through her sister's ramblings.

"No, ran to the restroom, but I'm heading out now."

"That's a shame," Tasha whined. "It's been fun."

"It has. Nice meeting you both. Mav, I'll hit you up later."

I dapped up Maverick, feeling the pout taking form on Tasha's face. It didn't matter. Years, no decades ago I'd made a vow to keep Kelly smiling. I knew the pout she would have from not following her would gut me more than the downturned smile of the woman who'd been all too eager to press herself upon me.

Leaving the table, I had one thing on my mind. Long, thick legs strong enough to crush even the strongest of men. Pillow soft cheeks that filled my hands and then some. A waist that narrowed in, leading up to breasts that longed to have my face cradled between their valleys. The soft skin of her chest, velvet on my lips.

I shook my head as I started my car. Driving through the neon-lit Houston streets and highways, images of all the times Kelly had indulged me, opened herself up to me, let me taste the sweet nectar hidden between the petals of her independence. I thought back to the very first time. I'd been in town with my father the summer she'd lost her grandmother, Ms. Sonya.

She'd been sitting on the steps of her grandmother's porch, her face sullen, anguish written into each lash. Quickly, I'd said hello to my aunt, then headed down the street. Seeing Kelly sitting there, all I'd wanted to do was take the pain away. For the next few days, I made it my mission to keep her spirits high, giving her refuge from the incessant arguing going on as her mother and uncle decided what to do with her grandmother's belongings. We'd done everything a broke sixteen-year-old could afford without robbing my father blind. Easily, spending time with Kelly became my favorite pastime.

Zay gave me flack about my choosing to spend my break soaked up in the world of Kelly, but he didn't get it. He didn't understand the way my heart swelled each time she was near. For as long as I'd known her, my favorite thing to see was the smile that lit her face, a smile so bright the northern star became jealous. That by the end of this week, I'd ask her to be my girl, even though we'd lived in distant places. Even if her world was wholly different from mine.

And I was almost successful. She'd managed to sneak away during a party at her grandmother's house. A rare moment of her mother and brother getting along, especially since her father had made it to town. We'd gone back to my aunt's house–my father and she were also attending the party–leading her to a barren room, save for a bed, a few boxes, and a Bluetooth speaker I'd use to play music from my iPod.

That night, she dropped the guard she'd built over the years, letting me in in more ways than one. I was nervous as hell, wanting to make the moment special for her, special for us. And it was. We were each other's first physically, but little did she know, she'd cemented herself as my love. When I brought her home, standing under the dim light of the porch, I started to ask her to be mine. Unfortunately, I was cut off due to the shouting coming from inside of the house. Seconds later, her father stumbled out, being dragged by her mother. Between the chaos of whatever happened between her father and uncle, I never got to ask.

This time would be different.

Thirty minutes later, I was at her door. I knocked, getting no answer. Glancing at my phone, checking her location, I saw she was still about five minutes away. I made myself comfortable, standing against the brick wall of her entryway. An eternity later, a car pulled into her driveway. She sauntered out, blowing kisses to the driver, Lynn, then stumbled as she turned and saw me waiting. Quickly, shock was replaced by intrigue as she made her way slowly to the door, ensuring every muscle and curve of her body rippled with each step.

I bit my lip, controlling the urge to take her right there. That was probably what she wanted. Always one to play games. I pocketed my phone as she stood in front of me. She rolled her eyes like she didn't care that I'd shown up at her door, ready to give her every piece of me if she'd let me.

"What are you doing at my house, Big Head?" A playful glint danced in her eyes as she stared back at me. The smile that melted my heart grinned back, daring me.

Instead of a reply, I circled an arm around her waist, pressing her body close to mine. With my other hand, I grazed the soft skin of her jaw, taking in the epitome of natural beauty in my arms. My hand trailed down to her graceful neck, my thumb playing over the pulse point thundering at the base. I squeezed gently, being met with a quick shudder escaping her lips as she closed her eyes. Her body shifted. That was the thing about Kelly. She loved being all steel and sarcasm, but if you looked closer, then you saw it. The softness she hid from the world. Even herself.

Holding her, the sweet, sharp scent of her perfume enveloped me. Her lips parted, ready with some smart-ass comment, but I didn't give her the chance. I touched her chin, tilting her face toward mine, and let my thumb graze over her full bottom lip. Eyeing the berry-pink painted lips, knowing the sweetness they housed, I covered them with my own, slow, possessive, in need of something that wouldn't be quenched with just this night.

Kelly's lips parted for me, soft and warm, remnants of sweet tequila lingering on her tongue. She kissed me back like she was mad at her body for betraying her mind. Mad that I was able to crack through her defenses and allow her to be fragile. Her fingers laced around my neck. Walking her backwards toward her door, I stripped the keys from her hands, unlocking the door, and leading us inside.

Upstairs in her bedroom, I savored her form as she laid back on the thick, beige comforter in nothing but the nude set she'd worn under her sheer dress. She looked at me, breathless. Her eyes flickered, a fight between her body and brain still waging.

I'd win.

I knew it.

She knew it.

But tonight wasn't about winning. We were done with the games. The incessant back and forth that'd been our friendship for years. It was time for me to show up. Time for me to prove I knew what she needed, when she needed it, even when she didn't know how to ask for it. I knelt down, kissing the hollows of her ankles, her citrusy-sweet scent sending a pleasurable ache to my dick. Loosening the thin straps, I peppered kisses along the arches.

"You didn't answer my question," she gasped.

Although she kept the devilish look to her face, the fidgeting of her toes let on that I was getting to her. Again, I refused her request for an answer. My mouth was too busy feasting on the satiny-smoothness of her legs, inching my way closer and closer to the valley between her thighs, making pit stops behind each knee.

"What happened to your little friend? I'm sure she was sad to see you go."

"You talk too much," I murmured against the softness of her thighs, drinking in the intoxicating smell of her arousal. "Let me give you a reason to be quiet."

Fire shot from her eyes when she looked at me. Her voice trapped in her throat, buried under the way I kissed between her breasts, unclasped her bra with one hand, and took her nipple in my mouth with the other. Softly, she cursed, her head falling back as I teased her, licking, sucking, pulling just enough to make her whimper.

I loved that sound.

Even with her body writhing beneath me, she tried to act like she was in control, like this was just sex. But with her thighs already trembling and her hands grasping through the curls of my hair, it was clear she needed something to hold onto. A life raft saving her from giving into something that was preordained from the moment we shared my chips, watching the *Jamie Foxx Show* in Ms. Sonya's kitchen.

"Khalil..." Her voice cracked, the first undoing of the armor she wore.

I looked up. Her lips were flushed, her pupils blown. "Turn that brain off, Lily-girl," I said, dragging my mouth down her stomach, my tongue leaving wet trails to my desired destination. "Let me back up all that shit you was talking earlier," I said, pulling the nude thong down in one smooth motion.

"I wasn't–"

I silenced her with my tongue.

She tasted like heaven.

Kelly bucked against my mouth as I kissed her, licked her, devoured her like I'd been starving. And I had. For her. Always her. I moved slow at first, then deeper, circling her clit just the way I knew she liked it, drawing those tight, needy sounds out of her one by one.

"This pussy sweet as fuck right now. You gon' keep it sweet for me later," I murmured between her precious lips, voice rough against the velvet skin. I sucked each lip in my mouth, savoring the plump sweetness, before attacking the hardened pearl.

She whimpered, her hips rising to meet my mouth. She didn't have shit to say now. No words. Just breathy, broken sounds. Music to my ears. She came fast, sharp, her thighs locking around my head, heels burrowing in my back as she cried out my name. She tried to catch her breath, her breasts rising and falling in rapid motion. I kissed up her body, tasting her pleasure coating my lips and tongue. Her eyes met mine glazed, unguarded. She wasn't thinking anymore.

I smiled, kissing her again. "Turn that ass over and arch that back, Lily-girl."

She nodded, biting her lip. She kneeled in front of me, ass to the ceiling, her center spread wide, blossoming and dripping with honey, ready for my taking. I stripped out of my clothes, watching her eyes track every movement as she peered over her shoulder, eyes filled with lust.

"I know you can arch that back better than that," I challenged, stroking my dick. Her eyes narrowed, her lips moved to say something, but it was lost when I ran my hand down her spine, gently pushing her head into the pillows underneath. *Beautiful.*

I settled behind her like I belonged there. Because I did. I slid inside with a low groan. She was tight, hot. *Perfect.*

Kelly moaned into the pillows, clinging to my hands as I gripped her hips. I moved slow. Deep. Purposeful. This wasn't about rushing. It was about breaking her open with every stroke.

"Keep throwing that ass back, just like that," I said, my voice a low husk, just louder than the slaps of her ass hitting my hips, her arousal leaking down her thighs. Spurred on, she met my thrusts with urgent fervor, seeking something she knew only I could give to her. When her movements became more sporadic and uncontrolled, I knew I had her.

"Turn over, let me see that beautiful face," I growled, pulling out. Never in my life had I seen a more exquisite human than Kelly lying before me, legs splayed wide, her center clenching, dripping for me, needy for me.

When I slid inside again, she shivered beneath me. Her moaning my name, so soft, so sensual, so desperate threatened to be my undoing. Her nails dragged down my back. Every time her hips lifted, I met her there. Every moan she let slip from her lips, I swallowed. Her arms clung to my shoulders, her hands gripping to the back of my head. As much as she said otherwise, her body couldn't help but tell the truth.

When her walls clenched around me again, I slowed, wiping the sheen gracing her hairline with my lips.

"Khalilplease"

"I got you," I whispered into her ear, then kissed the hollow of her neck. "Let go for me."

She came again, this time softer, deeper. I followed seconds later, groaning into her neck, her name breaking from my lips like a vow. I didn't pull away. Instead, I shifted us until she was lying across my chest, tucked against me like she belonged there.

Because she did.

Her fingers traced the tattoos littering my chest, spending extra time on the peace lily with 1 *Corinthians* 16:14. For once, she wasn't trying to fill the silence. She wasn't making jokes. She wasn't running.

She was here.

I kissed her forehead.

"I'm done playing games," I whispered, brushing my hand down her back. "You're a firecracker to the world. Let me be the soft spot to rest your head."

She didn't say anything. She stayed wrapped in my arms quiet, warm, vulnerable. And that said more than anything she could've come up with. Minutes later, her breathing slowed. She struggled to keep her eyelids open as she lay on my chest, her legs intertwined with mine underneath the thick comforter.

I swept my thumb over the delicate skin of her cheekbones, my other hand smoothing circles over her back. "Go to sleep, Lily-girl."

What little tension left in her body dissipated as her body melted into mine. Soft snores escaped her lips. I reached over to turn off the lamp on her nightstand. Staring at the ceiling, my feelings were set in stone. Lily-girl was mine. I'd crash out before I let another steal her away.

Chapter 4

Kelly

Summer 2010 - MawMaw's House, New Orleans, LA

THE SUN HAD NERVE TODAY. LIGHT-BLINDING, SKIN scorching audacity. It clung to everything—my scalp, the back of my neck, the swell of my cheeks—as if its mission was to remind people the world kept spinning, even when people stopped breathing. The stretch of street in front of my grandmother's house shimmered in the heat, save for the few potholes and jagged cracks in the pavement. Cicadas harmonized in the thick air, competing with the grumbling churn of the AC unit in desperate need of freon.

I sat on the top stoop with my knees pulled to my chest, my chin resting on top. I should have had a Kool-Aid pickle and a bag of Hot Cheetos with cheese and jalapeños in my hand. A card table should have been unfolded behind me, squeaky chairs holding the weights of my grandmother and her friends as they laughed and cussed each other out. Only now, there were no sodium rich snacks or sour sweet treats to stain my teeth. No smoke streak of Virginia Slims' fragrance in the air. Nobody sending me in the house for a cool can of malt liquor. Just a sagging silence wrapped around me, like the humidity. Too heavy to ignore, but too familiar to fight.

Inside, my parents were arguing again in hushed tones that didn't do a damn thing to hide the sharpness of their words. Mama was trying. She was trying so fucking hard, but you could only stretch grief so far before it snapped. And with Daddy and Uncle PJ circling each other like vultures battling for the decaying carcass since we made it to town, who could blame her. You could only take so much of being blame for something outside of your control. What was it today? Something about her not coming down enough, especially once MawMaw got sick. How that gave Mama no right to say what happened with her affairs now that she was gone.

Gone.

Everybody tiptoed around it. Around the growing reality. That the one who held the final thread of keeping her family together was gone, and none of us knew what to do with that. Especially me.

When one of my grandmother's friends stopped by after the funeral, she hugged me tight, rasping into my ear, "You're so strong, Kelly. Sonya would be so proud." And they kept saying it. Like it was a compliment. A badge of honor. As if it weren't a secret code instilled from my parents for, *keep your shit together so we don't have to.*

I stared out at the solar powered lights that lined the walkway to the mailbox. Watched as the heat made them bend at their necks to the drying grass. I knew people were wary of summer storms here, but today of all days I needed the reprieve from the beaming sun overhead. I was sure the oak trees and dry dirt would appreciate a little rainwater bringing to surface the old stories that lived in the cracks of this neighborhood.

A soft rumble of tires pounded down the street too fast, then eased up when it hit the dip near the corner. I looked just as a blue Maxima turned onto the block and slowed down in front of a house a few doors down. Khalil aunt's house.

I recognized him immediately as his tall frame stepped out of the car. Not because I paid attention to him like that, or wrote my name with his last name in the backs of my notebooks, or daydreamed about him when I became annoyed by the pretentious boys of my private school. Not like that. He just had a way of stepping into the world like it was made especially for him. All limbs and confidence. His usual wide coils tamed into braids that reached past his shoulders. Skin baked just right from what I was sure was his time playing football and training all summer.

When he got out, he stretched wide and glanced toward me before his dad popped the trunk. When our eyes met, the noise in my chest quieted. His face was all smiles as he waved to me from his aunt's driveway. He said something to his dad and started jogging toward me, leaving behind whatever his dad was unloading behind like it could wait.

Her heart. It had to have been my grandmother's heart that gave out. I wondered if it was genetic the way mine roared in my chest as Khalil got closer.

"Hey," he said when he got close, his voice low and noticeably deeper than I remembered. He stood at the edge of the stoop, eyes shaded under his lashes, hands in his pockets.

"Hey."

He didn't hesitate to sit next to me on the bottom step, close enough to bring the air around us up another 400 degrees. Heat stroke. *She went out in a literal blaze of glory.* That's what my obituary will say.

"I heard about Ms. Sonya," he said, his gaze fixed on me, reading my expressions so he could gauge my emotional state. "I'm sorry."

I nodded. Swallowed.

He leaned forward, resting his forearms on his knees. His fingers toyed with the tips of mine.

"You wanna talk about it?"

I shook my head. "Not really."

He bit his lip as he peered into my heart. "Cool. We don't have to."

And just like that, he gave me what nobody else had. Space. No pressure to be solid in my strength, just to make someone else feel like they'd done their part. He pulled out a pack of banana flavored Now & Laters, wrapped back the outer wrapper, and placed a pocket warmed square into the palm of my hand.

"Banana? What are you? Sixty?" I smirked. An uncontrollably smile tugged at my lips. I gave up the fight within seconds.

"Quit playing with me," he joked back. "Everybody and they mama know banana the best flavor... Sweet. Just like you."

My mind went blank. My. Mind. Went. Blank. Me, the one who normally had a sassy quip ready at the hip. All I heard was that Barbie rapper's new song playing on repeat. I was the toddler and his corny line was candy that I wanted more and more.

"Thanks," I said once my brain began functioning again. He watched me unwrap the candy and pop it in my mouth.

He looked behind me at the house. "You know, Ms. Sonya was happy when she moved to this house. Always had a pot of something ready to feed somebody. Man, I miss them neckbones and gravy."

"Yeah," I said, the candy watering my mouth. "She always had a way of feeding people. Aside from flowers, cooking was her favorite hobby. She liked sharing with others."

He glanced at me. "But she loved cooking for you most. When you'd visit, back in the day, she'd talk about it for weeks before and after. 'I gotta get some cold cups in the fridge for my Kelly-girl. Ummhuh Jeanne. She only like the red ones,'" he said, half-laughter, half-mimicking my grandmother's smoke-coated voice.

I looked away, cheeks warming. "They were my favorite. She's my... Was my favorite person."

"I believe that," he said, smiling. "You were hers, too."

"How do you know that? You haven't lived here since Katrina."

"Because I know. Y'all got the same energy. Light up a room when you walk in. Even when you ain't got shit to say."

I laughed. A real one, short and surprised. "You don't even know me like that."

"Yeah I do. I be seeing your posts on Facebook. I know you see me liking them bitches." He then proceeded to mock my signature pose. Head tilted, lips pursed, double-fisted peace sign.

I laughed again. Snorted something fierce. Gripped my belly as I tried to take him seriously. I grabbed one of his arms, begging him to stop his impromptu photoshoot. "Khalil, stop. I do not do that."

He took my hand in his, looping his finger through mine. "Yeah, you do," he said, licking his lips. "It's cute, though."

Our eyes locked as the cicadas picked up their song around us. "Stop looking at me."

"You right here in my face. Where else I'm supposed to look?"

I rolled my eyes, but I didn't look away. My chest tightened. Not in a bad way. Just in a way that made me feel seen and naked at the same time. A pause passed between us. Cars passed on the street in front of us.

"I'm angry she's gone," I said softly. "I hate everyone keeps operating in their own world, like they don't see me here hurting."

He didn't flinch. Just grabbed my other hand, locking it with the other one he still held. His thumb swept over the backs, slow and sure. "You don't gotta be strong with me," he said. "I told you way back when, I got you."

"Oh yeah? Me and how many other girls? Don't think I don't see the girls commenting on your posts."

When he laughed, he made the air feel easier to breathe. "You got jokes, huh? I wouldn't need them girls commenting on my shit if you wasn't always ghosting me."

I narrowed my eyes. When I opened my mouth to speak, his aunt hollering down the street cut me off.

"Khalil, bring your ass in this house and start packing these boxes!"

"Here I come!" he answered back, then looked back at me. "I'm gonna be out here the rest of the week. Let me show you what you missing out on when you start dipping out on a nigga. Help you take your mind off everything else."

"I guess," I replied, struggling to keep my excitement at bay. As he stood, I followed, swiping the dirt off of my pants. I looked at the ground, the porch behind me, the cars turning on the corner. Everywhere but him.

"Come here, Lily-girl." He wrapped his arms around my waist and pulled me into his chest. He smelled like Irish Spring soap and Old Spice. My body nestled into the embrace. "Fuck what everybody else got going on. You wanna be sad, be sad. You wanna cry, cry. You wanna laugh, laugh. You hear me?"

I looked up to see he was staring down at me. Tears lined the rims of my eyes. "How am I supposed to keep living and she's gone?"

He caught a runaway tear with his thumb. "Shit, it's gonna hurt like hell. But you'll be alright. Trust me?"

"Why should I do that?" I laughed between tears.

"Because you my girl. And I promise I gon' always make sure you good." He gave me one more squeeze, lifted my hands to his lips, and kissed the backs. "Let me go before my aunt come beat my ass. I'll send you a message. Respond."

"That doesn't sound like a question."

He laughed as he jogged back. "It's not." And with that, he ran back to his aunt's house, leaving me standing in the blazing sun.

Chapter 5

Khalil

MORNING LIGHT SEEPED THROUGH KELLY'S BLINDS LIKE it had the nerve to interrupt her peaceful slumber. Even still, she didn't stir. I slid from under her. We'd stayed in the same position all night her face on my chest, me holding her tight, not wanting to let go. Making my way to the door, I looked back at the sleeping beauty again. She was dead to the world, in desperate need of rest.

Becoming a doctor had her mind in overdrive since she'd started medical school. Even though she didn't say it aloud, I knew she was worried about her placement for her fellowship. On one hand, she wanted that placement in either DC, Boston, or San Francisco. On the other, she knew she'd escape one of her father's guilt trips if she were placed at Texas Children's here in the city. It was why she'd made that her first choice.

For the life of me, I couldn't understand why her father insisted on keeping her and her mother under the umbrella of his ego. Did he not see the shadow he casted over the women in his life kept them from blooming? If you asked me, as much as Kenneth Reid bragged and boasted about his life, he was fool's gold. I saw it. Kelly saw it. And I guess her mother, Charisse, was coming around to it as well.

Stepping into Kelly's guest bathroom downstairs, I turned on the shower, then grabbed a change of clothes from the drawer I'd claimed as my own after a few months of being in Houston. Begrudgingly, I washed the remnants of her off my body. Once fresh, I entered her kitchen, opening a window to let in the fresh morning breeze. The soft hum of children riding bikes with their parents and cars passing in the street cracked through the open space, mixing with the low sizzle of bacon cooking.

I stood at the stove, shirtless, flipping the pieces of bacon, concentrating to get them just right. I'd sautéed bell peppers, onions, and mushrooms for the omelets we'd share for breakfast. I thought about whipping up a batch of French toast, but that would be too much. She'd get skittish, regress back inside her mind. No, I only needed to do enough.

Just enough.

It wasn't lost on me the naturalness I felt being in her kitchen. How I knew which cabinet held the garlic powder and black pepper. That I knew her favorite coffee mug stayed tucked away in the dishwasher and never in the cabinet that housed her other glassware. I knew her better than she knew herself. Knew she liked sleeping cuddled up in a ball, burrowed under the sheets and comforter, no matter how hot it got. Knew to keep her fridge stocked and pantry full, or else she'd order take-out every night, then complain about it all going to her ass. I never complained about that. Knew the more hype she was on the outside, the bigger the inner turmoil she fought to keep to herself.

I knew she'd wake up being more casual than necessary. She'd walk into the kitchen, her head held high, ready to throw some witty remark about me still being here, right before sitting down to eat the meal I'd prepared. Say whatever she needed to assert her dominance again, even though she'd melted under my touch, shuddered each time my lips touched the innermost of her thighs, exhaled and cried each time I brought her to sweet release.

My phone buzzed on the counter, the screen lighting up with a name I hadn't seen in a few days.

"What's good, Pops?"

"Hey, son. Ain't talked to you since Zay's engagement party." His voice was heavy with a mixture of concern and unspoken judgment that Black fathers had mastered. "I know I'm probably interrupting your morning, but I wanted to check-in."

I whipped the eggs in the glass bowl with one hand, phone pressed between my shoulder and ear. "I'm good. Just cooking?"

"Oh yeah," he replied, pausing on the other end. "For you and who else?"

I chuckled low, sprinkling a few pinches of salt into the eggs then pouring them into the pan. "What you want, Pops?"

"I talked to your aunt the other day. Josie told her you still running behind that girl...Ms. Sonya granddaughter."

I blinked. Why parents felt the need to discuss your life with everyone except you was lost on me. I knew it'd be a matter of time before he came questioning me and Kelly's friendship. He'd done it when he caught the look on my face back when I was a teenager. When I brought Kelly to dinner with me when he'd visited back in college. And again, when I decided to move to Houston for good, following Zay.

"She got a name, Pops," I said. "It's Kelly, and you know we go way back."

He exhaled sharply, like he already knew where this was going. "Listen, you too old for lectures–"

"You say that right before starting a lecture." I smirked, flipping the eggs in the pan.

"I'm just trying to tell you to be careful. She got the same look in her eyes as your mama. You liable to get burned. Your mama done caused you enough hurt for one lifetime. Ain't no use adding on to it."

That made my jaw tighten. I glanced toward the hallway, listening for movement. She hadn't stirred yet.

"This ain't the same thing, Pops. You and I both know Mama was on that stuff bad. The only thing anyone could say Kelly's addicted to is working."

"Fix it up however you want. Addictions may be different, but the root cause is the same."

I paused, letting the soft sizzle of the pan fill the kitchen, save for my father's breathing on the other end of the call. "They're not the same."

"Women like that don't want no man telling her to slow down or sit still."

"I'm not telling her to slow down. Her ambition is the thing I love most about her." I clenched my jaw again, ready for this conversation to be over.

"Exactly," he snapped. "That's my point. It's going to come a time when you try and push her into something she don't want, you gon' lose her. Yourself too."

His words settled heavy in my chest. Even though his comments irritated me, I knew he only spoke from experience. It was all any of us could speak from. I remembered the silence after my mother left. My father moved through the house like a ghost. For months, he went to work, came home to eat, then went out in search of the love of his life. It was as if she vanished without a trace, her memory haunting us in the form of old photos and unopened mail.

"I understand what you're saying, Pops, but that's not Kelly. Things between us...it's complicated."

"Son, every damn thing in this life is complicated. Just don't fool yourself into thinking you can fix or trap her. Just when you think you caught her, she'll slip away like lightening in a storm."

I nodded, even though he couldn't see me. "Thanks for the wisdom, old man."

"Love you, too." He chuckled, deep and hearty. "Finish cooking. And stop moving around like you some kind of pimp. I raised you better than that. That's probably why Kelly ain't taking your ass serious."

He hung up.

I stood by the stove, heat rising from the omelet threatening to burn, trying to shake off the conversation. I knew Pops had good intentions, but I'd be lying if the words didn't leave me second-guessing.

Bare feet padded against the hardwood upstairs. The bathroom door creaked open, followed by the strong spray of water hitting the shower floors. I busied myself with plating our breakfast, and preparing Kelly's cup of coffee. Well, her cup of cream with a splash of coffee. When she stepped into the kitchen, I also dropped the prized mug.

She'd smoothed her fussed hair into a messy bun high on her head. A silk robe clung to her curves, her skin still dewy from her shower and the oil she'd applied to her limbs. She looked like the softest thing God ever made.

"Is there a reason you're still here?" she asked, folding her arms as she leaned against the counter. "It's Friday morning. Shouldn't you be at work?"

"When you the boss, you set your own hours."

She smirked, snatching the mug from my hand. "You're getting too comfortable here. I don't like that." She took a sip, moaning her satisfaction. My dick stirred in my pants. She looked up at me with affection-filled eyes buried under years of playing it cool.

"Sit down. I made breakfast."

"You're going to stop talking to me like I'm a child," she quipped, making herself comfortable at the kitchen table near the window. I added some toast to her plate and placed it in front of her.

"How did you know this is exactly what I had in mind when I bought these groceries?"

"It's my job to know." I smiled.

"Don't get carried away." She took a bite of the omelet and danced in her chair. "This is good, though."

Satisfied that she was satisfied, I grabbed my plate and sat in the chair opposite her. "I'm glad you like it. You can't survive off caffeine and lab reports."

She barked out a laugh. "How did you know that's my love language?"

"Seriously, though. You good?"

She chewed slowly, then nodded. "I'm decent, I suppose. Been working like hell trying not to think about my match. I don't have to tell you how stressed I am."

"You're gonna get it."

"You sound sure."

"I am sure. Even if it's not your first pick, you'll make the pivot."

She paused, holding her mug midway to her lips. "You know me too well."

"You know me too, and yet you're still convinced that this thing between us is just a situationship."

Her eyes narrowed playfully. "This is a situationship, Khalil. I don't have time for a relationship. You just happen to be the closest man with decent dick."

"Decent? Girl, I had that pussy speaking in tongues last night. Don't downplay my dick because you afraid of the truth."

She waved me off, sipping more of her coffee. Then it got quiet.

Not awkward, but real.

"I meant what I said last night," I said softly. "I see you, Lily-girl. Even when you trying to outwork your feelings."

She stared at her plate. "Don't do that."

"What?"

"Make this something more than what it is. Our situationship is perfect how it is. Simple. Clean."

"Nothing about us has ever been simple."

When she looked up at me, I saw it. Fear. Longing. Love she didn't know what to do with.

I reached for her hand. She didn't pull away.

"I'm not asking for everything," I said. "Just let me be here. However you need me."

She squeezed my fingers, then let go. "I'll think about it." She took a bite, filling her mouth with the omelet and toast. "But you're still doing the dishes."

I grinned. "Deal."

And just like that, we slipped back into our rhythm. Two people too stubborn to name the thing between us but too drawn to ever walk away. We didn't need a label because we both felt it.

This was us.

And damn if it didn't feel like home.

Chapter 6

Kelly

"Morning, Dr. Reid," one of the nurses called.

"Good morning, Carol," I replied, flashing my polished smile. "I see they have you holding down the unit again. You deserve a vacation."

"Oh, it's coming in a few weeks. Trust," the older nurse replied.

Pushing through the swinging doors of the pediatric ward, white coat flaring like a cape, hair pulled back in a low bun, I knew this environment was made for me. I could walk into any hospital and have three things happen in under five minutes.

A nurse would ask me to lead the morning rounds.

One of the junior residents would trail behind me like a baby duckling.

Some older man, intern, or "single" dad would try to shoot his shot.

I kept moving, sipping my latte as I made my way toward the board to check patient updates. Every step I made was measured but effortless. Not because I needed to prove anything. Just because any patient under my care deserved it.

"Dr. Reid," one of the new residents fell in step beside me. *What is his name? Jalen? Jordan?*

"Mmhmm?" Taking another sip, I didn't look away from the board.

"Got a question about our patient in 212A–the sickle cell kid?"

I arched a brow, finally glancing over at him. He was cute, in a baby-deer-in-headlights sort of way. Tall, unsure, definitely a future problem for some med schoolgirl or nurse with boundary issues.

"Her name is Janae, and she's not a kid. She's sixteen," I corrected. "And her pain plan should've been updated by now. You check the latest labs?"

He blinked. "I...uh, was just about to."

"Don't about to. Do. Sickle cell pain is real. Treat it like it's yours."

He nodded, nostrils flaring, and I moved past him toward Janae's room. Inside, I found her curled up in bed, face tense. I looked over my shoulder at the resident, letting him see the disappointment and frustration laced on my face. I could've drop-kicked him right there.

"Hey, beautiful," I soothed, approaching her with care. "Rough morning?"

She nodded without speaking.

I scanned her chart quickly, then knelt to eye level with her. "I'm going to make sure we adjust your meds, okay? You don't need to be in this much pain."

Her eyes welled. "It feels like they think I'm lying."

"They don't think that," I said, placing a hand over hers. "But I do know what it feels like to not be heard. That won't happen here. Not on my watch."

That was what I loved about my work—the precision, the connection, the power of being the person who could make someone feel seen in the middle of their worst moments.

After checking in with Janae and putting in her new pain meds orders, I stepped into the hallway just as my phone buzzed in my pocket. I pulled it out quickly, my heart skipping. Today was the day. I'd find out if I'd matched with one of my top picks.

Subject Line: Match Announcements–Fellowship Match System

I exhaled through my nose, lips pressed tight. I'd been checking my email all morning waiting for this. Now that it was here, I hesitated to open it. Fear took hold of my chest, even though the rational part of my brain said that a match was better than no match.

One of my attending physicians, Dr. Hightower, spotted me as I turned the corner. "Dr. Reid, just the person I wanted to see. You gave that presentation on pediatric blood disorders last month, right?"

"Guilty," I said, slipping my phone back into my pocket.

"Well, the board loved it. They're considering creating a teaching module from it for new interns. You've got a knack for making complex content...digestible."

I smiled effortlessly. "That's what happens when you grow up with a father for a doctor and Black mama who didn't let you half-step."

"I know that's right." She laughed. "You ever thought about staying here long-term?"

I appreciated the compliment, I did, but it didn't stick. That wasn't my goal. I was made for more. Of course, I could stay here and breeze on by. That would be easy. I wanted to specialize. I wanted to break ground.

"I appreciate that," I said. "But I've got my eyes on pediatric hematology-oncology. Somewhere I can make a bigger impact."

Dr. Hightower smiled softly. "Can't fault that. Just don't forget, the places that know you best are the ones you can grow in."

I filed that away as something old people said when they

wanted to tell you what to do without telling you what to do. Something my grandmother did before she died.

The rest of my shift passed with familiarity–charting, rounding, checking labs, making quick calls to consults. My name carried weight around here, and I knew how to wield it to get results. Make people feel safe. There wasn't a patient or parent on the floor who didn't trust me to give them the truth with a smile.

Even in my whirlwind of competence, I couldn't ignore the email burning a hole in my pocket. The decision lit a flicker of restlessness in my usually even-tempered heart. I knew choosing only the top, most competitive fellowships in the country wouldn't be easy. I wanted to know what it felt like to want again. To struggle a little. To stretch. I didn't expect it to be this nerve-wracking. What if all I'd done all the research, all the accolades, all the sleepless nights wasn't enough?

Sitting in the resident's locker room, I kicked off my sneakers. My feet were screaming, but my brain was still going full speed. I set my phone on the bench next to me. I gave myself a pep talk before my finger hovered over the email icon. I opened Instagram instead, skimming through my DMs, ignoring a half-hearted, "U up?" from a guy I used to hook up with. I rolled my eyes, moving on to the texts I'd left unread. Eyes emojis from my friends. Encouraging words from my mother, Aunt Viv, and Khalil.

My phone rang halfway through. Mama.

I debated letting it go to voicemail, but something tugged at me. I wiped my hands on a towel and answered.

"Hey, Mama."

"My Kelly Belly." I could feel her motherly hug through the phone. "You sound tired, my baby."

I sank into the couch. "I am. I don't know who's letting these new residents in. I had to correct a newbie today before he under treated one of my sickle cell patients."

"Oh, Lord," she said. "You didn't hurt his feelings too bad, did you?"

"I kept it cute. Professional. He'll survive." I sighed. "You know I don't play about my babies. No matter how old they are."

"You are your daddy's twin."

I stiffened. "Right…"

She didn't notice the tightness of my voice. "He used to come home heated about how certain doctors wouldn't take Black kids' pain seriously. Preached nonstop that if they had to prove their pain, something was already broken."

"I guess that means the two of you are talking again?"

There was a pause. Just enough to make my stomach tighten.

"Well," she started. "He did come by so I could help him pick up some groceries."

"Really, Mama? Groceries? Since when does Daddy need help buying groceries?"

"Don't do that, Kelly."

"Do what? Ask obvious questions?"

She sighed. "We're trying to be friends. For you."

I leaned my head back on the back of the couch. "Y'all don't do friends. You do drama and late-night phone calls."

"People change."

"Have you changed? Or are you slipping back into old habits because they're comfortable?" I scoffed, rolling my eyes even though she couldn't see me. If she had, she'd snatch me up so quick, I'd think I was a child, not a full-grown woman. But now, in this moment, she'd gone quiet. I knew that quiet. It'd become more and more prominent each year I became more aware of what went on between my parents. As I grew more comfortable calling them out on their bullshit, my mother perfected the role of playing peacekeeper when I wouldn't keep my mouth shut. It was her way of saying, *you're not wrong, but I don't want to admit it.*

"Mama," I started gently. "You deserve more than some halfway peace treaty with the same man who made you cry on and off for all my life."

"And you deserve more than running yourself into the ground chasing perfection," she snapped back.

Touche.

"I'm getting tired, Kelly. I just want to feel like I used to. Your father does, too."

There was no use arguing. I was surprised they'd been separated this long. Long enough for my mother to find her own place, even though I knew my father secretly footed the bill. Long enough for me to believe things would be different this time around. My parents were the reason I carefully crafted my life for no surprises. Nothing happened that didn't fall in line with my vision.

"I guess...Just don't let feeling lonely convince you that your past is your home."

"Stay in a child's place, Kelly." She paused. I knew she was glaring at me through the phone. Then she said, "It's decision day. Have you gotten your email?"

"Yes. Earlier today. I haven't opened it yet." Three beeps interrupted our call. I knew it was her FaceTiming me. I answered, and my mirror image, only older, stared back at me. Same almond eyes. Button nose. Smooth caramel skin. As much as she said otherwise. I was nothing like my father. I was everything like her.

"Share your screen, and let's open it together." Her eyes gleamed through the screen, her smile bright and wide. I wanted her excitement to leech onto me, but it wouldn't. Following her directions, I shared my screen, opened my email, and let the subject line that kept my heart racing throughout the day stare back at the both of us. Right before I tapped the email, my mom's screen cut out.

"Hold on, Kelly. It's your Uncle Doug."

While I waited for my mother to call back, I set my phone down and embraced the silence of the locker room. Seconds later, my phone was vibrating against the bench.

"Kelly!" My mother's frantic voice echoed throughout the

small room. "It's your daddy. They're rushing him to the emergency room!"

Hurriedly, I picked up my phone. Shaky footage of my mother's home moved around the screen as she rushed to gather her purse and keys. "Mama, what? What's going on?"

Tears welled in her eyes. Stress lines filled the corner and around her mouth. "I don't know, Kelly. Doug said they were talking to Khalil and Zay at one of the centers, then your dad started complaining of chest pains."

"What hospital are they bringing him to?" My nerves amped up even further. I rushed to change out of my scrubs.

"Memorial Hermann downtown. Meet me there, Kelly. If they tell me something bad, I won't be able to take it."

"Of course, Mama. I'm changing now. I'll be there."

THE HOUSE still smelled like his cologne. That rich, woodsy scent my father swore he didn't overuse, even though it lingered in curtains, pillows, and memories. He shuffled before me, my mother propping him up as they made their way to the living room, where he plopped down on the couch. My mother sat beside him, annoyance etched into her sharp cheekbones and luminous skin.

My father stretched out on the sectional portion of the couch, holding my mother close to his side. Leave it to Kenneth Reid to have a "health scare" on the most important day of my life. The scare? A bad case of gas.

I folded my arms as I stared down at the two of them. My father showered my mother's face with quick kisses as she feigned disinterest.

"Mama, we can leave. Daddy's going to be fine."

"Kelly, still ain't got any love for your old man? I just got out of the hospital," my father pouted, seemingly soothed by the circles my mother rubbed on his stomach.

"For heartburn?" I shuffled in my stance, sucking my teeth.

"That wasn't heartburn. It felt like somebody sat a Box Chevy on my chest."

"Because you eat like you're still twenty-five and made of steel. Smothered everything, hot links, fried this and that." My mother smirked, taking his jaw in her hand. "Your body gave you a warning, Kenny. Take the hint." They kissed again, this time deeply. I gagged.

"I'm leaving you two to whatever this is," I said, waving my hand in their direction. My parents chuckled into each other. As they stared back at me, I saw the weariness they shared. "I'm glad you're okay, Daddy," I added, genuinely happy it wasn't something worse.

My mother sat up, scooting over, breaking their embrace. She patted the cushion between them. "Sit down. We never got to open your decision email."

I hesitated. I didn't want to open it here. Not when there were one too many sets of eyes waiting to see my reaction. When my mother told me my father was headed to the hospital, I'd made it up in my mind that I'd open it at home, with a bottle of wine, and a few playlists ready for whatever the email would entail.

I opened the email and clicked the link leading to my Match Portal, my heart thumping hard enough to echo. One click. Then another. I held my breath.

Congratulations! You have been matched to the Seattle Regional Medical Center–Pediatric Hematology-Oncology Fellowship.

I blinked at the screen.

"Oh, my God," I whispered.

My mother moved closer, trying to read the words, knowing it was futile without her glasses. My father sat up straighter beside me.

"You matched?" My mother squealed.

I nodded slowly, letting the words sink in. "Seattle."

My mom beaned. "Baby, that's amazing! That was one of your top five, right?"

I nodded again, this time slower. "Yeah. Number four."

It wasn't Hopkins. Wasn't Boston. Wasn't Stanford. Seattle. Still top-tier. Still a win.

"Seattle? All the way on the other side of the country?" My father's face scrunched.

"It's a great program," I said automatically, still staring at the screen. "Research-focused, patient-first model. They're doing groundbreaking stuff with gene therapies."

"You can research gene therapies at Texas Children's." He tilted his head. "You go there, you're leaving everything behind. Your life, your people. What happened to you working at the clinic with me?"

I didn't flinch. I knew he was trying to rile me up, guilt me into staying. "Daddy, I've told you time and time again, I don't want to work in the clinic. I want to specialize."

"I don't see why you have to go halfway across the country when you're already helping people right here."

"It's not about proximity. It's about purpose."

"You don't think helping people in this community has a purpose?"

I clenched my jaw. "Daddy, you're twisting my words."

"Kenny, wait," my mother said, stepping in. "Stop antagonizing her. She just got the biggest news of her life, and you're ruining it with guilt."

"I'm not guilting her, I'm asking her to consider the people who raised her!" His voice boomed through the living room.

"And I'm telling you to respect her decisions like the grown woman she is," my mother snapped back.

I stood, sensing where this was headed.

My mother's voice softened. "Kelly"

"No, I'm not doing this with y'all." I grabbed my bag. "Y'all love to turn any moment into a back-and-forth about you. It's like you feed on the drama. I'm tired of it." I peered into my father's eyes. "Daddy, I came to make sure you were good, not defend my career."

He looked away from me, arms crossed, jaw set.

My mother let out a slow sigh, rubbing her forehead.

"I'm proud of you, baby," she said as I made my way to the front door.

"Thanks," I threw behind me, clipped.

I heard a rustle, followed by, "I mean it."

I nodded but kept moving. Tears pressed behind my eyes, threatening to break through. I wouldn't give my father the satisfaction of knowing he'd gotten to me. My mother followed behind me. We stood in the circle driveway of their home, the sun fading behind the horizon, a warm breeze cutting through the awkward silence between us.

My mother cradled my face. "He's just scared, Kelly."

"No he's not. He's just used to things revolving around him."

She gave a short laugh, rubbing her forehead again. "Yeah. But you know him. He loves hard, even though it comes out crooked."

"Is that what you've been telling yourself all these years?" I sighed. "I shouldn't have to keep explaining myself to him. I worked hard for this. But unless it's his way, he won't hear any of it."

"Oh, baby." She ran her hands up and down the sides of my arms as she looked up at me with tenderness in her eyes. "You're not wrong, but where do you think you learned it?"

I frowned. "Excuse me?"

"You walk around just as proud, expecting everyone to be okay with your choices and boundaries without extending that same grace."

"I don't know what you're talking about," I said, staring off to the side.

"So you didn't set up Nessa and Zay, even though you knew she wasn't ready to see him again."

I smacked my lips. "And now they're getting married and having a baby. Your point?"

"What do you mean a baby?" My mother shook her head, wanting to stay focused. "Marriage and a baby aside, what if it didn't end up that way. You busy yourself poking into everyone else's business, when you need to be paying attention to your own."

"My business isn't for anyone else," I said, crossing my arms.

She scoffed, placing her hands on her hips. "You think we don't know something's going on between you and Khalil? I knew you been feeling him since I caught that look on your face the last time we were in New Orleans. When your Uncle PJ almost pulled a gun on your daddy again."

"What do you mean again?"

"Listen to me, Kelly," she urged, grabbing my chin. "I see myself in you. Hiding your feelings. Telling everybody I was 'fine' while breaking apart inside."

I looked away, knowing everything she said was true.

"Your father and I loved each other hard. Still do. But for a long time, I didn't let myself need him."

"I don't need anyone, Mama," I said, defensive even to my own ears.

"No," she said. "You're scared to need someone. Scared it'll go away. That's why you love being in control."

The silence was heavier now.

She rubbed my shoulder then pulled me in for a hug. I settled into her arms, comforted by the peony and green apple scent of her Chanel perfume. "You can have your dreams, baby. You can move to Seattle, heal little kids, change the world. But don't convince yourself you have to do it with armor on all the time. Love will meet you where you are, if you let it."

I squeezed harder, biting my lip.

She stood on her tiptoes to kiss me on my forehead. "Call me when you settle your feelings on your fellowship. And Khalil."

She turned back toward the house.

I stood there for a long time, staring at the darkening sky, letting her words echo while the stars blinked into view–tiny, distant, guiding me toward something I hadn't let myself imagine yet.

Chapter 7

Kelly

"LOOK AT MY BABY MAMA." I LAUGHED, SNATCHING Vanessa into a hug.

"Don't let Zay hear you say that...Even if it is true." She giggled, squeezing me back. "How's Uncle Kenny?"

I scrunched my face, kissing my teeth. "Dramatic as hell." She peered at me, her round, brown eyes oozing concern. "I don't want to talk about it right now. Are you going to let me in or keep me standing here?"

Vanessa glowed, smiled brightly, eyes twinkling in the fading sunset. Impending motherhood looked good on her, natural. As if she'd been born to step into this role. As I stepped into her and Zay's home, the air smelled of drywall dust and new beginnings. Fresh paint lingered from the warm, white walls. The floors alternated between polished wood and bare concrete. Boxes scattered the hallway leading from the entryway to the living room.

Despite the chaos, the home felt cozy—a home being built on purpose. A perfect blend of Vanessa and Xavier. I was so happy for my friend. Even though her and Xavier had their moment, they truly were made for each other. I didn't care what my mother said about me getting involved. It was because I had played puppet master that the two had a second chance at a love so pure, nothing would break them apart again.

Following Vanessa into the living room, the low hum of male voices grew louder. Khalil and Xavier were sprawled across the large sectional taking up most of the space. Blueprints, laptops, and other documents spread across the coffee table. Khalil spread out, legs crossed, arms resting against the back of the couch like this was his home, too.

It was the same energy he'd used to claim parts of my home as his. The dresser drawer in my guest room. The cabinet space in my bathroom. The slides that stayed by the door leading to my garage. Wearing a white t-shirt that clung to his arms and chest, putting the sleeves of tattoos on display, his energy overwhelmed me. Xavier sat next to him, intensely quiet, his eyes narrowed in on a blueprint-domestic, casual, completely disarming. He was oblivious to the tormented way Khalil's eyes roved over me standing before them.

His eyes played investigator, always in tune with the emotions I kept buried beneath my charming smile. They spoke to me, whispering questions, seeking to understand the frustration that fretted about the lines of my forehead. He shifted to the side, dropping his feet from the long end of the sectional. I took it as my cue to sit.

Xavier finally glanced up, shooting me a warm smile. "Hey, Kelly. How's your dad? Nessa told us he had to go to the hospital. He seemed fine when we met with him this morning."

"He's fine," I replied. "Unless being a drama king is an actual diagnosis." Khalil's thumb stroked the back of my neck, soothing the tension coiling my muscles. "Is this the layout for the new center on the east side?"

"Yeah, Kenneth wanted to add a wellness clinic," Xavier replied, going back to his blueprints.

"That's smart," I said, sinking into the warmth the space offered me. "So many families skip the doctor because the hours are inconvenient or it costs too much."

Khalil looked at me with inspecting eyes. "We're gonna soft launch the clinic during the back-to-school event. Your dad said you'd help him give out vaccinations."

Of course he would. He and I knew there was a possibility I'd be halfway across the country starting my fellowship by that time. Anger settled in my chest for the third time today.

"I'll have to check my schedule." Khalil raised his eyebrow.

Before he could say something, Vanessa's voice rang from the second-floor landing.

"Zay, can you help me bring these canvases and paint from upstairs?" He quickly followed suit, jumping to aid his future wife. Once he was out of view, Khalil pulled me closer, wrapping me in his arms.

"What you mean 'I'll have to check my schedule?'"

"Exactly what I said. I may not be able to take off and fly out." I rested my head against the broad strength of his shoulder, finally exhaling from the anxiety-riddled day I'd had.

He tensed, a subtle movement that anyone else in the room would've missed. "You got your match results?"

I sighed. "I've had them since the morning."

"I called and texted and you ignored me." His heart began to race against my back, his body heating with nervousness.

"I didn't open the email until a few hours ago. The day's been a little distracting." I settled further into his chest, closing my eyes to rest my mind. "And don't ask me. I promised I'd tell my girls first."

The doorbell rung, followed by hammering knocks. Khalil stood and stretched, shooting me a look full of longing. Like he knew my time here wouldn't be long. Like he was preparing himself for goodbye, even though we'd never started. "You're lucky I like you."

"You love me, Big Head," I shot back, instantly regretting it when his smile deepened.

"As long as you know," he said casually. "I'm just waiting for you to stop pretending it's more complicated than that."

I couldn't look away from his gaze. He held me there, my heart skipping too many beats for comfort. We could've stayed there, lost in our tug-of-war of emotions and unspoken feelings, were it not for the cackling of laughter filtering in from the foyer.

"I'm sorry to kick you out, Khalil, but it's girls' night," Vanessa said, shooing him away.

"You mean I'm not part of the coven? I can cackle all night, too." Khalil proceeded to mock the laughter he'd heard moments earlier.

"Please, Khalil," Lynn started. "I'm sure there's something more useful you could be doing than running your mouth."

"Don't make me call Wesley, Lynn," he shot back.

Laughter chorused around the room as Lynn's eyes went wide, green pools of guilt letting on more than she'd ever admit.

"Come on, Khalil. I need help painting the rooms upstairs." Xavier turned to Vanessa, kissing her on the cheek before heading upstairs. "Call me if you need something," he tossed over his shoulder. Khalil followed behind him, mumbling something too low for me to catch.

Once they were out of sight, Vanessa said," Who's ready to try some mocktails?"

We stared at her in disbelief, mouths gaped open.

"Girl, if you don't go grab some wine," Lynn shouted. "Matter of fact, I'll find it myself." She brushed past Vanessa, entering the open-space kitchen.

"Find the tequila," I shouted from the couch.

"That's what I'm talking about," Nyah added, settling beside me. She pulled her fresh braids away from her face, tying the strands behind her head to stay put. Her eyes looked worried, tired, as they had for the past few months. Lynn walked back over to the living room, sitting in the chair next to the couch, a bottle of expensive tequila and plastic cups in her hands. She still wore the heels, pencil-skirt, and white blouse she favored when heading into her law office.

"I don't know about y'all, but I need something strong," Lynn said, kicking off her heels. "If I had $100 for every time I had to sit through a meeting with white men explaining structural racism to me, I'd be able to do pro-bono work for the rest of my life."

Vanessa settled on the couch with a glass bottle of blood-red liquid. "I hope you set them straight." She drank from the bottle, wincing. "Ugh, this tastes like dirt."

"What is that?" I asked. Nyah stole the bottle, swirling it around.

"It's beet juice. I saw a video saying it helps boost iron." Vanessa took another sip, wincing again. "They left out the part about it tasting horrible."

"Nessa, did your doctor say your iron was low?" I asked.

"No, it's just a precaution." Her eyes held the solemnity we all understood. Losing her and Xavier's baby the first time devastated her. Devastated all of us. It hurt worse knowing I couldn't be there for her, being I was away at medical school.

"Hey," Nyah started, taking Nessa into her arms, cradling her like the baby of the group that she was. "Everything is going to be fine. We're all praying for this baby. It'll be spoiled before it arrives." We all laughed misty-eyes giggles. Vanessa pressed the back of her hands to her eyes.

"I know. I just..." She reached for our hands. We met them, tangling our fingers together. "We want this baby so bad. I don't know what I'll do if I lose it again."

I moved to kneel in front of Vanessa, placing my hands on her knees. "You're not going to lose my baby." She laughed softly. "I'm serious. You were stressed out of your mind back then."

"I'm stressed now." She laughed, tears easing down her cheeks. "Scared shitless."

Lynn moved closer on the couch, wrapping her arms around Vanessa's waist. "Aww, baby girl. It's okay to be scared, but we got you, no matter the outcome." We allowed Vanessa to shed a few more tears until she collected herself.

"This baby is making me so emotional." She sniffed, wiping the remaining tears from her eyes.

Nyah, Lynn, and I stared at each other, immediately recognizing the flaw in her logic. "Now, Nessa, we all know it's not the baby making you cry."

She looked up at us, confusion causing fine lines in her otherwise smooth forehead.

"Don't look at us like that." Lynn smirked. "You know you're the crybaby of the group." Vanessa's mouth dropped, half-shocked, half-insulted.

"Nessa, it's true. You've been wailing at anything since you were born."

"So." She pouted, a half-smile inching around the corner of her mouth. "Anyways," she added, drawing the word out. "Can we finally know where you got matched?"

Lynn and Nyah leaned closer. I reached back to grab my phone off the coffee table. Slowly, I went to the email that held my fate, opening it and holding the phone up to my dearest friends, my sisters. Silence filled the space as they read the words I'd read earlier. Nyah was the first to speak.

"How do you feel?" Her hand covered my shoulder, a gentle squeeze preventing me from retreating into my shell.

Instead, I shrugged. I wasn't sure of my emotions. Seattle was a great hospital. I would learn a lot. It wasn't my top choice, but it was a top hospital. Still, something nagged away at me. Vanessa snapped her fingers in my face, bringing me back to the conversation.

"Stop that!" she scolded. "We all know you wanted Johns Hopkins or Stanford. It's okay to be upset."

"I'm not upset," I murmured. "I'm...indifferent."

"Here, take a shot," Lynn said, pouring me a round of tequila into one of the plastic cups. I threw it back, wincing as the liquor burned the nonexistent hairs off my chest. "Now take another one."

I side-eyed her but followed her instructions. When she started to pour another, I grabbed the bottle from her hands. "Lynn, enough. I have to drive home." I exhaled. "I'm fine. Seattle is a win. I'm proud of it. But…"

"It wasn't your first choice," Vanessa finished for me.

I nodded. "It wasn't. And now everything's picking up here. I don't know if I'm ready to leave it all."

"Kelly, it'll be okay. I know you. You'll make the best of it," Nyah reassured, rubbing my back.

"I don't know y'all," Lynn started. "I don't think Seattle is the problem."

Vanessa rubbed her belly, then looked at me gently. "I agree, Lynn. I don't even think it's leaving us behind that's the problem." She sipped more of her beet juice, fighting the gag as she swallowed.

My eyes narrowed. "What's that supposed to mean?"

"Stop acting ignorant, Kelly," Lynn said, tapping my hands. "You and Khalil love each other. Have loved each other for years."

"We're friends" I started before Lynn slapped my hands again. "Ouch!"

"Stop lying to yourself." This time it was Vanessa scolding me. "You walk around so confident, telling people what to do."

"I do not tell people what to do." I smirked, rolling my eyes.

"Oh please, you throw around orders just as much as Nessa cries." I looked to Nyah, hoping to garner some sympathy against the unnecessary attacks from my so-called friends.

"She's not lying," Nyah agreed.

To hell with these bitches.

All of them.

"Did you know he's been talking to Zay about settling down? Before you came in, they were discussing baby names and marriage?" Vanessa tender-hearted look was too much. It was all too much.

"Why won't you let yourself be with him, Kelly?" Nyah asked, her voice soft.

"That's exactly why," I said quietly. "He's my friend. I know what to expect from him in that lane. But once it shifts, everything becomes unpredictable. Risky."

"Kelly, it's already shifted."

She let me sit with my thoughts. All eyes grazed over my face, trying to read my mind. It had shifted. It terrified me. Not knowing what the outcome would be. I knew Khalil like I knew myself. We were one in the same. For so long, neither one of us dreamed of settling down. We liked our freedom, our independence, the ability to move around as we saw fit. But in the past few months, something changed. He became familiar in the same way I used the same coffee mug. Familiar like the laundry detergent brand I had on auto-buy so I'd never run out. I don't know when it happened. How it happened.

It just happened.

And I'd been blinded by its silent conquest.

"When are you going to tell him about Seattle?"

"I don't know." I shrugged. "It won't be long. He'll keep pestering me until I tell him."

"And you love it," Lynn cackled out.

"Hush up." I smiled back. "You make me sound like a lovesick teenager." I took my spot back on the long end of the couch, hoping a few traces of Khalil's scent were still trapped in the soft fibers.

"She's blushing!" Vanessa exclaimed. "She's in love!"

"Shut up before he hears you!" I squealed. "I'll never get rid of him."

"Come on, Kelly," Nyah said. "Admit you love him. We won't tell."

I fiddled my fingers into my shirt. Slowly, I turned my head to face my sisters, the people I could be my most authentic self with. A smile crept into the corners of my mouth. My face warmed as a lightness entered my heart. I bit my lip to contain the truth, but it didn't help. The truth was clear.

"I love him," I said just loud enough for them to hear. And as soon as the words escaped my lips, I wished I could take them back. Because now that they were out there, drifting in the realm of reality, it would hurt that much more to watch them be snuffed out.

Chapter 8

Khalil

Seattle.

Fucking Seattle.

Not Johns Hopkins. Not Stanford. But Seattle.

I didn't need to hear the full conversation to know Kelly was reeling from not getting matched with her first choice. I knew she'd start masking, pretending everything was fine. I heard it in the light laughter she gave her friends. I'd started to go downstairs to find more drop cloths when I'd overheard their conversation. The finality of it threatened to gut me had it not been for the last words she'd said.

I love him.

I'd never heard her utter the words before. Not in that way.

Some would say I had butterflies. Little flutters in my chest knowing the feeling was mutual. I'd tell them they were wrong. To me, it was always a low hum in my soul. Not panic. Not fear. Just energy. Coiled. Focused. Ready.

And it was all the sign I needed to know that this would be our time. Time to stop the games. Time to get serious. Time to be us. That was the feeling I took with me walking into the conference room of the new office Xavier and I shared. The walls were lined with mock-ups of the community center we were renovating. Blueprints of the new health clinic wing laid across the large table like war plans.

"You still getting nervous about giving project updates?" I asked, adjusting the collar of my shirt.

"Yeah, man. I didn't think it was possible. But it's Nessa's dad. I want to make sure it's right." Xavier nodded, tapping through the slideshow one last time. "They got a lot of faith in us. You got the outreach breakdown?"

"In my bag," I said. "And, I double-checked the budget proposal. And, I triple-checked the vendor approvals for the back-to-school event."

He glanced up at me, one brow raised. "You been triple-checking a lot, lately? What's with that?"

"I like knowing we got all our bases covered. You know Kelly bitch-ass daddy always got something to say. Like we don't know how to do *our* job." I smacked my teeth, irritated by the thought.

"Nah, you just like being the one in control." He laughed, shaking his head.

"I like making an impact." He smirked but didn't push it. "So, how you feeling, since you want to dig in my head?"

"Shit." Xavier exhaled through his nose. "Nervous as hell."

"No shit." I laughed. "You about to have a wife and a baby. I know you was applying pressure to get Nessa back, but I ain't expect y'all to lock it down that fast. You look calm, though."

"I stay calm because Nessa's already doing the hard part. What I feel? That's mine to manage. She deserves peace."

"That's your duty as the man."

"That's my duty because I love her." He let that sit in the air just long enough for it to take hold in my mind. "You thinking about settling down? Always asking me. You must be thinking about it?"

I didn't flinch. "Not tomorrow. But soon... With Kelly."

"She know that?"

"She do but she don't, if you know what I mean."

Xavier smoothed a hand over his head, laughing. "No, I don't know what that means."

I looked down at my hands. "See, with Kelly, she's always ten steps ahead of her own feelings. You can't say too much too soon, otherwise she'll run. Retreat inside of herself."

Xavier gave me a thoughtful nod, mentally checking off boxes. "You been in love with that girl since been."

"Yeah. I didn't know it then, but now..." I said. "I'd build a whole life with her if she let me."

"Let Nessa tell it. It's been the same on her end, too. Especially after you popped that cherry," Xavier teased.

"Shut the fuck up, Zay," I said, slapping him across the back of the head. "Besides, I know she love me. Kelly's just scared of what she can't control. I'm not going to rush her, but I'm not trying to lose her either."

"Well, decide what you going to do. She'll be leaving for Seattle in a few months."

Fucking Seattle.

Just then, the men we'd been waiting on walked through the room. Mr. Taylor had a look of exasperation on his face as Kenneth went on about something he found uninteresting.

"Zay. Khalil. Sorry we're late," Mr. Taylor said, patting Xavier on the shoulder and shaking his hand. "I had to wait on the old man over here."

Kenneth grimaced in his direction. "I know you not calling me old man."

"I'm not the one who went to the hospital because he thought he was having a heart attack." Mr. Taylor laughed. "Kenny, you're a doctor. You should know better."

"What I know is it got my wife back under our roof." Kenneth smirked, walking over to the conference table. He plopped down in a chair at the head of the table, leaning back like his name was on the marquee outside. "Let's get started."

Rolling my eyes, I launched into the pitch. I handled the community engagement, local partnerships, and event timelines. Xavier revisited the design efficiency, budget, and return on investment.

Kenneth cut in with questions that were already presented in previous meetings. "What's your plan to account for the lines I'm sure to have for the vaccines? My clinic can—"

"I've already contacted your clinic," I said, cutting him off. "We've finalized the logistics for vaccines distribution last month. It's covered in the meeting notes from last week. The ones you had me email to your secretary yesterday."

He nodded half-heartedly, dejected that he hadn't caught me slipping. I wouldn't give him that luxury.

When we wrapped, Mr. Taylor clapped his hands together. "Well done. We'll take this back to the board, but its got my vote."

Kenneth stood, flipping through the papers on the table. "I'm not convinced. I'm all for the community centers, but what happens when the money dries up? I can't be shelling out all this money all the time."

Xavier cut in, knowing Kenneth's digs were a sore spot for me. "The centers are funded through the upcoming fiscal year. We've already drafted the grant proposals for next year."

"Which we also talked about at the last meeting," I said through clenched teeth.

Kenneth looked at me, half a smile turning up the corners of his lips. "And if you can't talk someone into funding for next year, then what?"

I kept my voice even. "So far, we've gotten buy-in from three major local sponsors, including a few of the city's sports teams. All it took was a few conversations."

Kenneth didn't respond. He looked me up and down, as if trying to minimize the space I took up in the room to use for his inflated ego. I kept his gaze, matching his energy. Xavier busied himself with the papers on the desk. Mr. Taylor shook his head.

The meeting dissolved after that, but the older men remained, stating their wives were on their way with lunch. I stood by the window, sipping water, watching Kenneth and Mr. Taylor settle into the leather chairs across from our desks.

"Tell me, Zay," Mr. Taylor started. "How you feeling about fatherhood? It'll be here before you know it."

"I remember when I found out Charisse was pregnant with Kelly," Kenneth interjected, starting with a story no one asked for. "I was cocky. Thought I had that shit in the bag."

Xavier looked over at him, genuinely curious. "Did you?"

"Hell yeah." Kenneth laughed. "Told her doctor and the nurses to move out of the way. Brought my baby girl into the world myself. Didn't sleep for two weeks after that. But I *showed up*. That's what matters most. Love my girls with all my heart."

Mr. Taylor nodded. "You always did love hard, even if it didn't come out the best."

"Kids don't need perfect," Kenneth said, wistfully. "They need presence. I been around for every one of my Kelly baby's accomplishments."

I raised my eyebrow at that. Did he know how stressed she got trying to attain each one of those accomplishments? The late nights she stayed up pushing herself to be on top? The hypocrisy tickled me.

"You sure about that?" I said aloud to the room, not seeking an answer.

Kenneth turned to look at me. "You got something to say, son?"

"Last I checked, my pops was at home in Dallas. Don't son me," I said, glaring at the man who claimed to know so much about his daughter. "And presence is more than physically being there. You got to show up emotionally, too."

Xavier stilled. Mr. Taylor sat up in his chair, slight amusement twinkling in his eyes.

Kenneth narrowed his eyes, snarling his teeth. "You got something to say about the relationship between me and my daughter?"

"Nah," I said, sitting at my desk, unbothered. "Just might explain why she don't want to be around you like she used to."

The temperature in the room dropped. Xavier and Mr. Taylor looked on with caution, neither taking a chance on interceding.

Kenneth stood slowly, walking over to me. "You think you know her just 'cause you been sniffing around her since she had something to sniff?"

"I know her well enough to know you haven't known her since she was a kid." I looked him up and down. "And I ain't just sniffed."

Kenneth charged forward, clearing the space between us. "Watch how the fuck you talk about my daughter," he snapped, pointing at my chest.

Mr. Taylor shifted forward again. "Kenny, you just got out of the hospital."

Kenny. Weak ass nickname for a weak ass, excuse of a man.

"You talking a lot of shit." Kenneth smirked, taking a breath. "You think 'cause you got big ideas and talk a good game you ready for a grown man's world?"

"I think Kelly, and her mama, deserve more than being guilt-tripped for doing what's best for them."

Before Kenneth got the chance to fire back, the door swung open.

"Kenneth, enough. We heard you down the hallway," Mrs. Risse's voice rang out like a gavel. She stood with Mrs. Taylor beside her, bags of take-out in their arms, eyebrows lifted, eyes scanning the tension in the room like seasoned referees.

"Sit your narrow ass down before you wind up in the hospital again," she said. "This time it'll be my foot up your ass."

Kenneth turned. "Charisse"

"I don't want to hear it, Kenneth," she replied, cutting him off, rubbing her temples. "Doug, why is your friend out here still acting like his ego's on life support?"

"I don't know, Risse." Mr. Taylor laughed, sinking back into the leather chair. "That's your husband."

Mrs. Taylor handed her husband a bag, rubbing his back like the interaction between their friends was all routine.

When Kenneth went to grab the bag in Mrs. Risse's hands, she snatched it away, walking away to place it on my desk. "A whole grown ass man throwing tantrums because his daughter, who's successful in her own right, won't bend to his will."

Kenneth blinked. "I'm not"

"Khalil, come help me grab something from the car."

I followed Kelly's mother out of the office, meeting Kenneth's jealous face with a cocky smirk of my own. Once we'd gotten to her car, I looked through the windows for whatever she'd wanted me to grab. All the seats were empty.

"It's nothing there to get. I just wanted to talk to you without my drama king of a husband cutting in." She laughed.

"I'm not worried about him. I'll say what I need when I need."

"I know," she replied. "Let's go sit on the bench over there." Sitting down, I noticed Mrs. Risse was more resigned than I'd ever remember her being. When I was younger, she had this energy about her, much like her mother, Ms. Sonya. Now, it seemed as if Kenneth had sucked the essence from her to feed himself. What was left, she fed to Kelly.

"You talked to Kelly today?" she asked, peering at me with knowing eyes. "Of course you talked to her. You and her friends are her favorite people right now."

I nodded. "You and Kenneth don't give her much of choice in that matter."

"She's working herself to the bone," she continued. "I can feel it in my bones. I tell her to slow down, but she won't listen to me."

"You know your daughter better than that, Mrs. Risse." I laughed.

"She get that from her daddy. I never got their need for more," she said. "Been the top all their lives and still act like they have something to prove. Like being the best is a never-ending quest."

"That's just how they are."

"Exactly," she said, worry clouding her eyes. "That's the part that scares me. Not for Kenneth, but Lily-girl," she said, bumping my shoulder with hers. "I'm scared she's going to work herself to death. I put up with a lot so she could live easy."

I looked down at my hands, reflecting on what Mrs. Risse said. Kelly lit up any room she walked in–classroom, kickback, hospital. The only times I saw her close to softening was when she was in my arms. A rare solar eclipse–brilliant, brief.

"She doesn't know how to rest," I said finally.

"I agree." Mrs. Risse laughed. "My baby has all the book smarts, but slowing down? That's foreign to her." She let silence linger around us. "That's where you come in."

My gaze snapped to hers.

She looked at me–part challenge, part affection. "You love her."

It wasn't a question.

"I do." I grinned.

She nodded her head up and down, a smile filling her face. "I didn't need you to answer that. I know, been knowing for a while. When I walked on the porch after my mama passed and saw that look between the two of you."

I blushed, knowing she was talking about the night Kelly and I first had relations.

"Don't get bashful now. I would've cussed you out then, but it was crazy enough." She laughed, then sighed. "I also know you're the one that gave her that nickname Lily-girl."

Now it was my turn to laugh. "Ms. Sonya said she wouldn't say anything."

"Boy, my momma couldn't hold water when it came to Kelly. But we both saw it."

"Saw what?"

"You," she said. "You've been loving my daughter all these years. Patiently. Fully. Carefully waiting for her permission."

I exhaled. "And she acts like she has everything handled. Like she doesn't need anyone."

"She's just scared, Khalil." Mrs. Risse stared out into the parking lot. "That's my fault. I taught her to think love meant weakness. It's why her standards are so high. But you? You're the chink in the armor she works so hard to keep up." She chuckled to herself, then started to hum the opening to a gospel song I haven't heard since going to church with my aunt.

"Lily in the Valley," I stated.

"Ummhuh. My mama loved this song like she loved the flower." Mrs. Risse hummed a minute more, the humming turning to singing a few of the lyrics. Her voice was smooth and low. "You know what my mama used to say about lilies?"

I nodded my head. "They bloom in hardest of places."

"Kelly is the valley," she continued. "She keeps herself surrounded with work and chasing the next big accomplishment. And I love that for her. But you, you've always been the lily. Sure. Steady. Soft. Kelly needs that kind of love desperately. Deserves it. Especially after me and her daddy's bullshit."

I didn't know what to say, so I didn't say anything. The words rested in my soul like an echo of the hymn Mrs. Risse sung. Wetness clouded her eyes before she shook her head, laughing away the disappointment.

"I know we have the celebration dinner for her and Nessa coming up," she said, her eyes still twinkling from the unshed tears. "I was thinking, before she leaves for Seattle and busies herself again, could you take her away?"

"Like on a trip?"

"Doesn't have to be far. Just somewhere she can rest her mind. Enjoy life a bit. Somewhere she doesn't feel the need to perform. Just be."

I laughed. "You really think she'll go?"

"I know my daughter. She trusts you more than anyone," Mrs. Risse said. "She'll go."

"Okay, I'll take her."

"Good," she said, placing her hand over mine, sitting back with a satisfied smile. "And promise me you'll keep her soft, even when she's stubborn."

"I promise, if you make me one in return."

"What's that?"

"Stop saying she's stubborn. Kelly's a lot of things. Headstrong. Ambitious. Caring. Bossy." I turned to look Mrs. Risse in her eyes so she could see the conviction with which I spoke. "But she's never been stubborn. She's just a hurt little girl. I can make sure Kelly, the woman, is soft. But you and Kenneth need to do something for the little girl that had to grow up in the middle of y'all bullshit."

Chapter 9

Kelly

"MAMA, IF YOU BRING ME ANOTHER PLATE OF FOOD, I'LL be no good," I whined, pushing the plate filled with oxtails, rice, callaloo, and Jamaican meat pies. She stood behind me, one hand on her hip, lips pursed.

"You love this restaurant, Kelly Belly."

"I do, but that doesn't mean I have to eat like I won't be able to have it again."

"Tee Risse, if she won't eat it I will." Vanessa reached over and grabbed the plate for herself, chomping on the meat pie. "I haven't been able to keep anything down. This is the first meal my stomach hasn't revolted in days." She stuffed another meat-filled bite into her mouth as Xavier shook his head, filling her glass with more ginger ale like it was Dom Perignon.

"This baby is already spoiled," Aunt Viv beamed across the table, sipping her wine.

The laughter, the clinks of silverware hitting fine china, the overlapping conversations happening around me. It all felt like a moment I should have embraced. Instead, I was but a bird perched on the balcony above observing, speculating, reading the room for something that would take the joy away. And I found it. My father. Sitting just out of my view, like every bite offended him. His *"I'm not saying nothing"* silence louder than everyone else's joy.

If it weren't for the faint brush of Khalil's knee against mine, tethering me, I'd be awash in trying to regulate my father's emotions.

"You good?" he murmured under the noise.

"Mmhmm," I said, followed by a tight smile.

He didn't buy it. Just reached under the table, found my hand, and squeezed once. A silent *breathe, baby* in a language we only spoke. Across from us, Nyah sipped from her glass of wine like it might save her marriage. Her husband, Antonio, sat beside her, checking his phone under the table. Every now and then, she'd side-eye him like she wanted to break the glass over his head and shove the pieces down his throat.

Maverick, sitting two seats down from me, caught the glance. Watched Nyah. Watched Antonio. Then went back to his plate like minding his business was a full time job, even though his eyes said otherwise.

"Viv. Charisse. You remember that night we went down to Frenchman? Had these clowns," Aunt Lisa said, pointing to Uncle Doug and my father, "chasing behind us." She downed the champagne in her glass and raised it for Wesley to refill.

"Do I." Aunt Viv blushed beside Uncle Doug. "And for the record, it was you and Risse being chased. I already had my man." She smiled, pecking her husband on the lips.

"That's right, baby," he answered, rubbing the back of her neck.

Vanessa made a gagging noise beside me. "I think I jinxed myself." She winced. "Excuse me," she finished, pushing away from the table and hurrying to the bathroom down the hall.

Aunt Viv made a move to follow, but Xavier waved his hand. "I got it, Viv," he said, following behind his fiancée.

"Josie," Aunt Lisa started. "I had this dress on with a slit up to my hipbone."

"Mrs. Lisa, I just know you were that girl back then," Lynn hyped, raising her glass to Wesley's mom.

"And was." Aunt Lisa laughed out, downing another glass of champagne.

"I know that's right." Ma Josie laughed. "These children always talking about 'We outside. We outside.' They don't know what that is." The older generation laughed around us.

"Tell them, Lisa. We used to get down," my mother added, walking around the table to rub my father's shoulders. "Right, baby?"

"I remember y'all taking off playing games. That's what I remember," he replied, continuing to eat his food. My mother knocked off the comment like she always had. A kiss to his cheek, a tight smile that never reached her eyes, a slight sweep across her forehead to fix her mask.

Aunt Viv, wistful and soft-spoken, raised her glass. "I just want to say how proud I am of all my children. Vanessa, my baby, my heart. Kelly, my bonus daughter, who got her white coat and is heading to Seattle to nail her fellowship. And Wesley, my bonus son, ready to fill in his father's shoes." She patted a folded cloth napkin to her eyes. "Y'all make me so proud. Every day."

Glasses clinked around the table. But then came the pause. The one that signaled a storm brewing.

My father cleared his throat. "Well, since we talking about Seattle..."

"Kenneth, not tonight," my mother said between her teeth. Her hand wrapped around his, begging, pleading him to keep his mouth shut for once. I saw the muscles in Khalil's jaw tighten, even though he stayed silent.

"I just want to know what everybody else thinks about my baby moving clear across the country," he said, looking squarely at me. "Picking up and moving right now. Not giving people time to say their goodbyes."

"There's plenty time to say bye, Daddy," I echoed, my voice calm but clipped. "I don't start for another four weeks."

"Kenny, let the girl live her life," Aunt Lisa said quickly, grimacing back at him.

"Oh, you mean how you been living life?" he shot back. I noticed the way their friend group looked elsewhere as Lisa pursed her lips and went back to her champagne. "I just think" my father started again.

"Daddy, it's a fellowship, not a prison sentence."

"I know what a fellowship is, Kelly. I did plenty of them in my lifetime."

"But you're acting like I can't do the same! I'm a grown ass woman! You can't keep telling me what I can and can't do! I'm not Mama!"

"Kelly Marie, you better watch that tone!"

Khalil's hand flexed on my thigh, but he still didn't speak. The whole table froze. Not sure what to say. I didn't mean to say it aloud, but it was there now, floating like the wisps of smoke coming from the chafing dishes set out on the buffet. My father narrowed his eyes, but Uncle Doug jumped in like he'd been waiting for a detour.

"You know what we need? A change of scenery," he boomed, lifting the impasse occurring between my father and me.

"Ooh, yes. Mrs. Lisa, you, Mrs. Viv, and Ma Josie can show us how y'all used to get down," Lynn added, bringing some life back to the table.

"What you mean used to?" Ma Josie asked, feigning insult. "I still got it."

"I'm in," Aunt Viv said. "Risse, you're coming, too."

"Where y'all going?" Maverick asked, leaning forward, eyes on Nyah.

"I think they'll do good with 5015," I offered, grateful for the subject change.

"We should go, Antonio, especially since your parents have TJ." Nyah cut her eyes to Antonio, who still hadn't looked up.

"Nah, I'm tired and want to sleep in. You go ahead," he replied flatly.

"Cool."

Everyone started discussing logistics like which cars to take and how long we'd stay out. I tuned them out, the blood in my veins still humming from the words spat at my father. Khalil looked at me, something playful flickering in his eyes.

"What?"

He studied me before replying, "You good?"

"I guess," I said, shrugging my shoulders.

"You sure?"

I craned my neck to release the tension in my shoulders. I did a quick right to left movement with my head, then used my fork to push around the remaining food on my plate. Khalil brushed his thumb over the back of my hand.

"You gon' be alright. She know you didn't mean it like that."

I sipped the rest of the wine in my glass to clear the lump lodged in my throat. I looked around the table again. Vanessa and Xavier had made it back. She and Lynn recapped what had just happened in a corner with Lynn, while Xavier rubbed Vanessa's back. Our mothers were helping Mama clear the buffet before we headed out with Uncle Doug and Mr. Ted's help. And my father... He watched Khalil like he might spontaneously combust.

That simmer of tension between them hadn't cracked all night. No words exchanged. Just a cold war of glances and smirks. Khalil never flinched, much to my father's dismay. He just stood firm, his presence louder than anything his adversary could silence.

"He still can't stand you," I whispered, nodding between the two of them.

He shrugged. "That's still not gonna stop me from loving you," he said simply.

The words hit me in the chest and spread warmth throughout my body. I didn't respond. I glanced around quickly, seeing that it was only Khalil and I left at the table. I leaned in close, brushed my lips against his, then kissed him, slow and soft, and whispered, "Thank you."

He pulled back, rubbing our kiss into his lips. "Do me a favor tonight."

"That doesn't sound like a question." I smirked.

"It's not. Have fun with your mama and girls. Then come bounce on this dick later."

I laughed from deep in my belly. His smile matched mine, big and bright. "You know I can't stand you, right?"

He bit his lip as his eyelids lowered. "Yeah, but you love me, so it don't count."

You got me there.

"Come on, before we get left."

BY THE TIME we pulled up to Bar 5015, the night had finally shed its tension. That familiar glow bathed the block in a sultry promise. Yellow-orange streetlights buzzed low. A hum of various conversation interlaced with music spilling from the patio hugged my skin like it knew all my business. A small crowd lingered outside the entrance, dressed in varying degrees of grown and sexy. The bass from the DJ thumped through the sidewalk like a second heartbeat.

The parents walked ahead of us. My mom slid her arm into my father's and tugged him closer. She whispered something in his ear that made him crack a rare smile. They looked good together, even if the foundation was rocky. Nyah and Lynn walked arm in arm, Lynn urging her to scope out the scene. Maverick hovered close behind them, hands in his pockets, a grin playing at the corner of his mouth like he already knew the person she'd end up with.

I pushed myself to take it all in. Be present. Enjoy the rare moment of everyone getting along. From the open-air patio strung with string lights to the polished concrete bar that gleamed with years of drunken secrets.

At our section, the drinks came fast—lemon drops, top-shelf tequila bottles, whiskey on the rocks for my father. Music pulsed around us. We laughed loudly. Talked mess freely. I was tickled watching my mother and her friends pass the hookah around, as if it were natural. It probably was. I'd heard their stories growing up.

Nyah leaned close to me. "This feels like when we all got back to Houston after college. Like the before times."

"Girl, what before times?"

"When we were reckless and pretty and thought the worst thing that could happen was a bad eyebrow wax."

Lynn laughed. "We still pretty. We just got better insurance."

Khalil and Maverick sidled up with a platter of wings: lemon-pepper hot, fried hard.

"Y'all talking about insurance at the club?" he asked the group, his attention squarely on Nyah.

"It's a lounge," she corrected him. "We're classy now."

"It's a patio," he said, topping off Nyah's drink without her asking. "And it could be a garage, but if you there, it'll still be the most exciting spot in the world."

"Smooth," she said, smiling despite herself.

I looked over at my parents again. My mother leaned on my father's shoulder as they swayed to the line dance being played. I hadn't seen them like this in weeks...months, maybe. It made the ache in my chest go quiet.

Khalil pulled me into his chest as he sat on the top of the booth in our section. "You keeping your promise?" he asked, nuzzling his chin into the crook of my neck.

"Which one?" I smiled back.

"Shit, both of them," he replied, squeezing me tighter and gripping my ass. "Talk to me."

"I did already."

"You said you weren't sure about Seattle then deflected. Tell me why."

I exhaled, letting myself sink further into his arms. "Because it's far. Because I don't want to be alone. Because it feels like I'm choosing ambition over my family, my friends. Over...you."

He blinked slowly and nodded his head. "Nah. Choosing Seattle doesn't mean choosing against us."

"You say that now. But one day, you'll get tired of beating your own dick, and then what?"

He snickered. "I'll say it again tomorrow. And the next day. And the month and months after that. I'll keep saying it until you believe me."

I looked down at my nails. "What if everything falls apart?"

"I'll help you put it back together," he said without hesitation. "I'm not going to lie like I'm not going to miss you something bad. But you have to go, Kelly. You have to let yourself be great."

My eyes stung but I blinked the tears away. What would I look like crying in the club?

"You don't know how much I needed to hear that."

He leaned in, brushing his nose along my jawline. "I know exactly how much." Then he kissed me. And it wasn't the kind of kiss meant for public places. It possessed me, as our tongues danced together. His fingers slid lower on my waist, making their way to my ass, where he gripped tight enough to let anyone passing by know I was off limits. When he pulled back, his hazel-green eyes were deep emerald. His mouth curved devilishly.

"I'll be in Seattle every other weekend if I have to," he said. "I'll FaceTime you while you eat them dry ass sandwiches in the cafeteria."

I wrapped my arms around his neck and swayed to the music. "You really do love me, huh?"

"Since been. Never gonna stop."

"I like the sound of that."

He smiled wide like I'd just handed him a key he'd been waiting for. "Good," he said. "Now, let's dip out so you can make good on that other promise.

"Why are you always so nasty?" I smiled.

"Because you like it," he answered, then kissed my neck. "Come on."

Chapter 10

Kelly

THE FIRST THING I NOTICED WAS THE QUIET.

Not the kind of silence that clawed away at my mind when I was alone in my bed at night, save for the bright white light of my laptop screen. This was different. A weighted stillness. As I stared out of the window of Khalil's rental car, thick pines and red dust swirled with something in the air—maybe peace, maybe pressure, maybe both.

I leaned my temple against the car window as Khalil drove along the last stretch of a winding canyon road. The sun spilled across the horizon, gold flares towering over red rock cliffs. The shadows between each valley stretched long and soft like velvet across the desert floor.

I closed my eyes.

I shouldn't have come. There was still much left for me to do. Packing up my home, closing out patient files with my replacement, confirming start dates with my program director. I should not have been tricked into a trip that I didn't ask for. How convenient Khalil already had something in mind when he'd asked me while burying his bone deep in my uterus. Now who was going to say no to that. My phone buzzed in my lap, and I ignored it.

Beside me, Khalil let out a long, slow breath.

"You still mad at me?" he asked, his voice low and even.

"I don't like being set up," I huffed. "How did I let you guilt-trip me into this?"

"Guilt implies I feel bad about my actions." He brushed a finger along my cheek. "I don't feel bad about making you take a break, Lily-girl."

The SUV turned off the main road onto a gravel path lined with flowering cacti and wide stretches of open land. Nestled against the canyon wall ahead, the resort appeared like a mirage—earth-toned casitas with arched wooden doors and wraparound patios, each one blending perfectly with the landscape; it looked like the desert had grown it from the red clay.

When the car stopped, Khalil opened his door, then circled to open mine before I could reach for the handle.

"When did you become so soft and chivalrous?" He took my hand, unnecessarily helping me out of the large truck. A cloud of red dust settled at my feet.

"Hey," he said, tilting my chin up. "Let me have this trip. Let me spoil you a little."

I hesitated, entranced from the magnetic way his eyes held mine. I placed a hand over his. His grip was warm, sure, and easy in a way that made me woozy. His thumb brushed my lips. My heart thundered against my ribs. He lowered his face to mine, stilling just before our lips met. Then he laughed.

"Yeah," he growled, biting his lip. "We gonna get that mind to turn off for sure."

I punched his chest and walked off.

Walking into the casita felt like a different world. Shades of rusty reds, coppery browns, and golden yellows layered every surface. A rounded archway led into a sunken living room, grounded by a brick fireplace. The red of the brick mixed with the orange of the couch made me feel warm inside.

"Go take off your traveling clothes, like Ms. Sonya would say," Khalil's voice echoed from the doorway.

I walked over to him, eyeing him up and down. "You're getting too comfortable telling me what to do. I don't like that." I scrunched up my face as he walked over to me. He pulled me by the waist, strumming his fingers over my butt.

"You'll be comfortable with whatever I say you'll be comfortable with, understand." His voice was low, threatening in a too good sort of way. I started to respond, but he placed a finger on my lips instead. "Go change, then meet me on the patio."

I went to go change, but only because the compression of the workout set I was wearing was becoming uncomfortable quickly.

The sun dipped low by the time we sat down for dinner on the casita's private patio. The resort had set the table with flickering votives, cloth napkins, and an arrangement of lavender sprigs and desert roses. It was intimate–too intimate. Khalil and I had our thing, but it wasn't anything on the level of honeymooners trying to pretend the real world didn't exist.

A soft breeze tugged at the hem of my crocheted dress as I took a wine glass into my hand, sipping slowly. The chilled Sauvignon Blanc was crisp against my tongue, refreshing for the desert heat that lingered with the fading sun. Across from me, Khalil looked entirely relaxed, elbow draped over the back of his chair. The short sleeves of his linen shirt raised just enough to highlight the veins in his arms.

"You're sitting there being all calm," I said, taking another sip of the wine.

"That's the point of being here, right?" He cut into his salmon, slow and deliberate.

"Why are we eating here, instead of the restaurant?" I looked around the table. There was a pear and arugula salad with goat cheese and dried cranberries. A plate of Ahi tuna tostadas graced the center of the table, garnished with salsa verde and cilantro. R&B drifted in from the living space of the casita, filling the space with lover tunes. Khalil continued eating his salmon and potatoes. I looked at my own plate, my stomach urging me to begin eating. My mouth watered at the braised short rib with roasted carrots and mashed potatoes.

"What makes you think I want this? I don't recall you asking." I raised my eyebrow, toying with the silverware next to my hand.

"Do you want something else?" he asked, a smile flickering in his eyes. No. I didn't want something else. "Exactly, now stop asking so many questions and eat."

I rolled my eyes, picking up the fork, scooping a heaping amount of beef and carrots. The chile of the broth the beef was braised in paired well with the sweetness of the carrots. I closed my eyes and moaned. When I opened my eyes, Khalil was mid-bite.

"So, what's the plan for this trip?" I asked between bites. He shook his head, clearing his stupor from before.

"That's not for you to worry about." He held one of the tostadas to my lips. I opened and let him feed me. "You're here to relax."

I chewed, sitting back and crossing my arms. I washed down the food with more of my wine. "Why does everyone think I can't relax?"

"Because you don't. Your mind, brilliant as it is, runs nonstop."

My fork stopped halfway to my mouth.

"When's the last time you did something just because," he continued. "Not for awards or accolades. Or because it looks good on paper?"

I didn't answer. I couldn't answer.

The longer I held my response, the louder the silence became. How could anyone provide an answer when their whole life was rooted in achievement? For as long as I could remember, I pushed for the next big thing. Slowing down felt like quitting. I loved keeping my brain working. When it rested, when that twitch began twitching, the silence was unbearable. Resting felt like vulner-ability.

Khalil didn't press. He refilled my glass, held another tostada to my lips, waited for me to open up, placed it in my mouth, and sealed my lips with a brush of his thumb.

"This trip, you don't have to earn rest. You just have to receive it." He went back to eating his dinner, like he hadn't threatened to unravel me. "Now, eat. We have something planned after this. And no. I'm not telling you."

My chest tightened, then loosened. I just sat there, eating the food he knew I wanted, fighting myself to settle into the rest he thought I needed.

THE DOME WAS ROUND, warm, and dimly lit with hanging lanterns that swayed gently as people entered barefoot and quiet. Incense curled through the air in tendrils of sandalwood and some-thing floral, wrapping around me in feather-light kisses. I stood just inside of the threshold, staring at the arrangement of mats and cushions forming a circle across the stone floor.

"Khalil, I know you aren't about to have us join a cult," I whis-pered under my breath.

He chuckled behind me. "Do I look like somebody that would join a cult?"

"A little bit," I replied, trying not to smile. "If someone starts chanting in tongues"

"Chill." He laughed. "You trust me, right?"

He gave me a nudge toward the nearest set of cushions. I sat down stiffly. Around us, other couples stretched out on blankets, water bottles, and crystals. One woman had a rose quartz clutched to her chest like a prayer.

A hushed wave went around the room as a woman, small and serene, entered. Long, silver braids graced over her shoulders and went down her back. The cream linen tunic flowed from her shoulders to her ankles, its hems catching traces of red earth in their threads. She spoke softly about releasing tension and allowing the body to be a container for rest.

My head shot over to Khalil sitting behind me, his thighs bracketing me there. His hand turned my head around to the center where the woman stood without dropping his gaze. His hand dropped to my shoulder, anchoring me into the moment.

"Close your eyes if you feel comfortable," the woman rasped. "Begin to notice your breath. No need to change it. Just notice. Let the sound guide, move through you."

She struck the first metal bowl. It was a deep, resonant tone that echoed inside of my ribs. My fingers drummed on the thighs of my crisscrossed legs. I circled my head, cracking the pressure in my neck. My eyes darted between the people feeding into the sound waves rippling through the dome. Another tone reverberated around the room. Then another. Higher this time. Lighter. The vibrations danced up my spine like fingers brushing each vertebra.

I tried thinking of something else. My residency coming to completion. My fellowship gearing up in a few weeks. My patients I'd be leaving behind. With every thought, the sound pulled me back, dragging me into its lull of complacency. Not forcefully. Just...insistently. Like water dripping against stone, forging valleys in mountains that existed long before our time.

My fingers began a rapid tapping against the soft knit fabric of my dress. My manicured nails dug into the gaps of each stitch, threatening to pull threads from delicate yarn. Khalil's hand rested atop mine, stilling the movements. I felt him scoot closer, the warmth of his chest smoothing over my back. The scratchy coils of his beard tickled the crevice of my neck as his chin rested there. His heart beat methodically, in tandem with the ringing of the bowls by the woman centering the group.

Minutes passed, but it felt like hours. Time melted, as did my body against Khalil's grounding.

My breathing slowed.

My jaw unclenched.

I didn't realize I'd closed my eyes until the healer's voice returned, soft as the wind.

"When you're ready, begin to wiggle your fingers. Invite your body to return to you."

I blinked.

The dome was still there. The crystals. The flickering lanterns. The air felt fuller. My skin warmer. My thoughts...quieter?

Khalil didn't say anything as we stood and stepped out into the desert night. Stars blanketed the sky above—cold, clear, impossibly close.

"So, tell me, are we in a cult now," Khalil joked.

"Shut up, Big Head." I smirked back, rolling my eyes even though the tug in my chest felt otherwise.

"Come on. We have one more thing for the night." He took my hand as he led us back to our casita. Shadows danced along the desert landscape. Waist-high cacti with pointed tips. Tall, skinny grass laid at the roots. Weathered stones lined the pathway to the patio. Warm lighting glowed from within the adobe walls and flickered against the glass windows and sliding door.

Stepping into the casita, eucalyptus and neroli fragrant the air —minty, woodsy, with a slight sweet, floral citrus undertone. Soft R&B played through the hidden speakers from dinner. Khalil left the sliding door to the patio open just enough to let in the refreshing night air.

I circled the massage table placed in the center of the living room, eyeing the setup with suspicion. One robe, various bottles of massage oils, one pair of slippers. A perfectly prescribed dosage on unwarranted relaxation. A soft voice entered the space. The masseuse—an older Black woman named Lorraine with deep laugh lines and a calm aura—smiled gently as she stepped down beside the table.

"Welcome to Serenity Wellness Resort," she said warmly. "You're in for a special treat Ms. Reid. I'll be guiding Mr. Grant through one of our famous massages. My job is to set the tone, show him the technique, and help with pressure."

"Wait," I said, holding up my hand. "He's doing the massage?"

"Don't worry." He grinned. "I took anatomy in college. Don't forget, you helped me study." Before I could speak, he nodded his head side to side and pointed to the table. I peeled off my dress, leaving the nude-colored bikini on, climbed onto the table, and slipped beneath the warm sheet. A sigh escaped me as I settled onto the soft padding.

The lights dimmed. To my left, Lorraine poured a bit of oil into Khalil's palms, motioning him to rub his hands to warm up the liquid. "Khalil, you'll start with the shoulders, then follow my lead."

His first touch was tentative, carefully gauging my reaction to see how far I'd let him go, how much control I'd turn over in this moment. Dual sets of hands slid along the curves of my shoulders, then paused.

"It's very tense here, no?" Lorraine asked.

"Yeah, she carries her stress in her shoulders," Khalil replied.

"I see," Lorraine murmured. "Use firm pressure when you feel the knots like this, but don't rush."

Khalil's palms pressed down, slow and steady, working through the tension just beneath my skin. I inhaled sharply, sinking into the way the touch sent a wave of relaxation throughout me.

"You good?" Khalil asked.

"Too good," I replied into the pillow. He chuckled in response.

Then, his touch changed—softer, more deliberate. He moved to the base of my neck, his thumbs working in small circles down to my shoulder blades. My muscles melted into the table, breath by breath.

"How's that?" he murmured into my ear.

"If I cry, pretend I'm not," I said, my eyes closed.

"I got you," he said, as if it were a vow.

His hands moved lower, following Lorraine's guidance—over my back, my arms, even my temples. Each motion was slow, intentional, never rushed. He touched me like he was learning me all over again. Not to take. Not to fix.

There was no pressure to respond. No performance. No pressure to flirt or joke or seduce.

He took care of me.

I tried peering over my shoulder to see what the soft rustle and exchange of words were between Lorraine and Khalil. The soft click of a door being closed was followed by the soft thuds of Khalil's feet against the tile floor. He pumped more of the massage oil into his hands, then walked over to where I lay on the table.

His strong, oil-slicked fingers moved up the backs of my legs, slowly making their way to my thighs. The fingers kneaded into my flesh, fire crackling in every slow inch. The pads of his thumbs glided over the bare skin of my back like they'd done it a thousand times. I suppose in another life, they had. Perhaps in this life, I'd been too scared to let them.

"Relax," he murmured, his voice a low command against the shell of my ear. "I'm going to take care of you."

I should've bristled. That was my default, right? A reflex sharpened by years of masking my feelings through overachievement. But something about the weight of his palms against my ass, the slow drag of his thumbs against my spine, the scent of lavender and clove hanging in the air—all of it softened me, unraveled the apprehension lacing my muscle fibers one by one.

I breathed out shakily, my face cradled in the massage table's opening.

"That's it, Lily-girl," he praised. "Just breathe. You don't need to hold anything right now."

My thighs clenched under the sheet.

I cursed myself for reacting, but damn, his voice—deep, gravel-slicked. It had a *I know what you need* tone that melted straight between the cradle of my legs.

He pressed down into my lower back, circling his thumbs over the dimples just above my ass, and I gasped.

"You been carrying the weight of the world in this ass right here," he said, dragging his palms down, sliding the bikini bottoms I wore with them.

"I don't know how to turn it off," I admitted, my eyes fluttering shut.

He leaned down, his lips brushing just behind my ear. "Good thing you don't have to. You just have to listen."

"To what?"

"To me."

My stomach flipped. "Khalil—"

"Shh." He dragged his hands over my arms, his thumbs grazing the sides of my breasts. I arched toward his touch without meaning to.

"You're doing so good for me," he whispered, his lips grazing the nape of my neck. The warmth of his chest tingled against my back. His fingers pulled free the strings of my top. "So soft, So damn beautiful like this."

The sheet now covered nothing, as if it would've mattered. I was naked in every way that counted. Emotionally exposed, skin humming, pulsing in my ears.

"Let me see you."

I turned over without speaking. The sheet fell to the floor with a soft swish. My breasts peeked against the cool air dancing in the desert night. Khalil's eyes darkened, trailing slowly from my eyes to my throat to my navel, like he was mapping every place he planned to touch with his mouth.

"I don't know why you like hiding all this softness," he murmured, hovering over me, his body heat blanketing mine. "Listen to me clearly, Lily-girl. Softness looks good on you."

He bent down and kissed me, and I moaned into it–hungry, needy. The kiss wasn't rushed. It was deep, greedy. His tongue swept into my mouth, coaxing and claiming at the same time.

I reached for his shirt, fumbling with the buttons.

He pulled back just enough to whisper, "Ask me."

I blinked up at him, breathless. "What?"

"Ask me to touch you."

My pride flared with the arch of my brow, but my body had other plans. She was aching, every inch pulsing with need. And he knew it. He was teaching me how to say what I wanted without apology.

"Touch me," I whispered. "Please."

"Where?" he asked, licking his lips, the tips of his fingers tapping up my stomach.

"Khalil." I rolled my eyes. *Always the games*. "Everywhere. Fuck."

He smiled like I'd just passed a test.

"Good girl."

I was ashamed to admit the praise hit like lightening. I was a college-educated woman. A doctor for Christ's sake. But dammit if him telling me I did good didn't make me want him even more.

His hands slid down my sides, then lower, skimming the crease of my thighs as he lowered toward them. He kissed a slow trail down my stomach, his voice rough as he spoke against my skin. I pulled up on my elbows. Khalil kneaded my inner thighs, blowing gently against my sex. Lust pooled in his eyes.

"You're so perfect."

He kissed the tops of my knees, then higher.

"Let me see that pretty pussy."

I spread my legs, my knees hanging over the edges of the massage table. My heart raced as I stayed trapped in his reverent gaze; lost in whatever spell he'd conjured on me. The way he bit his bottom lip was sexy and sinister.

His hands trailed up to the juncture between my thighs, rubbing gently, stirring the molten lava swirling in my core. His mouth followed his hands, and when he tasted me, it wasn't tentative. He worshipped me as his soft lips lapped up the desire dripping from my lips.

"Oh my God," I choked, my hips arching.

"Ummhuh. Keep them legs open. Let me make you feel good."

And he did. He licked me like he was savoring something rare. Like I was his only need in the world. His fingers gripped my thighs, holding me in place as I writhed beneath him. He drew soft, slow circles around my clit with his tongue until my toes curled.

The build was maddening. He took his time, took pleasure in pulling me up into the throes of ecstasy until

"Come for me, Lily-girl."

And I did.

My body shook. My mind blanked. And through it all, his touch never left me. His hands anchored my thighs against his face. His lips sucked the soul from me as I rode the high. When I came down, he reached into his pocket and pulled out a foil packet.

Always prepared.

I reach up to touch his face. "Please," I panted, not able to say more.

He nodded, his eyes locked on mine, as he slid the condom on. "Anything for you."

He lifted me into his arms and carried me to the couch sitting in front of the lit gas fireplace. He placed me on the couch, knees planted in the cushions, a gentle hand arching my back toward the back of the couch. He kissed my shoulder, my neck. His hand grabbed the front of my throat, turning my head to assault my mouth.

"You'll keep that back arched for me," he whispered against my lips, pressing his dick against the crack of my ass.

I nodded, dazed. "Yes."

He slid in slowly, inch by inch, filling me, stretching me until I gasped.

"Fuck," he groaned. "You feel like heaven."

My nails dug into the back of the couch as I steadied myself, determined not to let my backbone slip.

He rolled his hips, deep and slow, one hand braced on my shoulders. The other gripping my hip, squeezing my ass. I looked back and we locked eyes. His eyes never left mine as he thrust back and forth, setting a rhythm all his own.

"You feel that?" he husked. "That's you letting me take care of you. And you're doing so good."

My walls fluttered around him, and he groaned again. Long, slow strokes followed deep hits into my core. I didn't think it was anymore possible to lose myself, but here I was, taking every inch, meeting his hips with my own. Desire grew hungrier and hungrier. I couldn't get enough. I moaned as his fingers dragged down my back.

Don't lose that arch, Kelly.

"That's it," he growled. "Look at you. So soft. So fucking beautiful like this. Mine."

"Yours," I gasped. "Fuck, don't stop. Please."

He didn't. He fucked me like he had something to prove. Like he was pouring everything he couldn't say into the way he moved inside of me. Deep. Focused. Sure.

And when I came again—louder, wetter, messier—he whispered, "That's it. Let it out."

Tears clouded my eyes as my hips moved sporadically, my body trembling. He pulled me against him, my back to his chest, as he continued his assault on my pussy. Kisses peppered my temples and the few teardrops that escaped the corners of my eyes. One hand gripped firm around my stomach, the other held my jaw in place. Waves trembled inside of me, milking his dick for everything it had to offer me.

"I got you, Lily-girl," he murmured against my ear. "Always."

And then he followed me over the edge, groaning my name into my skin like a prayer.

We laid there for a long time afterward, tangled on the couch in silence, the fire crackling beside us. He brushed my hair from my face, cupped my jaw, and kissed me again. Soft. Tender.

"You okay?" he asked.

I nodded. He kissed the tip of my nose. My legs trembled when he stood and scooped me into his arms again.

"Khalil" I protested weakly, burying my face against his chest, still flushed and floating.

"Hush," he commanded, kissing my hairline. "Let me do what I do."

The bathroom was already warm. Steam clung to the tile and mirror as he nudged the shower on. The spray flowed in a steady rhythm, soft and hot against the glass. He stepped inside the walk-in with me in his arms, still holding me like I was precious and breakable. When my feet touched the floor, I swayed a little. He steadied me with both hands on my waist. He didn't rush. He didn't talk much either, just kissed my shoulder as he let the water run over us. My head lolled backwards, resting against his chest while the water drummed against us, washing the heat from our skin but not the tenderness.

He reached for the body wash and lathered it between his palms, then began to soap me up. My arms. My back. My legs.

"Tell me if this is too much," he said quietly as his fingers smoothed between my thighs.

I shook my head. "Don't stop."

He kissed my temple, then my cheek, then the corner of my mouth. He washed every curve and crevice like he knew every spot but still approached it with discovery. I couldn't speak even if I wanted to. I just let him clean the parts of me I always guarded, always rushed through on my way to this appointment or that surgery.

He helped me rinse, then reached for a towel and wrapped it around me gently before grabbing one for himself. When we stepped out, he didn't hand me a robe. He dried me off, kneeling to pat my calves, my feet. Slathered my body with oil and butters then stood again meeting my eyes.

"I love taking care of you," he said softly, brushing a finger along the side of my face.

My throat tightened. "I don't know what to do with that."

He smiled, not pitying, not amused. Lovingly. "You don't have to do anything. Just let it be true."

Back in the bedroom, he guided me under the covers. I curled on my side, muscles finally loose, heart too full to speak. Khalil climbed in behind me, wrapped an arm around my waist, and pulled me back against his chest, his warmth soaking into my spine. His hand moved over my stomach in slow, calming strokes. Not greedy. Not suggestive.

"You know I don't need the perfect version of you, right?"

I swallowed. "I don't always know what version I am."

He kissed the back of my shoulder. "This one. Right now. The version that lets go."

My eyes burned, but I didn't cry. I let the silence stretch, safe in the arms of the only man who'd ever made me feel like being soft was a strength. Eventually, our breathing synced. His chest rose and fell behind me, steady and sure. Let sleep take me. No checklist. No deadline. No performance.

Just me.

Held.

Loved.

Enough.

Chapter 11

Khalil

SHE FELT LIKE PEACE. THE KIND OF PEACE I'D BEEN starving for since I could remember my first memory. The sunlight barely cracked the edge of the curtains, bathing the rust-colored walls in an amber glow, making her skin look softer than it already was. Her back pressed against my chest; our legs tangled like we'd done this a thousand times. Like our bodies remembered something she was still learning to say out loud.

She didn't move, save for the small rise and fall of her chest as she slumbered next to me. Lavender from the body oil I'd rubbed into her skin the night before clung to her braids. I didn't want to move. I wanted to stay in this. In this stillness with her.

But I felt it. The quiet tension in her body, like her mind had already started racing before she even had a chance to open her eyes. Like the fear of softness was hardwired into her more than anything else.

"You awake?" I murmured, my lips brushing the edge of her ear. Voice still low, still gravel and sleep.

"Mmm. Thinking about it," she said, her voice barely above a whisper.

I smiled. "Well, you thinking too loud."

"I am not."

"You are," I said, pressing a kiss behind her ear. "I can hear your brain gears grinding."

She didn't answer right away. I could feel her weighing how honest she wanted to be with me this morning. "So, you think you know me?" she finally asked.

"Yep," I said without hesitation. "Including how uncomfortable it makes you knowing I'm right every time."

She shifted, and I caught her gaze as she turned over.

Damn.

Golden light slid across her face, dancing in the curve of her cheekbones, the arch of her brow, the fullness of her lips. Her eyes were hazy and guarded but not closed off. Cautious. Like she was peeking through a crack in the door, deciding if it was worth stepping all the way in.

"I am comfortable," she muttered, climbing over me and straddling my hips. I caught the flicker in her eyes. Her stare lingered too long on my chest before blinking it away. "Just not delusional."

She was lying. I knew she wanted to stay like this, too. She was just too scared to admit it. I almost told her so. Instead, I pulled her close to my chest, inhaled behind her ear, smoothed my hand down her back, then smacked her ass with a *POW*! She screamed and rolled off me. I stood before she had a chance to retaliate.

"Fuck, Khalil. That hurt," she whined.

"Come on," I said, tossing her a lazy grin as I stretched and walked to the bathroom. "We going horseback riding at ten."

Her groan into the pillow was loud and dramatic. "You're evil. I thought this trip was supposed to be a break."

"It is," I said, stepping back to where she lay tangled with the covers on the bed. I bent down and kissed her forehead, taking my time with it. "And that includes making sure you don't have time to work that big ass" I paused, grinning at the way she scowled back at me, "beautiful brain of yours. And then later, I'm going to lay that ass out like communion again."

I flicked her nose and smacked her ass once again for good measure as I walked off, just to hear her half-heartedly spew a series of curses behind my name.

"And don't you bring Jesus into this!" she shouted from the bed.

I just chuckled, the sound echoing in the bathroom, knowing full well He already knew.

THE SKY HAD a sharp blue hue desert mornings were famous for; so clear it almost looked fake. The wind was light but inconsistent, tugging at my sleeves like it couldn't make up its mind. A stillness that didn't sit right hovered in the air.

We walked along the path toward the stables, shoes crunching in the reddish sand. The red rock cliffs towered in the distance like quiet gods, and even the birds seemed to keep their songs low. When we reached the horses, she stopped short, her whole body stiffening.

"I'm just saying," she hissed, adjusting her helmet like it was armor, her eyes locked in the black mare in front of her. "This horse does not fuck with me."

I bit the inside of my cheek to keep from laughing but couldn't stop the grin spreading across my face. I was already on Leo, a laid-back chestnut who matched my energy too well. He didn't spook, didn't strain. Just stood there chewing the air and blinking like he had all the time in the world. My kind of dude.

"Come on, Dr. Reid," I said, nodding toward her horse. "She just blinked." I meant to soothe her nerves, but she whipped her head toward me with that fire I loved a little too much. "Come back to me, Lily-girl." She stood firm, standing off with the animal in front of her. "You want to switch?"

She narrowed her eyes at me. "No."

"You sure?"

"Yes, I'm sure. I will not be outdone by a horse named Juniper. So, you can stop staring at me with your pretty-boy smile."

I let the smirk bloom slow, giving her all teeth. "You think I'm pretty?"

"Boy, I will push you off that damn saddle."

The guide stepped in to help her mount. I glared when his hand got too close to her lower back. He fixed that immediately. His partner gave us the standard safety rundown I barely heard. I focused on Kelly–the way her jaw clenched, the way her hands gripped the reins like the mare was a wild bull instead of a glorified house pet with hooves. Still, she got up there. Proud and slightly terrified. And I loved her for it.

The guide said something about terrain, maybe made a joke. I couldn't lie, I laughed, but mostly to keep her from noticing the way the wind shifted again, sudden and strange. The brush swayed sideways, not forward. A gust cut through the valley like it had secrets.

We started riding. The horses moved slow, trailing each other along the dusty red trail, winding through sun-warmed brush and jagged hills. I let Leo lead a bit, glancing back every so often to check on Kelly. Her posture was tight at first, rigid like her body hadn't decided whether to trust the animal. But after a few minutes, I saw her shoulders loosen. Her head tilted back slightly as she looked to the sky. She was breathing again.

I exhaled, too.

"This isn't too bad," she said behind me. "I could see how one would think this is peaceful."

"Stop expecting chaos, pretty girl," I called over my shoulder.

"I don't expect chaos." She smirked, her voice already softening. "It just finds me," she added with a fake pout.

"I love you like this," I said before I could stop myself.

"Like what?"

"Light."

She didn't answer. She didn't have to. I felt her hesitation in the silence that followed. I heard her walls trying to reconstruct themselves mid-trail. But I didn't push. I clicked my tongue and nudged Leo forward, giving her the space to breathe through whatever that four-letter word stirred up in her. Behind me, I heard her reins tighten, then loosen.

The rhythm of her horse's hooves synched with mine. Our guides continued joking as we made our way through the trail. She laughed and looked softer than the woman demanded her to be. The girl her parents needed her to be. I let myself believe we were solid, even if she hadn't spoken the words yet.

Chapter 12

Khalil

By the time we'd scrubbed off the red dust and horse sweat, napped and rested, the fading sun cast long shadows over the resort grounds. We'd taken advantage of the cooling night to walk the grounds, hand in hand. We were heading back to our casita when we passed a tucked away path behind the spa. Lanterns flickered above the sand-washed stone path, beeswax candles burning on low wooden tables arranged between clusters of tall cacti and shaded tents. There was something soft about the space. Intentional. Like it was waiting for us.

"Let's try this," I said, already reaching for an apron.

Kelly squinted at the sign written in chalk. "You and plants, I swear. What happened to getting another massage?"

I shot her a lazy grin as I tied the apron behind my back. "If you want me to stretch that pussy out again, just say that."

She didn't answer, but she didn't walk away either. She joined me, grabbing an apron and sliding onto the stool beside me. I watched her thumb through the herbs on the table. Delicate movements even though her jaw was set tight. She looked like she'd just touched a memory that still had teeth.

The instructor, a petite older woman with gray locs in a regal bun, greeted each person with a hug. Her name was Joi, and she moved through the garden like she belonged to it. Once she had everyone's attention, she told us the workshop was about intention setting through nature. We'd be building herb bundles to take home as reminders of what we needed more of in our lives.

I tuned her out for a while. Not because I wasn't listening, but because I already knew what I needed. My hands moved instinctively across the herbs, picking up sprigs, tucking them into a small pile without overthinking.

"You weren't the only one Ms. Sonya taught about plants," I said to Kelly, who was eyeing my bundle with intrigue. "You may have been her favorite person, but I was her favorite student. I know more about these plants than she ever tried to teach you."

She rolled her eyes but didn't argue.

Growth.

I focused back on the bouquet. Rosemary first, the smell of grounding and focus. My anchor when the world pulled me in too many directions. Then basil, sweet and strong. Something about it always made me feel like I deserved more. Next came lavender, for the nights when the weight of my past caught up with me. For the things I carried in silence. I held it for a second longer before placing it in, brushing the stem like it might recognize me. Cool and clean mint was next. As I crushed a leaf between my fingers, its scent lingered in the air. *Speak up*, it seemed to say. *Say it scared if you have to, but say it*. I finished the bundle with some dandelion wild, bright, and a little unruly.

Joi walked over and examined the bundle I'd built. "Very interesting," she started, her eyes flicking from the herbs to me. "I don't get many people straying from lavender or sage in these workshops." She turned to Kelly with a grin that made me wonder what she already saw.

Kelly tried to play it cool, but she was blinking more than

usual. Her hand hovered over a sprig of sage before she picked it up and handed it to Joi. "I'm not sure what else I need," she admitted.

"Sage is a great start for you." Her hands maneuvered through the rest of the plants with the same ease as me. "Let's add some motherwort, a little chamomile, few springs of thyme." She bundled the herbs and glanced at them, tapping her finger on the table. "Something's missing here?"

I reached over and handed her a bright gold flower with jagged petals, like sunlight that grew teeth.

"Oh, you know a little something, huh? This is perfect." Joi bundled it all and handed it to Kelly like it was fragile, sacred. She took it in both hands, not sure if she was ready to hold it.

"Motherwort for your heart, when it's been armored too long." Kelly's eyes went glassy, her mouth pressed into a thin line. Joi kept going. "Chamomile to rest without guilt. Thyme for courage. Sage for release. Calendula..." She paused, smiling. "To remind you that joy still belongs to you. Even now."

I'd known Kelly a long time. Knew her posture, her moods, the way her silence changed shape depending on what haunted her. The way she looked down at the bundle unfurled a softness she'd never shared with the world. Not with her friends, rarely with me. For damn sure not with her parents.

I wanted to protect it. I wanted her to feel safe enough to keep growing it.

When Joi asked us to write an affirmation for our bundles, I scribbled mine and kept it covered as I slipped it between the herbs. I stood to return our aprons and got caught in conversation with Joi about root systems and climate zones. I didn't realize Kelly had peeked until I turned and caught her staring at me with awe.

She held it in her eyes, swimming with our history. Traced the timeline between college nights spent together and breakdowns she thought she hid better than she did. She was finally beginning to see me, not as her homeboy, not as a safety net, not as a stand-in. But as hers.

She saw the words written on my slip of paper.

Peace looks good on you, Lily-girl.

And when I walked up behind her, wrapped my arms around her shoulders, I felt the shift. Small, but real. She was letting go. And this time, I wasn't alone in the bloom.

"Come on," I said, pressing a kiss to her cheek. "Joi said there's dinner under the main pavilion."

I grabbed our bundles before she could overthink and led us through the winding path lit with soft lanterns and firefly glimmers. The stars were already blinking awake above us. Walking into the covered space, laughter and shared air consumed us, a stark contrast from the candlelit, intimate dinner Kelly and I shared the previous night. Long tables stretched across the width of the space, benches covered with pillow cushions, table runners covered with crystal candelabras and family style platters of food. Strangers from all walks of life sat together, as if they'd known each other all their lives.

Plates passed hand to hand. Bowls of roasted vegetables, warm bread still steaming, and chicken kissed with something sweet and sharp. Handmade balsamic vinaigrette. Kelly and I sat shoulder to shoulder, our knees brushing beneath the table. I served her first without asking. She deserved softness even in the mundane. And she let me. The sweetest part of all was the way she leaned into me while I talked endlessly with the guests around us. Her laughter rang loose instead of guarded, music to my ears.

Someone brought out drums. The sound bath woman. Hippie Auntie, as Kelly called her. She led a chant that turned into a full-on circle of swaying and humming. Kelly eyed them with suspicion. I caught the exact moment her brain screamed *cult alert*.

I leaned over, wine glass in hand. "Look at you. Being present."

She rolled her eyes. "Be careful with that glass. You don't know what they laced this wine with."

I chuckled and slid my hand to her knee, tracing a small circle with my thumb. "Stay present, baby girl."

"I am."

"Nah," I said, watching her closely. "You're alert. Alert and present are two different things." I slipped my hand under the table, settled it against the inside of her thigh. Not to tease. Not to start something. But to anchor her. To remind her I was still here.

That I always had been.

LATER, after we'd slipped away from the crowd and the music, we ended up on the patio of our casita, sliding into the hot tub beneath a velvet black sky. The desert was still again, daring you to disturb it. Above us, a single cloud moved across the sky, slow and aimless. Stars blanketed in tiny clusters, secrets waiting to be spilled. The distant howl of a coyote rose, then fell, like a prayer answered too late. Sandstone cliffs loomed in the distance, dark silhouettes guarding our moment.

The steam from the tub rose around us. Kelly sank into the water across from me, her face flushed from the wine and heat, her eyes glassy with something heavier. She pulled her braids into a bun atop her head, but it'd already begun its own unraveling.

I leaned my head back, my arms stretching along the rim of the tub, trying to memorize this. Her. The way the lavender light from inside the casita haloed her profile. The way the dampness of her skin emitted an ethereal glow from within. The way she stared at me like she was seeing me for the first time, even though I'd been here all along.

"You like what you see?" I asked, my voice low.

"I do," she whispered, the sound of the jets punctuating her words.

I moved toward her, slow and sure, letting the water fold around my waist. When I reached her, I didn't ask. I just pulled her into me, walked us back until she was straddled on my lap, her arms around my neck, right where she needed to be.

She exhaled. That one breath told me more than her words ever could.

I kissed the curve of her shoulder, lips barely touching skin. "You good?"

"I don't know," she said, honest and raw. "But I want to be."

I pressed another kiss atop the thumping artery in her neck. Let my lips linger there to taste away the fear held close. "Then let me help."

Her fingers traced the tattoos on my chest like they were a map she already knew by heart. Her touch wasn't rushed. It was reverent. And I let her take her time.

"Why do you keep choosing me?" she asked, her voice like smoke.

"Because I already did. A long time ago." No fanfare. No pause. Just truthful reassurance she needed to hear.

She kissed me then. Soft, then deeper. Hungry. Her hands curled behind my neck as her body melted against mine. I knew she was done running.

"Take what you need, Lily-girl," I whispered into her mouth.

And she did.

She let herself need.

The kiss turned messy and slow as it unfolded in the darkness. My hand slid along her back, then up to cradle her head, her braids falling around my fingers. She let out a sound I felt in my spine, and I held her tighter, like she might slip away if I didn't. My hands dropped to grip her ass, pulling her closer to join us at the ribs. My thumbs loosened the strings of her bikini bottoms as I tugged them from her. Her hands tugged at the waistband of my trunks, freeing my dick. She slid down smooth and hot the most beautiful moan escaping her sweet lips. As she rocked her hips, I thrust into her, matching the rhythm she set.

Nothing else needed to be said. Us tangled in the heat and

steam and silence said everything. I didn't know how long we stayed like that. But I remembered the stars, how they flickered like they were blinking out one by one. I remembered how the air shifted, getting cooler, sharper, like something was waking up in the desert with us. Something I didn't see coming.

But for now, I had her in my arms.

And for once, she wasn't fighting it.

Part Two

"Ne Me Quitte Pas"

Nina Simone

Chapter 13

Khalil

SHE MOVED LIKE SHE DIDN'T WANT TO START THE DAY. Soft-footed, slow-stepping, lingering in every doorway like it might talk her out of leaving. The Kelly I knew—hell, the Kelly the world knew—packed fast and early. Always on the move. Always on go. Clipboard energy. Flight tracker on her phone, rolling her eyes at people who waited to pack until morning. But today?

She folded her clothes like they were made of spun sugar.

I sat on the edge of the bed, watching her move through the space like it was borrowed magic. The late-morning sun spilled across her shoulders, lighting up the gold undertones in her caramel skin. Her edges were a little wild from the hot tub and the shower and our sleep last night. My shirt hung loose over her frame, the hem grazing just over the plumpness of her butt. Her mouth carried a hint of a smile she hadn't wiped away yet.

This wasn't the woman who'd boarded the plane with me to Sedona a few days earlier. This was her without tension. Without the noise clouding her mind. Just Kelly. Soft. Bare. Breathing.

"You're being weird, Big Head," she said, raising a brow, continuing to fold and place her clothes in the suitcase.

"You're always weird."

"So you're trying to be like me?"

I hadn't realized how much I missed hearing her voice. The feather-lightness as she spoke at dinner. The deep, passion-filled moans as I brought her on an orgasm-induced high each night we'd been here at the wellness resort.

"You the one wearing my shirt."

She snatched it off and threw it in my direction, grabbing a tank from her suitcase. My eyes dilated, staring at the soft breasts that'd become my nightly pacifiers. A resting spot for my head, putting me into the best slumber I'd ever had in my life. I laughed and dropped my phone on the bed beside me.

"I'm not going to say I told you so, but–"

"Right before he says it." She smirked.

"But you needed this trip. More than you know."

She set down a folded dress and turned to face me, arms crossed over her stomach. She looked like she wanted to argue, but then she didn't. Instead, she walked over, plopped down in my lap, and wrapped my arms around her waist.

"I hate when you're right," she muttered.

"Why? Because I say it with my whole chest."

"You say it like a man who thinks he invented peace."

"Only for you." She exhaled and leaned back into my chest. After a minute, I asked, "You ready?"

"Almost."

I kissed her forehead, slow and sure. "You want your phone back before we go?"

She shook her head. "No."

"No?"

She pulled back enough to look me in the eye. "I want to hold onto peace a little longer."

Her words hit me in the damn throat. I knew how hard she fought for that stillness. Order. Stability. Knew how many years she spent carrying her parents' mess. Knew how rare it was for her to say out loud that she wanted something gentle.

"Okay," I said, massaging her scalp. "We'll stay put a little longer."

ON THE DRIVE to the airport, she leaned into me, threading her fingers through mine, resting her head on my shoulder as I drove the SUV through the canyons and brush-lined roads. She stayed curled under my shoulder as we waited for TSA to process our passes. I could feel her slipping into something foreign for her. Trust. Stillness. *Me.*

We didn't talk much in the terminal. She read from her Kindle, taking small sips of water every now and then. The brightness of her eyes and soft giggles sent warmth spreading through my chest. I let her bask in it. Being carefree.

At the gate, we boarded early. She curled into the window seat, asked for a ginger ale, and a pack of mixed nuts, then promptly dozed off on my shoulder. I watched her sleep for most of the flight. Eyes fluttering. Lips parted. Like she'd finally put her armor down.

And I'd never felt more protective in my life.

We landed in Houston to the usual wave of humidity and the sound of someone's baby wailing two rows up. Kelly stretched beside me and smiled, lazy and warm.

"Back to real life," she said, not unkindly.

"We'll bring the peace with us."

She bumped her shoulder into mine. "Look at you being emotionally evolved."

"Just how you got your degrees, I been studying, too," I said, adjusting her carry-on over my shoulder. "Only difference is, mine is a doctorate in Kelly Reid."

She didn't respond, just reached for my hand. She kept my hand in hers as we reached the departure terminal. Before we exited the building, she stopped me.

"I'm going to run to the restroom really quick. It's going to take us forever to get home from Hobby."

As she walked away, I pulled out my phone, powering it on.

That's when I saw them.

Eleven missed calls.

Six texts from Zay.

Three from Nessa.

My stomach dropped before I even tapped the screen. A kind of dread that sinks its teeth in before your brain catches up.

ZAY

Call me ASAP. It's important.

Khalil. Emergency, man.

It's Charisse. Don't say anything to Kelly.

Just call me ASAP.

Don't say anything to Kelly.

Please.

Just bring her to the hospital.

My fingers moved before I could think. I hit Zay's name. He picked up on the first ring, voice low and raw like he'd been fighting tears or a storm, or both.

"Yo," I said, stepping a few paces away. "What's going on?"

He didn't ease into it. "It's Kelly's mom. She collapsed this morning. Paramedics brought her here. They tried reviving her... but" he choked. "She didn't make it."

Everything slowed.

In front of me, Kelly was leaving the restroom, stopping by a kiosk hawking plastic nothingness. I turned my back on her and gripped the handle of her suitcase.

"Say that again," I whispered.

"She's gone, bruh. I—Me, Nessa, her parents. We're all here. It happened so fast."

I shut my eyes. Every muscle in my body clenched.

Xavier exhaled shakily. "Nessa says don't tell her. Just bring her straight here. We're at Memorial. Emergency entrance. Nessa said she'll meet you there and tell Kelly the news."

I swallowed hard. "I got it."

"Say, Khalil—" Xavier's voice cracked. "She's gonna need you."

"I know."

I turned back toward Kelly, who was now walking toward me, an easy grin on her face.

"You good?" she asked, eyeing me.

I nodded too fast. "Yeah. Car's almost here."

She narrowed her eyes but didn't push. Just kept walking ahead of me. The ride was quiet, but not in a bad way. Kelly rested her forehead against the window, fingers tapping absently on her thigh to some invisible rhythm. I stared out the opposite side, phone clutched in my palm like it might crack open and scream.

"Heard from anyone today?" she asked eventually.

My body stiffened. I cleared my throat. "Zay called me. Asked if we were on our way back yet?"

"Can't spend three days without each other, huh?" She laughed, then rested her head on my shoulder. "Nessa's probably blowing my phone up. She'll have to wait." She smiled faintly. "She's probably freaking out over her pregnancy. Or names. Every day I wake up to a new name suggestion. Just last week I had to talk her out of naming the baby something like Lavender."

My chest ached. "Khalil Junior is a strong name," I said, forcing a smile.

She laughed again. "We agreed you don't get naming rights until you're someone's husband."

"Technicalities."

She looked up at me then. Real soft. Real curious.

"You sure everything's okay?"

I nodded. "Yeah," I replied, then kissed her forehead. I hated how easy it was to lie when the truth would shatter her. *Nessa said she'll tell her.* But I didn't want to hand her off. I didn't want her finding out from anyone but me. Still, I promised. So, I sat in silence while she hummed along to the radio, completely unaware that her whole life had already changed.

As we got closer to the hospital, her body became tense, alert.

"Khalil, why are we headed to the hospital?"

I was frozen, stuck with how much, if anything, I should share. Instead, I decided to reply, "Nessa wants us to meet her there."

"Why? What happened? Is she okay?"

I wrapped my arm around Kelly's shoulders, pulling her close. "I'm not sure. She just said to head that way."

What was once an enjoyable moment soon became tense. Kelly's shoulders squared, her defenses heightened no matter how much I rubbed her shoulders. Her eyes flitted between the windows on either side of the car. Gone was the gentle humming from earlier. She sat there, furiously twiddling her thumbs, rapping of her fingers against whatever surface she could get her hands on. Muscle memory caused her to check her pockets for the phone she'd tucked away into her carry-on in the trunk of the car.

When we pulled into the entrance of the hospital, Kelly hopped out before I could even finish tipping the driver.

"She's just being overly cautious because of the miscarriage," Kelly mumbled to herself. "You know how worried she's been since she found out she's pregnant. She's fine, right?" Kelly looked to me for reassurance.

"We'll see," was all I could give her, as I ushered her into the emergency room lobby. Kelly's feet stopped moving when she saw who was waiting.

Vanessa.

Sitting motionless in one of the gray lobby chairs near the nurses' desk, Zay to her right. No frantic pacing. Just still.

Xavier looked morose as he soothed his fiancée. Nessa was different. Her hoodie sleeves were pushed over her hands, like she didn't know what to do with them. Her eyes—red and puffy, like she hadn't slept. Like she'd already been crying for hours.

"Wait...Nessa?" Kelly stepped forward to her best friend. Her sister.

Vanessa didn't speak. She stood slowly, arms loose at her sides. No smile. No relief. Just grief, raw and visible.

Kelly blinked. "You okay? Is the baby okay? Did something happen?" Her voice started to rise, panicked now. "What happened? Vanessa, you gotta say something. You're scaring me."

I moved beside her and gently touched her elbow. "Kelly."

She looked back at me, confused by me calling her real name instead of the nickname I'd given so many years before. Then, Vivian appeared from the hallway behind the glass doors, dressed in sweats, like she hadn't had time to put herself together. Her eyes weren't red, but they were hollow. Like she'd seen too much and still had to hold it together.

Kelly's breath caught.

"Aunt Viv?"

Vivian crossed the distance slowly. Every step deliberate, as if in negotiations with God himself. When she stopped in front of Kelly, she didn't rush the words. "Baby...I'm so sorry. Your mama didn't make it."

The silence that followed was loud.

Kelly blinked once. Then again.

"No," she said, barely above a whisper.

Not a scream.

Just a breath of disbelief.

"No. That's not...No."

She looked at Vanessa again, shaking her head.

"I thoughtI thought it was you. I thoughtAunt Viv, what are you talking about? Nessa, what is she saying?"

Vanessa opened her mouth, then closed it. Her jaw trembled. "I'm sorry," she whispered, her voice hoarse.

She took one stumbling step backwards. Then another.

I reached for her just before her knees hit the tile.

Her knees buckled like her body had stopped believing in gravity. I wrapped my arms around her waist from behind, lowering us both to the tiled floors.

"No. No. No," she kept whispering, clawing at my arms like she could unhear it.

She didn't sob. Not yet. She just trembled. Fisted my shirt in both hands and kept shaking her head like the world would listen.

"She was just here. We were just laughing. We were" she whispered. "I didn't say goodbye." Her voice cracked. Then the dam broke.

She screamed. One long, guttural, soul-ripping sound that tore through the lobby like a blade. The kind of wail that tore at your soul. Deep and jagged and endless. People in the waiting area turned to look, but I blocked them out. I pressed her face into my chest and let her beat her fists against me. I didn't say a word. Didn't ask her to breathe. Didn't tell her to be strong. I just held her.

Vanessa knelt beside us and reached for her again. "Kelly, I'm so sor–"

"Don't," Kelly wailed, burying her face in my chest. "Stop talking."

Vivian crouched too, but she didn't try to touch her. Just whispered, "She loved you so much, baby. You know that, right? You were her greatest joy."

Kelly cried harder. And I held her tighter. Xavier reached down to take a sobbing Vanessa into his arms, soothing her. His face was withdrawn, hoodie halfway zipped, eyes still red-rimmed. He didn't say anything. Just rubbed circles on Vanessa's back and gave me a nod. We were all helpless in that moment. And still, somehow, Kelly was the center holding all our broken pieces.

She whispered things into my chest I couldn't understand. Names. Pleas. Maybe prayers. I didn't know. I only knew I stayed with her. I didn't move. Didn't shush her. Didn't promise things I couldn't give. I just anchored.

Because everything that came next would hurt worse. And she needed to fall apart first.

Eventually, her breathing slowed. Not because the grief passed–grief didn't work like that. It just got tired of roaring and started humming low beneath her ribs. She lay in my lap, face swollen, braids scattered across her face, and chest hiccuping in shallow bursts. My legs had gone numb, but I didn't move. Wouldn't have even if a fire broke out against the floor.

She finally looked up at me. Her lips parted, but no sound came.

"You don't have to say anything," I murmured.

"I should've been here."

"You were where you needed to be."

She flinched. "That's the part that hurts the most."

Vivian brushed a braid behind her ear. "You want to see her?"

Her eyes filled again, fast and full. "I don't know."

"You don't have to decide yet. Just breathe for me, okay?" I asked, trying my best to console Kelly. Vivian continued rubbing her shoulders, tears lining her lower lids.

"I don't want to breathe without her."

My chest cracked.

"Take your time, Kelly," Vivian said, reaching to grab her. "There's no rush. When you're ready, I'll walk with you."

Kelly turned toward me instead. Not because she didn't love Vivian. But because in that moment, she didn't want history. She wanted safety. I stood slowly, lifting her with me. She didn't let go of my hand as we moved down the hall. Didn't let go when we passed the nurses trying not to stare. Didn't let go when we reached the private room with the frosted glass door and the brass plate that said *Family Only.*

I held it open. Kelly stepped in. Vivian followed. And I stayed outside. Back against the wall. Heart thudding. I listened as the door clicked shut. Soft. Final. And in that moment–standing alone in a quiet hospital hallway–I realized something I hadn't dared to name before. *Whatever came next, I wasn't walking away from her.*

Not after this.

Not ever.

Chapter 14

Kelly

There were too many shoes by the door. Loafers, beat-up sneakers, my mom's red-bottom heels too flashy for a day like this. I stepped over them without a word. The front door had barely shut behind me before the smell hitPine-sol, sweat, grief, and a pot of gumbo somebody had the nerve to put on, like food could make any of this any easier to digest.

I didn't want to be here.

But I couldn't be anywhere else.

"Kelly," Lisa's voice floated in from the hallway, warm and bracing. "Baby, I'm so sorry." She didn't wait for permission. She pulled me into a hug, arms soft but heavy with heartbreak. I let her. When she pulled back, I saw the strain in her green eyes, reddened from grief. "I'm here for you. You say the word, I'll handle it."

I blinked past her shoulder and caught the sight of the living room. My dad had sunken into his recliner like his bones had given up. Uncle Doug stood behind him, one hand resting on his shoulder. Xavier sat on the arm of the couch, legs crossed, lips pressed tight like he was swallowing a prayer. Wesley was off in a corner, scrolling on his phone, thumbs moving like if he stopped he might feel something.

Vanessa looked at me from her spot at the kitchen counter open to the living room. She tried to smile. I couldn't return it. Lynn and Nyah were sitting next to her, a tissue box wedged between them, already half-empty.

"Come sit," Lisa said. "I warmed up some gumbo your mama had in the freezer."

I shook my head. "I'm good. I just wanted to stop by before..."

"You not staying?" My dad's voice cut through everything. It was coarse. Demanding in the way it'd been all my life.

I looked at him. His eyes were still bloodshot and hollow, like he still wasn't fully inside his body. He'd been that way when I walked into the family room at the hospital. He hadn't even noticed I was there. Were it not for Aunt Viv telling him I was there, he'd still be crying on Uncle Doug's shoulder, inconsolable.

"I–yeah, I'll stay awhile," I relented.

His mouth trembled. "Your mama wouldn't want you off somewhere alone."

I nodded because anything else would've taken too much energy. He patted his knee like I was five again and he was calling me over for a story. Everyone looked on, an audience to our own Greek tragedy. As I walked toward him, their eyes tracked me like my mother's ghost was walking alongside me.

When I made it to my dad, he stood, wrapping me in his arms. But this time, I could feel how much of it was for him, not me.

"You know your mama was my whole heart," he whispered in my ear. "She ain't even tell me goodbye."

My hands tightened on his back. "I know, Daddy."

His breath caught. "I can't do this without her, Kelly. I swear to God I can't." I nodded again, but it felt like my throat was closing. He pulled back, his face wet. "Promise me you'll help me figure this out. Be strong for me, alright?"

That made something twist in me. Because of course I could. Of course I would. I always had. I didn't answer, just squeezed once more then kissed his cheek, and stepped away before I could drown in his sadness.

Vanessa stood up and took a few steps toward me. "You need anything? Water? A shot?" she laughed.

I shook my head. "I just need to go upstairs for a minute."

Khalil stepped to me. He hadn't shed a tear all day, yet the tears lingered in his eyes.

"You sure? I can come with you."

"No, I just–just give me a second."

I felt everyone's eyes on me as I climbed the stairs. My hand hovered above the banister before pulling back. Touching it felt like a disturbing memory. Each step creaked like it remembered me. It'd been months since I'd been to my parents shared home. My childhood home for as long as I could remember. My mother took her time filling every nook and cranny with trinkets and nonfunctional decor pieces just because. With her gone, and all her touches still here, it felt disrespectful. How dare they be here while she withered away in a funeral home.

When I pushed open the door to my old bedroom, I half-expected her to walk out of the closet, holding old clothes she'd collected to donate. I thought she'd stand up from fluffing the pillows on my bed or vacuuming the room that was already in pristine condition. But there weren't piles of clothes in the center of my room, or a bed in disarray, or the loud hum of a vacuum cleaner.

Silence.

That was all. Save for a glass vase housing a lone plant on my old desk by the window. A single lily, pinkish-white. Just as there'd always been one waiting for me each week. I'd come home from some school event and see a fresh flower waiting for me with a note. "For my sweet girl. Just because. Mommy."

I stared at it for what felt like forever. Then, I sat on the edge of the bed, and before I could brace myself, the first tear dropped. Quiet, simple. Then the second. Then a hemorrhaging of pain I couldn't stop. My chest caved. My body folded forward. The air felt too sharp to breathe. All I could do was cry. Not the kind people heard and rushed to comfort like I had in the hospital lobby. This wasn't that. This was the kind of crying that stayed low and buried, like it didn't want to be seen. I held my face in my hands and let it happen.

A knock came, soft and distant. Then the door creaked open. "Kelly?" Vanessa's voice. "You alright?"

I couldn't answer. Silent streams poured from my eyelids. The air in my lungs seemed thin. She stepped in, followed by Lynn. Nyah slipped in after, shutting the door, locking it behind her. She knelt in front of me and took my hands from my face. Her eyes welled up again when she saw mine. She stood and sat behind me, wrapping her arms around my shoulders, grounding me, empathizing with the pain in my soul. The missing piece that'd never grow back. Lynn and Vanessa sat next to me, completing the full circle embrace, resting their heads on my shoulder.

"You don't have to talk," Nyah whispered. "Just breathe."

I couldn't speak. I didn't want to. I wanted to scream. Shout. Yell at God for putting me through this. But I couldn't. No sound left from me aside from the small huffs of air as I struggled to catch my breathing. The room had gone blurry. And through it all, my friends held me.

In the hallway, I could make out a few soft strains of gospel playing from downstairs. I caught a few lyrics drifting under the small gap under my bedroom door. Something about having strength. Something about home.

But Mama wasn't coming home.

And I didn't know how to be strong anymore.

I looked over at the lily in the vase again, trembling in its glass enclosure like it wasn't sure it belonged in this world anymore. Maybe it didn't. *Maybe I didn't.* Outside, thunder cracked once, low and distant. I didn't flinch. Because the storm hadn't started yet.

But I knew it was coming.

Chapter 15

Khalil

The dream always started the same.

I'm six. Sitting on the carpet in front of the TV, eating a bowl of Froot Loops without milk. The colors blur on my tongue. The light from the screen flickers across the living room wall like we're at the movies. My dad's asleep on the couch behind me, one shoe on, one off. Exhausted from his night shift at the warehouse. His snores rattle like something broken inside of him.

And she's in the kitchen. My mama.

Singing along to the radio, cracking eggs in a mug, her earrings swinging like wind chimes every time she turns. She's singing "Before I Let Go," the words sloshing out her mouth with a troubled kind of gaiety I didn't understand at the time. Frazzled, strangled, not quite in tune with the harmonies of the song.

"Khalil, baby, go brush your teeth," she calls from the kitchen, loose and wild. And I do. Because even in the unstableness of her voice, she always said it in a way that made me feel like saying no would hurt her feelings. And I never wanted to hurt her feelings. When I come back to the kitchen, the mug filled with eggs is on the counter. The oil in the pan on the stove sizzles. But she's gone.

Just a hum of the fridge and the static echo of the song still playing from the radio. No one singing along to it. I walk over to the living room window and see the back of her walking toward a blue car. Her curly hair is wild. Her fair skin pale in the early morning sunlight. A blue bag is in her hand. No jacket. I don't call for her. Don't move from the spot by the window. My dad continues to snore on the couch, unaware that our world's changed forever. I don't understand it either, even as the car drives away, exhaust swirling into the air as they turn the corner.

And then–

I sat up, my heart pounding. The sheets were soaked. It took me a second to realize where I was. Kelly parents' guest room. Still Houston. Still the day after Charisse died. The house too quiet, grief too real. Even the walls seemed to be holding its breath, waiting for us all to wake up from an all too real nightmare.

I rubbed my face, trying to scrape the dream off my skin, but it lingered. It always did. A knock on the door pulled me out of it.

"Hey," Xavier said, cracking the door. "You up?"

"Yeah," I said, sleep still coating my voice.

"How you feeling?"

I shrugged. He didn't push. Just tapped the door in solemn agreement.

"Vivian made breakfast. Eggs, grits, sausage. Lisa brought some coffee."

"I'm good."

"You need to eat."

"I said I'm good."

He nodded again, leaning against the door frame. "You talk to Kelly? Nessa said she was silent all night up until we left."

I shook my head. "Nah. When I checked on her last night, she was asleep."

He watched me like he wanted to say something else. Then shrugged. "Everyone else is downstairs if you change your mind about breakfast. Let me know if you need anything."

I nodded my head again as he left. I laid back in the bed, gathering my thoughts. My dream from last night lingered in my mind fresh, raw. As if it happened just yesterday. I rubbed a hand over my eyes, then headed to restroom to freshen up. Now wasn't the time for me to sink into a dark place. Not when darkness shrouded my heart's world.

Downstairs, the air was heavy with somber whispers. People pretending not to see Kelly and her father falling apart before their eyes. Douglass and a man named Trent were posted near the front door like security. Lisa and Vivian were in the kitchen, making plates for all the visitors, washing dishes as they went. Kenneth was pacing back and forth by Douglass and Trent, mumbling something about Charisse's life insurance paperwork and her brother PJ. Nobody was listening.

Kelly was curled up on the couch between Nessa and Nyah. Lynn was close by, talking to Wesley. Kelly's hoodie was pulled tight around her face, her feet tucked tight beneath her. Her eyes were swollen. I sat on the arm of the love seat across from her. She didn't look at me. Vanessa glanced at me, then looked away. I knew I should say something. I just didn't know what. I was not the only one. Everyone was trying to do something, anything, to avoid the fact that Kelly and Kenneth were tilting.

"I was dreaming about somebody cooking eggs. Now I know why," I said with feigned lightness.

Nessa was the only one to respond. "It has to be this pregnancy, but these eggs are so good. I've had two plates." Xavier walked over to hand her another plate filled with sausage, eggs, and fruit. "Make that three. You sure you don't want anything, Kelly? You need to eat something." She pushed the plate to Kelly's face, who turned her head the other way in a slow, exasperated motion. Her fists curled in the sleeves of her hoodie.

Lisa walked over and handed me a plate. I chose to eat on the back porch, the fresh air a nice break from the stagnant air inside. In the distance, rainclouds swelled. My phone buzzed as I took the first bite. A text from my dad.

POPS

How's Kelly?

I started to type a response, then deleted it. How *is* she? Grieving. Silent. Gone without leaving. Just like Mama. I called him instead. When he answered, we were silent for a while. The kind that was not awkward. The kind that said, *I got you* even if we don't say it out loud.

"She's hurting bad," I finally said.

"I bet. Nothing can prepare you for that."

"What hurts me is she doesn't know how to say it. Not with words."

"Nobody knows how to process grief, son." We were quiet again. "Kelly's a strong woman. Just do what you can."

I shrugged, picking at the food on my plate. "I don't know what I'm supposed to do."

"She just scared, Khalil. Probably a little guilty. Probably mad at God and herself and the whole damn world."

"I get that. But why won't she let me in?"

"Has she ever?" He stayed silent so I could think. "I know y'all love each other, but some people love like a one-way street. Not 'cause they don't want to meet you halfway. They just never learned how."

I swallowed hard. "I just...I want to be there for her."

"And you think that's enough to keep her?" He said it so plainly. So quiet. Like a warning wrapped in an old truth he knew all too well. "I just wanted to check-in. Let me know when they get the details figured out for the funeral."

"I will." I picked at my food a bit more while staring out at the backyard.

The rest of the morning was a blur of friends and colleagues stopping by to pay their respects to Kelly and her father. Somehow, I'd fallen asleep on the patio after talking to Xavier about business stuff. While asleep, I dreamt about my mom again. But this time, I was older. She was standing in the kitchen with the same blue bag, hair twisting and turning in every direction. She turned around, looked me dead in the face, and said, "You can't save everybody, baby." I tried to speak, but my mouth wouldn't work. She walked out anyway. And I woke up gasping for air, choking on silence.

When I walked into the house, everyone left was fluttering around. Vivian was on a call. Douglass and Trent's voices were bellowing from Kenneth's office, seemingly trying to talk him down from something. Xavier was watching something on TV, a queasy Vanessa laying her head in his lap. That was when I saw him.

A man. Tall, wearing scrubs, standing with Kelly in the foyer. They laughed at something I couldn't hear. She was in sweatpants and a tank top. Her face was still grim, even with the smile pasted on.

They hugged.

It was not romantic. But it didn't have to be. The hug lasted one second too long. She opened the door. He left. She closed the door. And just like that, my chest split open. My thoughts became mute. I went straight to Kenneth's bar, picked a bottle from the top shelf, poured a shot of something brown, and knocked it back. And then another. And another. I leaned against the cabinets, breathing like I just ran ten miles. Because this right here?

This was what it felt like to be left all over again.

Chapter 16

Kelly

I HEARD THE GOSPEL SONG BEFORE I OPENED MY EYES. Just one line. "I know I've been changed..." Soft. Half a whisper in the back of my mind. Not playing from a speaker, not humming from anyone's mouth. Just there. Lingering. I blinked up at the ceiling of my childhood bedroom, the faint light through the blinds casting lines across the ceiling like jail bars. My mama's lily was still on the desk, reaching gently toward the window like it didn't know it was left behind. I got up, showered, dressed, and walked into the lion's den.

Once wet and reddened eyes were replaced by irises stuck in nostalgia. Toward the end of yesterday, pleas of whys turned into drunken memories of times with my mother. Her friends and my dad reminisced on simpler times, times when they thought they had more time, had eternity. That was, until my Uncle PJ banged on the door. Then the house became a war zone, everyone tiptoeing around the stand-off between he and my father. Two fragile egos fighting to reign supreme.

Walking into the living room, they were standing too close, both talking with their hands, their fists a breath away from making contact with each other's shoulders.

"I'm her husband, PJ," my father said, voice too loud. "I told you once before, everything to do with Charisse, I handle."

"She was my sister, too yeah," PJ shot back, his voice just as threatening. "Before she ever fucking met you and let you ruin her goddamn life. You don't know what the fuck she would've wanted. She barely wanted yo' bitch ass, that's for damn sho'. Should've shot yo' ass when I had the chance."

"That's bullshit! You always coming 'round here trying to start fights. Threatening to kill people. For what? And you expect me to believe my own wife wouldn't want me to know how she wanted to go in the ground?"

"Because she knew yo' bitch ass would make it all about you!"

"Shut up!" I snapped. Years. Years of arguing over nonsense. They were the reason I'd missed out on summers with my grand-mother before she passed. Hadn't they'd had enough? Enough of this tug-o-war they had over my mother. As if she weren't her own person and not for their possession. They turned, blinking like they'd just remembered I was there. Aunt Viv and Lisa stood in the kitchen with wide eyes. Uncle Doug and Uncle Trent were close by, trying to play referee, arms stretched between my father and uncle like human gates. I stepped forward, hands calm.

"My mother will be laid to rest in a white casket with gold trim," I said, my voice flat. "No open casket during the wake. I'll write the obituary. The service will be at First Baptist. Seven speakers max. Neither of you. The repast will be here. That's what's happening." I looked over at Aunt Viv and Lisa, I couldn't take the heartbreak filling their eyes. I blinked. "You got that, Aunt Viv and Lisa?"

Silence followed. Lisa gave me a look—half pride, half sadness. Vivian nodded. "Then it's settled."

PJ swallowed hard, his anger folding into something more frag-ile. "Okay, Lily-girl," he said, quiet. "You got it."

"Her name is Kelly," my dad gruffed, turning and walking to his bedroom.

That night, after everyone else had gone to bed or worn themselves out from crying laughter, I walked onto the back porch with a blanket wrapped on my shoulders. The night air had a humidity that was just thick enough to cling to your skin but not enough to rain. All day, Khalil hovered, worried words fraying the edges of his mind, even though they never left his lips. Making it to the steps that led from the patio to the lush, manicured lawn, Uncle PJ was sitting on the lighted steps, smoking a Black & Mild, his baseball cap pushed back off his forehead. His jacket draped over the railing. He swayed back and forth as he pulled deep inhales from the cigarillo.

"I was wondering when you'd come out," he said without turning around.

"Mama always said you were psychic," I said, sitting next to him.

He chuckled once, low, blowing out the smoke around us. I rested my head on his shoulder. The blanket wrapped around my shoulders trailed behind me like a cape I hadn't earned. We watched the yard in silence for a long time. The stars above were soft and stubborn.

"I'm not going tomorrow," he said eventually.

My heart dropped. I didn't turn to him right away. Just stared out at the grass. "What? Why?"

He flicked ashes toward the grass, then snuffed the cigar onto the steps. The blackened ash left a dark mark, matching the void in my soul. "That whole thing tomorrow? That ain't my version of her. That church. That casket. That choir. I don't belong in that world. I told her a long time ago."

"She just wanted peace," my voice cracked, the words breaking on my tongue.

"She had peace," he said. "In pieces. Even when the rest of y'all couldn't see it. But she was chasing something she thought was better. Kept tryin' to patch holes with your daddy like he wasn't half the wound himself."

I let that sit. It was too sharp and too true to touch.

"Doesn't make it right not to come," I murmured. "She was your sister."

"I know that," he said, his voice rough. "But I can't sit in that sanctuary and pretend. Not when everything in me is still mad at her. Not when I remember the her that laughed until she cried. Not the one who stiffened every time that nigga walked in the room. I don't want my last memory of her to be that."

He reached into his pocket and pulled out MawMaw's old locket. The one that used to hang off her rearview mirror like a lucky charm. Inside was a photo of him and Mama at her high school graduation. She was smiling wide, a simple dimple in her right cheek.

"She was the first person who made me feel I wasn't broken," Uncle PJ whispered. "And now...she gone. And I'm just some old man on a porch tryna remember how to breathe without the both of them in this world."

He handed me the locket and I held it tight. Traced her face with my thumb. "I don't want to remember her in a box. Like Mama," he said. "I want to remember her laughing like this," he said, tapping her picture. "Alive. Loud. Laughing like she don't owe nobody nothin'."

I didn't argue. I didn't beg him to change his mind. Because deep down, I understood. I'd been there living it. But it still stung, to hear it aloud. Another man I loved, backing away when I needed him to stay. Instead, choosing distance. Choosing self-preservation over presence.

"Even you are leaving me," I said, my voice low.

He looked at me now, really looked. His eyes softened. "That ain't fair, Noonie."

Noonie. The nickname he'd given me when I was three and stayed stuck to his hip a rare summer I visited my grandmother and he was around. It called me back to the little girl I used to be before life turned me to steel.

He kissed the top of my head. "I know I ain't perfect, Noonie. But I'm always gon' be one call away. Funeral or not."

I didn't respond. Just stared at the locket in my hand. Let the ache settle instead of trying to outrun it.

THE FUNERAL SMELLED like carnations and nervousness. The church was full. More people than I remembered her knowing. Old colleagues, members from different social clubs, cousins from places I hadn't heard from in years. Everyone was in their Sunday's best, faces tight with bereavement and caked on makeup. The choir opened with a medley as people took their seats. The organ trembled beneath the weight of it. Then came the soloist.

"*I know I've been changed...*"

There it was again. That damn line. Just that one line.

She sang it like a wail, like a promise and a warning all at once. It echoed off the walls, wormed its way into the curve of my neck.

"*I know I've been changed...*"

I didn't want to be different. I didn't want the life I'd carefully perfected to crumble just as it was falling into place. I wanted it to stop.

But it didn't.

It took up residence on the folds of my brain, coming back to me over and over, at random intervals—between prayers, between eulogies, between moments where someone shouted *Thank you, Lord!* And I wanted to scream back *What are you thanking him for?!* I sat in the front row next to my dad, who trembled from his shoulders, his face buried in his hands. A shell of the male bravado I'd seen my whole life. Their friends filled the rest of the front pew. My friends in the pew behind me kept me grounded. Khalil rubbed my shoulders every so often. I stared straight ahead.

The service unfolded like a play I already knew the ending to. Readings. Speeches. The choir began again. More crying. Then the preacher stood up and said something about my mother's strength. Her laughter. Her legacy. All I could think was, *everybody dies eventually*. That was all this was. A slow-motion rehearsal we all had to do. For the past ten years of my life, I'd been trained to break the same news to other families. Families couldn't get past the inevitable emptiness.

Everybody dies eventually.

So, I didn't cry.

Not when they rolled her casket out.

Not when they buried her.

Not when people clutched after me like I was the last piece of her left.

Not once.

Everyone else did. Vanessa sobbed so hard, her entire body shook. Xavier wiped his eyes behind his sunglasses. My father fell apart the second they rolled Mama's casket past the first pew and down the aisle. He would've been on the floor had it not been for Uncle Doug and Uncle Trent holding him up. Aunt Viv dabbed her eyes with a monogrammed handkerchief like her soul had cracked. She and Lisa held my hands as we marched behind my father.

But me?

I moved through it like a ghost. At some point, Lisa tapped me on the shoulder and led me to the upstairs hallway. Aunt Viv was there, too. We were tucked away from the loudness of people sharing stories of my mother, different versions of a woman that never really was. A woman I never knew. Bonding over plates of baked chicken, green beans, seasoned rice, and Sock-It-To-Me cake. Drunk off church punch and memories too sweet to be true.

I smiled. I nodded.

But I didn't *feel* anything.

Looking at my mother's best friends, they held something small between them. A folded envelope with my name on it.

"She wrote this when you were a little girl," Vivian said. "We all wrote one to give to our children on their wedding day."

"That's the day we made a pact," Lisa added. "If anything ever happened to one of us...the others would step in."

I took the envelope but didn't open it. What good were words on a paper when the person writing it would never say it with their voice?

"Thank you," I whispered. They nodded. Each kissed my cheek. I escaped to my bedroom after they left me on the upstairs landing. Sitting at the desk, staring at the now wilting lily, I tucked the letter into the desk drawer.

Hours later, I was finally free to head home. My home. My space. My things. Everything in order just as I needed it to be. It was getting dark, and the sky had a sick, orange glow, like it was trying to lie and say it wouldn't rain. Khalil followed me with a truck full of floral arrangements my father insisted I keep at my house. He claimed he had a black thumb and they'd die within the next few days. As if I weren't leaving the state in a matter of days. Said he couldn't stand to see anymore death for a while.

I stood in the kitchen, watching Khalil bring in plant after plant. At this point, I had enough to open my own flower shop.

"Last one," he said, placing a peace lily arrangement on the counter.

The moment I saw it, my stomach dropped. My grandmother used to keep them on hand in her flower shop. Said they were good for the soul. Said they absorbed negative energy. Said they bloomed best in quiet corners. Khalil topped off the plant with a bit of water, then took me in his arms.

"You okay?"

I turned and looked at him. "No," I muttered into his chest. "But I don't want to feel sad tonight." He opened his mouth, then closed it. "I want a drink. Take me somewhere. I want to celebrate her life, not sit with all these flowers bringing nothing but sadness."

He hesitated. I could see the thoughts forming behind his eyes. "Kelly—"

"I'm serious, Khalil. Please. I don't want to cry tonight."

I rounded my eyes and pouted my lips, knowing he wouldn't be able to refuse me. He didn't argue, just nodded. And that was how you start forgetting your mother died. One drink at a time.

We ended up at our favorite taco spot. The kind of place where the liquor and food was cheap, the lights were low, and the DJ played sets with bass loud enough to forget your thoughts. Perfect. Inside, the air smelled like tequila and grilled onions. The bartender wiped the counter with a towel that probably wasn't clean. An older woman in a rhinestone headwrap raised her glass at me from the end of the bar. I smiled politely. Khalil found us a corner booth. The seat squeaked when I slid in.

"What you want to drink?" he asked.

"Tequila. Straight."

He gave me a look but didn't argue. When he came back, he slid the glass across the table. The clear liquor trapped the colored LEDs of the DJ's booth.

"To Charisse," he said, lifting the glass.

I hesitated, then clinked mine against his. "To Mama."

The first sip burned all the way down. It felt good. Punishing. I wanted more. By the time we were two drinks in, the DJ played hit after hit. The bass vibrated through the floor, up the booth, and into my body. I let my head fall back against the booth and closed my eyes.

"I should be crying not throwing back tequila like it's water, huh?" I half-asked without looking at Khalil.

"You don't have to do anything," he replied.

"But that's what people expect. When you lose someone close, you fall apart. Be messy. Be broken."

He didn't answer right away. When I opened my eyes, he was watching me too closely.

"I'm not falling apart," I said. "I'm adapting."

"That's not the same thing."

"Isn't it?"

He leaned forward. "You want to talk about what you're feeling?"

"No," I said flatly. "That's the point of the drinks."

He sighed and rubbed his hand over his jaw. I could feel his judgment creeping in, even if he didn't say it. I downed the rest of my drink and signaled for another. When it arrived, I cradled it in my hands and stared at it like it held secrets.

"Can I tell you something?" I said, voice softer now, almost childlike.

"Of course."

"I didn't feel anything today."

Khalil's eyebrows pulled together.

"I mean it," I said. "At the church. At the burial. Even at the repast. I just...watched. Like it wasn't real. Like I was attending someone else's funeral."

His voice was careful. "That's not abnormal."

"But what if it doesn't hit later? What if it never comes? What does that say about me? The world fell apart, but I kept moving like business as usual."

He reached across the table, taking the drink from my hands. "Grief doesn't look one way."

His hand covered mine. I stared at it. It was warm. Steady. Too steady. I pulled back, taking my drink. We left the lounge before midnight. The ride to my house was quiet. The song was still stuck in my head. Just one line.

"I know I've been changed..."

It played in the rhythm of the tires on the road. It echoed in the space between us. It matched the taps of the bedframe as I worked to rid it from my mind atop Khalil. Riding him fast and hard before collapsing on top. But it never left. I went to sleep with it on repeat, a substitute for sleep. And for the first time all day, I felt afraid.

Chapter 17

Kelly

Spring 2013 - Xavier University, New Orleans, LA

THE LIBRARY HAD CLOSED HOURS AGO, BUT MY DESK lamp was still going strong, casting a buttery glow across my lab notes and a half dozen highlighters bleeding into the pages. My laptop was wheezing from being overworked, and my body wasn't far behind. I rubbed my temples and stared at the blinking cursor in my doc, daring it to type for me. If willpower could earn a degree, I'd have two by now.

That faint bass line of Bryson Tiller crept through the wall. Vanessa's room. She and Xavier had been holed up for hours now, no doubt whispering sweet nothings between kisses. I didn't mind it most nights. They were cute or whatever. But tonight? I felt like the last single bitch on Earth.

A knock came at the door from the kitchenette. Not a quick, polite knock either. This one was lazy and familiar. Only one person knocked like that. I cracked open the door. Khalil stood there in a purple and gold hoodie and gray sweats, hands tucked into his pockets, eyes sleepy but bright.

"Nessa and Zay keeping you up." He smirked.

I stepped back so he could enter the small living room space. "Nope. Even if they weren't fucking around like rabbits, I'd still be up studying."

"Always grinding, even when you know it all." He laughed, passing in front of me, heading to my bedroom suite.

"You say that like you haven't benefitted from me tutoring your ass every week."

"I didn't need tutoring," he said, flopping onto my bed uninvited. "I just wanted some time with you."

I rolled my eyes, but the warmth in my chest betrayed me. He made the room feel less heavy, like I could breathe again.

"Are you feeling better?" I asked, pulling up the sleeves of his hoodie to check the fading red hives that littered his body the past two weeks.

"Yeah, finally feel like I can breathe and my skin not on fire. Thanks to you, my favorite nurse." He smiled, then licked his lips as his thumb ran over my cheek and down my jaw. He reached over and picked up my highlighters, clicking it open and closed. "When's the last time you took a break?"

"I don't have time for breaks. I've got back-to-back exams, a presentation, and that volunteer clinic on Saturday."

He tilted his head. "So you working yourself into an early grave. Cool, cool."

"Khalil."

"Lily-girl." He smiled back.

We stared at each other, and then we both laughed. Same old game. He stood and walked out of the room, over to the cabinets in the kitchenette. I followed behind him. "Y'all got some snacks?"

"Check the fridge. Nessa's mom bakes the best fudge brownies. She brought us some when she came down last weekend."

He popped it open and whistled. "You must've known I was coming."

"No." I giggled. "You just somehow always show up starving."

"I show up," he said with a wink. "That's what matters." He

took a bite of the brownie and moaned. He looked comfortable, at ease, as he sat on the countertop, eyeing me as he chewed. "Come here."

The arched eyebrow on my face protested, but my feet were willing participants to his soothing command. I stopped just shy of the gap of his legs. Slowly, he broke a piece from the corner and held it up to my lips.

"Open."

And dammit, my mouth followed the same cues as my feet. My brain silently cursed my body for not following her explicit directions. Do not get close. Do not fall into the trap. The second his warm, thick fingers brushed my lips, I stopped talking. The sugar-sweetened cocoa powder exploded on my tongue. My eyelids shuttered closed as I savored the bite. A faint swipe of his thumb across my bottom lip energized me. My cheeks burned. I turned to sit at one of the couches before I got caught smiling too hard.

He followed.

"You remember when we used to sneak snacks from your grandma's flower shop?"

I looked up, surprised. "You remember that?"

"Hell yeah. You always made me wait until she was talking to customers. And clean up the back room first."

"Because we were raised right," I said, grinning. "Well, I was."

He leaned closer, throwing a too warm arm across my shoulders. "And you know the block parties was popping in the summer. Water balloons. Mr. Johnson's barbecue. The Candy Lady's frozen cups."

"Don't forget somebody blasting Frankie Beverly until your auntie kicked off her heels and started two-stepping."

"Then your bitch-ass daddy would pull up and ruin the vibe."

The smile on my face faded before I could catch it.

Khalil noticed. Of course he did. "What's wrong?"

I shrugged. "They're just...a lot lately. My mom and dad. Arguing again. More than usual. My mama swears she's leaving.

My daddy swears she won't. And she won't, not for long anyway. And somehow, I'm in the middle as if I don't already have finals to worry about."

He pulled me closer, close enough that I could smell the cocoa butter and Irish Spring soap he used from the shower I was sure he'd taken before coming over. A whiff of Polo Black touched my nose from the warmth radiating off his body. "You ever think about checking out of all that? No picking sides. Just picking you?"

"All the time," I admitted.

"Then start now."

I gave him a look. "What do you mean?"

"What do you need most right now?"

"A break. From everything."

"Come to this kickback with me."

I groaned. "Khalil…I am not trying to have somebody throw me on their shoulders and put their face between my legs."

"Chill." He laughed. "It's nothing like that. Some of the old heads in town and they doing a little something. Real lowkey."

"Y'all always throwing something.

"We believe in balance." He shrugged. "And you, Lily-girl. Need balance."

"I have to study."

"You already been studying. Come laugh. Drink a little bit. Be admired."

"Admired?"

He gave me that smug, pretty-boy grin. "You know what I mean."

I hesitated. He leaned closer, his breath tickling my neck. "And if you end up on anybody shoulders, I promise it'll be mine."

I swallowed. The thought made my body hum. "Fine. I'll go," I said, standing and stretching. "But if y'all get to barking, I'm out."

He barked once, loud, and I tossed a pillow at him.

THE KICKBACK WAS ALREADY in full swing by the time we pulled up. The house wasn't big. It was one of those shotgun-style rentals just off Claiborne, tucked between two cracked sidewalks and a leaning streetlamp, but it was vibrating with music and laughter. As soon as Khalil opened the passenger door, the scent of grilled chicken, weed, and cheap tequila punched me in the face. Somebody's cousin was on the speaker, blasting Boosie. I could already see a crowd spilling into the yard, red Solo cups in hand.

"I cannot believe I let you talk me into this," I said, taking in the scene before me. "This is not a kickback."

"It depend on what you define as a kickback." He grinned. "Besides, you need some fun."

Inside, the house was hazy with smoke and full of loud voices talking over even louder music. The kitchen table had been converted into a liquor lab. Half-empty bottles of New Amsterdam and Hennesy, plastic cups stacked like a pyramid, one lonely bottle of Malibu nobody was touching. People were already dancing in the middle of the living room, and when one of Khalil's bruhs spotted him, the shouting started.

"Ayeee! I thought you was dipping out on us."

"Never that." Khalil barked once.

Oh God.

"Was that absolutely necessary?" I asked, eyebrows raised.

He leaned down so only I could hear. "It's tradition."

"I see."

Before I could tease him more, a couple of his bruhs swooped in to dap him up, secret handshake in tow. One of them, a tall, chocolate-skinned senior with lashes too pretty for his own good, looked me up and down.

"And who is this?" he asked, licking his perfectly full lips, eyes twinkling, hands rubbing in a scheming motion.

"Chill," Khalil said, laughing, slipping an arm around my waist, pulling me in. "This my homegirl, Kelly."

My stomach did a little somersault and fell flat against the linoleum underfoot. He hadn't had to say it like that. *Homegirl Kelly*.

The guy chuckled and backed off with a knowing smirk. "My bad, bruh. Ain't mean no disrespect."

I rolled my eyes as Khalil led me through the crowd toward the back porch, fully aware of the pissing contest exchanged a few seconds ago. A few card games were already in progress. We slid into a corner, perched on the edge of an old patio sofa. For a second, everything just paused. I watched Khalil. The curve of his smile. The way his chin caught the light. How comfortable he was in his skin. How easily he fit into every room.

"You really do this, huh?" I asked.

"What?"

"Charm people for sport."

He took a sip from his cup. "Only person I'm worried about charming is you."

Too dangerous.

Still, I laughed. Leaned in a little. Let myself enjoy the attention. It wasn't long before a slow song started Miguel's *Sure Thing* and suddenly the whole room started vibing. Somebody's cousin pulled me into a two-step. I danced with him for a bit, laughing, letting my body grind into his. I could feel Khalil's eyes on me the whole time.

When I circled back to our spot, a group of girls had migrated his way. One was standing way too close, laughing a little too hard at something he said. Her hand brushed his chest lightly.

I didn't say a word. I sat on the arm of the couch, crossed my legs, and scrolled through my phone like I couldn't care less. But my chest was tight. He wasn't doing anything *wrong*. But he wasn't doing anything *right* either.

This wasn't new. This was always the thing with Khalil–the

magnetism, the easy way people wanted him. It didn't matter if we had history. It didn't matter if we'd shared beds, stories, or secrets. There were always going to be other women drawn to his orbit. And he didn't push them away fast enough. Eventually, the girl walked off, and Khalil looked up at me.

"You good?"

"Of course."

"You sure?"

I smiled, sweet as sorghum. "Enjoy your little fan club. I'm gonna go enjoy the night."

I was still perched on the edge of the patio sofa when the same guy from earlier, pretty chocolate skin and trouble in his smile, made his way back over. He grinned like he already knew the answer to the question he hadn't asked yet.

"You sure you wanna be wasting that pretty smile sitting over here bored?" he asked, as if we'd been in the middle of a conversation all night.

I raised an eyebrow, amused. "And you sure you wanna risk your life by talking to me in front of Khalil?"

He glanced over his shoulder, unfazed. Khalil was leaned back now, legs spread, a cup in one hand, deep in conversation with two girls in tight dresses who were giggling like they didn't care he hadn't laughed once.

"Your boy don't look too bothered," he said, turning back to me.

I shrugged off my annoyance. "That's his problem."

The guy smiled like he liked my answer and offered his hand. "Come on. We playing spades inside. You any good?"

"Baby," I said, slipping my phone into my back pocket. "I was raised on spades."

He guided me inside with a hand on my lower back, my hips swinging a little more than necessary. I didn't even look back to see if Khalil noticed. I didn't have to. He was always watching. That was the game. A constant push and pull. An invisible measuring stick of who cared more. A love song stuck on repeat, never quite reaching the chorus.

Inside, the house was warm and loud. Bodies pressed shoulder to shoulder. I slid into the chair opposite the guy, who'd let me know his name was Maverick. The table was talkative, trash talk flying like confetti. After two books and a clean cut, Maverick leaned across the table and grinned.

"Okay, I see you," he said.

I smirked, flicking a card onto the table. "Told you so."

We won that round, then another. The room buzzed, but I could feel his eyes watching me. Not like he wanted something, but like he noticed. When the next game started, we let another pair take our spot. We moved to the side and watched the ensuing game.

"So, what's the deal with you and my boy?" he asked. "Y'all together or what?"

"Depends on the night."

"Hmm," he said. "Tonight must be one of those nights."

"Nope," I said, throwing back the drink in my cup. "He's occupied tonight."

"You like him, though," he added. "More than you wanna admit."

I shrugged, softer this time. "It doesn't matter." My phone buzzed in my pocket. I took it out and saw it was Nyah Face-Timing me. I answered.

"Bitch! We are so fucked up," she half-laughed, half-screamed into the camera. She panned the camera around to Lynn who was bent over in laughter. Chaotic talking and laughter mixed in with the music from wherever they were.

"Who is that?" Maverick asked, getting closer to my screen, licking his lips.

"My other besties, Lynn and Nyah. They go to Texas Southern." I smiled at my screen, trying to make out whatever Nyah and Lynn babbled from the other end.

"Where's Nessa?" Nyah managed to get out. "I bet Zay got her addicted to the dick."

Lynn leaned her head on Nyah's shoulder. "Hell yeah! Got her ass dickmatized."

Maverick nudged my shoulder. "Let me talk to the one holding the phone," he urged.

"Boy, no. She won't even remember talking to you. Besides," I started, but didn't have to finish. Her boyfriend, Antonio, entered the screen, his face stoic as he whispered in Nyah's ear. She pouted in response as Lynn took the phone.

"Oh shit. We done got in trouble. Bye girl," she said, ending the call.

"Damn, man," Maverick said, smoothing a hand over his head. "All the good ones taken."

"What the fuck does that make me," I shot back.

He kissed his teeth and threw his hand. "Shit, you taken, too. Y'all just ain't figured the shit out yet." He poured himself another drink. "Let me bring you back to your man before he start fighting niggas."

I rolled my eyes as I followed Maverick back outside. As soon as we crossed the threshold to the backyard, Khalil's eyes met mine. He stood from the couch, leaving his harem behind. There was a slight edge to his eyes as he neared us.

"Where the hell y'all been?" he asked, trying to keep the question light.

Maverick sized him up, then laughed. "Stop being stupid, nigga." He laughed again, slapping Khalil's neck as he walked off.

Khalil stood in front of me, smiling now that we were alone. "You ready to go?"

I pursed my lips, narrowed my eyes. "Nope," I replied, smiling sweetly. "I'm just getting started."

Chapter 18

Khalil

THE SUN WASN'T EVEN UP YET, BUT THE WEIGHT IN MY skull made it feel like the day had already beaten me down. I lay flat on my back, fan blades slicing the air overhead, indifferent. The room tilted every time I blinked, like the walls were conspiring to hide something from me. I reached for my phone. No messages. No missed calls. Just the ghost of the message I'd sent Kelly last night. "Let me know if you need anything." I saw the three dots appear, brief as breath. Then nothing.

Them damn three dots haunted me more than the silence did.

My chest ached. Not sharp, not crushing. Just heavy. Like I'd slept under wet cement. I sat up and rubbed the back of my neck, staring at the stillness of my apartment. I used to complain about her constant need to work and wax poetic about charts and research—the frenzied hum of her voice, the shuffle of her feet, the half-laughs she made when speaking about something one of her patients said.

Now, silence was a punishment.

I'd gone from falling asleep with her breath on my skin to being a guest in her grief. The tile in the kitchen shocked my feet awake. I poured a cup of coffee I didn't want, adding oat milk out of habit. It tasted like bitterness, like absence. I dumped it without taking a second sip. I was doing all the things people said helped. Keeping busy, staying productive. Dishes always washed. Laundry folded on the same day. I'd added ten pounds to my bench press. My apartment had never looked more lived in, but it had never felt so empty.

I opened the group chat with Xavier, Wesley, Nessa, Lynn, Nyah, and Kelly. They were deep in a debate about some podcast arguing gender roles and relationships. The usual chaos. I scrolled, mostly bored, until I saw it.

Kelly had been active.

A few laughing emojis. A SpongeBob GIF. Her name mixed in with replies from everyone else. Participating. Laughing. Showing up. Just not with me.

ME

> So you can joke in the group chat, but you can't respond to my messages?

I almost typed something more. Something slick. Something real. Something that would've bled too much. I deleted it instead. Needy wasn't a good look. Not for me. Not with her.

I DIDN'T PLAN to drive to her house.

I just...kept driving. Searching the Houston streets for something to ground me. Then I was turning on her street like muscle memory.

Her car was in the driveway. Lights off. Curtains drawn like she didn't want the world to see her folding. I sat outside for a while. Fifteen minutes, maybe twenty, just watching the front door like it might blink or open or breathe.

Then I knocked.

Once. Twice.

No answer.

I stepped back, heart thudding the way it always did when I was trying not to care too much. That was when Xavier texted me.

ZAY

Say, nigga. Pull up and help me finish these floors in the nursery before Nessa break my neck.

I didn't answer right away. But eventually, I headed back to my car, reversed out of the driveway, turned my wheel, and left her house behind.

Xavier's place smelled like sawdust and baby powder. Nessa sat on a stool near the floor to ceiling windows of their living room, painting away on a canvas. She waved when I walked in behind Xavier.

"Khalil," she greeted me excitedly before scrunching up her face. "You okay?"

"I'm straight," I answered, following Xavier upstairs to the nursery.

We got to work, hammering away at the wooden planks. He didn't press. We joked a little, mostly letting the music and motions carry the moment. The sound of a hammer hitting something too soft to be the floor sounded, followed by a shouted curse from Xavier.

"Fuck!" He grimaced, holding his thumb.

"I told you I could've grabbed the pneumatic nailer from the construction site."

"Shut the fuck..." he shot back, annoyed. He threw the hammer away from him and sat back against the wall. "I'm taking a break."

As if on cue, Vanessa entered with two bottles of water. "Here," she said, offering me one. "Y'all look thirsty."

Her phone rang out from her other hand. She glanced at the screen and smiled.

She answered the FaceTime. "Lynn! Where are you?"

"Girl," she said, laughing. "Kelly got me out here drinking beer. Beer!"

My ears perked up. Vanessa looked over at me with wide eyes. She started to leave the room, then stilled when I shook my head. I stood and walked over to look at her phone. The screen lit up with Kelly and Lynn's faces. Both were seated at some outdoor table in a beer garden. Neon lights spilled over Kelly's cheeks. Her eyes were slightly glossy. The loose waves of her hair fell around her shoulders like she'd just stepped out the chair.

She smiled the fake ass smile she saved for strangers. Beside her, two dudes leaned in close, enraptured with her. Laughing too hard at whatever she was saying. By then, Xavier had made his way over and saw what I saw.

"Damn," he muttered low.

I leaned forward, exhaled deeply, my eyes fixed on the screen. "Let me see that, Nessa."

She blinked. "What?"

"Give me the phone."

"Kelly's right. You don't ask." Reluctantly, she handed it to me, pulling back slightly like she already felt the heat radiating off my skin. I tilted the phone toward me and spoke, calm but cutting.

"Kelly."

She looked up, blinking, shocked to see me on the phone. "Oh hey. Why do you have Nessa's phone?"

"How much you had to drink?"

"I don't know. I'm getting my fill before my days are all charting and rounds again." She smiled at something the guy next her said. "Oh, this is my friend, Khalil," she added, gesturing to the phone.

I laughed darkly, biting my lip. "Kelly, quit playing with me."

Her smile wavered just a bit. "Khalil, don't start. I don't have the energy."

"I ain't starting nothing. But I'll finish it if you keep acting like I'm just some name in your phone."

Lynn cut in fast. "Don't worry about Kelly. We're about to leave anyway."

"Drop her off at her place."

"Yeah," Lynn said, already shifting in her seat. "We're leaving now."

"Cool," I said, my jaw tight. "I'll meet y'all there."

Kelly rolled her eyes and leaned back in her chair, clearly drunk and detached.

"Whatever."

The call ended. I handed Vanessa back her phone and left without saying a word.

"Khalil," Xavier hollered behind me.

"I'm good," I shouted back, opening the front door and slamming it shut. Because I wasn't. Because she wasn't, even though she was pretending to be.

I drove back to Kelly's house, bypassing all the speed laws. I turned the corner just as Lynn's black Lexus crept onto the street ahead of me. We both pulled into the driveway at the same time.

Kelly was in the passenger seat; head tilted back, like the sun was too much. Her sunglasses were pushed high on her nose. I could see the outline of her closed eyes, like she was trying to hold onto whatever silence she'd found in the ride back home. She didn't move at first.

Then she opened the car door.

There was a wobble to her step. Barely there, but I saw it. She caught herself, adjusted, and when she saw me, her body didn't flinch. Her mouth smiled. Soft. Detached. Lynn peeked around the center console, giving me that friend-smile that meant, *Don't start nothing.*

"Appreciate it," I said, my voice hollow.

Lynn nodded, waved, and pulled off, her taillights fading down the block. I walked beside Kelly to the door. Her steps were slow, each one like a quiet confession she wouldn't say out loud. When we reached the door, she stopped.

"You can't just show up like this," she said, her words slurred but still sharp.

"When you don't answer my calls, yeah I can."

Her mouth tightened. "Last I checked, this is my house."

"You wasn't saying that when you let me cover every bill in this motherfucka."

She rolled her eyes. "It's still my name on the lease." She dug for her keys but didn't move to unlock the door.

"Can we talk?" I asked, my voice gentle now.

"I'm tired."

"I'm not trying to argue."

She didn't say yes. But she didn't go inside either.

"I came by the other day," I said.

"I wasn't home."

I stared at her. "Come on, Kelly. I saw your car. Lights on, tv blasting. You were home."

She looked away. "Stop watching me."

"I'm not watching you," I said. "I'm trying not to lose you."

"You're not losing me," she said quietly.

"You sure? Because it feels like you're disappearing. Piece by piece." She didn't answer. I lowered my voice. "I know you're grieving. I'm trying to give you space. But every time I reach for you, you take a step back. I'm not asking for much, Kelly. I just want to be here for you."

She looked down at her shoes. "You're being too much, Khalil."

I winced. "What does that even mean?"

"You love like you're solving a problem." She stared at the concrete. "And I'm not a problem."

"I don't think you are. But I know what it's like to be left. I just want to give you something to hold onto."

"I didn't ask you for that," she said. Her eyes met mine, tired and guarded. "You keep showing up like your love for me earns you special access. Keep expecting me to give you something I don't have in me."

"Then what do you want from me?"

Silence.

"I want things to go back to the way they were," she finally said, and the words slapped harder because they weren't yelled. They were soft. Certain. Measured. I stepped back, biting down whatever pride was about to drag me into a shouting match. She leaned against the door, like the weight of what she'd said was just catching up to her. "I'm sorry," she said, and her voice cracked. "I just...I'm flying out tomorrow morning. This fellowship is going to be tough. I'm already hanging on by a thread. I need to stay focused. I can't do us. Not right now. Not how you want."

I nodded slowly. Kissed her forehead. It felt like the last time. I turned without another word and walked to my car. Behind me, the door opened. Closed. And that was that.

I DIDN'T SLEEP. I tried. Tossed and turned all night. Downed some Benadryl. Soon as my lids shut, the dreams started. That was worse than being awake. I watched too many episodes of some cheesy show on Netflix. Went for a run while the night was marrying the day. Decided I'd see her off one last time. Reassure her, one last time.

The curb at Hobby smelled like burnt rubber, spilled coffee, and heartbreak. I had pulled up behind a rideshare car, hazards blinking in a slow, tired rhythm. Kelly's flight was early. Too early for the sun to be fully up but just late enough for the airport to already buzz with tension. The sky was the color of dishwater, low clouds curling against the concrete like they were trying to hold her back. She stepped out of the passenger seat before I could cut the engine.

Tight black leggings. Cream hoodie. Her hair was twisted back into the slick-backed bun she wore when she didn't feel like being perceived. She moved like someone on autopilot–shoulders tense, eyes shadowed, suitcase rolling behind her with a squeaky wheel that sounded far too loud for 6:30 in the morning.

She hadn't seen me yet. I stepped toward her, forcing my expression neutral even though my chest was already tightening. "Hey."

She turned, startled for half a second, then softened. But it wasn't the soft that reached her eyes. "Hey," she said, the word small and distracted, like she'd dropped it by accident. I reached for her bag, but she didn't let go. Just tugged it closer to her side like it was some kind of tether. "You didn't have to come."

"I know," I said, not knowing if I meant it. "But I wanted to." I wanted to see her. I wanted to remember how she looked when she left me. I wanted to be the last one to hold her gaze before the clouds swallowed her whole.

She gave a quick nod, eyes flitting past me to the sliding doors. "I should go in. TSA's probably packed." I nodded, too. Too much silence pressing in between us, stretching like old gum. I stepped forward anyway and pulled her into a hug, resting my lips atop her head. She let me. But she didn't melt. She didn't tuck her head beneath my chin like she used to. Her hands stayed mostly at her sides, brushing my back for a second before falling away. Her scent still wrapped around me–lavender, cocoa butter, something faintly citrusy. I could live inside it. I used to.

"You gonna text me when you land?" I asked, pulling back. My voice cracked a little, and I hated how it made me sound. Too tender. Too hopeful. Too much.

She looked at me, really looked at me for the first time that morning. And that was almost worse.

"I'll try to remember," she said. "I may get busy with getting settled."

I'll try. Not "*I will.*" Not "*of course.*" Just an effort, maybe.

She adjusted the strap of her crossbody bag and backed toward the check-in kiosks. Then, she stopped.

"Khalil?"

"Yeah?

She opened her mouth. Closed it. Looked down.

"Thank you for coming."

And then she turned. And then she walked away. I stood there like a man watching a memory leave his body. The wheels of her suitcase hummed, fading under the swell of car horns and flight announcements echoing from the loudspeakers. The glass doors slid closed as I left the building. I could still see her inside–standing in line, pulling out her ID, not once looking back.

I got in the car. I didn't drive off right away. I sat there, gripping the steering wheel, trying not to let my mind go too far down the path it was already sprinting toward.

This wasn't about Seattle. This wasn't about space. This was her pulling away from me like the tide. And me not knowing how to swim.

Chapter 19

Kelly

As the plane cut through the clouds somewhere between Houston and Seattle, I leaned against the cold window and closed my eyes. The feeling of Khalil's embrace lingered on my arms, his warmth a sleeve of comfort in the stuffy cabin of the plane. He knew how to show up for me. He also knew how to never stay in it without needing to prove something. Without needing to win.

But now, he was all in. Tired of the games. For the past year and some change, he'd learned how to use his words. Learned how to say what was on his heart with earnest and no reward. I hadn't said a thing about how I felt when we were teenagers, in college, or back in Arizona. And now, here I was again. Not saying a word.

It was easy then, staying silent while we surrounded ourselves with other people. Only this time, other women did not surround Khalil. He was standing alone. And I was still walking away...

I shook the feeling from my skin, choosing to stare out the large pane glass windows of Seattle Children's Hospital. The air was crisp in a way Houston could never be. It smelled like rain and trees. Everything was green. Quiet. Soft. Like the city had been dipped in chamomile. I told myself it was a good sign.

My fellowship orientation started today, and I wore navy blue scrubs and a smile that felt just believable. The first thing I noticed was how quiet everything was. Not silent–hospitals were never silent–but *calm*. Controlled. Like even the air had discipline. It was a far cry from the chaotic hum of Houston's emergency wings, where something was always beeping, crying, or breaking.

Here, the pediatric hematology-oncology floor was bright and painted in a palette of soothing pastels. Mint, sky blue, peach. Sunlight spilled in through the wide hallway windows and landed on sea-creature decals plastered across the linoleum floors. I passed a mural of a grinning dolphin in scrubs giving a high five to a cartoon jellyfish. The irony wasn't lost on me. We were in a place where children came to fight for their lives, but everything looked like a playroom.

I adjusted my badge. It still felt foreign around my neck. "*Dr. Kelly Reid, Pediatric Hematology-Oncology Fellow.*" The title felt too long. Too heavy. Like I had to prove it with every step.

Dr. Sayegh, my attending, was already halfway down the hall, lab coat flaring behind her like a cape. "Keep up," she called over her shoulder without turning around.

I sped up.

We started rounds with the senior fellows. One of them, Elena I think, had a tight bun and an even tighter tone. She handed me a patient's chart like I should already know the kid's background.

"This is Malik, nine years old. ALL, day five of induction. You'll be following his labs today. Don't fall behind on orders."

I nodded, even though I already felt like I was losing ground.

Dr. Sayegh swept into the patient's room without knocking. I hesitated before following. Malik was small. Smaller than a nine-year-old should be. His skin was grayish, lips cracked. His mother sat beside the bed with a blanket draped around her shoulders and eyes that hadn't slept in days.

"Morning, Malik," Dr. Sayegh said, her voice surprisingly warm. "How's the nausea today?"

He gave her a weak thumbs-up. His mom gave her a look that said *we're pretending it's fine.*

I stood at the foot of the bed, trying to find a place to exist.

When Dr. Sayegh turned to me, I straightened instinctively.

"Lab updates?" she asked.

I froze for half a second. Then remembered Elena handed me the chart. I flipped it open. "Hemoglobin low. Platelets even lower. ANC was tanking, like his immune system is going on strike." My voice didn't shake when I said the numbers aloud, but I could feel the sweat prickling at my back.

Dr. Sayegh gave a short nod. "Start transfusion orders before noon. And double-check his central line site. Last nurse said it looked irritated."

"Yes, ma'am."

She was already moving again.

By lunch, I was sitting in the staff's lounge alone with a turkey and cheese sandwich and bottle of water I hadn't touched. My hands were still cold. I'd washed them so many times, the skin between my fingers was starting to peel. Across the room, a group of second-year fellows laughed over a TikTok someone passed around. I smiled politely when one of them glanced my way, then looked down at my phone. No new texts. I clicked open Khalil's last message from the night before.

BIG HEAD

Don't let them rattle you. You belong there.

I hadn't responded. I typed "first day was fine," then deleted it. It wasn't a lie. It wasn't the truth either. That afternoon, I presented my first patient in rounds. My voice sounded too loud. Too clipped. I stumbled over the chemo protocol name and corrected myself mid-sentence.

Dr. Sayegh didn't blink. "Next time, prep your notes before entering the room. Confidence inspires confidence."

It wasn't said with venom. Just expectation. I nodded. Even

though her words landed like a slap. I knew better. I was better. By the time I made it home, my legs felt like they'd been filled with wet sand. My apartment was still mostly unpacked. Take-out containers littered the kitchen counters and trash. I kicked off my shoes, shed my scrubs into a corner, and collapsed onto the couch in a tank top and underwear. I stared at the ceiling. The silence was louder than anything I'd heard all day.

Mama would've asked how it went. She would've told me to treat myself to a little dessert. Something soft and sweet to cut the edge of a rough day. I swallowed hard. I pulled my phone out and scrolled Instagram like it might numb me.

THE NEXT MORNING, I left my apartment twenty minutes earlier just so I could breathe somewhere that didn't smell like antiseptic. Still + Stirred was a tiny corner coffee shop tucked between a bookstore and a yoga studio. The windows were fogged from the inside, plants hung in the windows like little green chandeliers, and a chalkboard out front read, "You survived yesterday. Here's to something warm for today."

I like that.

Inside, the walls were painted a faded terracotta, and Billie Holiday crooned softly from a dusty speaker in the corner. It was the kind of place where you could disappear without disappearing completely.

The barista, a light-skinned girl with bantu knots and a "BLACK COFFEE MATTERS" pin on her apron, smiled when I stepped to the counter.

"Hi, welcome to Still + Stirred! What can I get for you?" she asked.

"Double blonde espresso, oat milk, splash of hazelnut and a sprinkle of cinnamon."

"Coming right up." She smiled.

I took my drink and slid into the corner table near the window. The wood was chipped, but it had a perfect view of people pretending their lives weren't unraveling, too. Outside, a dad balanced his toddler on his shoulders. A woman walked by with headphones and a bouquet of flowers tucked into her bag. The world felt far away in the best way. I opened my laptop, pretending I was about to review new oncology protocols, but I kept staring at the blinking cursor in my empty Word doc. Instead, I clicked over to the group chat with my best friends.

NESSA ANN

tell me why I forgot to take the salmon out to thaw

all I want is a salmon bowl

LYNNIE MAE

again??? Come on Nessa.

NYAH MYAH

you're being dramatic. Just cook it from frozen in the air fryer

NESSA ANN

that's gonna poison me is it???

ME

no, it's not going to poison you

Just seeing their names made my shoulders drop a little. I didn't realize how much I missed them until now—our chaos, our arguments, the way we dragged each other with love. A notification popped up from Khalil. Just a heart emoji.

Nothing more.

That evening, after rounds and too many small mistakes to name, I got back to my apartment and collapsed on the couch again, fully clothed. It was past time for me to schedule a hair appointment. My edges would start to break soon if I didn't show my hair some love. The trash in the kitchen was beginning to sour, with me missing the cutoff time to place the bin outside for the valet to pick-up. I didn't care.

My phone lit up with a Facetime call from "Chaos Coven ." I stared at it for a second, thumb hovering. Then I answered.

Vanessa popped up first–barefoot, bonnet tied tight, holding another juice concoction and a bottle of stretch mark cream. Her baby bump was beginning to make the tiniest of appearances under her thin sleep tank. "My sweet Kelly," she choked, tears beginning to fill her eyes. "I miss you so much."

Nyah and Lynn's faces popped in behind her, all from different screens but somehow syncing all their energy, like we were sitting in the same living room.

"You're alive!" Lynn cheered, her eyes bright. "I was about to file a missing person's report."

"I'm fine," I said, propping myself up on a pillow. "Just... tired."

Vanessa squinted. "Tired or *tired*?"

"The former," I muttered.

Nyah shook her head. "I still don't get why you left the way you did. I mean, I get it–but damn, Kelly."

I looked down. "I had to. I was suffocating. I needed this fresh start."

Silence pressed at the edges of the screen for a second. Vanessa nodded, swiping away at a tear.

"Okay. But don't act like we're not here for you." She sniffled.

"Nessa, please don't cry," I begged. I couldn't handle tears. Not today.

"Nope. Hell no," Lynn quipped. "You need to cry. Talk. Yell. Binge Real Housewives, we got you."

I smiled, not the performative one. The real kind. Small but real.

"I appreciate y'all. I really do."

Lynn smiled wistfully and sipped her wine. "So have you seen any fine men in Seattle yet or is it just coffee and sadness?"

"Mostly coffee." I laughed. "I haven't had much time to explore."

"Speaking of men. When's the last time you talked to Khalil?" Lynn peered at me over her glasses.

"I don't know. When's the last time you fucked Wesley?" I shot back.

Vanessa and Nyah doubled over with laughter. Lynn's face fell flat.

"Fuck you, Kelly," she huffed. "It was one time! Besides, I have an actual suitor in my life right now."

"Does Wesley know this?" Vanessa laughed, wiping away happy tears.

"Shut up." Lynn pouted.

"It's so cliche," Nyah agreed. "I would write it into a book if I had the time."

"Oh, guess what y'all?" Vanessa ran around her kitchen then fumbled with her phone. "Look who's finally poking out!" She lifted the bottom of her shirt up until it hit below her bra. The belly I'd swore was still nonexistent when I'd left home had doubled, no tripled in size since I'd been in Seattle.

"Ahh!" Lynn squealed from her end. "Do we know what we're having yet?"

Vanessa shook her head. "No, we want to wait and do a reveal at the baby shower. Kelly, you'll be here, right?"

"I'll have to see. You know how hospital life is," I reassured. "When is it going to be?"

"Early November. Mama says I'm pushing it, but I think it'll be fine. It'll give Xavier and Khalil time to wrap up this community center."

"It'll be the perfect day," Lynn chimed in. "And we're all going to be there. I know it."

The conversation drifted toward updatesNyah and Antonio

were considering counseling, Lynn was preparing for a big trial, Vanessa and Xavier were still fake arguing about which brand of diapers they should use. I didn't say much. Just listened. Let their voices fill the room until I didn't feel so alone anymore. When the call ended, I stared at the dark screen of my phone. My reflection looked tired. Like the person I'd become had been quietly gnawing at the woman I used to be. I picked up the lavender candle on my coffee table and lit it.

One small light.

One small lie.

I'm fine.

~

BY THE START of my second month, I'd memorized the badge scanner code to the pediatric wing. I could navigate the supply closets without looking. I knew which elevator moved fastest and which nurse always had some snacks stashed in her purse.

What I didn't know was how to keep up.

It started with a blood culture that didn't get sent on time. A resident flagged it, not me. Dr. Sayegh raised an eyebrow during rounds but didn't say anything. I told myself I was just tired. Off my game.

The next day, it was a central line order that got duplicated because I hadn't documented it properly. One of the nurses—Janet, a kind but no-nonsense auntie type—gently pulled me aside.

"Look, I know you're new here. But this floor runs like clock-work. Patients like Malik can't afford even minor errors."

I nodded, throat tight. "Thank you for telling me." *As if I didn't know this already.*

"You okay, Dr. Reid?"

"I'm fine." The words tasted like chalk.

That afternoon, I stood outside Malik's room, pretending to review his file while Dr. Sayegh spoke to his mother. The boy had been admitted for neutropenic fever and was spiking again. The last labs showed some irregularities, nothing life-threatening, but enough to raise flags. I'd double-checked the notes. I *thought* I had.

But when Dr. Sayegh turned and asked, "Was his ANC trending down or stabilizing this morning?" I froze.

I had read the report. I remembered reading it. But couldn't remember the actual number. My brain was static.

"...I think it was–"

Dr. Sayegh raised a hand. "Don't think. Know." She turned to Elena. "Pull it up."

Elena had it up in seconds. "It's down. He needs new cultures and likely a broad-spectrum add-on."

Dr. Sayegh didn't say anything to me in the hallway. Not then.

But after rounds, she found me charting at a desk near the nurses' station.

"Dr. Reid." Her voice was calm. Low.

I turned. "Yes, ma'am?"

"You can't afford to live in your head here. These kids, their parents, need you present."

"I understand."

She studied me a moment longer, her tone softening just enough to cut deeper. "You're previous attending told me you're grieving. I know that. But if this is where you want to be, you'll have to find a way to carry it without letting it carry you."

I nodded again. It was the only thing I could do. My face stayed still. But inside?

I cracked.

Chapter 20

Khalil

Read 9:42 PM.

That was last night. This morning? Nothing. No follow-up. No "I'm okay." Not even one of those lazy "k" replies she used to send when she was mad but still wanted to keep the line open. Just silence. It was silence I'd started to memorize. The kind that crept up slow, thick like molasses, until I was drowning in it. But this one felt colder. Permanent.

I'd read her text over and over like there was a code hidden between the letters. *"I think I messed up today."* Did she mean work? Us? Both? My phone buzzed from a new message, but it was just Xavier telling me he was on his way to the community center we were renovating. I threw on a hoodie and grabbed my keys.

When I pulled up, it looked like every other construction zone I'd seen before. The drywall in the back classroom hadn't gone up yet, and you could still smell the wood glue in the foundation of the front office. A vision coming to life. Something we were building with our own hands. Something solid.

Unlike everything else.

Xavier was at the fold-out table we used as our "command center," flipping through blueprints with his laptop open beside him. The light caught the creases around his eyes, but his movements were steady. Reliable. Man was a damn metronome. Wesley perched himself on an overturned paint bucket near the window, in all-black as usual, sipping a coffee and talking mess between bites of an energy bar.

"You been ghost mode all week," Xavier said without looking up. "What's going on?"

I dropped my bag on the floor and pulled out a chair across from him. "Nothing."

"That nothing look heavy," Wesley muttered. "Let me guess. Kelly?"

I didn't respond.

Instead, I reached for one of the blueprints but couldn't focus on a single line.

"Nessa said she looks like she's doing okay. Doesn't believe it, though."

I huffed, sinking further into my chair. "She texted me last night. Said she messed up. Then, nothing."

"Grief will do that," Xavier said, voice low and even. "Make you reach out just to see if someone will catch you, then panic and let go."

"I just wish I knew where we stood," I admitted. "I don't want to push her. But I can't keep sitting in this damn limbo, waiting for her to choose me again."

Wesley leaned forward. "Are you waiting on her to reach out, or are you scared to admit she might not?"

That one stung.

Before I could answer, the front door swung open, and in

came Maverick, loud as ever, rocking some too loud cologne, gold chain glinting in the light, and a Shipley's box in hand.

"Y'all trying to build Wakanda or something?" he said, grinning. He looked around the room, settling his gaze on me. "Fuck wrong with you?" he asked, tossing the box of donuts on the table and flopping into the squeaky camp chair in the corner like he'd been invited. "What y'all talking about?"

"Kelly got him in his feelings," Wesley said, jerking his chin at me.

Maverick looked me over. "She still got your nose wide open. After all these years. Y'all know he was ready to square up back in college. I wasn't even trying to push up on her like that, just see how bad he had it."

"Chill," I muttered, rubbing the back of my neck.

"I'm just saying." Maverick shrugged, biting into another donut. "You walk around like you invincible. But anytime you and Kelly going through it, you look like you been listening to Brent Faiyaz on repeat."

I cracked a deep laugh despite myself. "I can't help it, bruh. She's in Seattle. I haven't seen her in months. Ain't really been talking."

Maverick sobered up a little. "Not even a text?"

"She texts. Sometimes. But she not really there."

Xavier leaned back and looked out the window. "When's the last time you felt like she was?"

I opened my mouth, then closed it. A tight swallow followed after. "Before Mrs. Charisse died."

"Then maybe she's still stuck in that moment," he said. "And maybe part of you is, too."

The table went quiet. We sat in that silence like men do, not uncomfortable, but charged. Each of us carrying something unspoken. That was what made this circle what it was. No performance. Just presence. Eventually, they started talking about some programs we could run by the community center director once construction was complete. I tuned in but didn't add to the conversation.

Xavier glanced back at me. "You quiet again."

"I'm listening," I said.

But I wasn't. Not really. I was already thinking about Seattle. About how many more days I could stomach not seeing her face. About how many times I'd check my phone before it broke me. About how many things I didn't say the last time I saw her.

Wesley stretched. "You thinking of going up there, huh?"

I didn't answer right away. Then, "yeah."

"You going to tell her you coming?"

I shook my head. "She won't respond anyway."

Maverick leaned forward. "So, what's the play?"

I stared down at the blueprints in front of me, lines criss-crossed with vision and purpose, and traced my finger along the paper, like it could tell me the future.

"I just need to see her," I said. "That's all."

THE DOOR CLICKED SHUT behind me like a period. Sharp. Final.

My apartment was dark except for the streetlight bleeding in through the blinds, throwing faint stripes across the living room wall. I didn't bother turning on the lights. I just dropped my keys into the bowl by the door and stood there, not moving. Not thinking. Just breathing in the stillness. It didn't used to feel this quiet.

There used to be movies playing in the background. Something old and classic that Kelly would inevitably fall asleep on. There used to be her voice from the kitchen, swearing up and down that her nachos were better than mine. Used to be one of her spare bonnets on the nightstand, her charger tangled with mine, her lotion still on my hands long after she left the room.

I walked to the couch and sat down slow, as if the air itself had weight. My hoodie still hung over the back of the chair from the last time she'd worn it. I reached for it without thinking, pressing it to my face. It barely smelled like her anymore. Just laundry detergent and my own indecision.

I pulled my phone out again, thumb hovering over her name. I didn't have anything new to say, and she didn't have anything new to tell me. But still, I opened the thread. Her last text glared back at me. What had she meant? Was she talking about the fellowship? About me? About pushing me away before she could really fall? Or was she already gone, and that message was just her final apology? I tapped the message field. Typed. Deleted. Typed again. Then I closed the thread. I had her apartment's address from helping her ship some stuff she couldn't take on the plane.

I opened Google to search flights instead.

My suitcase sat in the back of my closet, dusty but ready. I pulled it out and started tossing clothes inside. A few t-shirts. Two hoodies. The gray one she used to steal even though she swore it was "nothing special." I paused in the pantry. Grabbed an unopened bag of the spicy trail mix she loved from H-E-B. I tucked it in the front pocket of my suitcase. No not. No explanation. Just something that might make her smile. If she let herself.

By the time I zipped the bag, it was nearly 3:00 AM. My flight left at 6:00 AM. I sat on the edge of the bed, phone in hand, the screen lighting my face with a soft accusing glow. I opened me and Kelly's thread again. Typed.

ME

Let me know if you need anything.

Or if you just want somebody to talk to.

I'm still here.

You don't have to go through this alone.

Delivered.

No read receipt. No reply. I stared at the message until my eyes burned. Then I flipped the phone face down and turned off the lamp. The dark wasn't empty. It pulsed with the things I hadn't said. With the weight of being too late and wanted too little. I laid back on the bed, hoodie still on, heart thudding like I was already 30,000 feet in the air.

She didn't know I was coming.

But maybe, just maybe, she'd feel it.

Chapter 21

Kelly

ANOTHER NIGHT SITTING ALONE ON THE BALCONY OF MY apartment. Coldness clung to my bones, not sharp, not violent. Just persistent. The sky was steel-gray, a kind of muted Seattle dusk that felt like the day had been erased too early. I pulled my robe tighter around my body as I stared out at the evening commotion. A cold glass of wine rested in my hand. I sat back in the patio chair, my knees tucked tight under my chin. The frenzy from my day at the hospital had long since dissipated. All that was left was a subtle ache in my heart.

I missed my mom.

I missed being able to call her and say "today was hard" without needing to explain why.

I missed my old self. The one who could walk into a room and feel sure of who she was. The one who knew exactly where her edges stopped. It was as if my mother took that very essence of me with her to heaven. Now everything inside me felt blurred. Pulled thin.

I looked at my phone and took a sip of the tart, fruity wine. Khalil's last message lit up on the screen.

BIG HEAD

Let me know if you need anything.

Or if you just want somebody to talk to.

I'm still here.

You don't have to go through this alone.

The words hit like they always did. Gentle. Patient. *Him*. I stared at them for a long time. Felt them press against my ribcage. I wanted to write back. But what could I say? That I didn't want him to fix me, but was mad he stopped trying? That I missed him so much it made my skin itch? That I'd watched *Leprechaun in the Hood* almost every night my first two weeks here in Seattle just to feel like he were here with me? I could, but I didn't want to. I wanted to be mad, pissed. Khalil wouldn't let me. He'd make it so I could cry. I didn't want to cry. I placed the phone down in my robe's pocket and walked into the kitchen. Opened the wine. Poured another glass.

I took out my phone. Opened his message thread and typed: *I'm sorry*. Then deleted it. Typed: *I miss you*. Deleted that, too. Instead, I whispered it aloud–into the room, into the quiet, into the part of me that still believed he could hear me when I didn't speak.

"I miss you."

The wine glass trembled in my grip. I set it down. Curling into the corner of my couch, I hugged one of the throw pillows my mother kept in her living room, no matter the furniture. It still had the scent of wine-dipped florals if I pressed my face into it just right. I inhaled deeply as I sat in the dark, watching the single flame of the candle on my coffee table flicker. Silence hummed around me. Felt the creep of the ache unfolding for the first time since the funeral.

I told myself I needed air. That I'd been in the hospital day after day, for weeks, buried under fluorescent lights and the low hum of machines. That my brain needed a break, a reprieve from the charts and central lines and the way every hallway reminded me of my mother. I needed to feel invisible, if only for a few hours.

I needed a night out.

I hurried to change, throwing on a matching set and heels. I googled the nearest bar, set my makeup, and headed out for my first night out in Seattle. The bar was tucked into the basement of an old brick building on a side street. It didn't have a sign, just a single hanging light above the door and a narrow window fogged with condensation. Inside, it felt like stepping into someone's memory, dim and low-ceilinged, with warm amber bulbs strung like fairy lights above the bar and votive candles flickering on each table.

The walls were exposed wood and deep navy, softened by vintage concert posters and shelves of dusty books no one read. Jazz played from a turntable behind the bar, slightly scratchy, like the vinyl had lived a few lives already. It smelled like charred citrus, old whiskey, and something warm and spicy drifting in from the kitchen—maybe lamb sliders or duck fat popcorn. It was the kind of place you didn't just drink in. You sank into it. Quietly. Slowly. Like grief pretending to be elegance.

I took in the bar a minute longer before locking eyes with the guy leaning against the far wall. His eyes glanced over me, as if he'd been waiting on me all night. When he saw me, he straightened, slid his phone into his pocket, and smiled. It was soft, a smile that told you he noticed everything and wouldn't make you explain any of it unless you wanted to.

He looked good. Polished without being a try-hard. His simple t-shirt hugged his collarbone and the sharpened lines of his shoulders. He walked over, long confident strides carried by even longer legs. The warm glow of the vintage bulbs cast a smoky shadow over his face, deepening the impact of the manicured beard lining his jaw.

"I've seen you somewhere?" he asked. The warm air wrapped

around us. Hopefully the dim light blurred the frayed edges of my exhaustion.

"I've been told my face is unforgettable." I smiled, extending my hand.

"I know where. Still +Stirred. I get coffee there most days. What's your name?"

"Kelly," I replied, adding a smile-laugh. "Still + Stirred is becoming a favorite of mine."

"It's the best." He looked over at the semi-empty bar then the booths across from it. "I don't want to be forward, but do you mind if I buy you a drink?"

"Hmm, I don't know. They say you shouldn't take drinks from strangers," I said, coyly. "I don't even know your name."

He laughed, looking to the ground. "I'm Jordan."

"Well Jordan, now that we're not strangers, lead the way." I smiled.

We slid into a booth tucked in the back, half-shielded by a warped mirror and the leafy tendrils of a pothos plant that curved like it was listening. The booth cushions were aged leather, cracked but welcoming. There was a single candle on the table between us, its flame swaying like it was unsure if it wanted to keep burning.

I didn't plan on feeling this easy.

But once we ordered drinks—mezcal for him, citrus and vodka for me—the world outside the bar started to fade. And once the drinks came, and his leg brushed mine beneath the table, and I didn't flinch, it was like I was watching myself play a role I hadn't rehearsed but somehow knew all the lines.

"To beautiful not-so-strangers," he said, raising his glass, tapping it against mine.

The alcohol went down warm. He told a story about a business deal he had coming up and how he couldn't wait to stop dealing with people hunting for bargains. I laughed when he attempted to make jokes. Leaned in when he flirted.

"Stressed?" Jordan asked after a pause, voice gentler now.

"What makes you say that?"

"You just sighed like you hold the weight of the world on your shoulders."

I smiled, but my chest tightened. He watched me for a beat, then offered his hand across the table. I didn't take it, but I didn't look away.

"I've been talking all night. What do you do?"

"I'm a doctor. Pediatrician."

"Wow. What brings you to Seattle?"

"A fellowship for my specialty."

"That sounds exciting." He continued talking but I half-listened as he told me about his travels across the world. Jordan didn't ask questions I couldn't answer. Jordan didn't try to dissect the shadows under my eyes. He just let me be what I was without naming it. I needed that.

After the second round of drinks, we walked through Capitol Hill, past the streetcar tracks, through a blur of fog and faint music coming from someone's open apartment window. The mist painted everything soft and shiny, like the world was trying to romanticize my breakdown.

"You ever feel like you're watching yourself from the outside?" I asked suddenly as we passed under a crooked streetlamp.

He looked at me, surprised. "How so?"

I turned my face toward the light. "Like you're smiling and nodding and saying all the right things...but you're somewhere else entirely."

He nodded slowly. "No. I can't say that I have."

I wanted to cry. I didn't. Instead, I kissed him. Not dramatically. Not passionately. Just enough. A test. His lips were warm. Gentle. No rush. No hunger. Just confirmation that I was still real. Still reachable. That I could want something, even if I didn't understand why. We didn't speak as he pulled up the rideshare app on his phone. I gave him my address. He didn't ask if I meant for him to follow, just got in the car behind me. When we got to my building, I didn't look back. Just led the way from the elevators to my door, key trembling in the lock.

My apartment was dark except for the streetlights bleeding through the blinds. My wine glass from earlier still sat on the counter. I didn't care. I set my purse down. Turned around. Looked at him, still standing in the doorway.

"You sure?" he asked.

I nodded. "Yeah."

But what I meant was: I need to feel something other than this ache.

We didn't rush. We didn't talk much. There was kissing. Some slow undoing. But it wasn't about lust. It damn sure wasn't about love. It was about erasure. About quieting the memory of my mother's death. About smothering the echo of Khalil's voice in my chest. About surviving the night with someone who didn't know the whole story and wouldn't try to fix it.

Afterward, I curled into my side of the bed, facing the window. Jordan lay beside me but didn't press. Didn't pull. When he fell asleep, I stared at the ceiling. I grabbed my phone and opened Khalil's messages.

BIG HEAD

Let me know if you need anything.

Or if you just want somebody to talk to.

I'm still here.

You don't have to go through this alone.

My fingers stilled over the keyboard. I couldn't reply. A lone tear crept into the fibers of my pillow. Instead, I whispered into the dark, "I miss you."

But even I didn't know who I meant.

Chapter 22

Khalil

I landed in Seattle under a sky that looked like wet paper—gray, heavy, and creased with the faintest threat of rain. It was barely noon, but everything felt muted, like the city was holding its breath. The ride from the airport was quiet. The driver didn't speak, and I didn't invite conversation. I just stared out the window, watching the trees blur past, the skyline in the distance smudged like a memory I hadn't made yet. My heart was doing that thing again. Racing too fast for no reason, like it knew something I didn't. I told myself I wasn't nervous. Just ready.

Kelly's building was modern; all glass and steel, too clean to feel like home. I stepped into the elevator, pressed the button for her floor, and watched my reflection shift in the brushed metal doors. Hoodie. Black jeans. Sneakers clean. Bag slung over one shoulder. Heart in my throat. Each floor blinked past like a countdown.

Ding.

Her door was at the end of the hallway. The handle a matte black, minimal, and cold just like the rest of the building. I adjusted the bag on my shoulder, took a deep breath, and knocked. Waited. Knocked again. The door opened. And there she was. Lily-girl. Hair pulled up. Face bare. An oversized tee hanging off one shoulder. She looked like softness wrapped in silence. And when her eyes met mine, I saw it. Not surprised.

Guilt.

That shit hit like a gut punch.

"Hey," I said, smiling. Trying. "Surprise."

She didn't say anything. Just blinked.

"Khalil...what are you doing here?"

I tapped my bag like a peace offering. "Decided to take a weekend trip. You seemed off in your last message."

"Yeah. I just..."

Before she could finish, a voice came from inside the apartment. Male. Cocky.

"Tell whoever's at the door to leave so we–oh." He stepped into view. Clothes wrinkled. He looked between us, caught the tension like static, and straightened his posture. He walked past me, slow and quiet, brushing Kelly's shoulder gently. She didn't flinch. That was the worst part. "You got us breakfast delivered?" he asked, looking at her, not me. "Careful, sweetheart. It's too early to get clingy."

Kelly's eyes widened as she looked from him to me. She fidgeted with the hem of her shirt. My head spun, ears rung, as I tried to unhear what he'd just said.

"Kelly, who the fuck is this?" I asked, seething, trying to keep my lid from blowing off.

The guy turned to me with a slimy grin, extending his hand. I slapped it away.

"Kelly, what the fuck?" I hissed, trying to keep it together. "This what we doing now?"

Kelly stepped between the two of us, raising her hand to my chest. "Khalil, you need to calm down." Her eyes fretted all over my face. She bit the corners of her lips, as if looking for the words that would make this okay.

"Nah," I said, my eyes laser-focused on the dude behind her, still wearing that smug-ass grin. "If this what you on, I need to know."

"She ain't on nothing." Jordan laughed. "Well, could've been until you popped up."

I chuckled once, no humor, just heat. "Man, keep talking and see what happen."

He didn't take the warning, just kept moving his mouth. "You mad because she upgraded? She ain't your girl, bruh." He moved closer to grab Kelly by the waist and pull her to his chest.

She grappled with loosening herself from his hold. "Jordan, you need to leave," she urged.

He looked down at her with disgust. Dropped his hands, grabbed his things, and started for the door. "Waste of time. Bitch didn't even give up any pussy," he grumbled under his breath.

"Who you calling a bitch?" Kelly yelled.

I barely registered the response over the sound of my hand connecting to his face. Fist to jaw. He stumbled back into the table Kelly had in her entryway, slouching forward. Kelly screamed, trying to wedge herself between us, but Jordan flew at me, arms flailing around. I tucked Kelly behind me before swinging again, this time connecting with his ribs. Jordan folded over, grunting, continuing to stumble while trying to gain his footing.

"Khalil, stop!"

Jordan tried lunging forward with a slow swing. I ducked and followed with another punch to the bridge of his nose. He stumbled back, his hands flew to his face. Kelly tugged on the back of my hoodie, begging me to stop. I couldn't. I saw red. Not the flash of anger kind. Something deeper, like something split inside me, raw and deep. Not jealousy. Not betrayal. Like deepening a wound that'd just begun to heal. Something in my chest folded in on itself. The repeat of heartbreak. It didn't cut like the first time. No, this time was cleaner. Because this time, I knew exactly what I was losing.

Kelly yanked me back as my vision cleared. My ears still rang as heat radiated from my skin. Jordan stood straight, heaving, nose bloodied, pride gone. "Fuck this," he spit. "You can keep this bull-shit drama."

"Get the fuck out," she snapped, her voice sharp enough to slice concrete. As Jordan limped across the threshold and down the hall, we noticed the neighbor across the hall peeking from a crack in their door. "Mind your damn business," Kelly yelled across the hall, slamming her door closed. The silence that followed wasn't awkward.

It was war.

I stood there breathing hard. My chest pounded with the rage of a thousand storms over open sea. She looked at me like I'd burned her house down.

"Are you done?" she asked coldly.

"That's the type of nigga you trying to be with?" I spat back. "You going out sad, Dr. Reid."

"Why are you here?" Fury and fear blazed in her eyes, leaving me standing alone in the entryway.

I stepped inside without asking. Her place smelled like lavender and fresh linen. A candle burned low on her coffee table, a wine glass left stranded by the sink. I walked farther into the too small apartment, glancing into the bedroom. Her bed was half-made. The kind of messy that didn't come from sleeping alone. I dropped my bag on the floor next to the bar stools. Kelly stood by the door, arms crossed over her chest, like she was bracing for impact.

"You couldn't even wait until the dirt settled on your mama's grave, huh?" I swiped at my nose, pacing next to the bar counter.

"Don't," she whispered, her voice trembling.

"Were you going to fuck him?" I asked, my voice flat, straight to the point.

"No, Khalil! I swear. I just didn't want to be alone." Her voice was small, weak. The fury in her eyes transformed into pain.

I laughed. Not because it was funny, but because if I didn't, I might break something.

"You got me out here worried, praying for your ass, trying to hold you together from two thousand miles away. And this what you doing?"

She stepped forward. "Khalil, stop."

"No," I snapped. "You don't get to shut me up right now."

"I didn't do anything wrong."

I blinked. "The fuck you just say?"

"We're not together. You said you'd give me space. You said you'd wait. I didn't ask you to."

"You also begged me to stay in your life. Said you needed me."

"And I did," she snapped. "I do. But that doesn't mean I'm ready to be yours."

"That doesn't mean you fuck somebody else while I'm still trying, Kelly."

"You think this is easy for me?" she said, her voice rising. "You think I wanted this?"

"I don't know what the hell you want," I shot back. "Because all you do is push me away and then cry when I'm not standing there to catch you."

Her face changed. The pain hit like a delayed punch.

"You always do that," she said, trembling now. "You always make it about what you've done for me. Like love is a transaction. Like I owe you because you showed up."

"I don't need you to owe me," I said, quieter now. "I just wanted it to mean something."

"It did," she said. "But that doesn't mean it fixes me."

I looked away. The ache crawled up my spine like something alive.

She stepped forward, voice shaking. "You keep showing up like your love is a rescue mission. But I don't want to be saved, Khalil."

"You're drowning," I said, softer still. "And you don't even see it."

Her eyes filled. "And you think clinging to me while I sink is noble?"

We stood in opposite corners of the living room, two ghosts haunting the same space. Two people standing in the ruins of what they swore they would hold.

"You're selfish," I whispered.

She winced.

"You think you're protecting yourself," I continued, heat rising in my throat, "but all you do is hurt the people who see you. Who love you. You let people give and give and give, and when they're empty, you act like it's their fault they're tired."

"And you" her voice cracked, "you don't even know how to be loved unless you're being needed."

That hit something raw in me. A rusted nerve I didn't know she knew how to touch. I stepped back. Fists curled.

She didn't stop.

"You think loving me means saving me, but it doesn't. You show up, and you perform, and you pour out everything you have like it's the only way to prove you're worth staying for."

"You don't know what you're talking about," I said. I swiped at my nose again, heat creeping to the tops of my ears.

"I do," she fired back. "You don't love me, Khalil. You love being the one I might not walk away from."

"Shut up."

"Because your mother did. And you've been chasing women who make you feel needed ever since." Her words held a familiar bite she reserved for others. Reserved for her parents. Now that they were turned on me, they sank into my heart like venom-dripped darts.

I blinked hard. My lungs shattered.

"You want someone broken so you can feel whole." She continued poking and prodding at the deeper parts of me only she were privy to.

"Stop." I closed my eyes and inhaled, letting the air hang trapped in my chest.

"You keep showing up for me like I'm your redemption arc"

"Kelly."

"I'm not your second chance at proving you're needed!"

I slammed my fist against the counter. The wine glass shook like it had been slapped, then tipped to the kitchen floor, shattering.

"Fuck that, Kelly! That's the bullshit excuse you want to go with?" I snapped. "You think I like feeling like I'm the only one standing between you and collapse?"

Her breath quickened.

"You know what your problem is?" I said, voice low now, biting. "You been so busy playing peacekeeper in your parents' fucked up marriage, you don't know what healthy love looks like. You think running is freedom. You think pushing me away is strength. But all you doing is mimicking your mama's silence and your bitch-ass daddy's distance, calling it boundaries."

Her whole face shifted. That was the wound. The one no one else touched.

"You don't get to talk about my parents."

"Why not? They raised you into the woman who thinks love is war. Who expects men to leave so she punishes the ones who stay. I'm not your damn daddy, Kelly."

"And I'm not your mama," she spat. "I didn't abandon you."

"No, you're worse," I said. "You stayed. You let me believe we were building something while you planned your escape."

"I never asked you to wait."

"You didn't have to," I said. "You asked with your tears. With your silence. With that look you give me when you don't know what to say but still want to stay."

She stepped back like I slapped her.

"I show up for you," I said, quieter now, voice hoarse from hurt. "And all you give me is crumbs."

Her voice was barely a whisper as she looked to the floor. "Because all I have left are crumbs."

We both went still. Her arms dropped to her sides. My chest heaved like I'd just been pulled out to the ocean. Neither of us moved. Neither of us knew how to put it back together. The silence after the last words we hurled at each other wasn't peaceful. It was deafening. Hollow. Like the world had dropped out from under us, and now we were just standing in its ruins, pretending like the fire wasn't still burning.

I looked at her. She'd moved to brace herself against the counter like the granite beneath her elbows was the only thing keeping her upright. The candle on the coffee table flickered once, twice, and then died out completely. I bent down and picked up the bag I'd brought. Unzipped it slowly. Pulled out the spicy trail mix. Set it on the counter. She didn't move. Didn't speak. Just stared at the bag like it was a body I'd dropped between us.

"I brought this for you," I said, my voice steady, almost too calm. "Thought you could use something from home."

Her lips parted, but no sound came out. Her eyes, rimmed with thick, stubborn tears that refused to drop, followed my movements like she wanted to stop me but didn't know how.

I looked around the apartment one last time. This was the place I thought I'd visit to feel closer to her. All I felt now was distance.

"I know you think I came here to guilt you," I said, turning to the door. "But I didn't. I just wanted to be near you. I thought maybe...maybe that'd be enough."

"Khalil..." I froze. She was whispering again. "Let's talk this out. I don't want you to leave like this."

"Hmph," I said, not turning around. "You didn't want me to come either."

I opened the door. Her footsteps padded softly behind me. I felt the warmth of her presence at my back before she touched me. Her hand landed on my arm, small, unsure.

"Please. Don't go," she cracked. "Talk to me."

I turned finally, looked her dead in the eyes. The tears that wanted to fall clung to her lids like life preservers. Her lips trembled with all the words she'd refused to say earlier. She reached out again, fingertips brushing my chest. Like if she could just touch me enough, I'd forget what we just became. But I remembered everything. All the ways I'd bent. All the ways she never caught me when I folded.

"I can't keep loving you like this," I said, my voice catching in my throat. "It's killing me."

"Khalil. I–"

"You don't need to explain," I cut her off, shaking my head. "I know you don't have anything left to give. But I do. And I need to save it for myself."

Her hand dropped to her side. Tears slipped freely now, but she didn't sob. Just stood there, mouth slightly open, like she wanted to say something that couldn't stop the inevitable. But there was no speech that could undo what had been said. No apology that could rewind a wound so deep, it'd take decades to heal. So, I turned. Walked out. And this time I didn't look back.

WHEN I FLEW BACK to Houston, I didn't go straight home. I hit the gym, lifted weights for hours, ran a few trails at a park downtown. I needed air. I needed to feel something other than that hollow ache in my chest that kept getting wider the more I thought about her face when I left. By the time I made it in my apartment, the sun had long since set. I should've gone to sleep. Should've closed the curtains, curled up with the pain, and just taken the loss.

But I didn't. I refused to go out sad.

I texted Maverick.

ME
You out?

MAV

Always. Pull up. Sending you the address.

The club was a haze of lights and heat and motion. Bass thumped from the walls like a second heartbeat, and bodies moved through the air thick with sweat, smoke, and perfume. I found Mav near the bar, surrounded by women, energy, and noise. He dapped me up, drink already in hand.

"You good?" he asked.

"No."

He flagged the bartender down to bring me a shot. "Then fix that."

I threw it back without asking what it was. Let it burn.

Music blared. Women laughed. One of them caught my eye, but I looked away. Not yet. Not ready. But then I saw her. Tasha. Thick thighs. Brown skin lit gold by the strobe light. Hair laid. Eyes lined with black caterpillars. She saw me before I saw her. Tilted her head like, *Really? Here? Now?* I didn't blink. Threw back my fourth shot and made my way over.

She leaned in close, voice low and amused. "Didn't think I'd see you out tonight? Where's your entourage?" She looked around, waiting for a surprise popup that wouldn't come.

I smirked. "No entourage. Just me tonight?"

She raised a brow. "That right?"

I smirked. "You looking for somebody that's not coming."

She stepped closer, closing the gap between us. Her fingers toyed with the hem of my shirt. "I don't know. Last time, you said you free, then you ghosted me. I'm just trying to make sure your little shadow not coming out to play."

I almost flinched at the mention of Kelly, but I played it off with a laugh and shrug of my shoulders. "Nah, ain't no shadows. Just me."

"Aww. Got your heart broken?" Her tone was syrupy sweet as she dug for information that didn't concern her.

"You worrying about the wrong thing." I smirked, dragging my eyes down and back up her body. "You busy tonight?"

"Depends," she said. Her nails dragged up my body, from my belt to the chins around my neck. "You looking for company or consolation?"

I laughed. The first one that felt something like real. "You wild. Tell me what you trying to do."

"You're lucky you're cute as hell."

I leaned closer to her ear. "Cute? Come on, Tasha. You know I'm better than that."

She paused, looking me in my eyes. "I don't know. You seem a little dangerous."

"Nah," I said, licking my lips. "Never that."

She bit the side of her cheeks, hesitating. When she slid her hand down my chest, fingers playing with the metal of my belt, I didn't stop her.

"Come home with me," she whispered into my ear, like it was a dare.

I didn't hesitate.

~

HER APARTMENT WAS a mess of candles, incense, and chaos. But it was warm. Loud with color. Alive. We didn't talk much. We didn't need to. Clothes hit the floor. Hands gripped whatever they could find. This wasn't love. Wasn't even lust. It was something meaner. Heavier. A kind of mutual vengeance. A transaction of pain. She moaned my name. Clawed my back. Pulled my lip between her teeth like she wanted to take a piece of me with her.

And for a second, I let her.

After, I sat on the edge of the bed, pulling my jeans back on. My shirt was wrinkled on the floor. I didn't say anything. Didn't look at her. Tasha sat up against the headboard, watching me with eyes too clear for someone who was supposed to be casual about this.

"You can't even look at me," she said, laughing to soften the seriousness of her question.

I stayed quiet.

"You think I don't know what this was?" she asked. "You think you're the first man to climb into my bed just to spite the woman he actually wants?"

I finally looked at her. She wasn't mad. Just tired.

"Tasha, I" I started before she cut me off.

"You don't have to explain," she said. "I saw the way the two of you looked at each other in the club. I know I'm not her. I don't need the pretty version of the truth."

"That's not what I was going to say," I said.

"That's the problem with your type," she replied. "You never do, but you leave a mess anyway."

I grabbed my shirt. She didn't stop me. Just watched me with those sharp, unflinching eyes. The kind that saw too much and asked for nothing. My hand hovered near the doorknob. Then I turned it.

"I don't want to leave a mess this time," I said.

Her brow arched, skeptical. "What does that mean?"

"It means," I hesitated, the words bitter on my tongue even before they left. "Maybe I need to try something different."

"Different how?"

"I don't know. Something easy. Low-maintenance."

She snorted. "So, you're here to make me your low-maintenance rebound?"

"Chill," I said, laughing. "That's not what I meant. What I'm trying to say is that maybe I need someone who doesn't need saving. Just a place to land."

She crossed her arms. "And that place is me?"

"I don't know," I admitted. "But I don't want to leave this how I left everything else."

She studied me a long beat. "If you're looking for safe, I'm not that. But I am clear."

I nodded. "That's more than I've had in a long time."

A heavy pause filled the space between us.

She didn't smile. She didn't soften. But she looked toward the dim light of her bedroom, and said, "Let's start with breakfast in the morning."

That made me crack a laugh. Not because it was funny, but because it gave me just enough room to breathe. That would have to be enough for now. But as I laid back on her bed, her hand grazing a fiery trail up my ribs and over the lily tattoo on my chest, the ache didn't leave. I was building something new. But the blueprints were soaked in grief. And whether Tasha knew it or not, she was stepping into a house haunted by another woman's name.

Fuck.

Chapter 23

Kelly

T̲HE SILENCE CAME FIRST.

It slipped through the cracks after Khalil left, curling into the corners of my apartment, settling on my skin like a thin sheet draped over the furniture of an abandoned house. It was in the shadows behind my TV. In the hum of the refrigerator. In the hollowed-out breath I didn't realize I'd been holding since the door closed behind him. I thought I could outrun the noise.

For days, that turned into weeks, movies played in the background while I reviewed patient files. Music blasted while I took showers and got ready for work. I thought maybe if I filled the room with enough noise, I could drown out the words I didn't say. But even through the distractions, the silence stayed. Along with the weight in my chest and the ache beating the backs of my eyes.

I reached for my phone. The first message I sent not too long after the door closed behind him was short.

ME

Let me know when you make it home.

I waited hours for a reply. Nothing.

ME

You made it home safe?

I know I hurt you.

I didn't mean to. I just…

I didn't know what else to do.

Still nothing.

ME

Thank you for coming. I'm sorry it ended the way it did. I wish I could go back. Say things differently.

Say everything differently.

I'm sorry.

I'm so sorry. Please forgive me.

The read receipts popped up. I waited for the three dots to appear. They never did. Not that day or the next. Not that week, or the week that followed. Only messages I received were from my girls, updates from the hospital, words of encouragement from Aunt Viv and Lisa. My father called me when he had a question about something in the house. I let him talk to voicemail. Even my Uncle PJ managed to check-in once or twice.

After leaving the hospital for the day, I prepared myself for the routine FaceTime with Vanessa, Nyah, and Lynn. I was genuinely happy. For a few hours, my apartment would feel less like a tomb. Nyah picked up first, TJ hanging off her back as she put him down for bed. Vanessa followed, her face a tad bit swollen, belly poking a bit more from the last few pictures she sent me. Lynn was last to join, sipping a glass of wine, contracts in her hand.

"Damn," Lynn said gently. "You look…"

"Like I been through what I been through," I offered. "I know."

Vanessa rubbed her belly as she looked on. I didn't doubt she'd already heard Khalil's version of events. I wouldn't put it past him to vent to Xavier over a few beers.

Nyah tilted her head. "What happened?"

I didn't sugarcoat it. I told them about Khalil surprising me. About finding Jordan here in what should've been his space. I detailed the subsequent argument. The daggers we'd thrown with our words. I traced the painful steps of his departure, seeing his back walk toward the elevators head down, disappointed, heart shattered. Quiet, final, like turning a page that couldn't be unturned. They listened. They always did.

Nyah was the first to speak. "You were wrong."

"Excuse me?" I wasn't shocked she felt that way. More so stunned to hear it outside of the recorder that played in my head every day since Khalil left, giving credence to them.

"You were wrong," she said again. "Khalil may not be perfect, but that man showed up. For years. You pushed him away, and for what?"

Vanessa nodded, slower. "You've been spiraling, Kelly. We've been trying to give you space. We get it. But pain doesn't give you permission to wreck people you love."

My throat tightened. "I didn't mean to. I just wanted to feel something other than pain, if only for one night."

"We know you didn't mean to," Lynn said, softly but firmly. "We know anytime you pry into our lives, you never mean to. But you still have to be accountable."

I wanted to hang up. Wanted to disappear into my sheets and pretend none of this was happening. But I stayed. Because I needed to hear it, even if I hated every word.

"I'm trying to take accountability. I've called so many times, I've lost count. I've texted. I've said I'm sorry. He won't respond." The familiar burn in my eyes started again.

I noticed the uneasy way they looked at each other. The

unspoken words they fought to keep from me. Lynn sipped her wine and Nyah poured her a glass.

"What is it?"

Vanessa gulped before she spoke, peering over her shoulder. "I think Khalil's trying to move on."

"Move on? What?" I sat up. My ears burned. My nervous system went into overdrive. Little pricks of sweat touched my armpits.

"Tell her about lunch today, Nessa," Lynn piped up.

"Yeah, Nessa. Tell me about lunch," I urged.

She looked worried. Like whatever information she had threatened to push me over the ledge. She bit her lower lip, hesitating.

"Nessa, spill it," I said, clipped.

She exhaled. "I met up with Zay and Khalil for lunch. He seemed fine, I guess. I asked if he'd talked to you. He said no. We ordered, started talking about the community center renovations. Then he got a call. I knew it had to be a girl by the way he was smiling. I honestly thought it was you. Clearly, it wasn't. When he got off the phone, he said someone was about to pull through. Maybe fifteen minutes later, this girl, short, not gonna lie, she was cute, walks up to our table."

"Kelly, it was the girl from the club. Tasha," Lynn added, lowered the documents in her hand.

What could I say? What could I fucking say? Nothing. I could only blame myself. I half-listened as Vanessa recounted the interaction. I heard the drumming of my heart swell in my ears. Nyah, Lynn, and Vanessa dissected the interaction between Khalil and his new interest with precision. They swore up and down it was just a rebound. That he was just trying to get over what took place between us. Reassured me that once he got the hurt out of his system, he'd reach out. But I knew better. He was gone.

I fucked up.

I wanted to scream it. Cry it. Wail the words until my voice went hoarse. But I couldn't. Instead, I shut down. It was muscle-memory at this point. I'd perfected the art of disappearing without leaving. I'd mastered tucking the hurt deep behind a practiced smile. My teachers were those who gave birth to me. A mother who thought staying quiet meant strength. A father who absorbed the world around him and left nothing for anyone else. A life that never asked how I felt, instead expected me to cope.

As my friends continued gossiping and cackling, I smiled. Laughed at the right jokes. Added the necessary *"I know that's right,"* and *"Girl, I know you lying."* But inside, I was collapsing. My heart didn't ache anymore. It buzzed with a warning I kept ignoring. I paddled my boat made of denial and let the waves of grief carry me away.

Khalil was gone.

My mother was gone.

My childhood was gone long before them both. And now there was just me. Glass-coated and untouchable. A pretty picture in a cracked frame.

We wrapped up our call well past their bedtime. The sun was just beginning to set in Seattle. I stayed on the couch, watching the city buzz beneath me. A knock sounded at my door. I looked through the peephole, seeing a delivery person. I opened the door.

"Hi, I'm Margaret with Pet Pals. Are you Kelly Reid?" The woman held an animal crate in her arms. Her smile beamed bright in the hallway.

"Yes, I'm sorry, but I think you may be mistaken. I've never heard of a Pet Pals."

"Well, this invoice says I'm supposed to drop this off here." She placed the crate on the floor, then kneeled out to grab the whimpering animal inside. A French bulldog puppy. Fawn-colored. Big ears. A little blue collar with a note that read:

So you're not lonely when I head back. -K

"Someone loves you very much. It was no easy feat getting this cute thing here." She placed the puppy in my arms. We stared at each other, its round eyes blinking at me like I was its whole world. "I've got you set up with some food. My partner is on the way up with some other supplies. Little fella is trained, but we'll stay a bit to show you the ropes."

As Margaret and her partner set up all the extra equipment–puppy crate with a plush bed, water bowl, stored its foodI held the puppy in my arms. In a matter of hours, my apartment had gone from feeling empty to buzzing with energy. The puppy licked my arms as we got acquainted with each other. Eventually, Margaret and her partner wrapped up setting us up.

"His food will be delivered twice a month. Subscription's paid for the next six months. Also, you have a training package. Just give us a call to set up the dates and time that work for you. I believe Mr. Grant said you were a doctor?"

"Yes, yes, I am."

"Fancy," she cheered. She scratched behind the puppy's ears, still in my arms. "What are you thinking about naming him?"

"I don't know. I wasn't expecting this."

She and her partner laughed. "Well, don't take too long. You'll want to have a name when you start your training sessions." They walked to the door and said their goodbyes.

I held the French bulldog eye level with me. He yawned and ran a tongue across his mouth and nose. "Are you as tired as I am?" He whimpered in response. I placed him in the crate set up by the large windows of the living room, tucking him into the soft bed. He nuzzled himself into the soft comfort and half-closed his eyes.

I tried to call Khalil. Three times.

Straight to voicemail.

～

THE DOG, now named Karter, followed me everywhere. I couldn't pee without him crying on the other side of the door. Couldn't leave for work without him losing his mind. He made it harder to stay numb. When I worked on the couch, he watched from his crate by the window with perked ears and curious eyes. I envied his blank slate. He didn't know heartbreak, didn't know grief, didn't know what it meant to lose someone who wanted to love you but couldn't hold your weight. He just wanted a good belly rub and a bowl of food. He cried when I left and wagged his tail when I returned.

I used to be like that once.

Before I learned that some people walk away not because they stop loving you, but because loving you hurts too much.

Karter filled a space I didn't know I needed filling. Whereas before, we interacted with him in his cage and me on the couch. He slowly became my couch companion. One night, after cooking and eating dinner, I curled up on the couch, phone in my hand, Karter asleep beside me, and scrolled through the pictures of us on my phone. *We are so cute.*

I kept scrolling, looking at old pictures. I stopped at one. Me, blurry in a hoodie. Khalil, shirtless, brushing his teeth, smirking in the mirror. I scrolled to another. A photo of the chicken soup he made me when I had the flu last year. I stopped at another. We were tangled up on his couch, me asleep, him staring down at me as if I were his entire world. I'd snuck and shared the picture from my phone to his.

I tried calling again.

Voicemail.

I picked up Karter and nuzzled his head, placing him on his puppy bed to sleep for the night. I got into the shower, rinsed the day off, and fell into my own slumber.

Things started picking up at the hospital. I started showing up better. Not because I was okay, but because I had to be focused to survive the day. I dove into charts, into rotations, into everything except my feelings. Dr. Sayegh noticed.

"You're sharper this week," she said, nodding after rounds.

I nodded back. "Trying to be."

I was surviving. The feeling lasted for five seconds.

Because my first patient died.

His name was George. Six-years-old. Acute lymphoblastic leukemia. He loved Spider-Man and wore him on his socks every day. He insisted on calling me "Dr. Kelly Belly" because he thought it was the funniest thing in the world. Every time he said it, he burst into a fit of giggles like it was brand-new. I never corrected him.

His numbers had been slipping for days. We knew that. I knew that. But there was nothing emergent. His vitals were stable. He'd just been cleared to move from ICU back to the oncology floor. He'd been coloring with his mom that night. Laughing.

The next morning, he was gone.

Massive intracranial hemorrhage. Sudden. Irreversible. No warning. No time. I stared at his chart for ten minutes after they called time of death, flipping through labs, notes, med logs, vitals, looking for anything I might've missed. A decimal. A flag. A feeling. I'd followed protocol. Double-checked everything. I did all the right things. And it still happened. I didn't realize I was crying until a tear hit the page.

I don't remember how I ended up in the stairwell. I just remember the cold concrete against my spine and the sting of salt on my cheeks. I was folded in on myself, arms crossed tight over my stomach like I was holding my insides in place.

Dr. Sayegh found me there. She didn't knock. Didn't announce herself. Just sat down beside me like she knew I'd be exactly where she'd been once.

"You can't win them all, Dr. Reid," she said quietly.

I shook my head. "But he deserved to live."

"They all deserve to live. There was nothing you could've done."

My voice was weak. "Then why does it feel like I failed?"

She looked at me, eyes steady and soft. "Because you're the kind of doctor who takes it personally. That's a gift and a burden. It's why I picked you."

I wiped my eyes with the sleeve of my white coat, which suddenly felt heavy. A weight I hadn't earned. "I did everything right," I said. "I charted, I escalated concerns, I followed protocol. I knew he was fragile. I didn't miss anything."

"You didn't," she said. "Sometimes, things still go wrong. And that's what no one tells you when you sign up for this job." Dr. Sayegh reached over, touched my wrist gently. "You're one of the best fellows I've ever trained. You're sharp. Precise. Intuitive. But you're cracking under the pressure, Kelly."

I stared ahead at the stairwell, my jaw clenched so hard it ached.

"I'm fine, Dr. Sayegh. I just–"

"You're trying to outrun the break. I can see it. The perfection. The overcompensating. You think if you hold everything together, you can avoid it. But it'll still happen. It always does."

"Dr. Sayegh, I promise I'm fine."

She held a hand up to silence me. "You're not fine, Kelly. You're hanging on by a thread. I need you focused in this hospital. Fully. I can't have you here operating through a fog. So, I'm asking. No. I'm telling you to take some time off."

I wiped my eyes again, inhaled then exhaled. "Fine. I'll take the rest of the week. I'll be back Monday, ready to go."

She shook her head side to side, standing. "I'm placing you on required leave of absence. At least a month. At that time, we'll map out a return to work plan, contingent upon clearance from a licensed therapist."

"Why are you punishing me?"

"You're not being punished," she added gently. "You're being preserved."

I left the hospital after speaking with HR, a numbness settling into my bones. The world outside didn't care that a little boy died. It was still sunny. People smiled. Laughed. Lived. I wanted to scream at them. How dare you? Don't you know the world stopped?

I walked Karter through the same three blocks that became our routine loop. Past a yoga studio. Past Still + Stirred. He barked at a crow. I didn't stop him. When we got back to our apartment, there was a knock on the door. I wasn't expecting anyone. I opened it slowly.

A delivery man stood there with a potted plant. A peace lily. Bright green, tall, blooming.

"Kelly Reid?"

I nodded, confused.

He held it out gently, like it was a newborn.

"Someone sent this for you."

"Who?"

"No note."

He handed over the pot, tipped his hat, then left. I stood there in the doorway for too long, clutching another living thing I didn't ask for. Karter nipped at my heels as I closed the door, locking it behind me. I placed the pot on the coffee table. Karter sniffed it, sneezed, then trotted back to his cage. The plant sat there, glowing green against the shadows of the apartment.

It felt offensive.

I went into the kitchen to fix Karter's food and water. Then I glanced back. The plant stared at me. Alive. Steady. Needing things. Things I didn't have the capacity to give. I couldn't breathe. The walls were closing in. That little girl on the boat screamed. I tripped over Karter's water bowl, stepping into the spilled water. Something in me finally gave out.

I turned, grabbed the lily, and hurled it at the wall. The crash was sharp, immediate. Karter yelped from his cage. Ceramic exploded into shards. Soil spilled like blood. Leaves bent, broke, and curled; the stems snapped in half.

My knees buckled. I hit the floor hard. My hands tingled. My arms wouldn't move. My chest wouldn't expand. I was breathing. I had to be. But I couldn't feel it.

I tried to scream, but my jaw locked. My fingers clawed at the floor, desperate for something to ground me.

What's happening? What's happening?

The ceiling tilted. The air was thick. My heart slammed against my ribs hard as I pleaded with it to stop. I reached for my phone. Crawled across the floor, ceramic shards digging into my knees. I called Vanessa. No answer. Nyah. Voicemail. Lynn. Nothing. I pressed the last name in my call history. One I'd declined since being in Seattle.

"Hello?" my father's voice crackled through the line, sleep coating it. "Kelly?"

I couldn't speak. Just wheezed.

"Baby girl?" he asked again. His tone shifted. Panicked. "Kelly-girl, what's wrong?"

"I–I c-can't–" I gasped, the words broken. "I can't–breathe–I don't–know–dying."

"Okay. It's okay," he said, fully alert. "You're okay, baby girl. It's probably a panic attack. You're not dying. Listen to me, baby girl. Breathe with Daddy, okay. Just in and out, slow like when you were little and had nightmares. Remember?"

I clutched the phone like it was oxygen. My vision blurred as I struggled to breathe.

"Kelly, you hear me? In. One, two, three. Out. One, two, three."

My breath hitched. All my years of medical training were out the window. I clawed at my throat as the burn engulfed my chest. I managed to croak out, "Daddy...help."

"I'm booking a flight right now. You hear me? I'm coming."

The sobs came ugly, heaving, full-bodied bellows from the pits of my soul.

"Help," I gasped, choking on the words. "I'm...Scared... Alone."

"You're not alone," he reassured. "Daddy's coming. I'll be there soon. I got you. Your daddy's got you."

And for the first time in what felt like ever. I believed him.

Part Three

"I'm Tired (From "Euphoria"
An Original HBO Series)"

Labrinth • Zendaya

Chapter 24

Kelly

HE WAS TRUE TO HIS WORD. I'D STAYED ON THE PHONE with my dad until the tears subsided and I gained control of my breathing. He stayed on, giving me instructions to settle what little nerves I had left until I was safely tucked into my bed. Karter snuggled on top of the comforter by my feet. I dozed off to sounds of the airport–intercom announcements, beeping alarms. I remembered waking once and hearing my dad say he'd be there by the time I woke up.

And here he was. I didn't open the door right away. I could see his chest through the peephole, standing there in a navy windbreaker set, holding a carry-on suitcase, looking...small. Smaller than I remembered. His shoulders hunched slightly, wearied by what became of his life over the past few months. His mouth pressed into a thin, uncertain line surrounded by a beard and mustache that was more salt than pepper. My father, the man who used to walk into rooms like he was owed applause, now stood at my door like he wasn't sure I'd let in.

Karter barked once at my feet. Even he could sense the change in my energy.

I opened the door.

He smiled, cautious but relieved. "Hey, Kelly-girl."

I nodded and stepped aside so he could enter.

The moment he crossed the threshold, something in me wanted to run. Crash into his arms like I was a little girl again. Let him take care of the big bad terrorizing my mind, my heart, my soul. Instead, he dropped his carry-on, walked in front of me, and wrapped his arms around my shoulders, a hand holding my head to his chest. I broke down for the second time. He held me up but never told me to stop or be strong.

I calmed down after a few minutes. He stepped back, leaving a whiskered kiss on my forehead. He looked around the apartment slowly, like he was memorizing the place. "Your mama said this was a nice place. Threatened to get herself a unit if I didn't stop complaining about you coming out here." He laughed off.

I gave a lackluster sigh. "Thanks."

He knelt down and scratched behind Karter's ears. "Who's this little gremlin?"

"He's not a gremlin." I smiled, sniffling.

"He look like one," he teased. "A gremlin wearing a velvet hoodie." Karter began attacking my dad's ankles, knowing he'd just been insulted. Despite myself, I laughed. Just a little. And my dad smiled like he'd been holding his breath waiting to hear it.

The first few hours were mostly quiet. He rifled through my kitchen cabinets and fridge, looking for something to make breakfast. He'd started a pot of coffee, then realized I had not a drop of creamer or sugar. He had me get dressed so we could go out, mumbling away at nothing as he waited. With Karter on a leash, we walked to Still + Stirred, ordered our drinks, then sat in a booth in front of the window and drank. We didn't talk about the panic attack. Didn't talk about Mama. We focused on Karter's antics as he demolished a pup cup, smiling and laughing as my baby licked the cup clean. Eventually, Karter curled up under the table, his leash wrapped around my ankle. He snored softly, as if he hadn't had a care in the world. I stared into my half-filled mug.

"What's going on, baby girl?" my father asked, finally looking up from his cup.

I shook my head and shrugged my shoulders, staring out of the window. "I'm just tired, I suppose. I haven't gotten adjusted yet. I'll be okay."

He peered at me, knowing the truth laid buried somewhere but deciding which tool to use to dig it out of me. "You don't get panic attacks from just being tired. It's written all over your face, Kelly. Tell me what's going on."

I swallowed the knot in my throat and exhaled. "They're making me take a leave." I winced, blinking back the sting in my eyes.

"Who is?"

"My attending," I said, clearing my throat. "I'm not in trouble. I didn't do anything wrong. She just...highly suggested it. Because I've been off."

He nodded once, slowly taking a sip. "You agree with her?"

"No." I shrugged. "I mean, maybe...I don't know."

"Kelly."

"What," I said, louder and sharper than I intended. He set his mug down and met my gaze. I saw the hurt, the way he bit back the words he wanted to match mine. He inhaled once, then let out the breath as he stared out of the window, then down at Karter, dozing away.

"I should've told you to put off starting after your mother passed."

"Daddy, that has nothing to do with this. I'm just tired. I'm not spiraling because she's gone." I sighed, leaning back and crossing my arms.

"You said it, not me," he replied, calm as ever. "And I agree. You can't keep going like that didn't happen. Why do you think I haven't been back to the clinic?"

I didn't respond. I got lost in the swirl of foam and cinnamon around the rim of my mug.

"So, what now? How long are you on leave?"

"A month minimum. Says I have to get clearance from a therapist first, then they'll put together a transition plan. I'll catch up on tv and reading in the meantime."

"Still think you know everything. You got it honest." He chuckled softly. "I think you need to come home," he said, sipping from the cup.

"Daddy, I can't. I still need to finish my fellowship."

"I don't mean for good. Just while you're on this leave. Come be around people who know you. Viv and Lisa been driving me crazy making sure you okay."

"You told them?" I rolled my eyes and smacked my teeth. *Now everyone will know.*

"Well, when you put out a bat signal, you have to know everyone gonna try to come running." He laughed. "I promise I won't convince you to stay. I think it'll do you some good being around your friends. Your family. I'm sure Karter won't mind being spoiled."

I didn't answer right away. "I think so, too." I looked down into my cup, swirled it slowly.

"I'm glad you called me, baby girl," he said finally.

"I didn't have anyone else to call."

"That still counts," he replied.

The rest of the day was spent planning for me to fly back home. While I called to have Karter's food and medicines shipped to my parents' house in Houston, he and my father played around in the living room. While I packed, they wrestled on the floor. Later that night, we sat on the couch, eating from take-out containers.

"I'm sorry, baby girl," he said. "I'm sorry for how you had to grow up strong, dealing with me and your mama's bullshit. How tired it made you."

I finished the bite of Kung Pao chicken I had in my mouth,

washing it down with red wine. "Tired doesn't cover it," I finally replied.

"I should've been more aware. Especially after your mama passed on." His voice broke. I looked over at him. Tears filled his eyes. "I saw you breaking in the hospital. At the funeral. But I was too caught up in my own mess to remember I needed to be there for you."

I put the container of food in my lap on the coffee table. He did the same.

"For the past few months, I've been thinking, how could I have been better for y'all? Given you and your mother the life y'all deserved. Hearing you on the phone last night, and when you opened the door this morning." He shook his head side to side. "What did I instill in you to bring you to that point? To make you think you couldn't come to me."

"You left me with silence," I said. He didn't flinch. "You left me with a blueprint for emotional avoidance. I grew up in a house where no one said sorry. No one named their pain. Just tension and closed doors and long dinners with you and Mama either bickering or so caught up in each other you forgot I was there."

"I'm sorry, baby girl," he whispered.

"And I mirrored it. As much as I tried not to, I did. Took it with me into every room. Every relationship. And now, I don't know how to stop."

He didn't defend himself. Didn't shrink from the truth. He just reached for my hand, slowly, like he was asking permission without speaking. I let him take it. His palm was rougher than I remembered.

"I can't fix what I did wrong," he said. "But I'm gonna show up now. If you'll let me."

I swallowed, then nodded. He pulled me close, tapping his hand on my arm. I felt a version of safety I never knew I needed. My father, holding my hand, in the stillness.

∽

THE FLIGHT HOME WAS EASY. Karter snored in his carry-on crate under the seat in front of me. My dad read medical journals in the seat beside me, used the airplane Wi-Fi to look up therapists in Houston. I stared out the window at clouds that looked like bruises, my heart too tired to be anything but still. When we landed, the Houston heat slapped me in the face. The airport smelled like pollution, concrete, and despair.

We pulled into the circle drive of my parents' home just past dusk. The lights trailing the walkway from the driveway to the front door left a soft orange glow. Karter barked once in the back-seat. I stared at the house. At one point, I ran from it like it might swallow me whole. Every time I visited, the walls seemed to close in tighter. Now, it looked suffocating, a cage dressed up as a shell of a home. Familiar, but heavy with silence. A mausoleum of memories I never buried right.

My father cut the engine and glanced over at me. "They're here."

"Who's they?"

"You'll see."

It was then I noticed the extra cars lining the drive. I opened the car door and was instantly hit with the sound of familiar voices.

"Surprise!" Vivian and Lisa stood near the steps, both grinning like I was ten-years-old again. They rushed over and embraced me, showering kisses on my face. Nyah stood in the doorway with a glass of wine in one hand, a phone in the other. Vanessa waddled over with a glow that could only belong to a woman nearing the end of her pregnancy and the peak of peace, even though I saw the fretful worry in her eyes. Lynn, dressed in all-black, waved next to Nyah.

My throat tightened. I wasn't ready for this. But I needed it more than I wanted to admit.

There was gumbo on the stove and a random bowl of potato salad sweating on the counter next to it. The kitchen smelled like what welcome used to mean. Karter padded through every corner of the living room like it was his now, sniffing discarded shoes and swiping licks at everyone's ankles, wagging his tail like he'd been here all along.

I sank into the couch between Lynn and Nyah, a pillow shielding my lap, my hands balled into the sleeves of my hoodie.

"We missed you," Nyah said, pressing a kiss to my shoulder. "We came to see if you still know how to smile."

"I smile," I mumbled.

"Girl, that was not a smile. That was a polite exhale," Vanessa teased, spooning a combination of gumbo and potato salad into her mouth.

I rolled my eyes, but my lips twitched. "What happened to the juices?"

"I gave that up about two months ago. This baby wants some real food," she said, eating another bite. "Mama, can you bring me some more potato salad? Your grandchild can't get enough."

Vivian walked in with Vanessa's request and a photo album I hadn't seen in years.

"Kenneth found this cleaning out a closet. Thought you might want to flip through."

I opened it on instinct, and there we were—me in pigtails, my mama in a headwrap, my dad younger, tighter in the jaw, a little less round in the waist. Our faces frozen in moments I had forgotten I remembered. Happiness.

Nyah leaned over. "Our mamas loved them thick barrettes, huh?"

"The beads, too," I said.

"And the white socks with the lace ruffles!" Lynn cackled. "Somebody's Easter's best."

Everyone laughed. I forgot the heaviness for a moment. Forgot the grief. Forgot the letters and the silence and the exhaustion. I just sat there, surrounded by people who loved me, letting joy sneak in through the cracks, curling up beside me like a warm hand on a cold shoulder.

Later that night, when the dishes were stacked in the dishwasher to dry and the laughter had softened into yawns, I laid in my childhood bed, in a room too small for the woman I'd become and too big for the girl I used to be. The wallpaper hadn't changed. The photos of me in awkward braces and honor roll sashes were on the walls like they were tired of pretending, too. A soft hum came from the ceiling fan. Karter slept at the foot of the bed. I was surrounded by history. By memories. And by my girls.

Nyah and Lynn were sprawled on the floor with wine and snacks like it was high school all over again. Vanessa stretched out on the bed, rubbing her belly in circles, eyes half-closed in peace.

"How are you really doing, Kelly?" Lynn asked.

"I'm not okay," I said. "There's a hole I can't seem to fill, and I just want to not be okay for a while."

"That's real," Nyah whispered. "Losing your mother is hard. There's a piece of you you'll never get back. That void, it never fills. You just learn to deal with it. Learn to live with it."

"I'm just mad," I confessed. "So fucking angry. I don't want to feel this way forever."

"Feel however you need to feel," Vanessa said, patting the blanket.

We stayed like that until the wine disappeared and the conversation drifted into soft laughter and yawns you fought because you didn't want the night to end. "I can't believe I wasted my time on that boy. All he had going was a pretty smile." Lynn smirked, pouring herself another glass of wine. "It doesn't matter, because my dream man is right around the corner. I can feel it."

"Lynn." Nyah laughed. "How can you be so sure?"

Lynn took a sip and pondered Nyah's question, then said, "Delusion." We all collapsed into giggles.

"Lynn, you say that after every breakup. At this point, every man you come across is your dream man." I shook my head, leaning back to rub Vanessa's belly.

"I can't help I'm a lover girl. It's not my fault I can't keep them off me." She pouted.

Vanessa raised a brow. "And yet you fend off Wesley like a stray cat."

Lynn rolled her eyes. "That's because Wesley's annoying. Always talking in riddles like I'm supposed to understand his smart-ass haikus."

"But you have noticed the haikus," I teased. "At least once."

She waved me off but kept smiling. "Come on, y'all know Wesley's a grade-A, silver-spoon, asshole. He just hates me less than everyone else."

Nyah snorted. "Girl, he'd carry you across hot coals if you'd let him."

"And risk messing up his custom leather Louboutins. Girl, please."

I looked over at Nyah. Her head swayed from a muted melody as she twisted the hem of her shirt and drank her wine. "What about you?" I asked gently. "You good?"

She paused, training her eyes on something outside the window. "I suppose. I'll be better when you're good."

"You heard from Maverick?" Vanessa asked, nonchalant, but eyes curious.

Nyah blinked. "Why would I have heard from Mav?"

Lynn and I exchanged a look. "Because he stares at you like you're the sun to his moon," she answered for the both of us.

Nyah laughed, shaking her head. "That man is not checking for me like that. And did y'all forget, I'm married. I do have a husband. Y'all were in the wedding." We didn't press because we knew better. I supposed we all had our own delusional worlds we'd constructed to keep us from avoiding reality.

Vanessa shifted on the bed. "Khalil asked if he should come tonight."

I stilled. "He did?"

"Yeah, but I didn't know how you'd feel, so I told him maybe it wasn't for the best."

"Good," I said with no emotion. "He's doing his thing. I don't want to drag him back into my mess." No one said anything but I felt their questions pressing on me like the thick comforter we shared. "I just need time…To figure out how to be me again."

Lynn raised her glass. "To figuring shit out."

"To shedding dead weight," Nyah added, wetness filling her eyes.

"To whatever comes next," Vanessa said, rubbing her belly, catching the tear that fell down Nyah's cheek. We clinked our glasses and drank. For a moment, the ghosts quieted.

Lynn yawned dramatically before dragging herself off the bed with promises to call tomorrow. Nyah hugged me tight, resting her forehead against mine for a beat longer than normal. When my bedroom door clicked shut behind them, the room fell into a hush. Vanessa stayed behind, fluffing the pillows on my bed, as if they were hers.

"I'm spending the night," she said, getting comfortable under the covers.

I laughed. "What does Zay say about that?"

"If he knows what's good for him, he won't say anything," she fired back with a laugh. "Besides, he said the words before I had a chance to open my mouth. Already had my bag packed." We leaned back into the bed. She wrapped her arms around me as we settled in for the night.

"Thank you," I whispered into the pillows.

"You'll be okay," she whispered back, rubbing my back. "You're already on your way."

Chapter 25

Kelly

THE NEXT MORNING, I WOKE UP LATER THAN I MEANT to. Karter was curled up next to me, snoring soft little huffs. Vanessa's spot on the bed was empty. I picked up my phone, seeing her message and a few missed calls.

NESSA BOO

Headed to the studio. Call me when you get up.

Eventually, I made it to my childhood desk. It still had the faint pink shimmer nail polish stain from when I was thirteen. I swore I grew up to be a beauty guru. The top drawer squeaked when I opened it and there, nestled in the back corner, was the letter. The envelope was thick, luxury cardstock. My name scribbled on the front. My mother's handwriting. I stared at it for a full minute before I picked it up.

I didn't know what to expect—something angry, maybe. Something stoic. A last lesson. But it was... tender. Honest. Like her voice was echoing right over my shoulder.

To my sweet Kelly-girl,

If you're reading this, it means you've done something I should've done a long time ago. Find a love so pure and soft and sweet, you don't know what to do with it. I won't pretend I've been the best example. I stayed too long in something that didn't pour into me, and I wore my regret like armor, thinking it was strength. I forced you to watch me shrink inside myself, calling it love. I'm so sorry, my sweet girl.

But I'm writing this letter to let you know, I see you. Even when you think I don't. I admire your brilliance, your confidence, even when the world asked too much of you too soon. It makes me feel like I've done something right. However, you deserve a mother who leads with her whole heart, not just the pieces she thinks are acceptable. I'm still learning how to be her, if only for you.

What I know now, and what I need you to believe, is that love shouldn't feel like labor. You're not supposed to fight to earn it. You shouldn't fold yourself or carry it alone. The love I want for you, and hope you've found, is a gentle, quiet confidence. It's someone who sees your storms—you know the ones you work so hard to hide, but Mommy knows best— and chooses to stay anyway.

At this point in time, I don't know who this man is, but I have my suspicions. I see the way he looks at you whenever we visit MawMaw. I get tickled watching the way your face soften when you talk to him, even when you hit him with some sassy remark. Oh, and that little nickname he gave you, "Lily-Girl." Too cute. Okay, I'm done.

My sweet girl, wherever life takes, my hope is this. Choose softness, even when it scares you. Let someone hold you, not for what you do, but for who you are. You are enough and more. You always were from the moment I knew you were coming into my life.

I love you. Fully. Fiercely. Always.

Mommy

I didn't remember crying. Just the sound of my breath shaking in the quiet room. Then the creak of the door. My father stood in the doorway. I turned, the letter shaking in my hand. "She wrote me a letter."

He nodded. "I remember when I walked in on her, Viv, and Lisa doing that. You must've been around twelve or thirteen."

I clutched it to my chest. "I don't want to be broken anymore."

He walked over, knelt beside me, and took my hands into his. "You're not broken, baby girl," he said. "You're just a little bruised. And tired. But never broken."

"I don't know what to do with all this pain." I used the sleeve of my hoodie to wipe the tears from my eyes.

"You start by not holding it by yourself."

I looked down.

"I found somebody for you to talk to," he said. "Tell me you'll go?"

I nodded slowly.

I didn't argue.

THE OFFICE SMELLED like eucalyptus and something earthy I couldn't place. The walls were painted in warm browns and soft creams. A large window opened up to a garden full of sage and lavender. There was a faint hum in the air, like the room was still breathing even when I wasn't.

Her name was Ms. Reece.

She was in her fifties, maybe sixties. Dark skinned. Freshly pressed silver hair swooped over her forehead, curly and waving down her shoulders. A caftan that looked like it told stories. She didn't stand when I walked in. Just smiled.

"Welcome, baby," she said, like we'd met in a dream. "What brings you in today?"

"I need to get clearance so I can go back to work."

"Okay, straight to the point, I see." She looked me over, her eyes narrowing, a tight smile gracing her lips. "Why else are we here today?"

"I'm tired of feeling nothing and everything."

I sat on the couch. Tense. Clutching my palms together like they were the only thing holding me up. She watched me, like she already knew my story. The gaze made me wrap my arms around my stomach, stretch away the tension creeping into my shoulders.

"Hmph. You carry your trauma in your stomach," she said gently. "Right in that center. That's why it hurts when you sit still too long. Travels up your spine, coiling in your shoulders. You tense to keep from crying."

My eyes widened, then my brow raised. "How?"

"Our bodies speak even when we don't. Now. Let's get quiet and let it speak."

We didn't talk much. She guided me through breathing. Through movement. Through stillness. She touched my back, one palm between my shoulder blades, and told me to breathe into the spot where my mama used to rub when I was sick. I didn't think I could cry again. But I was. Not sobbing. Not loud. Just tears that poured quietly without shame. When I was done, I felt emptied. Wrung out. Like a bell that had finally been struck.

"I'm sorry," I whispered.

"Don't apologize for your pain. That's like telling yourself it's wrong for you to have feelings," she said. "I'm telling you now, I'm not clearing you until I'm sure you're ready. But you've started the journey. These first few sessions will be tough, but I have no doubt you'll persevere."

I wasn't ready to go back to my parents' house after meeting Ms. Reece. I drove around, hoping to clear my mind. No music. No destination. Just silence and streetlights. *I need tacos. And tequila.* I stopped at my old spot. The smell of carne asada hitting the grill in the back sent my stomach grumbling. I slid into a booth, placed my order with the waitress, and bobbed my head as Selena's light, aching voice rose above the sizzle of the grill as she sung about the wilting of a flower and a love gone too soon. I leaned back against the booth, letting the song wrap around me.

When the waitress brought my tequila sunrise, my fingers traced the condensation running down the sides of the glass, breathing for the first time in a long time.

The chime above the door jingled, but I paid it little attention. I sipped from my drink, the sweet, citrus flavors zinging my tongue. My shoulders swayed along with the velvet-smooth voice crooning a song so tender and tragic, the prayer-like words threatened to crack the glass in my hands. I knew none of the words, aside from "amor eterno," but it didn't keep me from feeling them. So I danced, closed my eyes, and let the music carry me away to something other than numbness and survival.

And that was when I felt it. The shift. A heat pressing into the space before I opened my eyes.

And then I saw him.

Khalil.

He stood before me, waiting for permission to enter the little sliver of peace I'd created since sitting down. He wore a chocolate brown, long-sleeve knit sweater that hugged the width of his chest, tucked neatly into camel-colored trousers that draped just right over glossy loafers. His standard gold chains glinted on his neck, subtle but sure. My mouth parted, but nothing came out. My pulse drummed in my ears.

"Khalil," I started, taking a sip now that my mouth had gone dry. "What are you doing here?"

"I promised Nessa unlimited babysitting if she gave me your location." He smiled. Then he raised a brow and nodded to the booth seat across from me. "Can I sit?"

I nodded my head, taking another sip, trying to calm the storm of nerves picking up in my veins.

"You look good," he said first, voice low.

"You know how Nessa has her pregnancy glow? Well, this is grief glow," I replied, trying to smile. "You don't look terrible either."

He chuckled, dry. We both fell quiet. "What's going on, Kelly?"

"I'm sorry," I said finally, stirring my drink like it might help me find the courage I'd been avoiding. "For Seattle. For all of it. Me shutting down and blaming you in one breath. You didn't deserve that."

He looked down at the table, then back at me. Not just at me, into me. "I know."

"I wasn't myself," I added, my voice splitting as I fought to keep the tears at bay. "But I also know that's not an excuse. I hurt you. And I didn't want to. Not ever."

"I know," he said again. And it sounded like forgiveness. We sat with that. Let it settle.

"The streets say you're doing okay, though," I said, quietly.

His jaw flexed. "I'm alright," he said.

I rolled my eyes. "Tell me about Tasha."

He blinked. Didn't hide his surprise. "Let me guess. The coven told you?"

"What can I say? There's nothing we won't share with each other," I replied, laughing.

He sipped my drink. "She's not you."

I met his eyes. "She's not supposed to be."

He looked like he wanted to say something more. But instead, he leaned back in the booth and watched me like I was a song he used to love but still knew the words to. He studied me for a moment longer, then said, "I've been trying to be okay. To move on. But some people leave their imprints, no matter how hard they try not to."

I let a pause whistle between us before responding.

"I'm in therapy," I said, softly. "I'm trying to be better."

"You already are." The look he gave me; I felt in my ribs.

I exhaled.

"Can we start over?" I asked.

"Like reset?" he asked.

I smiled. "Yes." When he smiled back, my stomach flipped like it did when we were sitting in my grandmother's kitchen so many years ago. The one that made me believe in us before we ever touched.

"Then yeah," he said. "We can start over."

I smiled. "Good. Because my tacos are ready, and with the day I've had, I'm starving."

I slid out of the booth and made my way to the counter, the scent of grilled meat and warm tortillas curling around me like honey on sopapillas. The worker handed over my tray, and I laughed to myself at the extra handful of napkins they added.

As I returned to the table, a familiar pulse of beat thumped low from the speakers. The brassy notes of trumpets and syncopated drums infused the small restaurant with a burst of energy. I bounced back to the booth, then slid in and began eating.

Khalil grinned wide, raising a brow. "You know what time it is?"

I shook my head. "Forget it. I'm eating."

"Nope," he said, standing and holding out his hand. "You need to dance. Work up a real appetite. The tacos will be here when we're done, Lily-girl."

That damn nickname. My cheeks warmed. My heart fluttered. I glanced around us. The restaurant was nearly empty, save for a couple tucked in the corner and a cook mopping in the back. There wasn't a dance floor in sight, just a small gap of space between our booth and the tables a few feet away.

When I stood, he pulled me into him, one hand at my waist, the other catching my wrist and swirling me around. The tequila-warmed laugh that escaped my belly shocked my ears. Baby girl hadn't heard the sound in months.

"What you know about *Suavemente*?" he asked, his lips near my ear as we swayed in sync.

"Boy hush." I giggled out. "You don't even know what the word means."

"Bet I do," he said, cocky and sure. "Dare me to show you."

"Tell Tasha to show you." I rolled my eyes, but when he dipped me a little too low and brought me back up, holding me firm against his chest, I couldn't breathe.

We were too close.

The bass vibrated between us, but it wasn't the music that made my skin tingle. He stared down at me, licking his lips, his thumbs caressing my spine. I couldn't look away. With the way he held me and the hypnotic caress of the music, the feelings I still had for him made their way to the forefront of my heart sharp, steady, and impossible to ignore.

I pulled away first. "I'm starving."

He let me go, but not really. Something warm, something waning, something real had passed between us between each vocal trill and exclamation made by the singer.

We spent the next couple hours learning each other while basking in our history. Shared laughs, stories, and a few more appetizers. It felt good for things to be nice and easy again, like the world had paused just long enough to give us back the version of us that didn't hurt.

Eventually, his phone buzzed. He glanced down. Pressed his lips together. "I should head out." His eyes lingered on mine like he didn't really want to.

I nodded, trying not to show the sting that settled behind my ribcage. We walked out, side by side, quiet again, but not in the way we were when he first walked in. A soft breeze wound its way through the late-evening air, holding its breath just for us. The sidewalk buzzed under the streetlamps turning on now that the sun was setting. Our shadows cut across the storefront windows as we closed the distance to the nearing car lot. I felt his eyes on me. The ones that saw through the version of myself I worked hard to curate.

"I'm glad you're home, Kelly," he said softly, then gave me a smile that didn't quite reach his eyes.

"I had no choice in the matter," I replied, scratching my forehead. "I'm hoping to head back after Nessa's baby shower."

He nodded slowly, resignation settling between his brows. He and I knew the clock was ticking on the peace we'd settled into. When we got to my car, we stood there, his hand not knowing where to land. Mine gripped the thin strap of my purse to anchor me. He stuffed his hands into the pockets of his trousers, trying to keep his heart from spilling out on the concrete beneath us.

"I really am sorry," I said, the words coming out breathless. "I know I can't go back and change things, take back what I said."

Fuck.

My voice caught at the back of my throat. The tears I thought I'd left with Ms. Reece punched the backs of my eyes. I blinked hard.

"I'm sorry for hurting you. I'm sorry for not giving us a chance. I understand if things are different between us moving forward. But know... I appreciated everything you did for me. Even when you called me out on my bullshit."

A tear slipped free when I blinked.

Khalil's thumb caught it.

His hand moved so gently, like I was made of something breakable. He cradled my face in both palms like it was the only thing in the world he wanted to touch. I let myself lean into him without armor that rusted long ago.

"I'm sorry, too," he said, his voice thick and low. "For pushing too hard. For not knowing when to let go and when to just hold space."

He pulled me to his chest, and I folded into him like a love note written on notebook paper, ready to be dished off between passing periods. My arms wrapped around his waist. His scent wrapped around me–sandalwood and smoke, like the afterglow of something still burning, calling me home.

"I missed this," I whispered into his chest. "I missed you." He pulled me tighter. I felt his jaw bury into the top of my head as we stopped there locked in the embrace, neither of us wanting to be the first to let go.

"And thank you for my new bestie, Karter," I said, smiling and stepping back. I pulled my phone out and showed him the pictures of me and Karter that threatened the storage in my phone. Us on a walk. Us lounging in bed. One extremely cute snapshot of me cuddling Karter and him nuzzled in the side of my face.

"Karter? What the hell kind of name is that?"

"A cute name for an even cuter puppy. Don't hate."

"Ain't nobody hating." He laughed, his eyes twinkling.

I grinned. "I can't picture you changing diapers. Unlimited babysitting, huh?"

"Your girl drives a hard bargain." He smoothed a hand over his head and bit his lip. "Besides, I was desperate."

He started walking backwards to his car, then paused. "Take care of yourself, Lily-girl," he said, stuffing his hands back in his pockets.

My heart skipped. That nickname. That damn nickname.

"You, too," I replied, unlocking my car.

I opened the door and slid into the driver's seat. He leaned on the side of his car, watching me like he didn't want to look away too soon. I gave a small wave. He nodded once. And then I drove off. I didn't cry again. Not because it didn't hurt.

But because it didn't feel like goodbye.

It felt like a comma.

Not a period.

Chapter 26

Khalil

I woke up in a bed that wasn't mine.

Again.

The sheets smelled like incense and coconut oil. Her perfume clung to the pillowcase like a second skin. The sun filtered through gauzy curtains, spilling across her hardwood floors in strips like faded film stock. It was morning, but not bright, just enough light to remind me I hadn't dreamed myself into this place.

Tasha was next to me, curled up on her side, arm stretched over where I had just been. She looked peaceful. Skin glowing in the hush of daylight, mouth slightly open, braids falling over her cheek like a curtain.

She looked like love.

But I felt like a stranger in the frame.

My bare feet touched the cold floor. That grounding kind of cold. The kind of cold that made you hyper aware of your body, of the way your chest rose too fast, like breath was trying to outrun whatever lived in your ribs.

I grabbed my pair of sweats from the chair, pulled them on quietly, and padded down the hallway into the kitchen. The house was too quiet. Not eerie, just blank. Tasha didn't believe in order.

Not physically. Not emotionally. She said everything should find its own resting place.

The walls were off-white, the cabinets stark brown. There was a live-edge dining table in the corner with four matching chairs. A few scratches and rings from heavy use.

The coffee maker was already going, the scent rich and warm, rising like steam off old regrets. She must've set the timer last night. She always did. To her, mornings shouldn't require extra decisions. Waking up was hard enough. The machine beeped. I poured coffee into the mug with her initials on it, then poured some into mine. Black. No cream. No sugar. It tasted like something burnt at the bottom of a memory. I leaned against the marble counter and stared out the window.

Houston in the early morning was still soft. The skyline in the distance peeked through a congested haze and humidity. Streetlights flickered out one by one, giving up the fight. A man walked his dog with a paper bag in hand, and a jogger bounced by, earbuds in, rhythm locked. And still, my mind went back to her.

Kelly.

Her face registered in my mind before I could prevent it. The way she looked that night at the taco bar, the soft, warm lights licking the curves of her cheekbones, her voice quieter than I remembered, like grief had lowered her volume. She hadn't smiled at first. She just looked at me like I was a bruise she forgot she had.

And I felt it again. That ache. That inconvenient, relentless ache.

She had no right to still live in my chest. But there she was, unpacked and unmoving. Even after all the silences. Even after the hurt. Even after I fooled myself into thinking I could move forward with Tasha.

Tasha padded in twenty minutes later, still wrapped in sleep. She wore one of my hoodies, the sleeves too long, the hem barely covering the curve of her thighs. She smelled like honey and sleep.

Her skin was warm where she leaned in to kiss my shoulder, her lips lingering just a second too long.

"You okay?" she asked, her voice still scratchy from sleep.

"Yeah," I said, sipping my coffee.

She didn't move right away. Just stood there beside me, one hip leaned against the counter, while her eyes studied my profile. She moved around me like we belonged here, together. She pulled the whole milk from the fridge, stirred it into her cup, and added two spoonfuls of sugar, clinked her spoon against the ceramic as she stirred. She liked it sweet, even when she was salty.

"You been up long?" she asked again.

"Just thinking."

She didn't push. She never did.

"About work?" she asked.

I didn't answer fast enough.

She smiled a tight curve that didn't reach her eyes. "You called her name in your sleep last night." That stopped me. She took a sip, then shrugged like she hadn't said it. "I'm not in my feelings, if that's what you're thinking. Y'all were close. You're allowed to still feel stuff. It's cool." She said it like she meant it, but the way she strangled her mug said otherwise. She was doing it again. Testing the waters, then skipping away when she saw how deep they ran.

"We said we weren't doing that. The mind games and shit."

She laughed, light and airy. I didn't laugh with her. She rolled her eyes and lifted her mug again. "The only one who should be worried about people playing mind games is me." Her jaw tightened as she turned away, like she hadn't cracked the surface just a little. At her dining table, she sat across from me, her legs folded beneath her, sipping her coffee like it held more answers than questions.

"You gonna tell me what you're thinking about?" she asked.

"Nothing important."

She didn't buy it, but she let it go. Sat there tight lipped as we finished our coffee. That was the thing with Tasha. She'd press close enough to make me wonder if we were getting too deep, then pull back like it didn't mean anything. And me? I let her play it that way. Because it kept me from having to answer the one question I didn't want to face.

What did it mean to miss someone who wasn't there while waking up next to someone who was?

WE SAT in a sun-drenched patio in midtown surrounded by her coupled up friends who laughed too loud and clinked mimosas like they were in a sitcom. Tasha talked animatedly with her girls about work, about her sister's engagement, about some trip to Tulum they were planning. I nodded at the right times. Smiled when I was supposed to. Kissed her temple when she made a joke that landed.

"So this is the mysterious Khalil?" one of them asked, raising an arched brow.

Tasha smiled. "The one and only."

I gave a polite nod and reached for my drink.

She leaned in, letting her lips graze my ear. "Babe, try the chilaquiles. You'll love them."

Babe? She never fixed her mouth to call me nothing like that before. She knew what we were. But in front of her friends, her fingers drummed on my left thigh, then rested there lightly, claiming me as hers.

I felt like I was watching myself from across the outdoor patio. Like I'd been cast in the role of *boyfriend* and didn't know the script. When her hand touched mine, I didn't flinch. But I didn't feel the spark either. I used to feel it. The pull. The heartbeat skip. That low hum in my blood.

I felt it with Kelly.

Even when I didn't want to.

Even when she was breaking me in half.

That night, I stayed at Tasha's again. We had sex. It was good. She knew what she was doing. She worked hard to make it feel like something. But halfway through, I caught myself thinking about the way Kelly used to look at me when I kissed her neck. That soft intake of breath, like she was surprised I still knew how to worship her.

Tasha kissed me hard, pulled me close, called me "baby" in a whisper.

But I wasn't present. My body moved, but my mind was elsewhere. Caught in the space between who I was pretending to be and who I actually missed.

After, she laid on my chest, fingers tracing lazy lines across my skin.

"I like this," she said.

"This?"

"You. Here. With me."

I nodded. Didn't speak. She didn't ask for more. That was the problem.

THE NEXT MORNING, I didn't mean to end up at Xavier's front door. But I did, a box of boudin kolaches in one hand. Sleep was still thick in my eyes. Regret sat heavier in my chest.

He answered the door in gym shorts and a hoodie, barefoot, sleep coating his eyes.

"Bruh...it's not even seven o'clock."

"I brought kolaches."

He opened the door wider, squinting at the box. "Let me get one before Nessa smell it and take them all for herself."

Inside, the house smelled like waffles and baby lotion. Vanessa's nesting energy was everywhere. Stacks of folded burping cloths filled the armchair in the living room. New paint samples littered the kitchen island. A stack of tiny pastel onesies hung over the back of the couch.

I followed Xavier to the kitchen where he poured coffee into a chipped mug with "Black Dads Matter" across the front. I set the kolache box down between us.

He raised an eyebrow as he bit into one. "Why you over here at the crack of dawn?"

"You said you needed help setting stuff up in the nursery."

"I ain't mean right now. I been up all night trying to satisfy Nessa's cravings. You look like you should be sleeping, too." He wiped his face, trying to wake up.

"I have been sleeping."

"Then why you look like you're haunted?"

I didn't answer.

He knew.

I leaned back in the kitchen chair and stared at the ceiling. "I pulled up on her."

Xavier paused mid-chew. "Who? Kelly?"

I nodded. "At our taco spot. Nessa got me trapped with unlimited babysitting."

"That's that business degree," he said, laughing at the end. "What'd y'all talk about?"

I ran my hand down my face. "We had a truce. Talked. Laughed. Apologized. She got the puppy I got for her. Named him some shit like Karter." I paused, thinking back to the pictures she'd shown me of her and the dog. "You know your girl told her about Tasha."

He whistled low. "Damn."

"She told me she was sorry. When she got in her car, I wanted to stop her. Wanted to tell her let's forget all the bullshit and pick up where we left off in Arizona," I said, pressing my thumb to the edge of my mug. "I couldn't bring myself to do it."

"How she doing? She look alright?"

"Always beautiful. A little sad, but who wouldn't be in her situation."

Xavier didn't speak right away. He chewed the kolache in his hand slowly, nodding as my words settled on the kitchen counter. "You still love her," he finally said, his mouth full. He set his coffee down and slid the box my way. "Eat man. Can't nobody deal with heartbreak on an empty stomach."

I sipped my coffee. It tasted like every morning I wished I woke up next to her instead of wondering where she went. I recounted the events to Xavier. But I didn't tell him how it felt to hold her again. How when I touched her cheek, pulled her close to my chest, it felt like I was home again.

Xavier wiped his hands on a napkin. "So what now?"

"I don't know."

"You like Tasha?"

"She's solid. Kind. She doesn't ask for too much."

"But?"

"She doesn't make me *feel*."

He didn't speak right away. Just watched me.

"I keep trying to convince myself that's a good thing," I said. "That maybe it's better to be safe than shaken."

"But safe don't sound like love, my boy."

I ran a hand through my curls. "What if I'm the reason it never worked with Kelly?"

"You *are* part of the reason," he said bluntly. "So is she."

I looked at him, annoyed.

He shrugged. "You want the truth or a hug?"

"Both," I muttered.

He laughed then he sobered.

"You loved her like she was your second chance. She loved you like you were her escape. Neither of y'all figured out how to love each other for the people you were becoming."

That sat heavy.

"You think it's too late?"

He finished his kolache, wiped the corner of his mouth, and leaned back in his chair.

"I think if there's still love under all that hurt, it ain't ever too late. Look at me and Nessa today."

"What about Nessa?" Vanessa asked, walking into the kitchen, her natural coils still wild from sleep. "Ooo, are those boudin kolaches? I smelled them from down the hall."

Xavier relinquished the box to Vanessa, who enjoyed the meal too much. I didn't miss the adoring way he looked at his future wife and mother of his child. Even as she stuffed her face and talked with her mouth full. I wanted that for myself.

"You look pitiful, Khalil. Regretting all that babysitting you owe us."

"Yeah, yeah," I replied, smirking.

"When are you and Kelly going to get it together?" she asked, munching away on the kolache in her hand as she stood between Xavier's legs. He rubbed her stomach while looking at her like she was the moon, the sun, and the stars.

"I know you not talking. How long you made this clown wait until you gave him a chance?"

"Hey now! I had to be sure," she argued back. "But now we're back like we were meant to be. My peace."

Xavier kissed his fiancée on the lips, then swatted her away. "So what you going to do?"

I sighed, thinking over my options. I knew what I wanted to do. I wanted to drive to her pop's house, tell her all was forgiven, and have us pick up the pieces together. But deep down, tucked away in a small, blue suitcase was the fear that held me back. Left me paralyzed.

Xavier stood and stretched. "Look, whatever you do, don't do nothing reckless?"

"Define reckless."

He squinted at me. "Khalil. I'm not trying to have nobody sue us 'cause you can't keep your hands to yourself."

I grinned. "Man, old dude asked for that ass whooping."

He rolled his eyes and headed toward the hallway with Vanessa following behind, her fingers laced with his.

"When you figure it out," he called over his shoulder, "see yourself out. We going back to sleep."

I stayed there for a while, alone in their kitchen, staring at the half-eaten box of food. My phone buzzed once, then again.

TASHA

Want takeout when you come over?

I'm thinking Rice Box. Their fried rice is calling my name.

Eventually, I grabbed my keys and left, letting the door click shut behind me. The drive to Tasha's was quiet. No music. Just the hum of the engine and my thoughts looping back to the way Kelly's face softened when I dipped her and picked her up in one swoop. By the time I pulled into the driveway, an ache stretched in my chest. I knew where I wanted to be. But I also knew you shouldn't touch a hot stove twice.

Inside, Tasha was curled on the couch, phone pressed to her ear, half-watching some low-budget movie. Peaceful. Pretty. Simple.

But I couldn't unsee what I saw in that booth with Kelly. Couldn't unfeel the ache of watching her drive away. For the first time since I'd met Tasha, I wondered if I'd walked into her life just to stop myself from drowning. And now that I could breathe again, I wasn't sure if I wanted to stay.

Chapter 27

Khalil

M y   f a t h e r   n e v e r   s t a y e d   i n   o n e   p l a c e   l o n g.   I learned that about him after my mother left. The longest place we stayed was my aunt's house the years he waited for her return. When we moved to North Texas, we changed apartments like babies changed diapers. When I'd gotten to high school, I begged him to stay put so I could have a normal high school experience. Have friends, play football. As soon as I graduated and left for college, he was on the move again.

Pack light. *Love light*. That was his motto. Move on before things get heavy. Before comfort turned to complacency. Before love became something you had to drag behind you like a busted tailpipe on a freeway. He didn't say those words out loud. Not once. But he lived them so loud I didn't need him to.

So, when he texted me that he was flying in for the weekend, no reason, just a *"Thinking about you son,"* and a screenshot of his Southwest itinerary, I stared at the message for five minutes before he landed. I knew something was off.

We hadn't visited each other in more than a year. When he called, he didn't do small talk, just jumped straight to the point. He did the important stuff. Paid for school fees, made sure I was at practice on time, taught me how to tie a tie. But he stayed emotionally in the shallow end, just far enough to say he showed up, never deep enough to drown.

Then, I got a follow-up message:

POPS

By the way, my lady's tagging along. Hope that's cool.

My fingers hovered over the keyboard. Your lady?

We'd talked here and there, checking in once a week. He never mentioned he was seeing someone. Not once. Especially not someone significant enough to want me to meet her.

ME

Yeah. That's cool. I'll pick y'all up from the airport.

Tasha was excited when I accidentally mentioned it during one of our morning-after conversations. She beamed, standing in my kitchen in a pair of biker shorts and hoodie, unpacking groceries. She pulled frozen chicken from a paper bag like it was a magic trick.

"Oh, we should all go to dinner," she said, tossing a box of couscous into the pantry. "It'll be a double date."

"Dinner?" I tried to play it cool, pulling a bottle of water from the fridge.

"Yeah," she said, not even looking at me. "It'll be cute."

"Cute?" I echoed, pouring myself a glass of water just to have something to hold. "I don't know if we need to do all of that. It probably ain't serious."

"He's bringing her to meet you. Of course it's serious."

I raised an eyebrow. "Maybe she's just tagging along," I muttered.

Tasha caught the look and laughed, leaning over the counter. She walked up behind me and wrapped her arms around my waist.

"Don't be weird about this. Maybe she's dope. Besides, I'll be there with you. I want to know where you come from."

It hit me that Tasha was serious about tagging along. I was silent, trying to figure a way out of this. Even if my pops was ready to introduce significant others, I wasn't sure if I was there just yet. Tasha took note of my silence.

"Do you not want me to come?" she asked, pulling back.

"Nah, it's not that," I lied. "This is all just new for me."

"Aww, baby," she cooed, kissing my cheek. "You'll be fine."

"Yeah."

But I wasn't.

Because part of me still remembered the smell of Mama's perfume on his collar. And the way it stopped showing up altogether.

SHE INTRODUCED HERSELF AS CHERYL. Light brown skin. Hair pinned up in a twist. Gold hoops. A mauve-colored wrap dress and a laugh that moved too easily in places where mine caught like gravel. She hugged me when they arrived at the restaurant. Real close. Real familiar.

"You look just like your daddy," she said. "It's so good to finally meet you."

I smiled with my teeth.

"You, too."

Tasha was already inside, fussing over the table, straightening menus, ordering wine like it was a business lunch. When she saw Cheryl, she turned on that charm like a dimmer switch flipped all the way up.

"Oh, you're stunning," she said, and meant it.

"Girl, stop." Cheryl laughed, waving her hand. "Look at you. That dress? The body? Please."

They clicked instantly. Shared a joke before we even ordered.

Talked skincare, astrology. And I just sat there. Stuck between past and present. Watching the man who raised me act like someone new. Someone lighter. My father reached for Cheryl's hand across the table like he'd done it a hundred times. He even smiled with his eyes. I didn't know he still knew how to do that.

"How long you two been... together?" I asked, careful with my tone.

Pops took a sip of his drink. "Few months."

"Six, to be exact," Cheryl added, flashing her dimples, beaming across the table at my father. He returned her look.

I nodded, chewing on the silence. My jaw clenched so hard; I had to take a drink just to loosen it. Tasha looked between us. Picked up on the tension like static. My father looked at me then really looked. And for the first time in a long time, he looked like he knew he might've hurt me. But didn't know how to fix it. Cheryl and Tasha picked up a conversation of their own.

"Looks like we both moved on," he said plainly.

I didn't answer. Because I wasn't sure if I was mad at him for being happy. Or mad that he got there without me. I watched he and Cheryl's interactions, the love that flowed between them easy, unconstrained. That wasn't Tasha and me.

The next day, Cheryl stayed behind for brunch with some cousin she had in Pearland, so it was just me and my father when we pulled up to Xavier's. He had the grill going and a fresh case of beer chilling in a tub of ice on the back porch. The speakers played Frankie Beverly low enough to talk over but loud enough to make you want to two-step.

My father shook his hand then embraced him like Xavier was his own son. "I can't believe the two of you really grown enough to have kids. How's Ted and Josie?"

Xavier grinned. "They're doing good. They'll be out here in a few weeks for the baby shower."

"I may have to double back," Pops said, hitting me in the chest playfully.

Later, when the food was gone and it was just the three of us, the conversation shifted.

"Cheryl seems cool," Xavier said, cracking open a beer.

"She is," my father agreed. "Solid woman. Knows who she is."

"She makes you happy?" I asked.

"Yeah, she does." He looked at me. "She makes it *easy*. Doesn't mean it's shallow."

I nodded slowly.

"But you gotta ask yourself," he added, "if easy is what you really want. Or if you're just tired of drowning."

We were halfway through a second round of beers when Xavier stepped inside to take a call, leaving just me and my father on the porch. The firepit had burned down to a soft, pulsing glow. Crickets sang in the brush beyond the fence. I leaned back in the chair, staring up at a sky I could barely see through the light pollution.

"You never really said what you thought about Tasha," I said finally.

My father looked over the rim of his beer. "I did," he replied. "Said she's nice. Easy."

"You mean easy like... compatible?"

"I mean easy like the thing that feels good 'cause it doesn't press on your sore spots."

He said it with no heat. No judgment. Just that matter-of-fact tone that made it worse.

"She's good to me," I said.

"I didn't say she wasn't," he replied. "But good to you ain't the same as good *for* you."

I hated how that sat right in my chest. "You think it's fake?"

"I think... you like the quiet she gives you. But you're not quiet, son. You've just gotten good at pretending you are."

I turned the bottle in my hands. Let condensation roll over my fingers.

"You ever felt like somebody loved you more than they should've?" I asked. "Like it scared you?"

He leaned forward, resting his forearms on his knees. "That's how I felt about your mother."

I glanced up.

"I loved that woman so hard, it felt like drowning. And I kept going back in because I thought *my* love was supposed to be the thing that saved her." He paused. Took another sip. "It wasn't."

I didn't ask more, but he kept going.

"Your mama was brilliant. Soft in ways the world didn't understand. But she had demons. And somewhere along the way, the demons started winning."

I listened, heart in my throat.

"I tried everything. Therapy. Church. Threats. Pleading. Silence. I thought if I just *stayed*, she'd get tired of the darkness and come back into the light with me." He looked up at me. "She didn't."

My throat burned. "So what'd you do?" I asked.

"I started saving myself." He let the words travel up to the darkening sky with the residual smoke from the pit. "And when I finally came up for air, I realized I was trying to raise a son in the middle of a war zone. So I gave up." Silence again. "How's Kelly doing? Josie told me she been taking her mama passing rough."

"She's doing better now. She's back home for a bit before she goes back to Seattle."

"What happened with you two?"

I exhaled through my nose. "It was... complicated."

He chuckled. "Love is complicated."

"She's smart. Passionate. Focused. She feels things deep but acts like she doesn't. She pushes everybody away to see if they'll come back."

"Did you?"

I nodded. "Too many times."

He looked over at me with something close to sympathy. "You still love her?"

I hesitated. Then nodded again. He didn't press.

Instead, he said, "Love like that don't die easy. But it'll take *everything* from you if you don't know who you are without it."

"I tried to help her."

"I know," he said. "But you can't save someone who don't want to be saved."

I swallowed.

"I don't think she didn't want to be," I said quietly. "I think she just didn't believe she was worth saving."

He nodded slowly.

"That's what scared me most about your mother. Not that she left. Not that the drugs changed her. But that she stopped seeing herself as somebody worth fighting for." He stared into the dying fire, eyes far away now. "If she'd been willing to save herself, I'd still be with her."

The sentence landed with the weight of a confession and a benediction. He didn't say it directly. Didn't need to. But I heard it anyway — the unspoken name floating beneath the truth.

Kelly.

Chapter 28

Khalil

THE PLAN WAS SIMPLE: DRINKS, A GAME OR TWO OF pool, and some much-needed trash talk. Me, Wesley, and Maverick hit up this old bar in EaDo. Wood-paneled walls, neon beer signs, music spinning low through a battered speaker. The floor stuck to your shoes, and the bartender didn't ask for a tab until you ordered three rounds in. It felt like college again with Wesley replacing Xavier. Back when none of us knew shit but all of us thought we were men. Wesley tossed the first round of darts. Missed the bullseye by three inches.

"Damn," I muttered, sipping my drink.

"That was a warm-up," he said, clearly lying.

Maverick leaned over the table, sizing up his shot. "Move out the way and let somebody with aim take a shot." Maverick hit the bullseye three times in a row.

Wesley scoffed. "I don't need to throw a football when my arm signs multi-million-dollar contracts just fine."

We laughed. It felt good. Simple. Until I heard that voice.

"Well, well, well. If it ain't the three stooges."

I turned.

Kelly.

Her smile could ruin mankind. Nyah stood next to her in a sage-green, oversized set, a cropped tank underneath. Lynn followed, all legs and attitude in a taupe knit sweater and suede skirt and polished brown boots.

Kelly strolled around, giving hugs to Maverick and Wesley. She had a white tee tucked under her breasts, just enough to show the curve of her waist. The skirt skimming over her hips did me in. Silky, leopard print hugged every inch like it'd been painted on. The red clutch tucked under her arm popped against the print. Her hair was slicked back into a low bun with two curled pieces framing her temples. She looked so good it hurt. I bit my lip to stifle the too wide smile threatening to cover my face.

Wesley did a double take. "Mmmm, Lady Lynn and her cackling hens."

"And who exactly is that supposed to be?" Lynn asked flatly, balling up Wesley's lips as she walked past him.

Maverick, who had just taken a swig of beer, paused, bottle still by his mouth.

Nyah looked over at him, one brow raised. "Maverick speechless? I'm shocked. You okay?"

He nodded quickly, wiping his mouth. "Yeah. Just... yeah, I'm straight."

She gave him a slow smile. "Well, don't make that a habit. I look forward to hearing the craziness that comes out of your mouth."

I laughed into my bottle, taking a sip. Kelly caught my eye and held it. Just long enough to say everything she didn't out loud. "Y'all joining us?" I asked.

"Depends," she said. "You buying?"

"First round's on me."

That was enough.

An hour later, we had taken over the bar like a familiar storm. Pool balls clacked, laughter bounced off the walls, and our drinks kept disappearing as fast as they showed up.

Kelly leaned across the table to line up her shot, hips cocked just slightly, tongue between her teeth. My dick twitched thinking back to how she looked bent over while I hit it from the back. I took another swig of my beer, my mouth suddenly dry.

"You know if you scratch on this, it's game over, right?" I teased, walking to the other side.

"I don't scratch," she said without looking at me.

And she didn't. Sank the ball with a tap and a smirk.

"Show off," I muttered.

"I learned from the best," she said, sipping her drink.

Wesley posted up at a nearby table, mid-debate with Lynn.

"I'm just saying," he insisted. "Drake is more relevant than Kendrick right now."

Lynn rolled her eyes so hard it looked like she was trying to see the back of her skull.

"Why should I trust your prep school music knowledge? You thought I forgot how you and the lacrosse team used him as hype music in high school. Just white-washed."

"Ouch," Maverick said.

"She ain't wrong," Nyah added, sipping something dark and dangerous.

Wesley narrowed his eyes. "So, you're team Kendrick?"

"I'm team talent," Lynn replied. "And taste. Which you have neither."

The tension between them crackled. Not mean. Not warm either. Something in between — like they hadn't decided yet if they liked or loathed each other. It was going to be fun to watch. Meanwhile, Maverick could barely keep his eyes off Nyah.

She caught him staring once and quirked a brow. "You got something to say or are you just collecting images for later?"

He choked again on his drink. "I mean—damn. Okay."

She laughed, genuinely this time, and he looked like he'd just found religion.

"You always that forward?" he asked.

"Only when I'm bored," she said, walking away toward the bar.

He watched her go, eyes wide, mouth slightly open.

"Mav," Wesley muttered. "You alright?"

"She's–"

"Better hydrate," I added. "She's married."

I stepped out for some air. The patio was quiet. String lights hung above the fence, glowing soft like candlelight. I leaned against the railing, drink in hand, breathing deep. Then I heard her behind me.

"Figured I'd find you out here," she said. "Got tired of losing to me?"

"I let you win."

She shrugged. "I still won."

I nodded. "What's on your mind, Lily-girl?"

"You ever think about how we always find each other in between things?" she asked.

I turned to her. "What do you mean?"

"In between life chapters. In between other people. In between the versions of ourselves we're still figuring out."

I had. Often.

"You make it sound like an accident," I said.

"Isn't it?"

"No," I said. "It's a pattern."

She looked up at me then, face lit by soft yellow light. "Patterns don't lie," she said quietly.

"No," I agreed. "But they do ask questions."

She sipped her drink. "You ever get tired of wondering?"

"Every day."

We didn't kiss. We didn't touch. Just lingered round each other. Something passed between us. The kind of tension that wasn't about sex. Or nostalgia. It was about recognition. Of what we could be if we ever caught each other at the right time.

Eventually, everyone spilled out onto the patio. The bartender cut the music. Last call. Someone lit a blunt. Nobody said anything as we passed it around. We sat in mismatched chairs, passing around drinks and stories like we hadn't all been through some kind of heartbreak this year. The air buzzed with what-ifs. Kelly laughed at something Wesley said. I watched her from across the group, knees curled beneath her, head tilted back, laughing.

That was when I heard another voice cracking above it.

"Oh my God. Khalil, why didn't you tell me y'all were out here?"

Tasha. She stood at the patio entrance with her arms folded, one of her over-dressed friends standing just behind her. She had her practiced smile pasted to her face. Her eyes were overly wide, bouncing over the patio, narrowing slightly when they met Kelly, until they landed back on me.

I stood, walking over to where she and her friend stood.

"Say, can we have a second?" Tasha's friend looked at her before walking off. "Tasha, we said we were cooling it. Giving each other space, remember?"

"I gave you space. I didn't know you'd be here," she said, sliding her arms around my waist, tugging tight. "It's not my fault we just happened to be in the same neighborhood."

I stared back at her blankly. "Tasha, quit playing games. I told you I was coming here."

"Well, maybe I forgot." She smiled again, arching her neck for a kiss. In the corner of my eye, I saw Kelly shift in her seat, smoothing her expression as she listened to whatever story Lynn was telling her. Her smile was tight as her eyes flickered under the string lights of the patio.

"Since I'm here, why don't you introduce me to everyone."

"Tasha," I said, my voice low. "This ain't the time."

She stepped back like I slapped her. "Oh? Because she's here? Y'all just passing blunts around like shit sweet." She laughed, sharp and a little unhinged. "My sister told me about niggas like you."

Kelly stood, cool and easy. "You good?"

"We're fine," Tasha replied, her eyes never leaving me.

"Chill, Tasha."

Silence held for a beat before Kelly dropped back to her seat and took the blunt from Maverick like nothing happened. She inhaled deeply, then let the smoke curl around her mouth as she exhaled. She passed it off to Lynn, who laughed at Kelly's smirk and rolling of her eyes.

"So this is what you mean by keeping it 'casual.' Sleep over at my place whenever you want, but when I want time with you, it's always a no."

"Tasha, it's late. Don't you have to get up early anyway?"

Tasha looked past my shoulders again, finding her target. "When she plays your ass again, you know where to find me." She walked off, meeting up with her friend near the parking lot. I could tell from her animated gestures, she was giving an exaggerated recap. I stared down at the spot she had stood, thinking about how loud the wrong person could be when you craved quiet.

Chapter 29

Kelly

BACON SALTY, SMOKY BACON PULLED ME FROM MY SLEEP. Not the kind on a greasy burger, but the homemade kind. The kind that made cast iron sizzle, fatty edges curling under the heat. A crispiness that came from a patience only fathers seemed to have when it came to frying things just right. I blinked against the sunlight cutting through the blinds in my childhood bedroom.

I'd been enjoying the time spent with my friends, the chances I'd been able to see Khalil, the morning walks with Karter, and nighttime dinners with just my father and me. There was no rush, no impending deadline pulling me from the present. I felt that way this morning too, were it not for my session with Ms. Reece. She'd said the first few weeks she wanted to take it easy, let me get comfortable. But today, we were getting to the root.

As I walked downstairs, my father hummed along to some old school R&B. Maze, *Golden Time of Day*. Mama would play that on Saturdays when she woke us both at the crack of dawn to clean up. When I walked into the kitchen, he looked up and smiled, wide and full of effort.

"Hey, Kelly-girl," my dad cheered from the kitchen. "Coffee or orange juice?"

"Coffee."

He poured it for me, adding just the right amount of oat milk and hazelnut syrup. I sat at the kitchen island while he assembled our plates. Bacon, scrambled eggs, toast buttered all the way to the edges. The two of us eating breakfast together was so normal. Karter ate from his dog bowl on the ground, laps of water filling the air.

"I appreciate this more than you know," I said, stuffing my mouth with bacon and eggs.

"You don't have to thank me for that."

"It's still nice to say."

He was quiet for a second, chewing. "I think I missed a lot of signs. Stuff I should've asked about. You just...you just always had it together. Me and your mama saw it as a blessing."

I looked at my food. "We all missed stuff."

"Yep," he said, sipping some of his coffee. "You ready for your session today?"

"Yeah, but it might be a little tough."

"Why is that? Don't you just sit on the couch and talk?"

"Not quite." I laughed. "My therapist takes a body-centered approach. You don't just talk. You feel. Move through it."

"Sounds hard," he said, polishing off his plate.

"It is."

He knocked on the table, like he was trying to enter a door neither of us wanted to open.

"I know you're angry," he started. "At me. At your mama. At everything. You don't have to carry that alone anymore." I nodded, swallowing the lump in my throat. He squeezed my hand, rough and warm. "Whatever comes up today, let it. Don't try to be strong. Just be real."

～

Ms. Reece's office was too calm for what I was feeling. Warm wood floors. Shelves filled with worn books and other random objects. A diffuser puffed out something herbal and grounding. Eucalyptus and frankincense maybe. The sun came in through gauzy curtains. In the corner, a faint trickle sounded from the tabletop fountain. Everything in the room said, *you are safe.*

But my body said, *run.*

I sat on the low couch, legs crossed at the knees, hands gripping my sides like I might float away. Ms. Reece sat across from me, house shoes adorning her feet like this was her living room and not an office in a medical building.

"How are we feeling today?"

"I'm not exactly in the mood to leave feeling drained, but here I am." I shrugged.

"Don't think of it as leaving drained. See it as releasing the old to make room for the new."

I nodded. "If it keeps me from unraveling in front of people, I'll take it."

She tilted her head, studying me. "I think you've spent more than enough time trying to be palatable to others. Performing perfection. Let's get a little messy." She had a glint to her eyes that made me nervous.

I didn't answer but my jaw clenched. That was my problem. My life was already a mess. How would getting messier help?

"I want to try something different today," she said, reaching for a spiral-bound notebook and a thick black marker. "No journaling. I know you don't like that. But no talking either. Just scribble."

I raised an eyebrow. "Scribble?"

"Yes. With your dominant hand. I'm going to ask you a series of questions. Your only job is to move your hand. Don't think. Don't write out words. Just let your body respond."

"I feel ridiculous."

"Good. That means your ego's on alert. Let's see if we can get beneath it."

I took the notebook in my left hand and held the marker like it was a foreign object. My fingers curled awkwardly around the barrel. Ms. Reece waited until I put the tip to paper, then she began.

"What did it feel like to hear your parents fighting through the walls?"

Immediately, I looked down at the paper and marker, a blackened dot growing as I processed the question.

"Stop thinking, Kelly, and scribble. What did it feel like hearing your parents fighting through the walls?"

I glitched, then exhaled, staring back at Ms. Reece. "You don't have an easier question we can start with?"

"I told you we're getting to the root today. We don't have time for easy. Scribble."

I rolled my eyes, then drew a straight line across the page. "There."

"Kelly, stop fighting it. If you're going to waste our time, you can leave." She stared at me, challenging me with her eyes.

I nodded for her to continue, turning the page.

"I'm going to ask you again, and when I do, hold my eyes, and scribble." She waited for me to hold the marker upright before she asked, "What did it feel like to hear your parents fighting through the walls?"

Scratch, scratch, scratch. I held her gaze as my hand moved across the page in tight, erratic spirals. I didn't stop until the marker snagged the edge of the page. I turned the page.

"What did your mother teach you about silence?" My shoulders tensed, but her eyes held mine captive. I scribbled harder, jagged lines overlapping, a growing storm on the page. "What do you wish your father would've done differently?" I hesitated. My heart raced. My ears were hot. My head spun, my eyes burned. I tried drawing an actual shape. A square. The marker never connected the four lines. It stabbed the paper over and over until the paper tore. She walked over and took in the pages, the scribbled lines written so forcefully they bled into the pages underneath.

"I'm going to ask you a question, and I want you to answer with the first thing that comes to your mind." I nodded. "Where in your body do you feel that rage?"

"My chest," I snapped. "And my hands."

"Then let them move."

I exhaled as she brought over a second, larger sheet of paper. Thick art paper. The kind Nessa had me carry with her to one of her art classes. Said she favored the brand because it held up no matter how much watercolor was applied. Never tore. Never crumbled. Ms. Reece taped it to the wall behind me.

"Stand up."

I did, slowly, heart pounding.

"Don't make it pretty. Just release." I stood in front of the paper, marker in hand, waiting for her next series of questions. "What did it cost you to pretend you weren't angry?"

My whole body jolted. Tears sprang. I gripped the marker like a weapon as I turned to Ms. Reece.

"I didn't pretend," I said, voice trembling. "There wasn't a point when it'd happen again."

Ms. Reece stepped closer, gently but firmly. "That's not true, Kelly. You wanted peace so bad you buried yourself to get it."

My vision blurred. "I had to! If I let it out it'd be a house full of people arguing. Over nothing. I would've destroyed everything."

"You were a child. Not a bomb."

The marker dropped from my hands. I took a step back, breathing heavy, my arms shaking. *Whatever comes up today, let it. Don't try to be strong. Just be real.*

"I hate them. I hate them," I whispered. "And I hate myself for feeling that way."

Ms. Reece didn't flinch. "Say it again," she said.

"I hate her," I said louder. "For staying. For pretending like it was okay. For never protecting me. I hate him for sucking the air out of her, leaving me nothing. I hate he's still here but she isn't. I hate there's nothing I can do about it. I hate I have to be here without her."

She stepped aside and gestured to the floor cushions. "Sit down. Let those feelings move through."

I sank into the cushion, legs folded, hands curled into fists.

She sat across from me and met my eyes. "I'm going to ask a few more questions. You don't have to answer out loud. Just feel what comes up."

I nodded, throat tight.

"Where does your anger live in your body today?"

"Here," I rasped, pressing a hand to my sternum. "It's sharp. Like something wants to tear out."

"What would it say if it had a voice?"

I closed my eyes. Heat rose in my ears, behind my eyes, in my gut. *Why didn't you choose me? Why wasn't I enough to make you leave? Why do I still need you to say I was worth saving?* My breath caught on a sob, but I forced it back. Ms. Reece didn't interrupt the silence. She just waited, patient and present. Then, a blood curdling scream escaped me. I grabbed the pillow in my lap, letting out another, and another. The tears flowed, thick and heavy. Sobs heaved from my chest, my throat felt raw. When I opened my eyes, she was still watching me. Calm. Unafraid.

"Say it," she said again.

"I needed her to leave," I admitted. "I needed her to save us. And she didn't." There it was. The truth. "I hate that I still want her approval. I hate that she's gone and I can't be mad at her."

"You can grieve someone and still hold them accountable, Kelly. That's not betrayal. That's honesty."

I didn't know what made me snap first. My own words, the echo of them in my chest, or the way Ms. Reece just *sat there*, like her calm was supposed to hold me together. But something cracked.

"I don't want to be here anymore," I said, voice low and mean. "This is not helping."

"You don't mean that," she said gently.

"I do. I came here to try to move forward, not get dragged back into the past like a damn time capsule of every moment that ever broke me."

"Then why are you yelling?"

"I'M NOT" I stopped, swallowed the scream halfway out of my throat. My hands were shaking.

Ms. Reece didn't flinch. She folded her hands in her lap and nodded slowly. "There it is."

"There *what* is?"

"The anger you've been wrapping in perfection. The fire under all that calm. It's finally speaking."

"No," I snapped. "You don't get to sit there and act like this is some kind of breakthrough. You don't *know* what it was like. Dealing with them. Being dragged in the middle like rope against hot sand."

"You're right," she said. "I wasn't there. But I've met hundreds of women who lived it. Who walked through fire, then told everyone it was just a little warm."

I stood up. My body felt too tight, too hot. "Don't patronize me."

"I'm not," she said. "But I *am* going to hold up the mirror. Because you came here for healing, not performance. And healing isn't quiet. It's not curated. It's not polite."

I clenched my fists at my sides. "Then maybe I'm not ready."

"Bullshit."

My head snapped up. I hadn't expected that. Not from her.

"I call bullshit," Ms. Reece said again, this time firmer. She stood slowly; her eyes locked on mine. "You *are* ready. You've been ready for years. You've just been too afraid to admit that the version of you, the version you built to survive... doesn't want to survive anymore. She wants to *live*."

I hated that her words hit me like that. Like bricks. Like gospel.

"I don't know how to let go without falling apart," I whispered, my voice cracking, timid because the little girl trapped deep down inside was begging for me to fight. Fight for her. Push through for us.

"Then fall," she said. "And I'll be right here when you do."

I shook my head. Tears blurred my vision. "You don't understand. I've held it together for everyone. My whole life. If I let go now, who am I?"

She stepped closer. "You're someone who deserves to be held."

That undid me.

I sank to my knees on the cushion again and let the sobs come. They didn't creep in—they *crashed*. Loud, ugly, full-bodied wails. The kind I hadn't made since I was small and still believed crying would change something.

"I hate them," I sobbed. "I hate that they made love look like punishment. I hate that I believed it."

Ms. Reece knelt beside me, her voice low and steady. "You get to be angry, Kelly. You get to rage. You get to scream. You get to *feel*."

I rocked forward, forehead to the floor, exasperated by the session. Ms. Reece let me gather my wits, staying next to me through it all. "I don't want to carry this anymore."

"Then don't."

She reached for the notebook again. "One more thing."

I looked up, eyes swollen. "What?"

"If you had the chance, if she were here right now, what would you say to your mother?"

I hesitated. "I don't know."

"You do know. Write."

I took the pen. Sat back on the cushion. Hands trembling. And I wrote.

Dear Mama,

You weren't supposed to leave me like this. You were supposed to do better. To tell me why it was okay to love a man who treated you like glass he was bored of breaking. You were supposed to tell me why you stayed. Why you made me stay. Why you made silence a virtue and obedience a survival skill. I loved you. I still do. But I needed more. And now that you're gone, I don't know what to do with all this fury. All this grief. All this need to be held by the one person who taught me never to reach out. I needed you to be brave. Now I'm the one trying to be. I hope wherever you are, you finally understand what you left behind. And I hope I forgive you someday. But not today. Today I'm still angry. And I think that's okay.

Love,

Kelly

I dropped the notebook in my lap and sobbed again, softer this time. Ms. Reece reached over, placed her hand gently on mine. "That's enough for today." I nodded. For once, I believed her.

Chapter 30

Khalil

Black people hosted baby showers like family reunions. It didn't matter that Vivian had rented some luxury event space with chandeliers for lights and upholstered chairs parked at tables with cream cloths covering them. Vanessa and Xavier made it a point to add all gifts would be donated to women's shelters to the custom invitations. Casual dress. A signal that this wasn't going to be some awkward, all-women, cupcake and pass the gift affair.

Between Vivian's event planner's vision and Ma Josie's insistence on having real food, it had become a bright, gold-accented, open-bar kind of event with catered food and a vibe that made you want to put on a two-piece linen suit or sundress. Pink and blue balloons twisted into arches flanking the entrance. A DJ was set up in the far corner by the dance floor. He mixed tracks while guests filled their plates while holding their cell phones in the other hand.

This was not a baby shower.

It was a function. And Kelly and I were the hosts.

Vivian floated around the room, wearing a pearl-colored jumpsuit and gold bangles that clinked every time she waved a finger.

Her heels clicked against the light hardwood, a glass of sangria in one hand. Douglass trailed behind her as they greeted everyone.

Kelly breezed past me, winking. Olive green knit hugged every curve like it was custom made for her. The sleeves skimmed her wrists, boots kissed her knees, and those damn legs went on forever. Her hair was swept into a bun, two soft curls at her temples, gold hoops catching the light. Fresh manicure. She balanced an armful of gifts like a pro. My eyes dragged up slow, stopping at the smirk she wore like a dare. God help me, she was a problem I needed to have.

"You good?" she asked, sitting the gifts on the table behind me.

"Yeah. You good? You over here being Wonder Woman and shit," I teased.

She gave me one of those looks, one that said *don't push it*, but her eyes still sparkled like she didn't mind the back and forth.

"When's your girlfriend coming?"

"Ha ha. You got jokes I see.."

"And yet, she met Pops," she said, squinting her eyes. "I'm grabbing me a plate before our hosting duties begin. I suggest you do the same." She walked away, switching her hips, her ass bouncing under the looseness of her dress. I followed.

At the buffet line, trays of wings, meatballs in a thick barbecue glaze, Rotel dip in ceramic ramekins, two types of mac and cheese, deviled eggs with smoked paprika and chopped bacon lined the tables. Toward the end, a full dessert bars with blue and pink candy-coated goods were displayed for the guests. I held two plates while Kelly piled on the food. We sat at the table with Nyah, Lynn, Wesley, and Maverick.

The DJ yelled into the mic, "IF YOU BROUGHT A GIFT, PUT IT ON THE TABLE! DON'T FORGET TO GET YOUR RAFFLE TICKET!"

"Tell me again why people are bringing gifts?" Maverick asked across the table. "Last time Zay had us putting some contraption together, it was baby stuff all over the house."

"Because it's not for her," Nyah corrected. "She's donating everything to women's shelters. I get to pick first to bring to a girl at my school who's not too far along behind Nessa."

"That's dope," Maverick replied. "You like teaching?"

"I guess you can say that. It keeps me busy and the kids are great."

"Look at Mav," I whispered to Kelly. "I already told him she married. He don't care."

"Mind the business that pays you," Kelly said between bites. "He didn't care in college. I'm not surprised he doesn't care now."

I rolled my eyes.

Vanessa and Xavier sat at the head table, looking out at their guests but still wrapped up in them. He grinned like a man who knew his life was about to change for the better. Vanessa glowed. Not in the cliche way people say about pregnant women. She really glowed, skin rich and warm, cheeks round and flushed, her full laugh carrying above the noise. She caught me staring and walked over with Xavier.

Kelly stood to hug her friend and let her sit down. "Thank y'all for hosting," she said.

I stood so Kelly could sit. "You know we got y'all."

At some point, Kelly passed me a baby doll wrapped in toilet paper and told me to hold it still while people tried to drop large pacifiers over baby bottles.

"What's the point of the doll?" I asked her.

"No point, just decoration, for the vibes." She shrugged, turning back to the game before us.

"Speaking of, how my big dog, Karter, doing?"

"Your big dog?" she laughed. "Karter is my baby. And, he's having a ball with my dad and running around the house."

"I mean, technically he mine, too. I did get him for you," I teased, wrapping an arm around her chair. "We can split custody."

She sized me up, narrowing her eyes. "And how would Tasha feel about that?"

Dammit. She had me there.

"Exactly. Now stand there, hold this baby, and try to look as cute as me."

She didn't know it, but there was no comparison. Not then. Not ever. Kelly was something the world didn't deserve but got anyway. A soft, golden kind of beautiful you didn't just see, but felt. It wrapped around you slow and warm, like sunlight after a summer rain. She moved like a song only I knew the words to. And that lightness she carried even when she didn't feel it, it radiated out of her, unbothered, unbent. Her soul refused to be anything but luminous.

Heaven-sent.

After a few games, the guests mellowed into that sweet post-plate itis where bellies were full and drinks continued flowing. Kelly stood, taking me with her to the center of the room. The DJ turned down the music just enough so she could be heard.

"Alright, alright! We have time for one more game. 'Who Knows the Parents Best!' Grab a partner. Parents can't play. Sorry Aunt Viv and Ms. Josie." She blew them kisses across the room. People shuffled, giggling, calling dibs on friends and cousins. Kelly pulled out a pair of index cards, like we were hosting an episode of Family Feud.

"Okay, question one. What's Vanessa's favorite pregnancy craving?" Kelly asked the crowd.

A few people yelled, "Pickles!"

I crossed my arms in an 'X.' "Wrong! It's actually Popeye's biscuits and ketchup."

"What the hell!" someone shouted from the back, followed by a chorus of groans.

"Hey, y'all leave my bestie alone," Kelly scolded.

"Yeah," Vanessa shouted out, laughing. "Don't knock it until you try it." Xavier kissed the side of her face, sipping his beer.

"Okay, question two," Kelly started, showing me the question.

"What color did Zay say he didn't want for the baby's nursery?" I picked up from where Kelly left off.

"Nah, we not playing this no more!" someone booed in good fun. Others laughed, feeling the good spirits of the shower. I glanced at Kelly. She was laughing, cheeks flushed, shaking her head.

I touched her lower back and whispered into her ear, "I think we should switch to something else."

She looked up at me. "I think you're right." Then she turned to the crowd. "I don't know about y'all, but I'm dying to know what Baby Morris will be."

"You already know!" Lynn yelled out, laughing.

Kelly placed a gentle hand on my back and whispered into my ear, "Go get the darts. I'm about to push everyone outside."

With everyone standing outside, the heat lamps took off the slight chill in an otherwise warm, early fall night. Guests crowded under the patio, staring at the large canvas with pink and blue balloons adhered to it. Vanessa and Xavier stood in the center of the crowd, holding the darts I'd grabbed. Chattering in the back started with people guessing whether it'd be a boy or girl. The DJ played Beyonce's *Countdown* in the background.

Xavier took the first throw, hitting a pink balloon filled with gray paint. Vanessa took the next throw, barely catching a blue balloon, also filled with gray paint. They kept rotating throws, keeping the guests in suspense. With each throw, Kelly held onto my arm, tighter and tighter. You'd think we didn't already know the gender. Suddenly, Vanessa hit another balloon, the color splattering everywhere.

"It's a girl!" Vivian and Ma Josie screamed at the same time, hugging each other. Xavier turned to pick up Vanessa, holding her in the air. Their kiss was magnetic. Tears filled her eyes. Her friends jumped up and down, waiting for their moment to hug her. When he put her down, they stayed connected. He whispered something to her over the cheers of the crowd. Kissed her tears away. Wiped the ones he couldn't catch. When they turned to us, joy wasn't even the word to capture the feeling on his face. They hugged their parents. Vanessa continued crying in her mother's arms. Her father finishing the circle. He stepped away to shake Xavier's hand.

Kelly and I looked on from the outskirts, letting everyone else have their moment. I looked down at her, seeing the tears streaming down her face as she looked on.

"Hey, you okay?" I brushed her cheek with my thumb. She shook her head side to side. "Come with me," I replied, taking her hand and guiding her out of the soft-lit world and into something quieter.

We ended up in a small bathroom off the catering kitchen. She grabbed some paper towels, wetting them in the sink and wiping her eyes. She took deep breaths to calm herself. I rubbed her back, smoothed my hands over her shoulders.

"Ugh, I'm so fucking tired of crying." She laughed, voice thin and damp around the edges. She looked at us in the mirror. For the first time, I think she saw herself. Not the woman she showed to the world. But the one still piecing herself together. The one holding everything up while still figuring out how to put it all down. She took a shaky breath, then another.

"It's okay to cry, Lily-girl," I said. I moved closer, reached to kiss her shoulder, but stopped myself halfway. Letting her breathe.

"I know. It's just. I've been crying and crying and crying. When does it stop?" She turned around and leaned against the sink, letting the cool porcelain ground her. I opened my hands. She placed hers there without hesitation, palms meeting mine. I traced slow circles over the backs of her hands.

"I'm not sad, though," she whispered. "I'm actually very happy. I'm just going to miss my sister. We been thugging together since the womb. They deserve this. Nessa and Zay."

"Yeah." I nodded. "They do."

She gave a soft smile, a little water round the edges. "You remember how we set them up?"

"Which time?" I chuckled. "It's been them and us since then."

"You make that sound bad," she said, tilting her head just slightly.

"It was never bad," I replied, voice low. "Even when it was bad."

She blinked slow, stepping into my space until I could feel her breath.

"It's still not bad," she whispered.

Her fingers slipped from my hands to my chest, flattening against my shirt. My arms drifted up to her waist, settling on soft fabric. We stood there, suspended in something hot and delicate, heartbeats crashing in rhythm.

She leaned in, and I did too.

Her lips brushed mine. Once. Then again, fuller this time. A question neither of us wanting to answer lingered there. It started soft. Gentle. Familiar. Then deepened. One hand at the base of her neck, the other gripping her ass. Our breaths hitched. Our mouths opened wider. A quiet hunger bloomed between us like something starved too long. I pressed her closer, hungry. She moaned into my mouth, wanting more.

But then she stilled. Pulled back. Rested her forehead against my jaw.

Her voice broke first. "I'm sorry. I shouldn't have"

"Don't apologize," I said quickly, still catching my breath. "You didn't do anything wrong."

She stepped back, looked down at the floor like it held the answers.

"I still feel things," she whispered. "But I don't trust myself right now to not break us again."

I nodded, slow. My chest ached, but not in the way it used to. This time it was clean. Honest.

"I still love you, Kelly," I said.

She looked up. "I think it's good I'm going home tomorrow. Maybe we give it time. Space. Try being friends for real." Her smile was small but real. She walked to the door. Paused with her hand on the knob. "Thank you, Big Head."

"For what?"

"For letting me be messy. And still seeing me."

I didn't say anything. Just nodded once. And when the door clicked shut behind her, I stood there with my back against the sink, head tilted to the ceiling. Trying not to ask what it would've felt like if I hadn't let her go.

Chapter 31

Kelly

Vanessa's house smelled like warmth and something sweet, perhaps from the peach cobbler Lynn reheated from the baby shower. The lights were dim, warm, and mellow. R&B played low in the background. Cleo Sol, Tems, and Solange. It was a girls' night. Maybe one of the last ones we'd have for a while, with Vanessa nearing her due date and me flying back to Seattle to finish my fellowship.

Khalil and the guys dragged Xavier out for one last night before fatherhood consumed his sleep schedule and his freedom. Vanessa wore a ribbed maternity dress and fuzzy socks. Her edges were slick and her twist out even fuller from the baby shower. She was glowing and exhausted and over it, all at once. Nyah and Lynn were posted up on the couch, passing Karter between each other. He ate up every moment all the belly rubs, cooing, the occasional nugget of chicken slipped under the table.

"I think Karter loves me," Nyah said as Karter rolled onto his back on her lap.

"He loves attention," I said, sipping tea. "Y'all just make yourselves easy targets."

"Well, he clearly has taste," Lynn added.

Vanessa shook her head. "Y'all clowning, but I'm telling you right now. I want my baby girl to be just like him. Low maintenance and always happy to see me."

We laughed. The baby shower was still fresh in our minds. The music, the food, the joy, the love, all of it was perfect.

"I still can't get over how beautiful it turned out," Vanessa said, rubbing her belly. "Mama and Ma Josie outdid themselves."

"They really did," Nyah said, sipping her tea. "But what I really want to know is where did you and Khalil sneak off to after the reveal?"

I raised an eyebrow.

Lynn perked up. "Oh, this is my kind of tea. Do tell, Kelly. Where did y'all go?"

I gave them the rundown of how I cried watching Vanessa and Xavier and told Kahlil I needed a moment. How he pulled me into the bathroom and waited with me. How staring there, looking at him—so attentive, so supportive, so caring I just couldn't help myself.

"Then I kissed him." Three pairs of eyes locked on me like I'd just admitted to eloping in Vegas. "It just happened. One minute we were talking, then we were holding hands. He put his hand on my back and pulled me close. I leaned in. He leaned in."

Vanessa smiled. "And what else?"

"And I pulled back. Said it was better for us to be friends while I work through my shit. I don't want to hurt him again."

Lynn raised a skeptical brow. "You two are exhausting. Fucking friends, Kelly?"

Nyah gave me a concerned look. "Is that what you really want?"

"No," I said, looking at my glass mug. "My love for him is still there. But he's trying to move on. I want to respect that."

Vanessa stood up, hand on her back. "Whew, this baby is active tonight. I'm gonna run to the restroom." She waddled off toward the hall. Karter hopped down and followed behind her, barking, before returning to the couch.

"You sure you're okay?" Nyah asked.

"I'm trying to be," I said. "But it's hard. I don't want to keep getting in the way of Khalil being happy, even if it is with Tasha."

Lynn looked me over. "You get to want stuff too, even if it doesn't live up some magical list of perfection you've concocted."

Before I could reply, we heard a sharp inhale. Then footsteps. Vanessa appeared at the edge of the hallway, gripping the wall.

"Kelly," she panted. "Something's happening."

I jumped up. "What kind of something?"

She winced. "I've been feeling pressure all day, but I thought it was just Braxton Hicks. Now? These are different."

I rushed over. "When did they start feeling different?"

"After the shower. But they were far apart. I didn't want to make a big deal."

"Nessa," I said through gritted teeth. "You should've told me."

"I know," she howled. She doubled over slightly. Another contraction.

"Nyah, time it," I said. "Lynn, grab her bag. Call Zay."

"What do I say?" Lynn asked, already unlocking her phone.

"Tell him his daughter's on the way, and he needs to get home now! Like now-now!" Nessa yelled through another contraction.

I crouched beside Vanessa and helped her breathe through the next wave. My palms were steady, but my heart was racing.

"Okay," I whispered, pressing two fingers to her wrist to count her pulse. "You're doing great."

She nodded, tears gathering in her eyes. "I'm scared, Kelly."

"It's okay, Nessa Ann. I'm here, okay?" She nodded, and a few tears dropped from her eyes.

Lynn turned to me. "He's not answering."

"Call Khalil."

"But"

"Call him!"

I pulled on gloves from the emergency kit Vanessa kept by the hall closet.

"Nessa, we're about to get even more personal, okay?"

"I don't care, just make sure my baby's okay," she cried.

"I'm about to check your cervix, see how far, if you're dilated." She nodded. When I checked her, my chest tightened.

8 centimeters.

"Oh my God," I muttered.

"What?" Vanessa asked. Her eyes were wide with fear. Nyah looked at me, holding her hand.

"Nessa, you're eight centimeters dilated." Nyah understood what I meant immediately. "We need to call an ambulance. This baby could come any minute."

"What do you mean any minute? Zay's not here. I'm not at the hospital." She was panicking.

Khalil's voice came through the speaker, crowds and music blasting in the background.

"Y'all bored without us?" He laughed on the other end.

I grabbed the phone from Lynn.

"Now's not the time, Khalil. Bring Zay. Now. Vanessa's in labor. The baby's coming."

"What? Hold on, I can't hear you." *Fuck.* I had to work double time to keep myself calm so Vanessa wouldn't panic more. I heard Khalil shuffle in the background. A car door slammed, then the engine started.

"Kelly, you on speaker. What did you say?"

"Nessa's eight centimeters dilated," Nessa howled in the background as another contraction pushed through.

"Kelly, that was two minutes," Nyah said, staying focused. Lynn held Karter out of the way.

"Khalil, I don't give a fuck about how many speed zones you break, get me home to my babies," Xavier urged through the speaker.

"Hurry, Khalil. This is moving too fast."

"On my way."

I hung up and turned to Nyah. "Grab towels. Boil water if you have to. Just keep the room calm."

"I got you," she said, moving like a soldier.

Vanessa's breaths came fast and shallow.

"I can't," she whispered between breaths.

"Yes, you can," I said, wiping her brow. "You are. You *are* doing it."

THE FRONT DOOR flew open twenty minutes later.

Khalil and Zay rushed in, eyes wide.

"She's in here!" Nyah called.

Zay dropped to his knees next to Vanessa. "Baby, I'm here."

"I hate you," she groaned as another contraction hit her. "I'm so scared, Zay." Xavier moved to sit behind her, supporting her back against his chest. He took a towel from Nyah and wiped her face.

Khalil came to my side by the kitchen sink. I was on my final scrub of antibacterial soap I found under a cabinet in the guest room.

"Need me?"

I didn't look up.

"I'm scared," I whispered. "What if I mess something up? That's not just a patient. That's my best friend. They already lost one child. I can't be responsible for another."

He touched my shoulder.

"I don't want to hear that right now. You are one of the best doctors around. There's nobody more capable of delivering this baby. You're Dr. Reid. Bad ass doctor that can do whatever. You tell us what you need. We got you. I got you. You hear me?"

His voice anchored me. Deep. Certain. I nodded my head and took a deep breath, exhaling as I walked back over to Vanessa.

Just as Vanessa gritted through another contraction, turning Xavier's hands a ghostly shade of purple, Lynn opened the door and two paramedics rushed in, red kits slung over their shoulders.

"Who's the patient?" one of them asked.

"Over here," I called from the floor, gloves on, hands steady despite the tremble in my heart. They knelt beside me. One reached for Vanessa's wrist to check her pulse.

"She's fully dilated," I said. "The baby's crowning. I've already checked for prolapsed cord and abnormal positioning. No signs of rupture. Vitals are elevated but stable. We don't have time for transport. This baby is coming now."

The other medic glanced down. "You a doctor?"

"Yes. Pediatric oncology fellow at Seattle Children's Hospital," I replied.

He nodded once. "Then lead. We've got your six."

I met his eyes, grateful. I wasn't letting anyone touch my sister but me.

"Sterile towels and suction," I said. "Zay, keep her calm. Nessa, you're about to start pushing, okay?"

Vanessa's voice broke. "Kelly... Keep my baby alive."

I looked up, meeting her eyes. The fear in them broke me while giving me all the motivation I needed to make sure nothing went wrong. Fate be damned.

"You know I got you always," I said to her.

"And forever," she responded.

"Another contraction should be coming in thirty seconds," Nyah shared, watching the timer on her phone. Karter barked chaotically in Lynn's arms. She nuzzled him close to settle her nerves.

"Okay, Nessa. Just breathe with me, okay? It's going to hurt a lot, but you'll feel so much better after. I promise."

Xavier kissed her temple. "We're right here. Yell as loud as you need. Squeeze my hand as hard as you need to, baby. I don't care if you break that motherfucker, you hear me?"

She nodded.

And as the next contraction built, I took a deep breath of my own and said the words I never imagined saying.

"Okay, Nessa. On this next one...push."

One contraction later, the baby slipped into my hands–slippery, perfect, crying like she knew she was loved. Her mother's daughter for sure.

A beautifully loud, wailing, healthy baby girl.

I wrapped her in towels. Placed her on Vanessa's chest. Vanessa sobbed. Zay held them both.

I sat back on my heels, breath caught in my throat.

The room had gone quiet aside from the rustle of towels, the soft cry of the baby, and Xavier whispering Vanessa's name like a prayer. My gloves were still on, streaked with blood and vernix. My body was still, but my breath had gone somewhere far away. Like my body knew to hold it for just a little longer, just until it was really over. I looked at the baby, red-face and hollering, impossibly small but already so real. A whole human. A whole beginning.

And I'd helped bring her here.

It didn't feel heroic.

It didn't feel like a movie.

It felt like pressure. Like terror. Like instinct wrapped in adrenaline. Like I had split open and stitched myself together again all within the span of a few minutes.

"She's perfect," Vanessa whispered, still admiring her and Xavier's little miracle.

I blinked back tears, smiling and nodding.

"You did that," I said.

But inside, my heart was racing from the fall. I backed away slightly, let the paramedics step in to do what they came to do. My body felt full and empty all at once. Then I started shaking. Khalil caught me when I swayed.

"You okay?" he asked.

"I'm fine." I lied. But the truth was written all over me. My hands shook. My eyes wide and far away. My throat was so tight I thought I might scream.

"Let's get you cleaned up," he soothed, pulling me away from everyone and into the guest bathroom.

He turned on the water, let it get warm before he wet a fresh towel. He pulled the gloves from my hands, disposing of them in a trash bag found under the sink. Slowly, softly, he wiped my arms clean. Afterwards, he pulled me in. Didn't say anything else. Just held me. Anchored me. Let me fall apart in the quiet space between his heartbeat and mine.

"She could've died," I whispered into his chest. "They both could've died." He pulled me tighter.

"But she didn't. They're both fine. You did good, Lily-girl." He kissed the top of my head. I squeezed him back tighter.

"Are they okay?"

"Yeah, they're okay. You're okay, too."

And for a few quiet seconds, I let go.

All of it.

The fear. The release. The knowing that I had just done something I couldn't undo. Something that reminded me exactly who I was. And who I still had the chance to become.

Chapter 32

Khalil

THE CINNAMON APPLES FROM THE PLUG-INS SHE KEPT IN every room, singed my nose when I stepped through the door. The lights were low. The curtains drawn. A candle flickered on the kitchen counter beside a bottle of red wine she'd already opened. Tasha moved around with her usual poised self, graceful, curated, aware of how to take up just enough room without seeming like she was trying.

"Hey," she said, looking up from the couch when I walked in. "You hungry? It's late, but I can cook you something."

"I'm good."

She nodded but lingered then settled, her hands busy with the remote, her eyes not really watching the screen. I set my keys down, dropped onto the far end of the couch. The space between us felt wider than usual. Not cold, just stretched thin. She waited a beat. Then another.

"You've been off," she said finally.

I looked over at her. She didn't say it like an accusation. Just a fact. I didn't respond right away. Because she was right.

Ever since Kelly flew back to Seattle, it'd been like I was wading through putty. I'd tried to stay present. I'd tried to be the version of myself that fit easily here. But something had shifted.

Liking Tasha was smooth.

Loving Kelly had been an ache.

But only one of them had made me feel.

"I'm just tired," I said.

I looked at her. Really looked and saw it in her face. The knowing. The waiting.

"You don't have to pretend," she said. "You've been somewhere else for weeks now. And it's because of her."

I sighed and rubbed the back of my neck. "It's not like that."

"It is," she said. "You just don't want to say it out loud. But it's because of Kelly." Tasha didn't get louder. She got sharper.

I closed my eyes for half a second. "It's not just about her."

"But she's part of the equation, isn't it? It's why you didn't want me to come to the baby shower."

"You got an invite. You decided not to come."

"It was a pity invite," she shot back.

I didn't answer because we both knew it was the truth. We'd been out for dinner with Xavier and Vanessa. She was so excited to show the invitations, she felt bad not including Tasha.

She sat back on the couch, crossed her legs, and picked at the hem of her hoodie. "You know what's funny?" she said. "You try so hard to make it look like you were present. As if I didn't notice when your mind wandered off, probably to wherever she was."

"Tasha"

"No, let me finish." Her voice rose. "You want to be a good guy. You want to do right by me. You show up, give what you can, but never all of it. I knew from the beginning you weren't going to stay."

I breathed through my nose.

"You're not wrong," I said. "And I'm not going to sit here and defend something that doesn't feel fair anymore. To either of us."

She looked at me, waiting for the part where I tried to deny it.

To chase her, get back in her good graces so we could live happily ever after. But it didn't. And I think that broke the spell.

Her lips curled. "Wow. That's it?"

"No," I said. "But I'm not going to argue the truth. You deserve somebody who can give you all of them. Not someone who keeps looking back at what he lost."

She flinched, even though I said it gently, it still stung.

"You know what the messed up part is?" she asked, her voice rising again. Now, she'd started pacing in front of the TV. "I believed you could be different. I thought I'd finally found someone who didn't come with ghosts."

"I tried to be."

"But you weren't."

"No," I replied. "I wasn't."

She stopped pacing, turning to me. "Why can't you give us a chance?"

"I did."

"No, you didn't. Not with your heart."

That landed. I nodded. "You're right."

Tasha crossed her arms. "So, what was I? A placeholder? A warm body while you waited for your feelings to change?"

"No," I said. "You were kind. You were honest with me. You gave me space when I didn't know I needed it. But I never stopped bleeding."

She blinked. "That's not love."

"I know."

"And it damn sure ain't healing."

"I know that, too."

She shook her head, jaw tight. "You men swear you're so self-aware just because you don't raise your voice."

I stayed still.

"I was trying," she said, biting her words. "I bent. I made space. I met you where you were. And every time you looked at me, I felt you measuring the distance between what I gave you and what you lost with Kelly."

"I didn't mean to"

"But you did! You meant to keep yourself guarded just enough so if I ever walked away, you could say you never really opened up."

"I couldn't open up something that was already locked down."

She was grieving the version of us she had dared to imagine. A version she dreamed of in her mind. A version we could never be.

"I don't hate you, Khalil," she said after a long pause. Her voice cracked. "But I resent how easy you look sitting there."

"It's not easy," I said. "It's necessary."

She looked away. Her lip trembled. I stood slowly, walked to the door. Paused with my hand on the knob.

"I hope you find someone who makes you feel chosen. First and full. No fractions. No doubts."

She didn't say anything as I turned the knob. Before I walked out, I heard her whisper behind me, soft, but sharp enough to stay with me. "Go be with the woman you never stopped loving."

The night air hit my skin like a cleansing. I didn't feel triumphant. I didn't feel relieved. But I felt free. Not from her. But from pretending. Pretending that I could detach myself from what I wanted most. Pretending that I could hold onto comfort while craving clarity.

My phone buzzed in my pocket. A text from Xavier:

ZAY

Took us a while to settle on a name, but here it is.

I smiled at the picture of my goddaughter wrapped up like a baby burrito. For a second, it felt like the world was shifting into alignment. I walked toward my car, the city humming in the distance.

Ready.

Rooted.

Part Four

"Put It On Me [Remix]"

Ja Rule (feat. Lil Mo ✦ Vita)

Chapter 33

Kelly

SEATTLE GREETED ME WITH RAIN. NOT A DOWNPOUR. Not dramatic. Just a constant mist that blurred the city into watercolor, dampening the air, softening the edges of buildings, coaxing leaves from green to gold. I stepped out of the rideshare, rolling my suitcase behind me, Karter in his soft carrier slung across my chest. He whined low, then yawned, his tiny face peeking out beneath the mesh.

"We're back," I whispered, looking up at my building. He blinked once like he agreed.

The apartment felt unfamiliar at first. Too clean. Too untouched. Like a life I had walked out of and returned wearing someone else's skin. But it didn't scare me this time. I unpacked slowly. Put lavender in the oil diffuser. Piled all of Karter's new dog toys my dad spoiled him with in his cage. He was too cute wrestled with a chicken looking thing that squeaked. With everything put away, I made myself some tea and decided to sit on the patio.

When I stepped out on the slightly damp concrete, I saw the peace lily plant tucked away in the corner. The same one I'd thrown against the wall before breaking down. She'd been placed here in her original plastic pot, most likely by my father. It'd been a few months since I'd last seen her, but here she was, growing, thriving, even with her droopy leaves speckled with rainwater.

I sat my tea down and brought the plant inside the warmth of my apartment. Sitting her on the sink, I grabbed a soft towel and wiped the excessive water from her leaves in the same gentle way my grandmother taught me. I searched for a bucket to re-pot her, let her roots stretch, let the excess water drain away. Eventually, I got her situated in a white mop bucket and sat her by the window. Call me crazy, but her leaves seemed to raise a little higher. Like she'd chosen to heal herself, even in subprime conditions.

"Go ahead and breathe, baby girl," I whispered against her leaves. "We got this."

I grabbed my tea and snuggled on the couch, calling Karter to sit on my lap. Outside, a slow heavy drizzle started, a soft rain that felt more like a confession than chaos. Clouds thickened overhead, curling into themselves like grief no longer needing to scream. Leaves danced with the wind; their golds and crimsons muted under the weight of moisture.

Karter shifted on my lap, his cheek pressed to my chest, the steady rhythm of his breathing syncing with mine. I curled my hand around his tiny back, let my eyes drift to the window, and watched the world blur. This wasn't the kind of rain that drowned you. It was the kind that stayed, lingering until it seeped into your clothes, your skin, your spirit until you surrendered to it.

That was the point. Not to push through the heaviness. Not to outrun it. But sit in it. To sip tea in it. To hold your son and your breath and your bruised peace lily and say I was still here. Somewhere beneath all that gray, I was beginning to unfurl too, slowly, softly. Like a leaf that didn't mind the fall.

THE FIRST DAY back on rounds felt like returning to a play you'd rehearsed in another lifetime. Same halls. Same white coats. Same pagers and protocol. I walked differently, not because I wanted to be noticed, but because I didn't want to disappear. I greeted the few colleagues I remembered by their name. Asked about their kids, their specialty tracks. I smiled more. Not wide, just enough to signal I was really there. Present. Choosing this version of myself on purpose.

Morning rounds started with a familiar cadence. Vitals, labs, review the charts, check the boards. But my pace was different. Intentional. Unrushed. I didn't move like I had something to prove, only something to give.

Room 408: *Janelle, age 9, Wilms tumor, post-nephrectomy and first round of chemo.*

I was greeted with bright eyes and a high ponytail carefully brushed by her mother this morning. She showed me her unicorn stickers as I checked her port's site dressing. She said the sparkiest one was for her nurse if today didn't hurt too bad.

"You like unicorns?" I asked.

She nodded. "They're magic."

I leaned in. "You know what else is magic?"

"What?"

"How fast your body's healing, growing strong, even with just one kidney."

She grinned. "Dr. Kelly, you sound like my grandma."

"She sounds like a smart woman."

We fist-bumped. Her mom mouthed *thank you* behind her.

Room 412: *Noah, age 6, sickle cell anemia, admitted for pain crisis.*

He was drawing on the whiteboard when I walked in, his tiny frame bundled in dinosaur pajamas. He offered me a green crayon and told me the T-Rex was him big and strong even when it hurts.

"How's your pain today, buddy?" I asked, crouching to his level.

He shrugged. "My legs still feel like fire a little."

I nodded gently. "Fire legs are tough, but you're tougher."

"The heating pad helped," his dad added. "And the red popsicle."

I grinned. "Medicine and popsicles. Best combo there is."

His dad chuckled from the corner. "You're the only one that can get him to say more than a few words."

"It's because I know the secret."

"What secret?" Noah piped up.

"Dinosaurs don't quit," I whispered, tapping his nose. The boy squealed.

Dr. Sayegh caught up with me near the nurses' station. "I've been watching you today," she said, arms folded. "Taking notes on how you're doing."

"Better or worse?"

She gave me that soft, rare smile she saved for meaningful moments. "Centered."

We made our way to the NICU. A quiet reverence always lingered there — low lights, soft beeping, the hush of hope and fear woven into every breath. We checked in on twins born at twenty-eight weeks. Their mother, no older than me, had tear tracks on her face but fire in her eyes.

"They're fighters," I said gently. "So are you."

She didn't say anything. Just nodded and kept her hand on the incubator window. Sometimes, that was enough.

While I missed my friends and family back home, it felt good to be getting back to what I loved most. Showing others healing didn't mean you had to have pain. I thought it'd take me a few weeks to get back into the groove of things, but being back in the halls, seeing the smiling faces of patients, the sage advice from nurses, it felt like a part of me that was hiding was coming to the forefront.

At lunch, I didn't eat in the breakroom. I walked down to the courtyard instead, sitting beneath a cherry tree that hadn't bloomed yet, journal in my lap.

I wrote:

I'm not the same woman who cracked.
I'm rebuilding without hiding the fracture lines.
I miss her. But I don't miss losing myself.

Once I'd soaked up what little sun the cloudy Seattle sky offered, I headed back to the office I'd been using to write reports and do research. On my way, I peeked into patients' rooms, checking in with their parents, passing out stickers here and there. Up ahead, I saw Dr. Sayegh speaking with a different attending in cardiothoracic. She flagged me down before I could turn the corner. When I reached her, she pulled me into her office before the next rotation.

"I wanted to tell you something," she said, sliding into her chair. "You're excelling. Not just technically. Emotionally. Professionally. You're modeling exactly the kind of doctor we want leading this next generation. The doctor I chose."

My throat caught. "I—thank you."

She leaned forward. "Whatever you did while you were gone? Keep doing it."

I nodded. "I'm trying."

"You're not trying, Kelly. You're doing."

Later that afternoon, I was reviewing a new chart outside of Room 516, peds respiratory, when I saw the name: Kahlia. Ten-years-old. Persistent wheezing. History of RSV. Standard. Familiar.

I knocked on the door, stepped inside. And everything inside me froze. The woman standing at the foot of the bed looked up. And I knew. Same bone structure. Same eyes. Same grief in the corners of her mouth. She wore her hair in a curly updo, a neutral wrap around her head. No trace of makeup. Just a plain black sweatshirt and hospital bracelet from checking her daughter in.

This bitch.

God had to be playing with me. All these years, all those quiet conversations. The heartbreak I thought I could soothe. The void he worked tirelessly to find and then replace. Stood there, right in front of me.

"Hello," I said, my voice somewhere between panicked and professional. "I'm Dr. Kelly Reid. I'll be overseeing Kahlia's care."

She smiled. But something passed through her eyes brief, sharp.

"Nice to meet you," she said. "I'm LaToya." She said her name like a test.

LaToya. LaToya.

I wanted to push it over the edge of a cliff as it passed around my mind. Instead, I nodded, even though my pulse was sprinting ahead of me.

"Dr. Reid, the symptoms?" Dr. Sayegh asked behind me.

Don't react. Don't assume. Don't break.

I turned to the tablet in my hands to keep my hands from trembling. "How long has the wheezing been this persistent?"

"Couple weeks," she said. "It got worse after her last cold. I thought it would pass, but..." She exhaled like she'd been holding her breath since she'd walked out of the house with that damn blue suitcase. "It didn't."

I nodded again, mechanical. My jaw ticked as I fought to hold back the words I really wanted to say. "Any fever? Chest tightness? Difficulty sleeping?"

"Some nights, yeah. I tried giving her some fish oil to loosen it up, but it didn't help not a bit."

My eyebrow raised when it caught the distinct way she said oil with an 'r' added to the pronunciation. It was the same regional fleck my mother and grandmother had anytime they said "boil" and "foil." I kept my voice neutral, the way I'd been drilled to do so from so many years of medical training. But inside my chest, boom after boom went off.

Because I knew. Knew the arch of that jaw. The hazel eyes with small flecks of green catching the light like fire. The guarded way she held herself like the world had asked too much, too often. As if she hadn't left a hole of emptiness in the heart of one of the best people in the world. And here I was, struggling to maintain my composure. Be professional. When all I wanted to do was curse this lady out from here to hell. And she had the audacity to sit here with another child. Like the one before didn't matter. "Does she have any known allergies?" My voice cracked slightly on the word allergies. Dr. Sayegh raised a brow, but let me continue with the examination.

"She had a bad reaction to something when she was younger. Bactrim. My poor baby broke out in hives all over. They told me it was a Sulfa allergy."

I froze. My stylus hovered over the tablet. Sulfa allergy. Hives. The same hives I'd made fun of when Khalil had them while trying to recover from his sinus infection. Little red patches covered his body. I'd enjoyed making him my fake patient, rubbing ointment over his back and nursing him back to health.

My throat tightened. "Any other allergies?" I kept my voice neutral when all I wanted to do was scream, *How could you leave him?*

"Nope. Just that one. I'll never forget it. Kahlia was miserable for days," she said, smoothing her hand over the girl's forehead.

I gave a tight smile. "I'll be sure her meds are updated accordingly."

"Thank you, doctor," she replied. The word sat heavy between us.

I managed a smile that probably looked more like a grimace. "You're welcome." In my rush to leave the room, my badge caught on the IV pole. I muttered a quiet, "I'm sorry," as I untangled it.

LaToya didn't say anything else as Dr. Sayegh and I left the room. She just watched. Waited. Maybe wondered. Dr. Sayegh rambled off what she thought might be the cause of Kahlia's illness. I listened intently to still the rampant frenzy happening in my veins. My ears ran hot. When Dr. Sayegh dismissed me to my office, I closed the door with a huff. I leaned against it, my breath shaky.

She's alive.

She was alive and has another child. A girl that looked just like Khalil. Same eyes, same curly black hair. And he didn't know.

What am I supposed to do with that?

~

AFTER WORK, I walked into my apartment in a daze. I took Karter for a walk, picked up and disposed of his poop. Took a long, skin-scorching shower. I couldn't believe the day I'd had.

Khalil, his mother, and sister all shared the same eyes that quietly observed the world before speaking. The knowing wouldn't let me rest. It pulsed in the base of my throat, itched at my palms. My mind kept looping every detail. The cadence of her voice, the faint scars on her forearms, the way she kept her distance even while thanking me for being kind.

What am I supposed to do with this?

The next morning, I sat on my couch, laptop on my lap Karter tugging at a bone by my feet virtual session open and waiting. Ms. Reece appeared a minute later, hair wrapped in a bold purple scarf, gold hoops catching the light through her window.

"Morning, baby girl," she said. "You look like your spirit's holding its breath."

I exhaled so fast it made me dizzy. "You're not wrong."

"Let's start there. Tell me what's going on?"

"I think I met Khalil's mother yesterday."

Ms. Reece blinked once, then nodded, slow and knowing. "You think?"

"No," I admitted. "I know. I'm almost positive it's her. They look just the same. Same face, same eyes, same curly hair. She was there with her daughter, Kahlia. She didn't recognize me, but I recognized her."

"Hmm," Ms. Reece murmured, leaning forward. "So now the question is: what does that recognition ask of you?"

I swallowed. "That's what I don't know. Should I say something? Should I keep it to myself? I don't know."

"You know," she said gently. "You're just scared of what comes with it."

"I'm afraid of what it'll do to him if I tell him," I said. "I'm even more afraid of what it'll do if I don't tell him."

Ms. Reece nodded. "Say more."

I stared at the glass mug sitting on the coffee table. The tea bag stilled, the water having gone cold. "He's wanted this for so long. Answers. Closure. Her." I closed my eyes, inhaling and breathing out the strain in my chest. "Am I the right person to give him that news?"

Ms. Reece tilted her head. "Are you afraid it will undo him? Or you?"

She waited. Patient.

"I'm scared it'll undo the version of him I'm letting myself believe him. The one who isn't looking backward anymore."

"And what if the truth is the very thing that frees him forward?"

She let me gather my thoughts in the silence. Karter stirred beside me on the rug.

"I have to tell him, don't I?"

"Oh Kelly, I think you already know you need to."

I pressed my fingers to my eyes, sinking back on the couch. "God, this is too messy."

She smiled. "So is healing."

Chapter 34

Kelly

THE HALLWAY SMELLED LIKE ANTISEPTIC AND ORANGES, a weird combo that had somehow started to feel like comfort again. We moved in a triangle me, Dr. Sayegh, and Elena. I'd grown to admire Elena in recent weeks. She was sharp, observant, asked good questions without trying too hard to sound like a know-it-all. It was funny I resented her five months ago.

Our rounds had been smooth that morning. A post-op check-in on a six-year-old with a pin removal. A consult for a teen with unexplained bruising. And an impromptu appointment with a toddler that had a stubborn ear infection who kept calling every woman in a white coat "mommy." I was finding my rhythm again. I smiled when it made sense. I cracked jokes about my terrible handwriting with little patients and their nurses.

We were walking down the hall when Dr. Sayegh stopped, flipping through the last chart on her tablet.

"Kahlia Baptiste," she said. "Persistent wheezing. History of RSV, no hospitalizations since infancy. Symptoms escalated after a mild respiratory infection two weeks ago. Asthma medicine isn't working as well as expected. We ordered more testing when she checked-in."

Elena looked over her shoulder. "Could it be misdiagnosed?"

"Possibly," Dr. Sayegh replied. "We're waiting on spirometry and chest imaging. But there's a chance we're looking at a developing case of pediatric bronchiectasis. Could also be early signs of a connective tissue disorder." She turned to me. "What are your thoughts?"

I nodded. "She presented stable but resistant to typical bronchodilators. I flagged the inconsistent response."

Dr. Sayegh gave me a subtle nod. "Good catch. Let's check in. Dr. Reid, you'll present."

When we entered the room, Kahlia was sitting up in bed, drawing in a sketchbook. She looked up and grinned when she saw me.

"Hi, Dr. Reid."

"Hey, Little Basquiat. You feeling better today?"

She gave me a shy head nod side to side.

And then I felt it. That slow burn at the side of my neck, crawling up my cheeks and ears. I looked to my left. LaToya stood near the window, arms folded loosely, head tilted slightly like she was trying to figure me out through layers of time. Her expression wasn't hostile. Neither was it casual. It was curious. Inspecting. Like she'd seen my face from a memory she couldn't quite place.

I cleared my throat and stepped forward, tablet in hand.

"We're seeing some signs that point us toward an atypical presentation," I said, speaking more to Khalil's mother now. "Given Kahlia's persistent wheezing, history of RSV, and recent lack of response to short-acting bronchodilators, we're moving forward with a chest CT today."

LaToya's brows creased. "Dr. Reid, I barely made it out of high school. Put that in plain English."

"I'm sorry." I smiled. "We're noticing a few things that aren't following usual patterns when treating asthma. Because Kahlia's still wheezing, has a history of a bad RSV infection, and hasn't been getting better with breathing treatments, we want to get a clearer picture of what's going on in her lungs. We're hoping the CT scan, or detailed X-ray, can help us get a clearer picture."

Toya nodded her head. "So, it's not just asthma?"

"It could be," I replied. "But we want to rule out other possibilities. One thing we're checking for is a condition where the airways get stretched out and hold mucus, which can cause long-term breathing problems. We're also looking to rule out anything related to the immune system that could be affecting her lungs. In kids Kahlia's age, it's not unusual for these things to show up a little while after they've had a big infection."

"Okay." She nodded slowly.

"I'll be checking in again after the scan results are in, but for now, her breathing's stable and we're managing the inflammation."

Kahlia looked up from her notebook. "Does this mean I still have to use the mask thing?"

"For now." I smiled. "But I promise to find you some good color pencils. Deal?"

"Deal," Kahlia agreed and smiled, going back to her drawing.

I tucked the tablet under my arm and made a note to return in a few hours. But as I moved to leave, I felt Toya's eyes still on me. Quizzically narrowed slits that matched my movements. Not watching.

Remembering.

When I returned later on with a fresh pack of deluxe coloring pencils, the floor was hushed. It was a calm that normally descended after dinnertime in pediatrics. I knocked softly before entering.

Kahlia was asleep, her chest rising and falling beneath the knit throw her mother had brought from home. Her sketch pad had slipped from her hands and onto the bed beside her. The light above her was dim.

LaToya sat in the corner, still in the same black sweatshirt, hair pulled up in a high, wild ponytail. She looked tired in a way I understood all too well. It crept up on you slowly and settled into your bones out of nowhere, refusing to leave.

I checked the monitor, adjusted the nebulizer mask on Kahlia's face, then turned to leave.

"You from New Orleans?"

The question caught me mid-step. I turned. "No, ma'am. Born and raised in Houston."

"Hmph." Toya sat forward slightly, her voice steady but low. "You sure you don't have no people from the city?"

I tucked my hands into my pockets. "My mother was from there. My grandma and uncle."

"What's the names?"

I cleared my throat. "Sonya Green. Her kids are Charisse and Paul. Charisse was my mother."

The look on her face wasn't just recognition. It was a gut-punch.

"Lord," she whispered, drawing the word out. "You Ms. Sonya's grandbaby?"

"Yes, ma'am."

She sat back, blinking, trying to refocus a blurry photo in her mind. "I knew your mama," she said finally. "Not well, but enough. She was loud and fine and too smart for her own good. How's she doing?"

"She passed about six months ago."

"I'm so sorry to hear that. I used to see her going to your grandma flower shop when I walked home from school. She always had this look on her face like the world owed her softness yet had the nerve to give her thorns." I didn't respond. LaToya exhaled. "That seem like a lifetime ago."

I stepped closer to Kahlia's bed, gently adjusting her IV line where it looped around the rail.

"You're Khalil's mother, aren't you?" I asked, staring straight into her eyes.

She laughed, even though her eyes reddened and strained.

"People always said he was my twin." She grimaced, her eyes going glossy. She looked down at her hands, her fingers knotted tightly, knuckles going pale. "Do you know him?"

Do I know him?

Khalil carried my heart in the comforting embrace of his arms. Nurtured it, tended to it when I left it for dead. He saw the parts of myself I kept hidden, even from myself, and never looked away. Not once. How could she sit here and ask if I knew him? He was the love of my life. *The love of my life.* And here I was standing in front of the woman who had broken his innocent heart, a heart so pure, so golden.

"You must know him well. I can see it in your eyes, the defensiveness." Her jaw clenched. "I never meant to be found like this."

"Like what," I gritted low between teeth. "An apparition living a whole new life while the one you left behind learned how to move forward, piecing the puzzle together. Alone."

The tears grew heavy in her lower lids. "They were better off without me," she murmured, her voice watery.

I shook my head, trying to remember I was a doctor at this hospital and not a random person off the street. I sat in the empty chair beside her. Close, but not too close. "So, what happened?" I asked quietly.

"I left because I was drowning," she said. "And I knew I'd pull them under with me." She paused. "No one understands what addiction is really like. What it really takes from you. You hear stories. You watch the movies, the afterschool specials. But nobody talks about the mornings when your baby's crying and you can't feel anything. The days you look at your man and hate him for trying to love you when you feel like dust inside."

My throat tightened.

"I didn't want Khalil to grow up watching me fade," she said. "Didn't want him to spend his life trying to fill in what I made hollow."

"You don't think leaving hollowed him out, too?"

Her eyes glistened. "I know it did."

"He waited for you. His whole life," I added. "Even when he stopped saying it aloud, he was still waiting. He built this whole magnificent, brilliant life trying not to look like he needed you, but he did."

She covered her face with her hands. "I always knew he'd turn out alright."

"He did, but not fully. He's been carrying your shadow all his life."

She was silent, then whispered," I didn't think I deserved to be his mother anymore."

"That's not your choice." I looked over at a still sleeping Kahlia. "I have to tell him. He deserves to know."

Toya nodded slowly. "I'm guessing he'll want to come here. Meet me." I nodded. She looked at her daughter. "I figured. He's my twin, but his daddy's son all the same."

"I need you not to run."

She looked up at me, steady, through the tears held in her eyes. "I won't."

IT TOOK me two days to pick up the phone. Not because I was unsure. But because I knew once I did, nothing between us would ever sit in the same place again. Every time I hovered over his name in my phone, I thought of the last time I saw him. The softness in his voice when he said he was proud of me, the quiet ache in his eyes when we pulled apart before anything dangerous could happen.

He was doing the work. Trying to be whole. Trying not to need me.

And here I was, about to unearth the part of him he'd buried deeper than either of us knew.

I sat on the edge of my bed, fresh out the shower, hair covered in deep conditioner in four big twists, phone clutched in my hand like it weighed more than it should. Karter sat beside me, head tilted, sensing the shift in my breath. I ran my fingers through his fur, more to ground myself than comfort him. I took a breath and hit "Call." It rang twice before he answered.

"Hey." His voice caught me off guard. It did something to me I hadn't quite figured out how to turn off.

"Hey," I said, trying to keep my tone steady.

"You good?" he asked.

I exhaled. "I'm not calling to start anything."

"I didn't think you were." My mouth opened, but the words clung to the back of my throat. "Lily-girl, you didn't call just to hear me breathe, did you?"

"I found your mother." It came out quick, quicker than I expected. "Khalil," I said softly. "She's here. In Seattle."

Still, no sound on the line. Just his breathing, shallow, too careful.

"She came in with her daughter. Kahlia. Ten years old. Respiratory issues."

When he finally spoke, his voice was dust.

"How do you know?"

"She told me. After I told her who I was. She didn't know at first. But when she realized... it was like her whole body remembered you. She looks just like you."

Another pause.

"What did she say?"

"That she wasn't ready to be found. That she thought she didn't deserve you."

His breath shook. I heard it.

"I told her I was going to tell you. I told her not to run."

"Is she—" His voice cracked. "Is she still there?"

"She is."

I didn't say more. Didn't have to. After a long silence, he asked the only question that mattered.

"I'm coming. Can I stay with you?"

My throat tightened.

"Yeah. Yes, of course."

"And Kelly?"

"Yeah?"

"Thank you." His voice broke at the end.

And it broke me. My heart palpitated in my chest and tears lined the rims of my eyes. My heart broke for Khalil. Years of learning to live without the love and nurturing of a mother. Years of saving, bearing the weight of needing to save everyone around him because he couldn't save the one who needed it most. I swiped at my cheek to wipe away the tears that fell.

Chapter 35

Khalil

THE WHEELS HIT THE TARMAC HARDER THAN expected. I didn't exhale until we reached the gate. The chaos of deplaning began. People in middle rows stood first, reaching over those in aisle seats to grab their belongings from the overhead bins. Folks stretched in the aisle like they'd been sitting longer than the four hours of the flight duration. But I moved slow. Methodical.

I stepped off the plane and into the tunnel of glass and steel, Seattle's gray skies pressed flat against the windows. The air smelled like jet fuel and coffee. The walk to the rideshare pickup felt longer than it should've. Every step, my mind spun tighter—around her voice, her face, the ghost I'd carried in my ribs since I was a kid and now may have to face with skin and breath. And another child.

LaToya Baptiste.

Not just a name. Not just a wound.

My mother. Breathing. Somewhere in this city.

I climbed into the backseat of a black car. My palms itched. My throat felt too dry, and my stomach hadn't stopped its quiet somersaults since I boarded the plane in Houston. The ride blurred by. Tall buildings. Wet pavement. A skyline that didn't belong to either of us.

But she did.

Kelly.

And that was the only reason I wasn't coming undone.

She opened the door before I could knock twice. Hair tied up. A thick hoodie and leggings covered her body.

"Khalil, I told you I would pick you up from the airport."

I stepped inside. "You got something to eat?"

She arched an eyebrow. "You're really asking me for food right now?"

I grinned, but it was weak. "I was hoping you'd take care of your guest since last time didn't go so well."

She didn't say anything at first. Just walked forward and pulled me into a hug. And that was it. All that cool I'd rehearsed on the flight? Gone. Melted into the sleeves of her hoodie. I wrapped my arms around her and didn't let go for a long time.

"Okay," she whispered eventually, voice warm against my chest. "You don't have to be strong for me."

I swallowed. Didn't speak. Just stood there, eyes closed, letting the weight of what I'd carried fall between us. Karter trotted over like he owned the place, tail wagging, eyes full of judgment.

Kelly pulled back and kissed my chest. "Let me get you a drink, my sweet boy. I guess you can have one too, Big Head."

I laughed, following her to the kitchen. She handed me a bottle of ginger ale and leaned against the counter.

"How are you feeling?" she asked, softly.

"I'm all over the place." I drank from the bottle. "How's her daughter doing?"

"Tomorrow's the earliest we'll have full test results back. Dr. Sayegh's still leaning toward post-infectious bronchiectasis."

"And her mom?"

"She's still here, if that's what you're asking," Kelly said. "Not in denial, not in panic."

That landed heavy in my chest.

"She know I'm coming?"

Kelly hesitated. "Yes."

I nodded.

"You don't have to see her if you're not ready. The choice is yours."

"No, I do."

We moved to the couch, Karter wedging himself in the middle like a self-appointed chaperone. Kelly tossed him a tiny treat from the coffee table bowl. "He's been my emotional support baby. He has official papers and everything."

"I thought that was my job," I muttered, sinking into the cushions.

Her leg brushed mine, not on purpose, but she didn't move it either. "You okay?" she asked again, this time quieter.

"No," I said honestly. "It's like... there's a part of me that's still six. Still looking out the window, watching her drive off, waiting for her to come back." I looked down at my hands. "And now I'm supposed to walk up to her and be...what? Cool? Calm? Thankful?"

"You don't have to be anything but honest," Kelly said.

I looked over at her.

"She's not a monster," she added. "But she made a choice. And it cost you something she'll never be able to repay."

I exhaled hard. "How'd she look?"

"She looked worn. But not destroyed. Healthy."

I leaned back, letting my head rest against the couch cushion.

"I don't know what I'll say."

"You don't have to decide tonight."

She handed me the remote. "Pick a movie. Something that doesn't make me think."

I scrolled, then smirked.

"What?" she asked.

"You should already know what I'm putting on." I smiled genuinely.

"Khalil, I swear if you make me watch *Leprechaun in the Hood* again," she said. "You know what? I'm picking, give me the remote."

"Always hating," I said, handing her the remote. She searched through Netflix until she landed on *The Wood*. Karter climbed into Kelly's lap like he had seniority. She pressed play, and the opening notes of the soundtrack filled the room. We didn't say much after that. We didn't have to.

Kelly leaned back onto the couch, one hand absently stroking Karter's fur, the other tucked beneath the blanket she'd wrapped them in. The soft flicker of the TV cast light across her face, warm and golden.. I glanced over at her when Omar Epps made his awkward entrance, and she was smiling. Not the kind she forced for everyone else. This one reached her eyes and laughed back at the character's antics.

Outside, the rain tapped gently against the windows. Inside, something calmer bloomed, like the thick, white petals of the peace lily next to her windows. It wasn't fireworks. It wasn't a rush. Just an ember catching again, slow and steady.

For once, it didn't feel like goodbye was just waiting around the corner.

MUTED CONVERSATIONS in the hospital cafeteria echoed off tile and glass. Wide windows stretched along one side of the room, revealing a wintry courtyard outside. Stone beaches formed a circle, empty planters spaced between them, a fountain long turned off for the season in the center.

Kelly walked beside me, her pace unhurried, her shoulders brushing mine every few steps like she was reminding me she was still there.

"There," she said, pointing to a table in the corner.

My mother sat alone, hands curled around a white paper cup. The wild, curly hair I remembered as a child was pulled up high, secured by a scarf. She looked out of the window, studying the barren cherry blossom tree—its stretched out branches, leafless. When she turned and saw me, her whole body tensed, not in fear, but motherly recognition. Bone-deep regret.

Kelly placed a gentle hand on my back.

"I'll be back after I check on some patients," she said softly.

I nodded, watching her walk away. Then, I walked forward, sitting in the chair opposite the woman who birthed me. For a second, we didn't speak. Just stared at each other, mirror images.

"You want some coffee?" she asked.

"No. I'm good."

Silence. The kind stitched with old wounds and too many words that never made it out.

"You look good," she started. "Part of me was nervous you'd change your mind about coming."

"Then you don't know me at all," I said through my teeth. I swiped at my nose and looked out at the courtyard.

She nodded once. "That's fair."

I studied her, every line, every weathered curve around her mouth. She looked like someone who had survived being forgotten.

"I know you got questions," she said. "Ask me."

"You remember the last thing you said to me?"

She flinched. "To brush your teeth."

"Then you ran off. Like you were making groceries. But you didn't come back."

She swallowed. "Yeah."

I leaned forward, my voice dropping another octave. "You know what it's like to walk into every room wondering if the woman who made you can still breathe your name?"

"No. I can't."

"For years I hated myself for wanting you to come back. It's why I went back to New Orleans, hoping you'd turn a corner and make it right."

She looked away, eyes brimming.

"I'm sorry," she whispered. "For all of it."

I shook my head. "That ain't enough." The tree outside danced in the wind, leafless. "You got a daughter," I said.

She nodded. "Kahlia."

"You love her?"

"With everything I didn't know how to give you."

"Why–" My throat tightened. "Why couldn't you learn how to give it to me?"

"Because I was broken," she said, voice shaking. "And the only thing worse than watching your mother fall apart is thinking you're the one supposed to catch her. I didn't want that for you."

"So you gave me nothing," I rushed out.

"I thought that was better than giving you a version of me that could've ruined you."

"You ruined us anyway," I said. "Pops just now starting to move on. I can't be with somebody unless I feel like I need to be doing something for them."

Her face fell. She didn't answer.

"I became the kind of man who gives everything and expects nothing. Who waits for the people I love to leave, even when I'm standing right in front of them."

Her eyes glistened.

I kept going.

"I don't know how to hold anything without wondering when it's going to slip away. I give love like a warning. Like a debt. Like... if I just do enough, they'll stay."

Her hand was still between us, motionless.

"I did that to someone," I added. "Someone who means everything and then some."

Her eyes found mine. Wet. Sharp. Mother-soft. "Someone like Dr. Reid?"

I didn't answer. Didn't need to.

She smiled, sad. "She look at you like she already knowsyou bleed for the people you love. And she chooses you, too. Put me in my place good-fashioned when I admitted who I was."

I swallowed hard, staying quiet.

She leaned forward, resting her hand against her chest, like she was steadying something deeper than her breath.

"You don't have to forgive me," she said. "I wouldn't blame you if you never did."

I stayed quiet, turning away.

"But don't," she added, voice trembling. "Don't spend the rest of your life feeling like you gotta earn being loved."

Silence rang. I stared out at the courtyard. That tree looked dead. But I knew better. It was just waiting. Like I had been. Still, I didn't take her hand. I caught her eyes, let her see me hurting. She sat back slowly, like the truth knocked something loose in her spine.

"I thought about you every day," she said, looking out into the courtyard. "Wondered how tall you'd gotten. If you still like them Hubig pies your daddy would bring home after work...I kept telling myself you'd forget me. You wasn't old enough to remember anyway. It'd be a blessing in disguise."

"The day you left haunts me," I said matter-of-fact.

"I know. It haunts me, too," she replied, her voice cracking. "But when people see a Black woman breaking, they ignore the fear. They say she bitter. Fast. Crazy. I had a baby on my hip and grief in my chest, and nobody said a damn thing. Gave a damn."

"You want to talk about your grief," I spat out. "What did you have to grieve? You're the one that disappeared."

She looked down into her folded hands resting on her lap. "I don't know, baby"

"Khalil," I corrected.

"I don't know, Khalil. Maybe from being born in a house where women didn't cry. Maybe from loving a man who loved me more than I knew what to do with. Maybe from waking up every day, knowing I wasn't okay and still had to be a wife and mother. I needed an escape."

"So you left," I said. "To grieve while you killed everything in your wake."

"No." She shook her head vehemently. "I left because I thought I was the poison, and the people I loved kept drinking from me." She reached her hand over the table, waiting for mine. I stared at the foreign fingers and looked back out into the courtyard. "I thought I was finally safe when I met your father. He did everything right. But I didn't know how to be held. I didn't know how to sit still inside a good thing without clawing at the walls. It wasn't his love that scared me. It was being seen and having nowhere to hide. And he saw me. Saw my fear. Saw the little plastic baggies I tried to hide. Saw through my glazed eyes."

She reached into her purse and pulled out a photo. It was me around eight-years-old, missing a tooth, eating a cold cup while talking to Xavier at a block party. I couldn't make out the full expression on my face from the far angle the picture was taken, but I could see the happiness and laughter.

"There was one time I thought I could come back, then I saw you like this. Happy and too stinking cute. Bad as hell, I'm sure." She laughed softly. "I changed my mind. Snapped the picture then went and got my next fix. Took me about a year before I could develop the film. I think I'd made it to Colorado by then. Told myself I was gon' get my life together, even if I never saw you again."

I stared at it. The color had started to fade, and the edges were worn.

"You go to meetings or anything?" I asked quietly.

She nodded, a subtle beam to her eyes. "I quit cold turkey for a while. Then found out I was pregnant with Kahlia. Figured God was giving me my second chance. First couple of years were good, then her no good daddy left. Things got tight. Found me a group so I wouldn't go back down that road. Got my ten-year chip last spring." She offered a small smile I turned down.

I looked at her again. Really looked. The ghost I remembered as faded away, making room for the human. "Why reach out now? If you never ran into Kelly, we wouldn't be sitting here."

She exhaled. "Dr. Reid made me see if I really loved you, I couldn't stay away. I needed to show up for you, even if it might be too late."

I rubbed my jaw. "You missed a lot."

"I know," she whispered. "But I'm here. And if the only thing I ever got to tell you is how sorry I am and how much I love you, I'll do that. Until the day I die."

I rested my head in my hands, taking deep breaths. My body warmed as my heart cried inside my chest. "I don't know what to do with you," I admitted. "Where you belong in my life now."

"You don't have to decide today. I just hope you'll give me a chance."

"And what about your daughter?" I asked. "Kahlia?"

Her face softened. "She knows about you. She's gotten to the point where she knows enough to understand what happened. She asks about you all the time. Made her promise me she wouldn't reach out to you on Facebook or wherever. She knows I'm talking to you now. Wants to meet you, but I said it was your decision."

I inhaled and exhaled, trying to breathe past the knot in my throat. She reached across the table again to place her palm on my arm.

"I can't go back and change my mistakes. But I'm here now. If you'll let me, I'll keep being here. Even if it's just a few texts here and there. Or a call on the holidays."

I looked at the hand still on my arm. "I don't forgive you. But I hear you."

She squeezed slightly. "I'll take it."

I stood from my chair, shrugging her hand away from me. I walked away with the photo still in my hand, leaving LaToya Baptiste sitting there with her cup full of regret. When I turned the corner and passed the line of trash cans leaving the cafeteria, I didn't look back. But I didn't throw the photo away either.

I SAT on Kelly's couch with my jacket still on, a bottle of water sweating in my palm. Karter jumped up beside me like he belonged to the both of us now, his soft body pressing into my thigh without a sound. Kelly was in her bedroom, moving around, shedding her doctor layers. The shower spray started, then stopped. She walked out of her bedroom looking refreshed, her hair loose, skin beaming, body tucked away in another oversized hoodie and black leggings.

"How you feeling?" she asked, stealing Karter from my lap, plopping down beside me.

"I'm just trying to make sense of everything," I said, leaning forward on my knees.

She nodded. "You want to stay in? Rest?"

I shook my head. "Not really."

"Come on." She shrugged. "I haven't had a chance to truly explore Seattle. I'm off the next two days. Let's make it count." She strapped Karter in his matching blue harness, stuffed some dog treats, foldable water bowl, a few tennis balls, and shit bags into the small purse slung across her chest.

"You packing more stuff for him than yourself."

She picked up Karter, nuzzling his face. "Cause he's my baby." She pouted. "Now, hush before I put you on poop duty." She walked out the door and I followed behind, smiling.

We ended up on the waterfront, walking like we didn't owe anything to the evening air. She pointed out the sculpture garden, told me about the first time she took Karter for a walk here and how he almost made her slip on the cobblestones, trying to chase a squirrel. The air was sharp, but not cruel. The water glistened in a cold, poetic way cities like Seattle had mastered. Kelly laughed with her head tilted back when Karter growled at a gnome set. I hadn't seen her do that in a long time.

"You look lighter," I told her.

She looked at me. "I wish I could say the same for you, but I get it."

We made a quick run back to the apartment to drop off Karter. He barked once he realized he was being left behind.

"It's getting dark outside, my sweet boy, and you know you get scared," Kelly cooed as she set him up in his cage.

"Why you talking to him like that?" I crouched down and stared Karter in the eyes. "Listen, lil nigga. Your ass can't come 'cause you try to attack everything that pass by you. You not about to have me busting my ass like you did your mama."

Karter tilted his head and widened his eyes. Then came the howl, loud and dramatic like we'd left him at the ages of hell.

Kelly looked at me and deadpanned. "Oh, he's cursing you out." She cackled.

"Man, I ain't worried about him," I said, smacking my teeth.

After leaving Karter to soothe his betrayal, we wandered a few blocks to Communion, a Black-owned spot she told me she'd been wanting to go to for months. The place was humming—soft laughter, clinking glasses, the smell of catfish and cornbread so good it made your heart ache. We squeezed into a corner booth and split a plate of oxtail sliders and crispy greens. She stole a fry from my plate like it was muscle memory. We didn't talk about Houston. Or the hospital. Or anything that felt like breaking. Just music. Food. Jokes. The way Seattle looked at night, like it was giving us a little grace for once.

"I've been wanting to come here for months," she said. "But I've been working my ass off at the hospital."

"Nah, you still got a good grip back there. Let me check for you." When I started reaching around to cop a feel, she pushed me away, giggling.

"Don't make me regret letting you crash on my couch." She smirked.

"The couch? Wow. You going to do your man like that?" I amped up a feigned hurt look on my face. She wasn't buying it.

"My name's not Tasha," she quipped back, taking another bite of a slider.

Oh." I laughed. "So, we going there?"

She rolled her eyes and continued nibbling on the remaining fries on the plate.

"You know that's dead, right?"

She shrugged. "How unfortunate. I thought maybe I was in for a surprise guest."

"Nah, you don't have to worry about that."

"Boy, stop playing with me. I was never worried. You should be the way she kept popping up on your ass. Next thing you know, I'm giving a green screen interview on some Netflix documentary."

I let her enjoy her moment while watching her eat. At some point, her foot brushed mine under the table and neither of us moved away.

"You been checking in with me since I got here," I said, wrapping my arm around her shoulders and pulling her close. "I appreciate that, but how you been?"

"Good, well until I ran into your mother." She rested her head on my shoulder, as she fed me the last few fries. "I have my days, but I'm finding healthier ways to deal with it."

"Like what?"

"Don't laugh, but I found this rage room. I just go and break a bunch of shit when I'm feeling overwhelmed or furious about everything that happened. Helps keep me grounded."

"Shit, I could break some shit." The waitress brought over dessert—peach cobbler and a scoop of brown sugar ice cream. We took turns feeding each other small bites.

"Want to try it out? I can see if they have some time slots for tonight," she said, reaching for her phone.

"Nah, maybe next time," I said, feeding her a spoonful of peaches and ice cream.

"What makes you think you're going to come stay with me again?" She mumbled around the food.

"Because you love me," I said nonchalantly. Before she had the chance to reply, I snuck another bite into her mouth. "I love you, too, Lily-girl." I bit my lip to contain the smile upon seeing her face soften and cheeks blush as she sat there chewing.

We lingered over dessert until the restaurant thinned out. Neither of us wanted to say it was time to leave, but eventually she stretched, soft and slow, like she was easing back into her own skin.

Outside, the city had dimmed but hadn't gone quiet. Car headlights glossed the slick pavement, and the low murmur of nightlife buzzed in the distance. We walked side by side, close enough for our shoulders to brush now and then. I heard her teeth chattering lightly and pulled her close for warmth as we walked faster back to the apartment. She didn't flinch when I did. Every so often she pointed out some landmarks she'd seen while taking Karter out for daily walks. I barely heard her words. I was watching the way her hands moved, how her voice got soft when she talked.

"I forgot how much I like being with you," she said, almost like it surprised her.

"I didn't."

She glanced up at me, eyes soft and a little unsure. "You always say stuff like that."

"Because it's always true."

We stopped at a crosswalk, the little blinking hand holding us in place. The streetlight caught her in that moment, turning the gold undertone in her skin a sensual amber. Her hair framed her face in soft shadows.

I wanted to say something. Ask something. But instead, I reached for her hand, slow and steady.

She didn't pull away.

We crossed the street like that, her fingers laced in mine. No declarations. No promises. Just skin and warmth and the kind of silence that felt earned.

By the time we reached her building and entered her apartment, Karter was curled up in his cage, snoring softly. We took turns freshening up and changing into pajamas. Cuddled on the couch, she draped a thick blanket over our laps, her head resting on my shoulder as I wrapped my arms around her neck. She put on *Selena*.

"Really," I groaned.

She grinned. "You need balance. And culture. Besides, can you really say you're from Texas if you've never seen *Selena*?"

As the movie played, we shifted positions to lay on the couch, her legs tangled with mine, her head resting on my chest. Karter continued snoring like he paid rent. Kelly whispered quotes under her breath. I rolled my eyes as she repeated the Tejano singers dances under the cover, singing along.

And when the last scene came—the candles, the voiceover, the lone white rose thrown to the stage—I realized she'd gone quiet, save for a few sniffles. I turned her face to mine. Her eyes were glassy with red strains. Anguished.

"What's wrong, Lily-Girl?" I asked, wiping her tears.

"I haven't watched this movie since..." I felt her breath stutter against my chest. "This song just hits something in my chest now that Mama's gone." I pulled her up my body, so her face was level with mine, pressing a kiss onto each cheek and her forehead.

"Khalil," she started. "It's not my place to tell you what to do because we all know I hate people telling me what I should do. But if my mother were still here, and I had the chance to forgive her, I would."

My jaw tightened. Kelly said the one thing I didn't want to hear out loud. Not tonight. Not while the re-opened wounds were still raw from seeing the woman who left me like a damn ghost story no one ever finished telling.

"Not because she earned it," she continued. "But because I'm tired of carrying the burden of everything she couldn't fix."

I looked away, blinking slowly. My chest pulled tight, like her words laced around the hurt just tight enough to squeeze it free. Kelly didn't flinch. She held my gaze.

"She looked me in the eye and told me she thought leaving me was better than breaking me."

"And she was wrong," Kelly replied gently.

"I know. My brain knows that, but my body doesn't. My muscles tighten every time I think about the birthdays she missed. The first days of school. Fuck. I used to go to sleep at night, hoping, praying I'd wake up and she'd be back in the kitchen making breakfast."

Kelly's hand slid over my chest, grounding me.

"I don't want to hate her," I admitted. "But I don't want to forgive her either."

"Forgiveness isn't for her," she said, her voice soft. "It's for the part of you still waiting by the window for her to turn around."

I closed my eyes and let her words settle, choosing not to argue. She held me. I let her.

"And if you want to hate her and never talk to her again. Then fuck that bitch. Just have a conversation and hear her out first."

Chapter 36

Khalil

KELLY BROUGHT UP ME TALKING TO LaTOYA AGAIN once more. I promised I'd go and try to hear her out. As I waited for the elevator to reach Kahlia's floor, there was still a knot in my chest. Still a tremble in places I couldn't name. But there was also curiosity. I counted down the room numbers, until I got to the one Kelly texted me. I stopped outside the door and looked through the glass. Kahlia sat up in bed, sketching. Big curls were pulled into two ponytails at the base of her neck. Toya sat beside her, reading something off her phone. Her eyes flicked up as I approached. She stood slowly. I pushed the door open and stepped inside.

Kahlia looked up, eyes wide, glancing between her mother and me.

"Hi," I said, voice low.

Kahlia blinked. "Are you the guy my mama said looks like me?"

I laughed, caught off guard. "I guess I am."

She squinted. "You kinda do. But your ears are bigger."

Toya covered her mouth to hide a laugh. I walked forward and crouched beside the bed.

"I'm Khalil."

She nodded. "I'm Kahlia."

"I heard you draw."

She grinned. "Wanna see?"

"Absolutely."

She flipped to the back of her sketchpad and held it up. A colorful drawing of Kelly in her lab coat, curly hair pulled up, stethoscope slung low, smiling, filled the page. The words, "Dr. Kelly Belly," floated above in big bubble letters.

"She said I could call her that," Kahlia added proudly.

I laughed. "That's what her friends call her."

Kelly stepped in just then with Dr. Sayegh, and her eyes softened the moment she saw the sketch.

"Is this for me?" Kelly asked.

"Yup." Kahlia nodded and tore it out carefully. "You can have it."

Kelly took it with both hands, like it was a painting that belonged in a museum.

"I'll frame it."

Kahlia beamed.

Kelly stepped forward and shared the final test results. Bronchiectasis confirmed, but mild and manageable. A treatment plan was outlined. Pulmonary therapy sessions scheduled. All hopeful.

"She's gonna be okay," Dr. Sayegh said, her hand on LaToya's shoulder.

"Thank you," LaToya whispered.

Kelly gave Kahlia a soft pat on the head and turned to me.

"Is it okay if we keep you here a few more days? Just to be sure," Kelly asked the girl. *My sister*.

"Yes," Toya shot. "And thank you so much. For everything."

"Anytime." Kelly smiled then left with Dr. Sayegh.

And just like that, it was just me and them.

My mother.

And my sister.

LaToya shifted in her chair; her fingers curled around a Styrofoam cup. "She's a good kid," she said softly, watching Kahlia as she flipped to a new page in her sketchbook. I nodded, arms crossed, eyes fixed on the slow rise and fall of her little shoulders. "She got your humor," she continued. "And your stubbornness."

"Mama, I am not stubborn," Kahlia corrected.

"Don't hold that against her." I laughed under my breath. "We probably get it from you."

"Yeah, you're probably right," she said. A pause stretched between us, more comfortable now.

"How's your daddy doing?"

"Good. At peace. He said to tell you hi."

"I really am sorry, Khalil." she said, making room for me on the couch by the window. I took the space. "After I got...right...I didn't want to live with myself for what I'd done. I was ready to end it all," she whispered. "Would have, had it not been for Kahlia. Found out she was cooking and took it as a sign that we all had second chances. You don't know this, but I managed to find out where you went to high school. The day you graduated, I stayed in the parking lot all day, watching droves of people leave. Then, I saw you and your dad. Your auntie, some skinny chocolate boy, and some woman that must've been his mama. You looked so happy."

"You should've gotten out of the car. Walked over, said something."

"It was a lot of things I could've done, but didn't. I wasn't going to take that day away from you. My showing up would've been me making it all about me."

She grabbed my hands.

"It was wrong of me to leave, but you turned out good. So good. I've been spending the last ten years grateful, I got a second chance, but you never left my heart. Not once."

My throat choked up. My eyes burned. I pressed my hands to my eyes. My mother didn't hesitate. She pulled me in her arms and rocked the pain away. Decades of what-ifs, evaporating, as if they'd never existed. She laid my head in the crook of her neck and shushed me. I looked over her shoulder and saw Kahlia looking on intently, paused from her drawing. When she pulled my face back, she kissed my curls, my forehead, my cheeks.

"I meant what I said," she added, tone low. "I know I don't have a stake in this... but I like Kelly. For you." I took in her motherly smile. "She got the kind of love that don't ask you to be perfect," she said. "That kind of love's hard to find. Harder to keep when you think you don't deserve it."

I didn't say anything. Just nodded once, slow and sure.

"Me, too," I finally said.

She took my hands in hers, gave it a light squeeze.

"I wanna do better," she said. "Not just with Kahlia. With you. I don't expect miracles. But I want a chance."

I looked over at Kahlia, who was still watching from the bed.

"You don't need miracles," I said. "You just gotta keep showing up."

She nodded, her lips fighting to hold her tears at bay. "I'll do that."

I STEPPED through the door and paused at the sound of overlapping voices — baby coos, teasing jabs, that distinct rhythm of women who'd known each other long enough to skip past politeness.

"She's got Zay's eyes," Kelly was saying.

"And my cheeks," Vanessa added, her voice proud and tired.

I turned the corner and there she was, perched on the couch in a giant hoodie, phone propped up, hair piled on top of her head like she hadn't even tried, and still looked like Sunday morning peace.

"Y'all don't think she looks like me?" Vanessa asked.

"She looks like she stole Zay's entire DNA strand," Lynn replied. "You contributed nothing but hair and vocal chords."

Everyone cracked up.

Kelly leaned into the screen. "Zaria girl, blink once if your daddy been making you listen to Luther."

"Not too much on my man!" Vanessa laughed.

That was when Karter noticed me. He jumped up from his spot on the rug and trotted toward me, hopping with his front paws in the air, begging for me to pick him up.

She finally noticed me standing there and sat up straighter. "Y'all, I gotta go. Company just walked in."

"Oooh?" Lynn said, dragging the vowel out.

"Bye," Kelly said pointedly, ending the call with a dramatic sigh.

She looked over at me as I dropped the rental car keys in the dish by the door.

"Sorry," she said. "You know how they are."

I shrugged. "Nah. That sounded like you were excited I'm home."

She smiled. The kind that started in her eyes.

"How'd it go?" she asked, voice softer now.

I walked to the kitchen, grabbed a bottle of water from the fridge, and leaned against the counter.

"She's trying," I said. "It's weird. But it's real. And Kahlia's... something else. Bright. Weird in a good way."

Kelly walked over to me. "You okay?"

I nodded. "Yeah. I think... I'm going to try and get to know her. Now. For Kahlia, if nothing else."

Kelly reached over and squeezed my hand once before letting go. She turned to reach for something behind her and when she did, I stepped closer. Cornered her without meaning to. Or maybe I meant to. Her back pressed to the counter. My hand found the space beside her hip. She looked up at me. Eyes big. Lips slightly parted. Still soft from the smile she'd just given Zaria through the screen.

"You okay?" she asked again, barely a whisper this time.

"No," I said. "Not even a little."

Her brows drew together, but before she could speak, I stepped into the space between us, unhurried but measured. Close enough to feel her breath catch. Close enough she had to tilt her chin up to meet my eyes.

"You've been holding me together since the second I got off that plane," I murmured. "Giving me peace. Giving me light."

She blinked.

I wasn't done.

"But every time you touch me, Kelly... I feel how much you're holding back. And I can't do that anymore."

Her breath hitched.

I leaned in, my mouth a breath from her ear.

"I want the real thing. Not just your comfort. Not just your friendship."

She didn't move. Didn't speak. So, I kissed her. Not softly. Not sweetly. But like I'd been dying of thirst and she was the only water I'd ever recognize. She gasped, but her mouth opened for me. Her hands found my shirt. Clutched it. I pressed her into the counter, one hand cupping her jaw, the other braced beside her hip. She melted against me like she'd been waiting for this just as long. We kissed like people who didn't know how to stop once we started.

When I finally pulled back, my breath ragged, eyes locked on hers, she looked wrecked in the most beautiful way. Lips kiss-swollen. Cheeks flushed. Fingers still curled in my hoodie.

"It's my last night here. I'm taking you out," I said, voice rough. "Not as your friend. Not as a placeholder. As the man whose been waiting for you to stop pretending we're anything less than everything."

She swallowed. Nodded once, dazed. "Okay."

"Say it," I whispered, brushing her bottom lip with my thumb.

"Yes," she breathed.

I kissed her again, slower this time. Deep. Certain. And in that moment, everything I thought I'd lost started feeling possible again. Because loving her had never been the problem. It was believing I was allowed to.

Chapter 37

Khalil

SHE DISAPPEARED INTO HER ROOM AFTER SAYING YES, leaving me standing in the kitchen with a mouth that still tasted like her and a heart trying to play it cool. I leaned on the counter, arms crossed, listening to her move around. Water rushed, bottles clinked, a blow dryer hummed. Even her getting ready had a rhythm. She was orchestrating a moment she didn't know was already perfect. Karter padded over and plopped down at my feet, growling, like he knew what was coming.

"You supposed to be my big dog," I muttered, bending down to scratch behind his ears. "You and I both know she's about to knock me out, huh?"

He yelped once, like confirmation.

When she finally stepped out, I forgot how to blink. She'd changed into a black sweater dress that hugged her curves and stopped high on her thighs. Sheer, black stockings covered the thickness of her legs, which were stuffed into knee high black leather heeled boots. An oversized denim coat hung off her shoulders. She'd put soft curls in her hair, sweeping the thick strands into a high ponytail with two pieces curling toward her temples.

Lip gloss covered her lips like honey, meant to ruin somebody. Ruin me.

She looked up, caught the stare I couldn't hide, and raised a brow.

"What?"

"I'm trying to be cool," I said, my voice low. "But you come out looking like that, make me want to bring you back in that bedroom."

She huffed a quiet laugh and shook her head, stepping closer, her heels slow against the hardwood. "You always talk reckless when you're nervous." Her mouth tugged into that smirk she saved for moments when she got caught off guard, but was secretly flattered. That *stop talking before I climb you like a tree* kind of smirk.

"I'm not nervous," I said, my voice a low growl.

"Hmm," she murmured, smoothing a hand over my shirt. Her eyes were warm, dancing in the light of the kitchen. "You keep saying stuff like that," she added softly, "and we're not making it out the front door." Then she brushed past me, just close enough to leave the scent of sweet cashmere and citrus in the air.

"Let's go," she called over her shoulder. "You're looking like you want to feed me something without nutritional value."

"Stop playing with me, Lily-girl. You know vitamin D does a body good." I followed her down the hall of her complex after locking the door, thinking to myself tonight was going to be a long night.

THE RESTAURANT WAS a quaint place near the edge of Capitol Hill. It didn't look like much from the outside but made you feel like you were walking into something lowkey special. Brick walls. Hanging plants. A small bar with two shelves of whiskey and guy behind it who looked like he was also the owner, the waiter, and the backup cook.

Kelly shrugged off her coat and sat across from me, her eyes scanning the handwritten chalkboard menu. The way her dress hugged her body had me mentally undressing her for the second time since we'd left the apartment. As she decided on a meal, she sat unfazed, unaware of what she was doing to me.

"You're staring again," she said without looking up.

"I like what I see."

She snorted. "You eye-fucking me is going to make our waiter uncomfortable."

"I'll leave them a big tip. They'll be aight."

We ordered braised short ribs, grilled salmon, and duck fat potatoes. She made fun of me for calling her water bougie Sprite without sugar. By the time the server left, we were leaned in, elbow to elbow, like the whole restaurant was ours.

"You know what I miss?" she said, pushing a piece of bread into the basil olive oil dip.

"What?"

"Nothing in particular. Just the feeling that I'm not missing anything?"

I watched her for a second, the way she spoke so lightly but meant so much.

"Seattle's been good for you," I said.

She shrugged. "Seattle's been quiet to me. There's a difference." She paused. "I used to chase noise, running from my own troubles," she added. "Now I chase peace, even if I'm not always sure what it looks like."

"Maybe peace is just being around someone who doesn't need a translator to understand you."

She looked at me, eyes softer than they'd been all night.

"Is that what you think this is?"

I didn't blink. I broke off another piece of bread, swirled it in the olive oil, and held it in front of her mouth.

"I think you feel like home. And I'm not trying to fumble that again."

Our food came. We made fun of the fact she cut her meat like a surgeon. She used the salmon to show me a new stitching technique she'd been practicing. She stole bits from my plate. I didn't say anything when she ate half the braised short ribs and most of the potatoes. Halfway through the meal, she dropped her napkin. I bent to grab it and let my hand travel up the length of her exposed leg, stopping just under the hem of her dress.

"You're annoying," she said, breathless, chest heaving.

"Keep saying that," I said. "I'll show you annoying."

She rolled her eyes. But her body moved closer to mine, her foot resting lightly against mine.

We left the restaurant in no rush. The air outside had a chill misty and soft making Kelly lean into my side without saying why.

"You full?" I asked.

She sighed dramatically. "Beyond full. You might have to carry me home."

"That's fine. I got strong shoulders. You trust me?"

She pinched her fingers together. "A little bit." She laughed.

We cut through the side streets, my mind remembering the directions for our next stop. Warm light glowed inside the second-floor apartments. An occasional dog barked behind fenced court-yards. I liked walking with her like this. Unrushed. Unbothered. It was a short walk to the private theater. One screen. Twenty velvet chairs. The guy at the door barely looked up as I handed him the code.

"This feels like a trap. Is this when you make me join a cult," she muttered, walking behind me.

"Chill, Lily-girl. You gotta stop watching those documentaries."

Inside, I handed her a warm popcorn box and a tiny bottle of wine. We settled into a lone loveseat at the back. The lights dimmed. *Love Jones* lit up the screen.

"Wait…" Kelly paused, sitting upright in her chair. She looked around, her eye flitting between the still empty seats around us and the screen before us. "Did you rent this place out?"

I shrugged, but my smirk gave me away. "Something like that. It helps when you know people."

"And how did you get them to play my favorite movie?"

"Because I give a damn about making sure you have every-thing, love."

She blinked, then turned wide-eyed, biting her lip. "Thank you."

"Anytime, Lily-girl."

I didn't talk much during the movie. I didn't need to. Kelly whispered the poem scene. Smiled at the parts that used to make her roll her eyes when we stayed up late watching the film in college. Halfway through, she curled into me, resting her head on my shoulder. When Darius said, *"Let me love you just like that,"* she shifted, like she felt the line in her soul. I looked down at her, the glow of the movie dancing across her face in blue and gold tones. She glanced up, catching me watching her, and I knew I was stuck.

"You're not paying attention," she whispered.

"I am," I said. "Just not to the movie."

She rolled her eyes but didn't pull away. Instead, she leaned in, pressing her lips to my jaw just once. Just enough to set the air between us on fire. When the movie ended, we didn't rush to leave, even when the credits faded to black and the screen went dark. We exchanged soft glances, as she let me taste the sweet warmth of her throat and hold the soft curves of her hips. She never stopped me.

Long after our food settled, after the end credits rolled, after we'd made it back to her apartment, we stood by the large windows of her living room, staring out over the Seattle's night sky. I walked behind her, pulling her tight against my chest. Her head rolled back to the space between my jaw and shoulders. She breathed softly.

"I used to think love was something you earned," I finally said.

"Like if you showed up enough, got it right enough, people wouldn't leave." She didn't say anything, just waited for me to continue. "I realized, I spent so long trying to be someone worthy of love, I forgot how to be someone who could just receive it." I turned her to face me, my hands resting low on her back, forehead pressed to hers. "I love you, Kelly," I whispered against her lips. "I want to do this right."

"You are," she replied.

The kiss was slow. We were writing it as we went, letting it build with no urgency, just intention. Her hands curled at the nape of my neck. Mine slid up and down the slope of her spine. We didn't rush the moment. Just let it unfold.

By the time we made it to her bedroom, it wasn't about heat. It was about finally being here. Together. Present. Breathless. Unafraid.

We didn't rush. We undressed each other in pieces. Not for the reveal, but for the permission. Each layer a question. Each touch an answer. Her dress slid over her shoulders like water obeying gravity. My hands followed its path, mapping familiar territory I'd been aching to claim as mine again. She tugged my shirt over my head like she needed to feel the skin underneath just to believe I was real.

When I kissed the curve of her shoulder, she sighed like she'd been holding her breath for months. Like this moment was her oxygen. Her fingers traced the tattoos on my chest, soft at first, then pressing into me like she was grounding herself. When she whispered my name, I felt something in me settle. Anchor. Break free.

"I got you," I murmured into her skin. "Let me talk to you."

She looked at me, pupils blown, lips parted, so damn beautiful I felt it in my bones. I slipped a hand between her thighs, slow, deliberate. Her breath caught. My lips ghosted over hers. "Tell me what you need, Lily-girl."

"You," she breathed, voice trembling. "Just you."

"You don't know what you do to me," I whispered, palms

finding her waist. I slid them up slowly over the curve of her waist, the swell of her breasts and when I leaned to take a pebbled nipple into my mouth, she shivered. Like my mouth was the only thing that had touched her in months.

A few seconds later, I heard soft whimpers and scratches against the wall by Karter's crate. I groaned, forehead dropping to her shoulder. "Your child is cockblocking me."

She giggled, breathless. "He thinks you're hurting me."

Reluctantly, I pulled away, went to my bag and grabbed some calming CBD treats I'd picked up earlier. I knelt down to his cage, cracking the door. He sat there, ears perked up, eyes wide, tongue hanging like he wasn't trying to ruin my night. I gave him two chews and pointed toward his bed.

"Night night, little nigga." He huffed but padded off. I shut the door and double-checked it was locked. "Now, where were we?"

She undid my pants with shaky fingers; eyes locked on mine. "Take them off then," I commanded, soft but firm, like she needed my permission to gain access to something that was solely hers. When I stood bare in front of her, she touched my chest again like she was memorizing the moment. When I kissed her again, it wasn't tender. It was hungry. Possessive. Desperate. Months of tension, months of longing, all pouring out at once. Our teeth clicked, tongues fought, hands held onto whatever they could find to stay grounded. I walked her backwards to her room, to her bed, lips never leaving hers, and laid her down like something sacred. I dragged the soaked panties down and off with one hand slow, teasing her nipples with the other, each pinch brought another delicious moan from her swollen lips.

"You already wet for me?" I growled, pressing my fingers to her slit. She was drenched. "Damn, Lily-girl...all this for me?"

She nodded, biting her lip. "It's always been for you."

I dropped to my knees. Spread her thighs wide. Took one long lick from her entrance up to her clit. She gasped, full body twitch.

Then I did it again. Sloppier. Slower. I wanted her to feel every stroke of my tongue like a confession. I buried my face between her legs, moaning into her like she was the only meal I'd had all year. Her hands fisted in my hair, grinding against my mouth like she couldn't help it.

"That's it. Ride my face," I growled, sucking her clit and releasing it with a juicy smack. "Don't hold back. Let me have it."

She came hard, thighs shaking around my head, moaning my name like a prayer turned curse. But I didn't stop. I didn't want to stop. I licked her through it, fingers sliding inside her, curling just right. Her back arched, hands smacking the bed. Ruined.

"Too much," she whimpered.

"No," I said, voice thick. "Not yet. You can take it. I got you."

When I finally pulled back, her pussy was glistening, twitching, needy. I climbed up and kissed her, slow and filthy, letting her taste herself on my tongue. She wrapped her legs around me, pulling me down, begging without words. I lined up at her entrance, dragging the head of my dick through her wetness, teasing. "You stay calling me Big Head...You ready?"

"Yes," she gasped. "Please," she whined.

"I want you to feel this," I said, voice low in her ear as I pushed in slow. Her mouth dropped open, her body stretching around me, taking every inch like it belonged there. I filled her to the hilt and stayed there, buried deep, letting her adjust, letting her feel what she did to me. She was so fucking tight. So wet. So warm. It took everything in me not to come right there.

"Fuck... you feel like heaven."

We moved together in a rhythm that didn't start with bodies. It started with knowing. With trust. With love worn raw by time and healed with need. I rocked into her, deep and unhurried, letting her walls milk me slow. She gripped my back, hips lifting to meet every thrust, eyes locked on mine like she was looking through me.

"That's it. Take it. Let me in."

I flipped her over, pulled her ass up, and slammed back in with a groan. She screamed, hand flying to her mouth, and I yanked it away.

"Don't hide. Let them hear you."

I fucked her hard, deep strokes that made her toes curl and the bed knock the wall. She threw it back, meeting every one like she was trying to keep me. Trying to break me. I slapped her ass and she moaned louder, wetter, begging with every breath.

"You mine?" I growled, hand in her hair, yanking her head back.

"All yours," she gasped.

"Say it."

"I'm yours, Khalil. *Fuck*, I'm yours."

When she came again, her whole body convulsed, walls fluttering around me, squeezing, pulling. I lost it. I drove into her one last time, deeper than I thought possible, and came with a growl that shook the room.

We collapsed together, tangled, soaked, barely breathing.

Minutes passed. Or maybe hours. She lay in front of me, her spine flush against my chest, her skin warm and slick with the echoes of us. My arm curled tight around her waist, holding her like she might drift away if I let go. I pressed a kiss to the back of her neck. She exhaled as if I'd reached her chest and touched something sacred.

Karter's snores rumbled from the living room like a lullaby. Somewhere out there, the world kept turning. But in here, it was just us. She reached down and laced our fingers. Her thumb brushed over mine.

"You good?" I asked softly, lips against her shoulder.

She nodded. "I feel full in every way possible."

"This wasn't just sex," I whispered.

She turned to me, her eyes heavy, glassy, but clear. "I know."

"I meant every part of what I said. Every word. Every touch." I kissed her again. "I love you, Kelly."

Her breath hitched, and I felt her swallow. "I love you, Khalil."

I pressed my fingers to her lips. "Say it again."

"I love you, Khalil," she repeated, laughing, a single tear escaping.

"I'm here," I promised. "I'm not going anywhere."

We stayed like that, our hearts syncing, skin cooling. I pulled the blankets up around us, careful not to let the air steal the warmth between us. She sighed and tucked herself deeper into my hold. In that breath between heartbeats, I didn't just know she was mine.

I knew I was hers.

Chapter 38

Kelly

I woke up reaching for him. The other side of the bed was still warm, but empty. Khalil had left before the sun even rose. I'd barely closed my eyes after seeing him out and getting back in bed before Karter started his barking from his cage. I rolled over as the sharp yips filtered into my bedroom. I inhaled, smelling the remnants of him–smoky sandalwood lingering in the threads of my sheets.

He was gone.

My chest ached like a bruise I'd forgotten was still tender.

I rolled out of bed, padding to my living room where Karter nipped at the door of his cage. His head popped up at my sigh while his tail thumped on his doggy bed. "Good morning, my sweet boy," I said, my voice still groggy from sleep. He licked my face and jumped out of my arms, trotting around the apartment looking for his new favorite adversary. When his hunt went futile, he gave a quiet whine.

"Yeah," I murmured, rubbing behind his ears. "I miss him, too."

After filling Karter's food and water bowl, I freshened up and journaled by the window. The Seattle morning was cool and gray, mist curling around the trees like it was trying to hold onto its secrets a little longer. The rising sun made the little water droplets sparkle like gossip ready to spread like wildfire.

I put on a workout set, got Karter in his harness, and decided to take us on a walk. Music played in my headphones, but I didn't hear it. Karter and I walked the same path we'd taken a few days ago with Khalil. While it looked the same, it wasn't the same. My heart stirred. My nose prickled with the tell-tale sign of tears to follow. I let myself feel it all. The lingering warmth of his presence in my soul. The ache of his absence in my heart.

My cell phone buzzed in my crossbody bag. I took it out and a picture of my dad filled the screen. I answered with a smile and sat on a nearby bench.

"Hey, baby girl," he answered, big and boastful.

"Hi, Daddy," I replied. Karter barked from his perched spot on the ground.

"I told you I taught the dog how to speak English," he said, cocky as ever.

"He's only barking because he thinks you can give him treats through the phone." I laughed.

"How you feeling?"

"Good. Taking it day by day."

"Why you look so sad then?"

I laughed again, swiping away at a fallen tear. "Because I am, but I promise I'll be okay."

My father looked me over again, realization clicking in his brain. "You sad because that Khalil boy left, huh?" He smacked his teeth and took a sip from the mug in his hand. "I thought it was just him stuck on you, but I guess you got it bad, too."

We talked for a while. He told me about the community center clinics and how they were doing. He'd finally gone back part-time to his practice, even though he was considering retirement to dedicate more time at the community centers and be present for me. I shared the progress of my fellowship and how I finally felt I'd gotten into a good groove.

"But really," he added, "I just wanted to check in. You look good, baby girl."

I looked away from the screen, swallowing. "I'm getting there."

"I can tell," he said. "You got your mother's eyes. You know that?"

"She used to tell me that all the time. *'You got my eyes, but your daddy's spirit.'*" We sat in the pause, soft and quiet.

"She still looking down and smiling on you. She would always say you were her greatest accomplishment. Mine, too."

"Thanks, Daddy," I choked out, wiping my eyes.

"Let's say you and me go put some flowers at her gravesite the next time you're back home."

I didn't have words, just a storm of emotions trying to work itself out in my chest. I just nodded my head and busied myself with picking up and holding Karter in my arms. He and my father had a conversation on their own while I gathered myself.

As soon as I hung up, I got a text from Lynn.

LYNNIE MAE

Kelly belly. I need to crash with you. My flight changed and I have an overnight layover. I'll uber to your place. Boarding plane to Seattle now. Will call when I land

"Come on, Karter," I said, checking his harness. "Auntie Lynn's coming for a visit."

On the way back to my apartment, I scrolled aimlessly on social media. Soon, I felt Karter's leash tug, followed by his usual attack-mode barking. I tried reigning him in, threatening, "Karter, if that's not Lynn, you better hush it up, right now."

But it wasn't Lynn.

It was Khalil.

The leash slipped from my hand, allowing Karter to take off

with a mad dash, tongue lolling out of the side of his mouth. Khalil picked him up, his bag still slung over his shoulder, a sheepish smirk on face.

"What are you still doing here? You left four hours ago."

"I couldn't leave," he said simply. "Got to airport. Watched my first flight board and take off. Thought about buying another ticket, and couldn't."

I blinked.

"Every part of me felt like I was walking away from something I finally got right." He stepped closer. Not too close. Like he was giving me space to choose. "I don't want to rush anything. You can have your time. But know you're mine. I just want to be where you are, even if I'm splitting time between here and Houston."

My body relaxed. I fell against him, wrapping my arms around his waist, burying my face against his chest. "I want to be with you. I don't need time to tell me that."

Karter barked in agreement, wagging his tail. We both laughed. Khalil wrapped his free arm around my waist, pulling me into a kiss that stole my breath. His hand lowered to cup my ass and squeezed.

"When you go back to the hospital?" he asked, sucking on my neck.

"Day after next," I rasped, leaning on him for support.

"Let's get inside. I need that," he growled, kneading my ass again.

STEAM CLOUDED the mirrors of my bathroom. My forehead pressed against the cool tile wall, one hand gripping the recessed shelf, the other braced against Khalil's arm circling my waist. He was deep and determined.

"You keep squeezing me like that, Lily-Girl," he growled into my ear. "You gonna to make a nigga come too soon."

"I'm not trying to," I breathed.

"Nah," he said, sliding his hand down my stomach and circling his thumb over my clit with precision. "I just want you to feel. Let me take care of the rest." I moaned against the tile. My knees nearly buckled.

"Khalil, I can't"

"Uh uh," he whispered, his lips brushing the shell of my ear. "Stay with me, Lily-girl. I know you not ready to tap out now." I heard a knock at the front door, followed by Karter's barking.

"Fuck, it's Lynn," I panted.

"Oh shit, you got to go let her in, huh?" he asked, his voice lazy and amused while continuing to bury himself deep inside me. "I need you to let that shit go on me first. You'll do that for me?" He pounded deeper, left trails of kisses along my shoulder, neck, and temples. Karter continued barking. Lynn continued knocking. Khalil continued stroking the fire inside of me with the same control he used in the boardroom.

"Come on, Kelly," he taunted. "You can't leave your girl out there like that."

I couldn't think. Let alone reply.

My phone started ringing on my nightstand. Karter scratched at the bathroom door. It was all too much. Khalil pulled out, and suddenly I wished I'd listened the first time and came already.

"Wait" I whined, feeling empty and pissed. I didn't have to wait long to feel him again. Khalil turned me to face him, then picked me up, bracing my back against the shower wall, my legs gripped in the crooks of his arms.

He continued his assault on my pussy with long, languid strokes, filling every inch. He moved like he had time. Like I was the only thing that mattered. His mouth covered mine, threatening to suck the soul out of me. The tingling started in my toes, combed up my thighs, coiled tight in my belly. Khalil matched his strokes to Lynn's knocks on the door. I counted fifteen before I was tossed over the edge, pussy clenching, moaning into his mouth.

"Fuck, fuck, fuck," I cried, biting his shoulder, legs shaking as I came hard around him.

"Yeah, that's it," he murmured. "Just like that. I told you you could do it." His rhythm turned frantic, each thrust deeper, more purposeful, until he broke too, groaning into my neck as his release spilled between us. When he came down, we fought to catch our breath, then ended with a laugh.

"Finish showering. I'll go let her in," he commanded, leaving me wobbly-legged and knocked-kneed in the shower spray.

By the time I left the bathroom, Khalil was feeding Karter and Lynn was on the couch, one brow raised and a glass of wine in her hand. Khalil walked into the bedroom then continued showering, whistling like he hadn't just rearranged my organs and had me begging for it.

"You good?" she asked, scooting over. "In fact, I already know the answer. You walking out here with a limp, your skin glowing. Yeah, you're good."

I tried to fight the smile tugging at my mouth as I sank into the couch beside her. "You're annoying."

"Mmhm. And you're in love. Down bad." I grabbed her wine and took a sip. She grinned. "And we're not denying it?"

I shrugged. "What's the point? That's my man."

"Not my man, my man, my man." She giggled. "It's good to see you like this. Not just post-dick glowing. From this dreamy smile pasted on your face, I'm assuming ten out of ten. But...It's nice seeing you step into your softness."

"That's how he makes me feel," I admitted. "Like I'm not carrying it alone. It's always been like that, I was just too stubborn to accept it."

"That part," she whispered, leaning her head back on the couch. "Not the feeling of not being safe. Just having that person who matches your energy. Brings out the best in you." We sat in silence for a bit. "I'm trying this new thing. Ever since the firm let me go, I've been changing my mindset. What's for me is for me. The man of my dreams is going to walk into my life out of nowhere. I promise I'll dive headfirst."

I side-eyed her. "Lynn, you can't manifest your way out of capitalism and fuck boys."

She held up a finger. "Yes the hell I can. I tell myself everything works out for me, even when I have zero evidence."

"So, you manifested being let go?" I quizzed, trying not to roll my eyes.

"I wasn't clear enough. I said I was going to leave that job. I should've added it wouldn't happen until I secured another one." She cackled at the end.

We talked about her job search, how tired we both were of pretending to be okay all the time, and how the soft life wasn't soft at all. Khalil came out of the bathroom, clean and smug in a hoodie, dapping up Karter like they were cousins. He walked over to where I sat on the couch, and leaned in.

"Told sis I'd meet up with her and Toya," he said. "You need anything?"

"Oh," Lynn replied. "You're going to leave us unsupervised? I'd hate for the coven to put a spell on you."

"I trust y'all," he said, never taking his eyes off me. He kissed my temple, making me blush. "No tequila shots, Lynn. My baby need her rest."

"No promises," Lynn replied.

Once the door closed, she turned to me, falling back dramatically on the couch. Karter jumped off the cushion with a yelp and trotted to his cage.

"Shower sex, forehead kisses, eye contact. You win," she whined. "Universe, send me my man. I'm ready. I swear I'm ready."

"And you still won't give Wesley a chance?"

She shivered. "No. And I seriously considered it, when we... you know. He's too emotionally constipated for something real."

"I could see that," I said, sipping more wine.

"Besides, I don't care how good his stroke game was, y'all are not about to clown me in the group chat."

I reached over and grabbed her hand. "Lynn, if he makes you feel good, even for now while you wait on the universe, that's okay. You deserve softness, too."

She sighed, her eyes glossing. "That's the problem. I know I do. It's just hard not to feel like I'm chasing something I'm not supposed to keep."

I squeezed her hand. "I don't know. Maybe it's about letting it keep you."

Lynn wiped the corner of her eye and reached for her wine. "If you keep saying stuff like that, I'm going to get emotional, and I can't touch up my Botox until I secure the bag. Fuck what Khalil was talking about. Where's the tequila?"

The rest of the night unfolded like one long exhale. I pulled out popcorn and the tequila. We laughed and it felt like medicine. We took shots until my chest warmed, and my cheeks hurt from smiling. Lynn made a playlist called "Soft, Rich Bi$h" and we danced until the room swayed.

Lynn poured another round of shots. "To hoe phases and healing."

"Bitch." I cackled. "Not too much on me."

She laughed until she braced herself at the waist. "I'm sorry, girl. How about, to softness and second chances."

We clinked glasses, threw the shots back, and continued dancing and singing. It was silly and sacred. Exactly the kind of night that reminded me I wasn't doing life alone.

Chapter 39

Khalil

I SAT IN THE PARKING LOT OUTSIDE OF SOME LOUD-ASS arcade and restaurant hybrid. Neon lights from the large sign atop the building bounced off my windshield like a warning. Kahlia had picked the place. "Something casual," she'd texted me. "So it won't be awkward." But the second I pulled into the lot, my stomach dropped. Because I wanted to see them. See her. My mother. And that made it worse. I stared at the steering wheel, the engine still running, then reached for my phone.

Pops answered on the second ring.

"Hey, son. Everything alright?"

"I decided to stay," I said, swallowing the knot lodged in my throat.

"Where you at now?"

"Some game place my sister suggested." I blinked. *My sister.* How was it the recognition flowed so easily, yet I stayed stuck in the driver's seat. "Just been sitting in my car."

He chuckled softly. "You want me to say you ain't gotta go?"

"No. I want to go in."

Silence stretched between us. I heard the buzzing of his ceiling fan and his girlfriend yapping away in the background.

"You nervous?" he finally asked.

"Yeah."

"Don't be. You remember when I taught you how to swim?"

I smacked my teeth. "You mean when you tossed me in the water and stared at me from the edge?"

"Sounds about right." He laughed. "You weren't scared of the water, just how deep it was."

"Hell yeah. I could've drowned."

"That's all this is. You don't know how deep the water is. You don't know if your mama's who she say she's become." I swallowed hard. "Trust me when I say this. Your mama had her issues, but she loved you more than you know. I spent a long time being mad at her for breaking the part of me that believed we could make it. Thought I was enough."

"She said she left because she was broken."

"She was. Took me awhile to see it. Understand why she did what she did. That don't mean it's your job to pick up the pieces."

"But what if I want the relationship. With her. With Kahlia."

"Then let her earn it. Take her for who she is today. Decide if there's room for that in life now." I nodded even though he couldn't see me. "I'm forever proud of you. You always show up, even when it's hard."

"Even if I'm sitting in the car like a bitch?" I laughed.

"You and that damn mouth." He chuckled back. "Especially then."

We paused and listened to each other's breathing.

"I love you, Pops," I said quietly.

"I love you too, son. No matter what happens in there, you're not the little boy waiting by the window. You're a man. A good one."

I hung up before I could cry. I turned off the engine, got out of the car, and walked inside.

Chapter 40

Kelly

HANDING OFF THE LAST CHART TO MY ATTENDING nurse was the best thing I did all day. I stepped into the low-lit elevator, desperate to escape the too bright, too cold air that'd consumed me for the past few hours. When the sliding doors hissed shut behind me, the tightness in my chest didn't move. It just settled in deeper as I descended toward the ground level.

The sliding doors on the hospital opened to a watercolor painted Seattle—wet sidewalks, the smell of coffee beans, and rain mixing. I walked fast to my approaching Uber. Movement meant I didn't have to think about the mother who needed answers I couldn't give yet. As my driver maneuvered through the thickening traffic, I focused on the passing buildings blurring with lights from passing cars and traffic lights. And yet, all I saw was the brave child lying in bed in pain, the same way grief sits in a corner, waiting for you to look at it.

My phone buzzed in my pocket. I let it ring as I put in my earbuds, then answered. "Hey, Big Head," I said, my voice thin.

Khalil's face filled the screen, his soft caramel skin warm under the lights of his apartment. He wore a white graphic t-shirt, sleeves cut off, that made his shoulders look like the perfect resting spot for my thighs. "Hey, Dr. Reid. You made it home yet?"

"Almost." I flipped the camera to show the wet street, the neon sign of a Ramen bar on the corner, the bouncy trot of a wiener dog in a raincoat leading its owner through the damp drizzle.

"You sound tight, Lily-girl."

"Because I am." I sighed, flipping the camera around so he could see my pout. "It's been a long day."

"I can see it in your eyebrows."

"My eyebrows are none of your business," I replied, rolling my eyes.

He smirked. "Everything about you is my business."

"Khalil—" The car pulled to a slow stop in front of my building. "Let me FaceTime you when I get inside." I huffed a quick thank you to the driver and made a mad dash into the building. By the time I trudged across the threshold of my apartment, my clothes felt like they were glued to my skin. I kicked off my tennis shoes, dropped my bag next to Karter's cage, picked up and snuggled him close to my heart. He huffed and nuzzled my chest like the world was simple.

"I know, sweet boy," I told him. I walked us over to the couch and plopped down, setting my phone against a stack of books on my coffee table, and called Khalil back. He answered before the first ring finished. Karter began yipping at the phone as soon as his face filled the screen.

"Wazzam, lil nigga," Khalil joked into the phone. That only caused the French bulldog to yap more into the screen, bouncing all over my lap. Khalil talked back, egging him on.

"Okay, okay," I interrupted, placing Karter on the floor. "Y'all are doing the most."

"You know I had to catch up with my big dawg." He stared at me through the phone, biting his lip, mischief lingering in his eyes. "You not comfortable, are you?"

"Almost, why?" I asked, raising a brow.

"Get up and go change. Put on something you can move in."

"What?" I groaned, scrunching up my face. "Uh-huh. My shoes are already off. I'm ready to call it a night."

"Nah, you gotta let out some of that tension."

"I don't want to." I pouted, folding my arms.

"Kelly."

Him saying my name wasn't a warning. It was a gentle hand at the small of my back, guiding me. How could I refuse? I rolled my eyes so hard I could have seen my amygdala, but a smile tugged at the corners of my mouth anyway.

"What are we about to do?" I asked, pulling myself off the couch and making my way to my bedroom. I paused in front of my dresser, a thought coming to my head. "Are you here?" I smiled brightly, the ache in my chest loosening a notch.

"No." He laughed. I heard the jingle of his keys and a quick beep of a horn. "I'm still in Houston. About to walk into my gym."

"The gym? Khalil, seriously, what are we about to do?"

"Workout date." He smiled. The bright, white lights of the gym made it glow. He nodded to someone in the distance as he walked deeper into the gym.

"Workout," I shrieked. "Oh, nuh-huh."

"Yeah," he said, like it was obvious. "You about to work out that little funky ass attitude."

"I do not have a funky ass attitude," I said under my breath, pulling out a sports bra, biker shorts, and one of Khalil's hoodies he'd left here.

"Come on. You can't be upset if you too tired from doing burpees."

"I am not doing burpees."

"Fine. No burpees," he said, charming me into his crazy idea for a date. "For me. Please?"

The plea did something to my spine. I set my phone down and

changed fast. When I stepped into the camera, he barked obnoxious and entitled.

"Is this okay?" I poked my booty into the camera, as he bit his lip, thirsty as ever.

He sat back on a bench, sipping water from a bottle. "More than okay. Turn around again and bend over this time. I need to double-check."

"Focus," I said, trying not to laugh.

"I am focused." He stood, dragging a mat across the floor with his foot. "So I only have three rules. You don't think about anything for the next hour. You do what I do. You breathe. Deal?"

I blew out a long breath. "Deal." I walked into my living room, turning on a few more lights and propping my phone up on my TV stand. I rolled out my pilates mat that'd been collecting dust in a corner since I moved to Seattle. Once I was ready to begin, I stood, waiting for my first set of instructions.

"Go ahead and give me a shake. Gotta let go of some of the tension in our limbs." He shook his arms, shoulders, and chest as if he were made of loose wire, then grinned. "You look like one of those inflatable things at the car dealerships along the highway."

"I'm adding a rule. No jokes," I said flatly. He walked me through a few more stretches before we jumped into the real workout—high knees, jumping jacks, jumps. I hardly had time to think about the room with beeping monitors or the way the mother's hands shook when she asked me if her child was going to be okay.

"Feeling better?" he asked.

" A little," I admitted.

"Good. Now we can get to work." He widened his stance. "Pretend you have a boxing bag in front of you. Give it quick jabs, right then left."

I smiled despite myself, then "hit." The first few were sloppy. The next few found a rhythm. Right, left, right-right. I kept up with Khalil's cadence as he boxed the bag in front of him. I started making little sound effects with each hit. He chuckled on the other end as I snorted, the sound surprising both of us.

"There she is," he said, his eyes warm. "Next, we got squats. Go grab Karter and hold him to your chest."

"That sounds terrible," I said between quick breaths.

"You love me anyway."

I paused. Not because I hadn't heard it before, but because he said it like a fact we both lived inside now, not a question thrown into a storm. I didn't answer. I didn't have to. He saw the agreement in my face and nodded his reassurance, like he'd put something gentle on a shelf to admire later.

I moved to grab Karter, then continued following Khalil's directions. Karter jerked against my chest while I did slow squats, where Khalil reminded me to press through my heels and let my knees hover over my toes. He let me know when I clenched my jaw. The weighted squats turned to lunges with Karter being raised over my head. Between balancing his movements above me and trying to keep my form, I'd long forgotten about the stress of my day.

Khalil's phone tilted a bit when he demonstrated a plank. He propped it up against the feet of the bench and dropped back to his forearms. "Thirty seconds. Breathe through it. Feel how strong you are."

I held the plank, my body a straight, shaking line. Sweat stung my eyes. My brain tried to sprint again. Khalil counted down. When he reached zero, I collapsed to the mat, breathing hard.

"That was one. Four more to go," he huffed.

"Four?! Nah, I have one, maybe two more in me."

"Let's go." He counted us off. The burn started in my shoulders then traveled to my core.

"Fuck! I should've stuck with pilates." I tried catching my breath, but it was futile. "Fuck, fuck fuck."

"Breathe through it, baby. Halfway there."

I looked at my phone's screen. He seemed to be calm, too still, like we hadn't just done a whole other set of exercises that had my body screaming. By the time Khalil started his countdown from five, my whole body shook like a stripper.

"Zero," Khalil groaned. "Ready for the last one?"

I shot lasers at him.

"You doing so good, Lily-Girl. Give me one more?"

"I hate you," I lied, breathless.

"No you don't. Let's go."

We started the last hold. Karter trotted over and stuck his nose against my bun. He licked the sweat at my temples and backed up, tilting his head. He barked once, and I swore I saw a devilish grin cross his mouth. He trotted to my side and placed a paw on my back.

"Karter, no," I rushed out between breaths. He paid me dust as he climbed on my back and made himself comfortable. "Fuck! Karter, get down!"

For the first time, Khalil's steel composure in each move broke. He shook with laughter as he tried to keep his form.

"Don't laugh at me!" I snapped, trying to shake Karter off my back. "Karter, get down now!" The stubborn dog stayed put. My arms cried out for relief. My eyes went bleary from the sweat pouring into them.

"Thirty more seconds," Khalil called out.

"The fuck do you mean, thirty more seconds?" I rushed out.

"We gotta finish strong." He smiled. I looked down at the mat, working hard to calm the burn building in my muscles. I felt Karter stand on all fours as he barked back at Khalil. My mind started to run wild, frenzied, and unfocused. I pulled it back by my breath like a kite string. I counted a slow four count for each inhale and exhale like a metronome I could lean against. The apartment softened around the edges.

This time, when he reached zero, I collapsed to the mat, laughing into the crook of my elbow. It sounded loud in my living room. Karter cursed me out through his barks and went back to his bed.

"How we doing?" Khalil asked, on his back now, chest rising like a tide.

"Murderous...but I'm too tired." I watched as he wiped down his equipment and made his way back to his car, taking occasional gulps from his water bottle.

He started his car and leaned back in his seat. The soft glow from the dashboard outlines the chiseled features of his face, still dewy from the sweat of our workout. An ache rose within me, this time from the heated juncture between my thighs.

"Tell me one thing about today that doesn't involve a frown."

The questions sat with me. "This morning, we had a patient who's a magician in the making. She did this card trick that had us all stumped."

His grin showed on its own. "Tell me another."

"My attending nurse makes the best cornbread."

"Lies. Ma Joise makes the best cornbread."

"I'm serious." I laughed. "She has her beat. Either that, or I was starving after running around between patients all day."

He tilted his head, satisfied. "Another."

I bit my lip, thinking of something else that went right in a day that felt so wrong. "Dr. Sayegh said my notes were consistently 'clean and compassionate.'" I tried making my voice flat, but pride was hard to smother when it was honest.

"Because they are," he replied. "Because you are."

We admired each other through the screen, the two of us breathing like we were in the same room. Rain tapped on my window like a drummer keeping time.

"Lily-girl," he said after a minute, his voice low.

"Hmm?"

The corner of his mouth curved in a dangerous way. "I'm gonna need a little more of your time."

"For what?" I asked, but the question came out soft, already halfway to surrender.

"For me," he said. "For you, really. Stand up, get a glass of water. I need to borrow your hands for a few minutes."

I rolled over to my side, my bones humming. When I turned on the lamp next to the couch and cut off the overhead lights, the living room gentled. I filled a glass, took a long sip, and let the water settle in my belly like rain on dry soil.

"Okay," I said, coming back into frame. "Hands, borrowed."

"Go to your bathroom," he said, a gentle command wrapped in honey. "Keep me where I can see you."

I carried my phone into the bathroom, set it on the counter, and propped it up against a bottle of perfume. I sat on the rim of my tub, hands bracing the cold ceramic rim. My pulse was suddenly everywhere, a drumline marching toward a battle of the band's showdown.

"Closer," he said, and I moved the phone a little. "Perfect."

He continued to lean back low in the driver's seat of his car, his shirt draping over his chest in ways that should be illegal. His eyes dragged over me with a hunger that wasn't impatient. It was reverent. As if he'd finally gotten the prayer he'd asked God for.

"Take a breath," he said. "Let the day go for real this time."

I did. It came out shaky as I stared back at him.

"That's it." His voice stroked my skin. "Now tell me one thing you wanted today."

You. The answer leapt up, simple as gravity. But I didn't want to play coy tonight.

"You," I said, and watched as the word hit him.

"Say it again," he murmured, then bit his lip.

"You," I repeated as heat rose to my ribs.

"Come here," he said, useless across two thousand miles, but my body leaned forward anyway like his voice had a string on it. "I want you to let me watch you feel good."

"Khalil—"

"Uh-uh," he said softly. "Take them clothes off and sit back down."

The room tightened to the size of the screen. Slowly, I peeled off the damp biker shorts and sports bra. He didn't rush me. A faint moan came through my phone as my panties landed on the floor. I sat back on the edge of the tub, waiting for further instructions. He talked me through a slower body scan, but this one was all wanting. It started with my lips, my throat, the hollow base of my neck. It laced around the tightened buds of my breasts, trailing to the throbbing nub between the slit of my legs. All the places he'd learned like a song. Praise threaded through the air, all low and shameless in a way that made my core yearn and ache for him. He told me I was beautiful as my fingers he'd borrowed found a majestic rhythm in my center.

"Look at me," he said, and I did. His gaze held me. Held me open, held us together. "That's it. That's my Lily-girl. Keep those fingers pumping, slow and steady." Raspy restraint coated his voice. The words sank straight into the muscle memory of every time we'd been together. I felt them in the tender places he refused to let me hide. My breath turned to a tide. The distance between us thinned to a wire thrumming with both our heartbeats.

"Good," he murmured. "You're doing so good for me."

The praise knocked something loose in me. I let go. A wave rolled through me in slow motion. My vision went staticky as I tried to keep his gaze. I rode it until it set me down.

"Fuck," I breathed, laughing at nothing, because joy makes fools of us all.

"Fucking right," he said, equally wrecked, equally pleased. We stayed there, smiling at each other in the hush afterglow. The rain against my bedroom window kept writing its poem against the glass.

"Tell me something dumb that happened today."

"The vending machine wouldn't drop my chips," I mumbled.

"That's why you thought that cornbread was good."

I smiled as I started my bathwater. "I miss you."

"I'm right here," he reassured, and he was. "You'll be back in Houston soon enough."

"Soon," I echoed.

"Let me head home before you make me get a ticket for public indecency."

"Don't hang up," I pleaded softly. "If that's okay."

"It is."

As I bathed the remnants of the day, luxuriating in the silky water, Khalil talked my ear off about his day—new construction sites, some business Mav wanted to start, the last time he babysat Zaria, and she had a poop explosion on his favorite t-shirt. I listened, hanging on to every word. I laughed as he tried to convince me to wear a silk lingerie set instead of the boy shorts and oversized shirt that would bring me much more comfort. By the time he made it home, I was tucked under my comforter, Karter snuggled at the foot of the bed by my feet.

"Close those eyes for me, Lily-girl."

And I did. I didn't fill the silence with anything but my breath. If he repeated my name, it was somewhere between waking and dreaming. The last thing I registered before sleep caught me was the ripple of his muscles as he dried off after showering. With the knowledge that he was on the other end, my body unclenched into peace like it was the only prayer that mattered tonight.

Chapter 41

Khalil

I hit 610 with the windows cracked. My first stop was the barbershop, then a flower shop, which had become a ritual like grocery shopping, and finally the airport to pick her up. On the way, I called my mother before I could talk myself out of it. She answered on the second ring, voice careful but warm.

"Khalil, it's so good to see you calling."

"Hey," I said, switching lanes in the steady traffic. My chest tightened as I tried to sound casual. "Y'all good?"

"I'd say so. Kahlia's doing better with this new inhaler."

My sister's voice cut in from the background, sharp and unfiltered. "Did you ask him? Did you ask him?"

I laughed. "Ask me what?"

I heard the deep sigh my mother gave before she answered. "Don't mind her. Kahlia was wondering when she'd be seeing you again. She has it made up in her mind that you two will be in a good place by summer so that she can visit for a few days."

"Look Khalil. I know you and Mommy are working through your stuff, but I'm innocent in this," my sister clarified, loud enough to make sure I heard her.

"Let's talk about it the next time I'm in Seattle. How does that sound?"

"Fine," she huffed through the phone. "I'm going to work on my English homework."

"She hasn't stopped telling her friends about you," my mother said warmly. "It's always 'My big brother this' or 'My big brother that.'"

"She's pretty cool, too. I told my sis-in-law about Kahlia. She's an artist. Said she'd want to bring her to her art studio if she ever visited."

"That'd be nice. Kahlia would love that." We both got quiet, save for the honking horns and muscle cars revving their engines as they zoomed by on the highway. Neither one of us knew what to say next. My mother decided to start first.

"Thank you for giving me a chance. You didn't have to, but you are, and I'll forever thank you for that."

A knot formed in my throat. I pulled into a parking spot. "Thank you for learning from the past. I know we're a work in progress, but I need you to keep showing up."

"I'll do that." I could hear the slight wince of emotion as she responded.

"I didn't want anything. Just wanted to say hi and check-in."

"Don't be a stranger. Text me anytime," my mother said. "Hold on, Kahlia wants to tell you something."

"Hey big bro, next time you're in Seattle, we have to try this new Boba shop." My heart squeezed at the new nickname Kahlia had given me.

"Bet. You paying?"

"Me? You're the adult. I'm but a poor child. Older siblings are supposed to take care of the younger ones, am I right?"

"Yeah." I laughed. "I got you, okay?"

"Okay then." I could feel her smile through the phone.

I walked into the barbershop, where Maverick had already hyped up the customers as he signed autographs. He sat in a chair near the back, cape around his shoulders like a king who knew his crown was in the cut. The shop smelled like alcohol and oil sheen. Clippers sang from different stations. Zay sat a few chairs down, eyes tired but bright with joy.

"Look what the cat dragged in," Maverick said, holding his hand out for a handshake. "Boy been glued to his phone since he came back from Seattle."

"Shut your ass up, bruh," I said. I dapped up Zay, then sat in an empty chair to wait my turn.

"When do you have to pick up Kelly?" Zay asked, checking his line in the mirror.

"Couple hours. Zay, y'all got everybody showing out for Zaria's ½ birthday."

"Man what? Viv and Ma been planning this for months. You'd think it was a sweet sixteen. But hey, after the party, they're tag-teaming Granny daycare for a few days." Zay squinted at me through the mirror. "You look different."

I smiled as a text from Kelly came through on my phone.

WIFEY 🖤

boarding now 😊 see you soon

ME

I'll be there waiting for you

The barber popped the cape and dusted Maverick's neck like he was blessing him. Maverick slid out of the chair, checked his angles, then bumped into my chest. "Who you texting right now?"

"My future wife."

"Like I said, glued to the phone," he joked, moving out of the way so I could take his spot in the chair.

"At least my girl is somebody I can be with. You trying to play me, but ain't Nyah married, Zay?"

Maverick shrugged off my comments. "Not for long. She just don't know it yet."

Zay laughed in his chair. "Mav, what you gonna do when she and Antonio come to this karaoke thing Nessa got us doing tonight?"

Maverick scrunched up his face as if he'd been insulted. "You busy asking me what I'm going to do. Y'all need to be asking what his lame ass is going to do. Fuck you talking about."

~

I LEFT the shop with a crisp line and smooth fade, feeling cleaner than a confession. The sun was bright overhead, but bearable. I had one more stop at the flower shop before I headed to the airport. When I walked in, the woman behind the counter saw me and grinned.

"Long distance must be going good."

"Better than ever," I said, tapping the glass counter. "Give me my usual, except no delivery this time."

She bundled the bouquet like she was filling a treasure chest and slid it to me.

By the time I hit arrivals, traffic was bumper to bumper. I texted Kelly to let her know I was pulling up outside. I parked on the curb and watched the doors slide open and shut like a pair of lungs. Then she walked out, rolling a small suitcase and carrying Karter's carrier on her shoulder. Even in the chaos of the airport, she was a problem I wanted for life. Long body waves blew around her face, fanning out in layers, gold hoops caught the rays of the sun, and a matching leggings set hugged her body too right. I got out and took the suitcase handle with one hand and her waist with the other.

"A fresh cut? Just for me," she teased as I nuzzled my face into her neck.

"Most definitely."

She curled into me, one arm around my neck, the other gripping my chin as she stood on her toes to meet my lips for a kiss.

Heat rose clean and fast and I had to pull away to ground myself.

"I missed you," she whispered against my mouth.

"I missed you, too," I replied, feeling fourteen, and not thirty-years-old. We broke when a security guard in a neon vest gave the universal keep-it-moving look. I got Kelly into the car and strapped Karter in the backseat, her suitcase next to him.

When I got in the driver's seat, she had the bundle of flowers close to her nose, inhaling the floral scent. "I do believe you're keeping the lily industry afloat."

"Me?"

"Umm-huh." She sniffed the flowers again and looked at me as I pulled away from the curb. "I know I'm only here for a few days, but I'm going to enjoy every bit."

"I'm just trying to make sure I get my time in," I said. "Everybody's been waiting on you to come back in town."

"Then I came back on time." She took my hand across the console. "And they'll have to wait their turn, because I need my man to dick me down a few times before I go back."

I laughed. "You ain't said nothing but a word."

We rode like that, our fingers tangled and her humming along to the music playing through the speakers. As we merged onto the interstate, the downtown's skyline came into view, slow and grand. And in that moment, a small quiet traveled between two people who'd been missing each other something fierce. A soft clicking of a key fitting right where it belonged.

HOURS AFTER ZARIA'S CHRISTENING, Vanessa had Zay book a private room at a karaoke spot where the floor lights changed color every time you breathed wrong. The host led us down a hallway of doors until we hit our room. There were couches along three sides of the room with a screen on the fourth, a low table in the center with two mics, a tablet with more song choices than a DJ at a wedding.

"I'm pumping and dumping tonight," Vanessa sang at the table, before throwing back another Green Tea bomb with her friends.

"Bless it." Lynn winced, shaking off the sting of the alcohol. "That was strong as hell."

"Nessa baby, you sure you want wings? You know you and spice been enemies since Zaria was born."

"I'll worry about heartburn tomorrow." She shrugged off, flipping through the tablet of songs.

Kelly slid beside me and propped her legs over my lap. She tilted her face toward me with a look that would set heaven on fire. She leaned in close and whispered in my ear, "I want a repeat of this morning. The dick felt too good." I kissed the base of her neck and squeezed the skin of her thigh that was exposed from the way her dress rose. The soft moan that left her lips had all the blood racing to my dick.

On the other couch, Nyah sat between Maverick and her husband Antonio. Maverick popped a bottle of something fizzy and poured Nyah a glass. She replied with a quiet 'thank you' as her husband looked on, a tightness in the corners of his mouth, as if smiling cost calories he was trying to conserve.

The first round of songs were predictable—old-school R&B everyone knew by muscle memory, rap songs that had us reliving our glory days in college. Lynn and Nyah tag-teamed a drunken duet of Beyonce's *If I Were a Boy*, much to Antonio's chagrin. When they finished, we all clapped. Antonio clapped too, but his was the slowest, a clap out of obligation, not appreciation.

Kelly and Vanessa went next, howling their way through Monica's *Why I Love You So Much*. When Kelly's voice croaked on a high note, they fell into each other in laughter, lost the beat, but didn't care. They were proof that confidence couldn't buy a note. As they wrapped up, a waitress brought in hot wings, fries, and another round of drinks that made everyone behave worse. Everyone noticed the tight look Antonio gave Nyah as she sipped from her glass.

"You did your thing up there with Lynn," Maverick said, breaking the tension.

"We were just having fun," Nyah replied, avoiding his eyes.

"Fun looks good on you," Maverick replied. "Nessa, Zay, where we going for this joint bachelor/bachelorette trip? I still don't understand the concept."

"Vegas. In June, so everybody clear your calendars!" Xavier shouted above the music.

"Why Vegas?" Kelly asked.

"I don't want to go too far from Zaria," Vanessa replied. "Anywhere out of the country and I swear I'll cry every day."

The tablet of songs ended up in my hands. I passed it to Kelly. "Pick a song for us."

She scrolled with a wicked smile. "You trust me?"

"Always."

She queued up the song and pulled us to the front of the room. A heartbeat of quiet filled the room, then the early-2000s strings followed by a drum loop cut through like oversized jerseys and baggy jeans. The room erupted as Lil Mo's backup vocals came through. It took my brain a second to catch up. Then the hook cue flashed on the screen, and I started laughing because of course she picked this song.

Kelly passed me a mic, mouthing, "Surprise."

"Oh, this is perfect for them," Lynn cooed from the couch.

The track rolled, and I fell into the pocket like muscle memory. I lowered my voice to take on Ja Rule's distinct gravelly rasp and looked straight at Kelly. I rapped the promises of showing up and holding it down, no matter what the world brought. She answered me back through Lil Mo and Vita's words. Pretty soon, our duet turned to a church choir, our friends singing from their seats.

"Hey, this song is for me and my man," she half-shouted, half-laughed back at them. They ignored her and continued singing. At the end, I kissed her shoulder. As we walked back to our spot on the couch, my grin hurt my face. Maverick and Xavier took a turn as Kelly and I faded to our own bubble.

She kissed me again. "You did good."

"You too," I agreed, looking at her like a thief looked at a prized jewel.

She brushed her thumb over my lower lip. "My man," she said softly.

"My woman," I answered. I kissed her temple because that was all I could do without making a scene. She moved to sit on my lap and leaned against my chest as she watched Lynn and Nessa sing another song. I wrapped my arms around her waist and rested my chin in the warm space between her neck and shoulder. For the first time in a long time, I didn't feel like I was balancing on something that might crack. Vanessa and Zay continued to enjoy their night off from being parents. Lynn and Nyah fed into Maverick's antics while Antonio stayed rigid.

Kelly turned around and kissed me again. Sweet, steady, sure. I didn't need to see the smiling faces of our friends to know we were already building forever.

Chapter 42

Kelly

MY FATHER AND I STOOD SIDE BY SIDE. WE'D JUST finished leaving flowers on the headstone that still looked too new to me, even after all these months. The letters of my mother's name cut cleanly into the granite, as if they were afraid to bruise the stone. Karter trotted the paths between the plots like he understood he needed to be quiet.

"I'm happy you came." My father wrapped an arm around my shoulders. "I'll give you a second." He kissed my temple, then walked away with Karter following behind him.

I nodded. It was my first time at my mother's gravesite since the funeral. It still didn't feel real, standing here with her beneath us.

"Hi Mommy," I said, my voice fighting its way around the knot in my throat. "I know it's been a while, but I finally made it. I'm sorry it took me so long. I probably should've come a lot sooner, but I couldn't. Even still, I've been carrying some words around in my mouth, waiting for the jagged edges to turn smooth so I could lay them down. They're ready now."

"There are days I am mad at you for leaving. For dying. For all the sentences we didn't get to finish and the hugs that went unfinished. I didn't know what to do with that anger except hold it like a fever and not give it to anyone else. I thought I could continue living with this fury in my heart, but I couldn't. I fought and fought, but I got tired. And in that tiredness, a window opened to let forgiveness in."

"I grew up thinking softness was danger. I thought softness meant I wouldn't be able to do the hard thing, that it would make me less sharp. But I'm learning a different medicine. The softer I am at home, the more I allow myself to be held, the braver I am, the more capacity I have to hold someone else's love. I think you were trying to teach me that in your own way. I hear you now."

"I miss you in the tiny ways most. Your bossy voice when I'm doing 'too much.' The way you'd hum instead of giving me an answer to a problem only I could solve. I miss your hands. The way they knew how to make magic in the kitchen to heal, hurt, and honor hope—the soothing way your fingers knew where to rub to calm my racing mind. When I'm at the hospital and I feel my jaw lock and my chest go tight because I don't have an answer for a parent worried about their child, I press my fingers to the nape of my neck in the same way you would, pretending it's your hand. It helps."

"I know you can't come back, not physically, but I wanted you to know I found the parts of you you left on purpose. The parts that knew how to look at a mess and find joy in the cleanup. I will carry those forward, not as weight, but roots. You are with me. In my hands, in my mouth, when I say thank you. In my chest, when I breathe, it hurts. In my laugh when it escapes. In the little girl who wanted, and the woman who knows what to do with wanting now. I understand. I miss you. I love you."

I crouched down and hugged my knees to my chest. A mourning dove flew and perched atop my mother's headstone. I dried the last falling tears as my father and Karter walked back up. He reached out his hand to grab me and pull me up, tucking me under his arm.

"Did you say all you needed to say?"

"Yeah, I think so."

"I'm proud of you."

"Thank you."

"Let's go cook something good. I feel your mama's spirit near." He laughed, holding me tight.

The drive back was the kind where the radio was a murmur in the background and the city rolled by like a slideshow of memories. Karter sat in my lap, his front paws on the console, staring out the window like he was on patrol.

Once in the kitchen, my father pulled out a heavy-bottomed pan while I chopped bell peppers and onions. When the oil in the pot was hot, I threw in the holy trinity. The onions went glossy, the celery went soft, and the bell peppers gave up their green. I added flour to the pan and watched it turn a light shade of brown before adding some seasonings, water, and crawfish tails. My father sang along to a song by an R&B group from the late 80s as he seasoned and floured catfish filets and prepped them for the fryer he'd pre-heated on the backyard patio.

When the song entered the second verse, he cleared his throat. "You want to invite Khalil?" he asked, never looking up from the breading station at the kitchen island.

"For dinner?"

"Yeah." He hesitated like the following words had thorns and he was trying to hand them to me without sticking either one of us. "He's a good man, even if he is a little cocky sometimes. And I guess if I had to have anybody else protecting you, it'd be him."

Tears pricked my eyes, and not from the onions. "Daddy."

"If he's good to you, he's good with me," he said, opening the drawers for a spoon like he hadn't just ended his cold war with Khalil.

I wiped my hands on a towel and called Khalil as my father went to the backyard to fry the fish. The call barely rang once.

"Tell me something good," he said, smiling.

"I want you to come over and have dinner with me and my dad."

"He cool with that?"

"It was his idea." Khalil was quiet for a beat.

"I'm on my way."

By the time he knocked on the front door, the whole house was fragrant with a buttery, rich crawfish etouffee and piping hot catfish fresh from the grease. Khalil followed me to the kitchen, placing a Chantilly cake on the island, making my dad's eyes go wide. Karter made his rounds—sniffing Khalil's shoes and waiting for a head scratch.

Dinner was easy. The first bites made the table hum. After polishing off slices of cake, my dad left us to meet up with Uncle Doug. Khalil and I washed dishes then moved to the living room to watch tv. We settled on streaming *The Jamie Foxx Show*. He reached across my lap to pull me into his chest.

"Can I ask you a question?"

"You can ask me anything," I said, looking up at his face.

"When you picture home," he said, his words careful, "what's in the frame?"

I thought for a moment. "This," I said. "Food that tastes like someone loves me. Laughter in the same room as quiet. A dog with firm opinions. You."

His jaw worked once. "Me, huh?"

"Yep. What about you?"

He didn't blink. "You. Work that matters and doesn't own me. Sunday dinners where we argue about absolutely nothing then wash dishes until our fingers wrinkle. A little chaos mixed with a whole lot of softness."

"These sound like the same pictures."

"Kelly," he said, my name a vow. "I want you..." He stopped short and shook his head like he was promising himself not to jump the gun. "I want this always."

"Me, too," I said. "Always."

He reached for the plate of cake that sat on the coffee table. As episode after episode of Jamie Foxx reruns played, he fed us bites of cake in between kisses. Eventually, I found my mother's old quilt and he covered it over us. Tucking me into his side, he kissed my temples, then my lips. Karter circled the floor beneath us twice and settled like a punctuation mark. The show's laugh track blared into the quiet comfort. It was a softness I'd fought all my life and finally learned how to lie in it.

Tomorrow I'd be flying back to Seattle, going back to a life of rounds and distance from the people I loved most. Tonight, I was in a house that held my dearest memories, a dog that was my spirit animal, and my man who said my name like it was a door he'd build a home behind.

Epilogue

One Year Later

THE LAKE LOOKED LIKE IT'D BEEN POURED STRAIGHT out of a dream. Still as glass, surrounded by pines so tall they touched the clouds. An A-frame cabin sat nestled in the trees, all dark wood and big windows that drank in the water. Karter barked once, then took off down the dock, paws slipping on the damp wood before he launched himself into the water with a splash that made me laugh out loud.

"You sure he was meant to be a city dog?" I called out, watching his tiny body paddle with Olympic confidence.

"He's a Gemini," Khalil said from the porch, lifting his coffee mug. "They adapt."

I turned, giving him a look. "You're making stuff up now."

"You let him eat off your plate yesterday when you thought I wasn't looking. I get to make stuff up."

It was our third day in the mountains. A long overdue escape, far from Seattle, far from pagers and labs and hospital rounds. No itinerary. No plans. Just us and Karter, living his best wilderness era.

I sat on the edge of the dock, legs dangling, coffee warming my hands. Khalil came behind me, draping a throw blanket around my shoulders before sitting at my side.

"You good?" he asked.

"Mmhmm."

He leaned in, kissing the corner of my mouth.

"Still the best choice I ever made," he murmured.

"Booking this place?"

"Loving you."

My heart tugged, familiar and full. "In all my years of knowing you, not once could I say you were poetic."

"Nah," he said, sipping his coffee. "Sometimes I just say it plain. You're my person."

I bumped his shoulder. He bumped back, then pulled me to his side, wrapping his arm around my shoulders like a tether. He whistled, calling Karter.

"Big Dog, come see!" he yelled out to the water. Karter swam back toward the dock, whimpering theatrically until Khalil helped him up, wrapped him in a towel, and sat back down with him in his lap.

"His name is Karter," I said, snatching my baby back. "Not Big Dog." Karter sneezed, making us laugh.

"God bless the truth," Khalil muttered, grinning.

The sun climbed higher behind the trees. Somewhere in the distance, a hawk called out, its wings slicing the sky. The day stretched ahead like an open palm.

By day two, I noticed something with Khalil was off. Not loud or obnoxious, just enough to give me pause. Twitchy. Too agreeable. Folding blankets that were already folded. Checking his phone like he expected news from a number from the deep beyond. That morning, I caught him cursing the firepit, rearranging logs like they'd personally offended him.

"You good?" I asked, using his usual question against him. I leaned against the railing. Karter and I looked on, curious. He trotted over to Khalil, barking at the logs as Khalil moved them around.

"Yeah," he said quickly, not looking up. "Just making sure the coals catch."

I raised my eyebrow. "There's no fire, Khalil."

He shrugged. "I'm being proactive."

I narrowed my eyes. "You're being weird."

Finally, he turned to me and blinked, expression innocent like he hadn't taken ten minutes to stack three pieces of wood. Karter barked at me, defending him.

"Really, Karter? You're supposed to be on my side."

"I told you that's my Big Dog."

I rolled my eyes. Still. I knew Khalil too well. He was hiding something.

Later, we walked the trail behind the cabin, just us and Karter. The little bulldog bounded ahead of us through the trees, like he was on a very important mission involving moss and squirrels, fetching the lone stick Khalil threw seconds ago. Khalil reached for my hand as we walked. His grip was firm, like he was anchoring himself. I squeezed back, saying nothing. We reached a clearing overlooking the lake. The view was postcard perfect. Blue water mirroring an even bluer sky. Golden light slanting through pine branches.

Khalil stopped beside me, a hand in his coat pocket, breath slow.

"I brought you here for a reason," he said, voice a little louder than a whisper, yet echoing in the clearing.

I turned to him, my pesky brow raising. "Because of the view?"

His eyes met mine and didn't move.

"Because of what you once said, about chasing peace. How you were always running toward it but never catching it." I stilled. The wind tugged softly at the edge of my jacket. "It made me think...Maybe peace isn't something we find...It's something we choose. A person. A decision."

The wind rustled through the pines around us. Not cold, just present, holding space for us.

"But then you..." he exhaled; the sound caught between strength and surrender. "I've seen you grieving and soft. Seen you fierce and focused. Afraid. I've watched you hold everyone around you, even while you were falling apart. I've watched you rebuild yourself and still show up for love."

My throat tightened. My eyes burned.

"And I want to spend the rest of my life learning to love you like that," he said. "In every season. Without condition. Without hesitation."

He whistled once. Karter leaped over dropped branches, the stick in his mouth. Khalil kneeled, taking the stick, fiddling with a string wrapped around it. As the string untwisted, a gold ring caught the light. Simple. Stunning. A clear, round-cut diamond set in rose gold. Beautiful, not flashy. It looked like it belonged only on my hand. A few feet away, Karter sat with his head tilted, ears perked up to the sky, like even he knew what was happening.

"I don't need perfect," Khalil said, his voice breaking just slightly. "I just want real. And I want it with you. All of it. Always."

Tears slipped down my cheeks. I didn't wipe them.

"Kelly...Lily-girl," he whispered.

I didn't wait for him to finish. I stepped to him, heart first. "Yes," I said. "Yes. Yes!"

He laughed, a low breathless sound that only came when he forgot to guard his joy. He stood, hands shaking as he slid the ring onto my finger. When our lips met, warmth bloomed, history course-corrected. The lake stretched wide behind us, gold spilling across the water like a promise too sacred to be spoken. Karter barked once then trotted over, pressing his snout into my shin like he was claiming both of us as his family.

We laughed into the kiss.

In the stillness that hung between us, tangled in pine-scented air and morning light, love in every breath, I knew peace didn't live in a destination. It lived here. In the man that stood in front of me. In the life we were building.

Where did we go from here?

Anywhere.

Together.

Always.

Acknowledgments

To every readers who loved *Loved By You, The Choices We Make Pt. 1, and Lily In The Valley*, thank you for believing in me, for showing up, and for making room in your hearts for these characters. Your messages, reviews, and support have meant more than you'll ever know. You've carried me through some of my hardest days.

To my incredible alpha and beta readers, thank you for your time, your feedback, and your beautiful (and hilarious) comments that made me laugh, cry, and push through the hard parts. Your words reminded me that stories aren't just written, they're shared. I'm endlessly grateful you shared this one with me.

To my editor, thank you for seeing the heart of this story when I couldn't always see it myself. Your patience, guidance, and skill helped shape *Lily In The Valley* into something I'm deeply proud of. This book would not have been finished without you.

This book was born from a valley. My own season of darkness, grief, and transition that I didn't think I'd make it out of. Writing it forced me to confront the pain I'd tucked away, and in doing so, I found pieces of myself I thought were gone. *Lily In The Valley* isn't just a story of love. It's a story of healing, of choosing yourself, and of finding the light again after the storm.

If you're reading this and walking through your own valley, I hope this story reminds you that it's okay to sit with the darkness for a while. It's okay to fall apart. Healing doesn't look perfect, it looks human. But I promise, there's beauty waiting for you on the other side.

This journey has been my way of processing, forgiving, and

growing. If evening person finds comfort of hope within these pages, then every tear, every rewrite, and every late night was worth it.

With all my love,
Alexandrea LeChelle

Double Back In 2026

Thank you for reading!

I'm so grateful you've joined me on this journey with *Lily In The Valley*—it means the world to me! If you want to stay connected and follow along with my author adventures, be sure to follow me on TikTok, Instagram, Threads, and YouTube: @alexandrealechelle! Your support keeps me writing, and I can't wait to share even more stories with you. Speaking of... keep reading for a special sneak peek of what's coming next! 🩶

Lynn

I AM THE LUCKIEST GIRL IN THE WORLD TONIGHT. NOT because the moon and the stars owe me anything, but because I decided at 1:13 PM today. My arrival in Vegas a few hours ago and subsequent job offer resting in my email confirmed it.

"I don't chase, I attract. What's meant for me will never miss me," I tell my reflection, tapping rose gold highlighter into the bow of my top lip and tops of my cheeks like a until I glowed like Beyonce at the BET Awards.. "Okay universe, bend over backward and make me smile. I need another win this weekend."

Behind me, Vanessa pops a bottle of Ace of Spades, and champagne flares into the mirror like liquid diamonds.. "Cheers to the bride-to-be–Me!" she cheers in a sing-song, slightly off-tune pitch, warbled from the liquor she'd been downing since we stepped foot on Wesley's private jet.

"I'd blame you being drunk already on this being the first time you're drinking after having Zaria, but you've always been the lightweight of the group. Isn't that the second bottle of Ace of Spades?" See, Lynn-of-twelve-hours-ago would have been calculating the price, numbers ticking away in my head, and comparing them to which bill would go unpaid this month.

Student loan payment? Nope, skipped them twice already.

Cell phone and internet? Need that for applications and interviews Lynnie Mae.

A stream of air silently escapes my lips as I touch up the strip lash I've started using as a backup to my usual appointments with my lash tech. Nope, not this weekend. Lynn of now has her entire life back on track...Well, almost on track. I turned around, fixing my face, tipping the bottle of champagne. Glittery bubbles crest over the flutes in Vanessa's hand like a done deal.

Xavier peeks around the doorway with his usual soft, private smile he reserves solely for his future wife and daughter. "Y'all almost done? We gonna be late to dinner, Nessa baby."

"You can never be late when you look this good," I correct, grinning and pressing my lips together so the gloss sets.

"Amen to that," Vanessa sings, letting Xavier drag her to the living room overlooking the Vegas strip. I follow behind them and see my friends amping themselves up for the night ahead.

Wesley sprawled across the seat of the green velvet chaise like the tag on this Versace dress I'm praying doesn't pop off...Just in case... Wesley's black shirt flays open at the throat, his collarbone on quiet display, the gold chain catching the chandelier light like it knows it's sin. He's got the kind of face that looks better under expensive shadows–darkened rooms barely lit with sultry lights, The Weeknd playing hauntingly in the background as lips trail the heroin-laced kisses down your throat and atop the crests of your breasts. You want to fight back, argue against the commands because every word out of his mouth is a dare, but–

"You manifesting us missing the reservation?" he asks dryly, not even looking up from the phone in his hand.

I pass him on the chaise, and my clutch knocks the phone to the ground. I shoot him an apology look so bright, LED lights would be jealous. "I manifested you loosening up for once. Smile. It's free."

His mouth doesn't move. His eyes do, flicking from my hemline to my face with a heat that feels like a hand on my knee. "You don't want me smiling, Lynn."

"You're right," I say, tapping my clutch on his chest. "That would be too much like right."

"Careful what you wish for."

He said it like a promise and a threat, and my spine reacted first, a dancer's reflex, lifting like a whistled signal I couldn't ignore.

As we spilled into the private elevator of the penthouse suite, laughter filled the enclosed space. More than once I felt the soft brush of Wesley's shirt, the subtle strength beneath the expensive fabric, brushing against my skin. If it weren't for the laughter, I was sure everyone could hear the drumline in my chest, every cadence the marking of every bad decision my soul begged to make. I concentrated on my friends: Vanessa and Xavier, magnetic as ever; Kelly dolled up in an emerald satin slip that looked illegal in most states, Khalil enjoying every inch of it. Maverick boasted a story about him and Khalil during high school, coaxing Nyah out of her shell. Antonio stood off to the side, half-brooding, half-suspiciously charming at her side. I just know they're a whole storm of a book we haven't read yet.

Me? I'm a glittery ball, humming in the middle. Because I'm employed, finally, after a year of robbing Peter to pay Paul. Because my bank account can breathe again. When I saw the offer pop up in my email after lending, I signed it in record time and blew a kiss to the clouds. I texted a screenshot to my family's group chat and waited for the spill of capitalized praise that made me tear up. Today was proof that the world was finally aligning in my favor. Tonight, I'm allowed to be a bit ridiculous.

Exiting the elevator, we parade down marble and gold emblazoned halls, through the casino that smells like citrus-cigar smoke and money. The secrets of Sin City smooth a cool hand across the back of my neck, guiding me to a night of endless possibilities. Free drinks appear without being summoned. A woman wearing a sparkling headdress, tall as my dreams, calls me "Goddess."

Dinner happens in a blur of perfectly charred steaks and truffle everything. The waiter brings a dessert topped with sparklers and *Congratulations, V + X*, piped in chocolate. We clink. We toast. Vanessa's eyes are their regular glassiness from the overwhelm of emotions.

Then we're out again, cruising the strip in a rented SUV, black as the night with seats long I could grand jete across the roof and still have room to spare—the bass of the music thrumming from the speakers threads through my ribs. I bask in the river of neon provided by the Strip, a leaf that said yes to being carried.

Maverick presses a button, and the sunroof glides open, adding a touch of gilded-edge merriment to the car's ambiance. He shoots up, carrying Nyah with him halfway before Antonio pulls her back down with a possessive hand. She continues to laugh, shrugging him off with a smile.

I look ahead of me.

Wesley watches me instead of the city. Although I never meet his eyes, I feel it, as heavy as the crown atop my head. Those sage green eyes shoot lasers across my skin, each look counting every speck of glitter of dusted across my body. Our knees are almost touching. If this car took a hard left, we'd be pressed together by physics and a merciful God.

"Drink," Vanessa half slurs, half commands, shoving a shot glass of tequila to my lips. "We are not living timid tonight."

"I'm not timid," I protest, throwing the shot back without a wince. She wobbles toward Kelly and Nyah and practically force feeds them rounds of shots.

I look at Wesley and have to stop myself from slapping the annoyingly handsome smirk off of his face.

"You are absolutely timid," he says, his mouth curving a

millimeter. "When it's something you want. A perfect ball of chaos coated in politeness."

"And you're sunshine pretending to be a thunderstorm," I shoot back.

"So you like the rain. Noted."

The driver drops us off at a club with a ceiling that rains confetti. A bar with a mechanical bull has Vanessa and Kelly competing to see who could last longer. Song after song, my heels never left the dancefloor. Each transition made by the DJ had me rising to the balls of my feet, ready to hit an eight-count, reliving every Homecoming at my alma mater. Every time my body arched and curved to the beat, I spotted him. Glancing. Waiting. Sipping his bourbon straight. Smoky, emerald eyes preying on my every move. I let the thrill of being his private dancer washes over me as the liquor coursing through my veins sends me to a new high. I'm about twelve different glitter smudges and crooked lashes by the time I realize we've stopped.

"Where are we?" I ask no one in particular.

Vanessa gasps. "Fate," she cries, her eyes widening.

The building is smaller than a secret and twice as loud; white painted wood, pink neon hearts adorning the walls, plastic roses that should look tacky but add to the charm and aesthetic. It's the kind of chapel you point to when you have a story you'll never tell your mother.

"The Little White Lotus Chapel," Kelly reads off a sign, squinting. "For the low price of $150, you can be married by the pop icon of your dreams."

"It's fate," Vanessa repeats, softener now, the words landing somewhere in her chest. Her fingers knot with Xavier's, her round eyes pleading. "Let's get married now, without all the fuss our mother's have been adding to it."

"Nessa baby, you can't be serious." Xavier laughs, but his eyes are soft. Their love, pure and sweet, changes the air around us.

"Let's just do it," Vanessa pleads again, gesturing to the neon hearts and chapel behind us. "We wanted small. We wanted us."

Xavier looks from her to the plastic roses. He takes a breath. And, just when I think he's going to oblige his love's request, his gaze snags the ring finger of her left hand like a hook. The ring he redesigned, the proposal playing fresh in his mind. It's not like family members neither of them know are planning to fly in. It's not like Vanessa's second cousin twice removed, who could've had a fantastic singing career, was already practicing the live rendition of the wedding songs. Even TJ had been practicing rolling the wheelbarrow that'd bring Zaria down the aisle between football practices.

Instead, he swallows. "I want to," he admits. "But I want what I promised us. The whole day. Zaria clapping as we say our vows. Our people drunk off their ass from the open bar. Dancing with you until the stars get jealous of how bright you shine underneath their glow. "

Vanessa's eyes close like a door shutting without a slam. When they open, they're bright and clear. "You're right." She tucks a stray coil behind her ear. "We'll wait," she says, sealing the promise with a kiss on Xavier's lips.

There's a pocket of silence as devotion finds its seat again. And then chaos.

Fake Michael Jackson slides out from a beaded curtain in the doorway. White sequined jacket and glove in check, with the slightest curl of dark hair centered on his forehead. When he shouts, "Hee-hee," we all lose it.

"Nessa, you can't seriously think getting married here would be a better memory than what's already been planned?"

Just then, Fake Prince walks next to Micahle, plastic purple guitar strapped across his chest, lashes darkened with mascara. I glanced around, waiting for taxidermied doves to be perched somewhere.

"Let's go lovers," he croons. "Are we ready to kiss your way to everlasting commitment?"

Kelly and Khalil double over with laughter. Wesley's pearly-white teeth show for the first time tonight.

"We have packages starting at $500 tonight. Twenty-minute ceremony including vows, cubic zirconia rings, and one verse of 'Lady In My Life' performed by MJ over here."

"Hee-hee."

"Is that all he says?" Maverick questions, looking down at a speechless Nyah. "You and you man should renew your vows. Seems like the perfect place for what y'all got going on," he laughs out. She elbows him while fighting a smile down.

"How about you two," Prince asks, pointing his guitar toward Wesley and me.

The sentence is a spark thrown into tinder. My friends shouts twelve versions of "Do it!" that ricochet off the wooden walls.

Wesley looks at me.

I don't know who moves first. I just know the "yes" lands on my collarbone like a songbird, and I hold out my hand.

"You barely like me," Wesley responds, flicking his eyes toward my outstretched hand.

"I don't even like how little I like you," I correct, too honest. "Let's give everyone a show. What happens in Vegas, stays in Vegas, right?"

"Don't be afraid of what happens next, Lady Lynn" he smiles, his lips curling around his straight teeth, slow and cruel.

"I'm never scared," I charge back, giving him a warning smile of my own.

His tongue swipes his lower lip, then he bites down, a private promise tucked away for later. "Good girl."

The words hit the place in me that wants to argue and kneel at the same time. Heat curls around me like chaîné turns, round and round until I'm swimming in the atmosphere Wesley's built around us. I toss my chin to the air, straightening my spine, dignity a jacket I can't seem to keep on.

"Don't say that. And don't call me Lady Lynn, like I'm yours or something," I say, and hear the lack of conviction in my voice.

"Okay," he replies, taking my hand and walking us to the slightly raised platform at the back of the building. "Mrs. Wesley Wright sounds better anyway."

I crane my neck to say something, but Prince throws ceremony options in our face like a car wash menu. Wesley pays the $500 plus an extra $25 for the wedding album Khalil insists we need for the memories. I wear a veil that looks like it belongs on a Barbie. Wesley declines the sequined top hat.

We stand underneath the plastic arch adorned with faux peonies and dust-covered greenery. Our friends fill the few rows of chairs, glowing and loud. Vanessa's hands are clasped over her mouth. Nyah records the ceremony on her phone like a proud mother. Maverick sings "Adore" softly off to the side. Antonio's smile doesn't quite reach his eyes, as if it ever did.

The small room smells like artificial rose spray and possibility.

"Dealry beloved," Fake Michael starts, adjusting his glove. His voice rises into a shine. "We are gathered here tonight to celebrate the love of these two beautiful souls."

Laughter breaks like crystal against marble tile.

He leads us through the vows, fast and funny and somehow still catching something real by the hem. "Do you promise to love, respect, and occasionally let him think he's right. Even when he's wrong?"

"I do," I say, surprising myself with how steady it sounds.

"Do you promise to love, cherish, protect, and tolerate her playlists, even when she's feeling 2000s R&B nostalgia at 2 a.m.?"

"I do," Wesley answers, steady and sure.

"Do you both promise to be there for each other until the end of time?"

My heart beats like a hummingbird as we both respond, "Yes." The intensity in Wesley's eyes let me know I'm not alone.

We exchange rings that threaten to turn my finger green. When I push the silver ring onto his finger, I have to bite my tongue not to make a joke about ownership. A thought pirouettes across my mind so fast I barely catch it. I admit to myself that I like the idea of him taking things that belong to me —my hand, my attention, the air around my mouth. I also enjoy making him ask.

Wesley tilts his head down, and everything slows like syrup. He is not a man prone to spectacle. He is a man who makes the room move around him, pretending not to notice. But right now, under plastic flowers, neon lights, and the wild raucous of our friends, he looks straight at me and lowers his voice until it's just us.

"I don't make promises I don't keep," he whispers against my lips.

"Lucky me," I reply, getting lost in his glare.

"Lucky us," he corrects. His hand tightens around my waist, a firm press that says hold till. The pressure, the control in that slight touch, makes my knees go weak. He registers it and bears my weight, pulling me closer to him. As I concede, his eyes flare just enough to be illegal.

"By the power vested in me by my manager and the State of Nevada," Fake Michael flourished with his glove, "I now pronounce you man and wife...at least until you sober up or make it legal. You may kiss your person."

The kiss isn't soft.

It isn't wild either. It's calibrated, like he picked a point between restraint and ruin and settled his mouth there. His hand comes to the back of my neck, warm and sure. He doesn't pull me closer. He doesn't have to. My body leans into his like it already belongs there. His kiss is a study in patience and subtext I'm not ready to unpack.

Applause detonated behind us. Confetti shoots from cannons someone had to have paid for separate. The Polariod clicks and spits out truth in a square; he and I, our mouths locked enough to make pretend a reality. We sign the novelty certificate with glitter pens. The chapel hands us a bag with our "unity gift": a mini snow globe with a tiny Elvis. There's a moment afterward, when the group heads back to the car, leaving Wesley and me standing by the counter alone for a breath that tastes like candy.

"You put on a show back there," I breathe out.

"I don't put on shows," he replies, the smile long gone. "And now you're Mrs. Wesley Wright for the next few hours." He chuckles when I grimace.

"I'm nobody's."

He smiles like he knows an addendum I haven't read. "We'll see about that. Come on, Mrs. Wright."

We all go back to the suite. There are more bottles of champagne and greasy food spread across every counter of the kitchenette. There's a toast to Vanessa and Xavier's real day, for which Wesley and I were merely a dress rehearsal. It takes ten tries to get the perfect group photo. There's a moment on the balcony when Wesley's palm finds my waist, and my spine becomes an idea I once had. There is nothing I will admit happened or didn't after that because I am a lady. But also, because my brain refuses to process it all.

I remember laughing, loud enough to feel my chest crack open and light get in. I remember removing the veil and placing it on Maverick, who solemnly vowed to be a faithful husband to the love of his life. I remember Wesley's mouth near my ear when everyone else drifted into their corners of the night, his voice a ribbon tied around my ribs. "Come here."

I remember...then the remembering gets blurry and soft around the edges, like the Polaroid before it develops.

And then—

Morning slaps me with a dry mouth and a wall of sunlight.

Vegas at 9 a.m. is a hungover apology. The bedroom is a quiet battlefield—a gold heel on its side like it fainted, half-empty champagne bottles that look haunted on the dresser. My head is a cathedral of bells. There's a makeup print of my face on the pillow. A satin robe tie falls from my wrists as gold confetti drops from my hair. A slight oily sheen covers my skin, smelling faintly of amber and something florally sweet. *Ridiculous.*

I groan myself upright and realize I am not in my room.

This room is colder, neater, and smells expensive in a way you can't buy at the mall. The sheets are a million-thread-count cloud. The view is a slice of Strip and mountains wearing hazing morning shades; the Bellagio and Cosmopolitan are nestled on either side of the view. On the dresser, a watch, cuff links, and a black shirt folded with military precision. My dress is on the back of a chair, like it put itself in time-out. My body is in a T-shirt that is not mine. It says The *Echelon* in bold typeface, with *Wright Horizons* in tiny letters underneath, and it hurts my feelings how good it feels against my skin.

I follow the sun's trail to the balcony.

Wesley is there. He looks like an ad for something I can't afford–barefoot, gray sweatpants, a coffee mug big enough to baptize me in one hand, sunglasses shielding the sins behind them. He's leaning against the railing, letting the morning gild his shoulders.

For a second, I just look...because I am just a girl. And because last night, I might have been lucky, but this morning, I am honest. I like beautiful, complicated things that look like problems and feel like answers.

When I slide the floor-to-ceiling door and pad out onto the balcony, he doesn't turn when he speaks. "Good morning, Mrs. Wright." He inhales another sip of his coffee.

The name is a drop of honey in lemon tea. It melts into every part of me.

I snort hard enough to choke on air. "I beg your pardon."

"I'm sorry," he says, turning to me, removing the sunglasses from his face. A smirk lingers in the corners of his mouth.

"Good morning, Mrs. Wesley Wright." His smile blazes my cheeks.

"Aww," I pout, pinching the bridge of my nose. "Your eight hours are over. I'm back to being Lynn Malveaux now."

"Mm." He walks to me, putting the mug to my lips. I drink from his silent command. The subtle glint in his eyes lets me know he's proud. "We have brunch in an hour. Kelly says don't be late. I have my assistant bringing up clothes for you." He walks past me to the dresser, stops to fasten the watch, leaving me on the balcony.

"Don't give me orders."

He doesn't say anything. Just smirks again and heads to the ensuite bathroom. The shower spray turns on full force. He comes back to the doorway, gestures with two fingers like he's summoning me.

Heat flares low in my belly like a bad idea lighting a cigarette. I squash it with both hands and a lecture. "I'm heading back to my hotel."

"Why would you do that? We're still on our honeymoon."

"We," I start, pointing between Wesley and me, "are not anything. We did a bit. The bit is over. We're back to boundaries," I tell him, gathering my dress and my clutch and what's left of my pride. "I need a shower to wash whatever this is off my spirit."

He tilts his head, amusement lazy as noon. He starts to walk toward me. "You can leave if you need to. Drink water. Stop pretending like last not didn't scare you."

He gets too close. I start my march toward the private elevator. "It didn't."

"Then act like it."

My ching lifts on instinct. "Stop giving me orders."

He says nothing, but his slow saunter says it all. My back braces against the elevator door. I hit the button to call the carriage with my clutch. I step back once the door opens, holding it open with my clutch. Wesley stops in his tracks.

"Goodbye, husband. It's a shame we couldn't work this out."

He grits his jaw, then lets out a sinister laugh. "Bring coffee when you come back. Black. Two sugars."

"I'm not coming back."

His jaw grits again, then he swipes his nose. "Luck circles...and so will you."

I let the doors close, then exhale as I begin the descent to the hotel lobby. I square my shoulder. Lucky girls don't run; we exit in a huff and make the universe chase us.

About the Author

Born and raised in Houston, Texas, with roots stretching across Louisiana, Alexandrea has always felt a deep connection to the stories of the South. Having lived in both Texas and Louisiana all their life, she noticed a gap in literature representing the real, complex issues faced by people in these regions—particularly within the Black community. This gap sparked their journey as a writer.

Inspired by a desire to bring untold stories to life, Alexandrea writes to shed light on critical topics like gentrification, mental health in the Black community, parental wounds, and the importance of creating safe spaces for Black women and men to express their emotions. But above all, her work emphasizes the beauty of healthy Black love and the power of Black women being cherished and celebrated.

An avid reader, bullet journaler, crafter, and cook, Alexandrea finds creative fuel in everyday activities and the work of influential authors like Toni Morrison, Zora Neale Hurston, Beverly Jenkins, and Kennedy Ryan. Many of the themes explored in her debut and future novels are drawn from personal experiences or those of close friends and family, making each story a deeply personal and authentic reflection of life.

For anyone aspiring to write, her advice is simple: "Just start. There is someone out there who needs to hear your story."

Also by Alexandrea LeChelle

Loved By You: The Double Back Diaries Book 1

The Choices We Make Pt. 1: A Double Back Diaries Novella

Lily In The Valley: The Double Back Diaries Book 2

The Choices We Make Pt. 2: A Double Back Diaries Novella (coming soon)

Lady In My Life: The Double Back Diaries Book 3 (coming 2026)